Shadoe's arms circled her waist, and he pressed his cheek to her thick hair. When the edge of her hat grazed his temple, he said, "Why do women wear these wicked things?"

"So that we will look pretty," Isabel said, dropping her head against his as if it was the most natural thing in the world. Then, quietly, she turned into his arms and smiled at him. Her mouth parted, exposing straight white teeth. Her tongue wetted her upper lip.

"Women shouldn't do that when a man is holding them," said Shadoe.

"Why not?"

"A man takes it as an invitation."

"An invitation to do what?"

"This—" His head dipped and his mouth tenderly grazed hers. When she made no protest, he deepened the kiss.

"Don't—don't—" she whispered, attempting to withdraw from his embrace. But he held her firmly, refusing to let her go, and she lifted her trembling mouth to be claimed again by his own.

Was it still November? Was she dreaming? Isabel knew only that there was nowhere else she wanted to be. Being in Shadoe's arms seemed as natural as drawing breath.

CAROLINE BOURNE

LOVE'S PERFECT DREAM

ZEBRA BOOKS
KENSINGTON PUBLISHING CORP.

ZEBRA BOOKS are published by

Kensington Publishing Corp.
475 Park Avenue South
New York, NY 10016

First Printing: June, 1993

Printed in the United States of America

Prologue

On the range of the Circle Pine Ranch, Oklahoma, 1878

"Did I ever tell ya 'bout dat time I got pitched of'n my hoss after a big ol' storm an' when I picked dis here face up out'n de mud, dey wuz a feller starin' at me, what wid de flesh all scraped of'n his haid an' two big ol' empty holes a'starin' me in de eyes?"

"Don't reckon you did," absently replied Hotch Trumble, who'd grown accustomed to the wild stories told by the ex-slave Philbus. "I guess this all happened down there in Louisiana where you was raised?"

A throaty chuckle echoed among the rough walls of the line cabin in which the two men rested. "Sho' did." In one swift move, the aging cowboy put floor beneath his boots, leaving the impression of his massive frame in the narrow cot he'd just vacated. His footfalls carried him to the single window covered only by rotting gauze, which he swept back so that he might look out on the hot July sky covered, now, by the veil of absolute darkness. "Louziana nights —" he reminisced, his mind wandering back to those days long past. "Dey ain't like here in Oklahoma. Louziana, it has what dey call *personality.* Why, ya wake up on a Louziana night an' dey be's de sound o' crickets a scrapin' dey legs in de awfullest way, yet it be's real peaceful. When de rain fall on a Louziana night, why it be's like music from de heavens . . . Lawd, I sho' does miss Louziana. Dey is de smell

5

o' gardenias and honeysuckle in de air, not like cow dung here in Oklahoma. An' deys the purtiest li'l ol' black-skinned gals, all round in de right places an' sum'tuous . . . Lawd, do they be sum'tuous! Sometimes, ol' Philbus, he kick hisself in de butt fo' leavin'. Did I ever tell ya why I leave Louziana, Hotch?"

"No less than a thousand times," responded his cabin mate and friend as he absently dug the remainder of his supper from his teeth with his pocket knife. " 'Cause you was a slave an' wanted to be a cowboy. But you ain't told me 'bout that dead fella you come face to face with."

Philbus dragged his fingers through coarse, gray-fringed hair. "Dat white fella what I found back in '57, he come a'lookin' fer dat gold what Massah Wickley s'posed ta have buried on de plantation. An' he got hisself kil't by 'nother slave what's name was Swainie." Again, Philbus chuckled. "When I found dat dead fella, sho' did stir up a hornet's nest at Shadows-in-de-Mist, an' de new owner, dat Yankee-doodle gambler Grant Emerson, why he sho' had a mystery on 'is hands. Lawd, an' he already had 'nough to handle, what wid Missy causin' him a poker full o' trouble 'nough to drive him to think 'bout killin' hisself an' endin' de mis'ry, I reckon. Lawd, why'd I leave dem good folks . . . I's jes' never know!"

Philbus stood at the window, seeing the sky over Oklahoma, its darkness suddenly paled by a stretch of nondescript moonlight, and imagining the mysterious Louisiana nights. He thought he heard the gentle currents of Bayou Boeuf rushing along its haphazard journey and the mournful cries of night creatures echoing across the distance. Was that Mozelle's voice calling his name? He still loved his first—and only—wife, and never a day passed that he didn't think of her. He was getting older now; the past was important to him. If so much time hadn't passed, he might even return.

6

"You goin' to tell me about that dead fella and the gold, Philbus?"

Startled from his thoughts, the hard muscles of the black man flinched. "Maybe 'nother time, Hotch." Turning back to the cot, Philbus said sadly, "I sho' does miss dem folks down there what wuz my family—"

"Those Wickleys you told me about, Philbus?" queried an indulgent Hotch Trumble. "Hell . . . you was their slave."

Philbus stretched out on the cot and tucked his hands beneath his gray head. "Sho', Hotch, I wuz dey slave. But when I's jes' a li'l fella, my massah what I had befo' Mistah Wickley, he whooped me real good an' I jes' 'bout died layin' wid a bad fever in de punishment shed. Massah Wickley, he wuz visitin' an' he took a shine ta me, an' he offered to buy me of'n my mean massah. An' massah, he sol' me, an den Mistah Wickley, he took pity on me 'cuz I wuz bein' took from my mammy an' my pappy, too, an' he bought 'em an' he brung us all to Shadows-in-de-Mist. Ya know, Hotch, I wuz so mean an' stubborn, I never thanked Massah Wickley fo' what he done. Sho, I was a slave, but I weren't treated like no slave. We wuz family, sho 'nuff, Massah an' his gal, Missy . . . me an' my folks . . . dem folks what be black like me, but Massah Wickley an' his gal, dey don't look at dey own skin an' see white, den look at de skin of de slaves an' see black. Dey just see folks. An' I never even said thank ya, what wuz de least I could 'a done." When Hotch gave no response, Philbus sat forward again, then dragged a small wooden box from beneath his cot. Holding it on his lap, he said, "Hotch, you be jes' 'bout my bes' friend here. If anything should happen ta ol' Philbus, will ya promise to send dis here box to de Wickleys in Louziana? Dey address in de box. Will ya do dat, Hotch?"

"Ain't nothin' goin' to happen to you, Philbus—"

"But if it do, Hotch, will ya promise?"

7

Hotch shrugged. "Sure, if that's what you want."

Drawing a deep breath, Philbus edged the box into its place beneath the cot. Then he again stretched out, dragged one of his arms forward and covered his eyes. Now, we need ta git some sleep, Hotch. Still got a hun'erd or so strays ta round up in de mo'nin."

Had Hotch noticed the waver of emotion in his voice? Philbus imagined that he had and was being polite by not mentioning it. When Philbus thought about Louisiana, Shadows-in-the-Mist and the Wickleys, he didn't think about being a slave. Rather, he thought about home and family . . . and being together. As he closed his eyes and thought about being there, he remembered the good times, and being loved by the Wickleys, not as a slave, but as a friend. True, by law he had been Angus Wickley's property, but if the truth be known, if he'd taken off, Angus would merely have shrugged his shoulders and wished him good luck. There would have been no bounty hunters, runaway posters, or whips.

He was especially reminiscent tonight, perhaps because he was getting on up in years and family was important. There were so many things he would do differently if he could only turn back time.

One day, Missy, he thought, remembering the last time he'd seen Delilah Wickley. *One day, ol' Philbus, he'll find a way ta rightly repay ya fo' ya kindness. One day—*

Part One
Beginnings

One

The city of New Orleans drowsed under the violet and gold hues of a cool November morning, its picturesque appearance hardly in keeping with the activities of the many warehouses on Tchoupitoulas Road. Isabel Emerson moved swiftly along the roadside, hugging her shawl to her and hoping that her cousin had not yet awakened and found her gone. With luck, she would return to her aunt's silent wooden mansion with its vast verandas well before either had awakened for the day.

Just the night before, Dustin had forbidden her to journey alone to the rough business district, and that fact had given her the incentive to make the trip. No one in the world, especially her overprotective cousin, would prohibit her from doing anything that she chose to do! After all, it was 1879, the South was only now recovering from the full effects of the War Between The States, and the Southern aristocracy had long ago crumbled, giving women the incentive to display their intelligence as well as their gentle charms. Dustin would simply have to remember that she would not be suppressed.

Though any woman in the vicinity of the warehouses was an oddity, the rough, grizzled workers gave Isabel little more than a perfunctory glance this overcast morning as she moved swiftly along. Draped as she was from head to toe in a somber black cape,

11

she might as easily have been a pickled old witch as the lovely flaxen-haired, blue-eyed daughter of Grant and Delilah Emerson. Soon she found the warehouse where her great-aunt Imogen's much younger male companion worked, purchased from him the cameo brooch he had said would be a perfect gift for her birthday on Saturday, and began the short trek back to the house on Royal. It couldn't be much past the hour of seven, and both her great-aunt and her cousin customarily slept until eight.

When she entered Royal, her glance automatically cut to the astonishingly jagged rooflines cut into the blue strip of intervening sky. Every conceivable angle met her: gables and eaves, dormers and triangular peaks of slate, projecting corners of balconies and verandas, jutting from houses of every conceivable tint. Whether the houses were canary or chocolate, gray, red or pale rose, all had sap-green batten shutters and the balconies balustraded with elegant wrought-iron arabesques. It was just such a house whose courtyard she turned into a few minutes later.

She stood for a moment in a garden enclosed on three sides by spiked railings, and remembered how brilliantly it had flourished in mid-summer, with its prolific beds of marigolds, periwinkles, and heather. Now only a few ruby-red roses clung to a strappy bush, and a single gardenia rested against the dark green leaves of its host. The chill weather had turned the ground to a carpet the color of sand, and the bursts of bright green that had graced the summer were pale and copper and burnt-looking. Heaving a weary sigh, she chased away her moment of melancholy and entered the foyer. Everything had its season, and the garden would flourish again.

There in the doorway, her hands drawn to her wide hips, stood Mercedes, her cheeks shining like

12

new copper. "Where ya been, Miss Uppity Britches," she demanded in a low, quiet voice. "Gonna tell me, Missy, or tell yo' cousin when he gits up out o' his bed?"

Dropping her reticule to a nearby chair, Isabel took the hands of the black maid. "I do declare, Mercedes, you treat me like a child," she responded, touching her mouth in a gentle kiss to the woman's cheek.

"Don't ya be tryin' ta charm me, Missy. I ain't a gonna conspire with ya if ya's up to no good."

Retrieving the reticule, she removed the lovely gold and ivory brooch she had purchased from Mr. Thackeray. "What do you think? Will Aunt Imogen like it?"

Only now did Mercedes allow herself to smile. "I think she will like it very much, Miss Isabel. She has black cameos, and other colors, but she ain't got one like this, with all them pearly lookin' colors shinin' in it. Yes, indeed, she'll be right pleased!"

"Where have you been, Isabel?"

Isabel turned swiftly, meeting the narrowed gaze of her cousin who slowly descended the stairs. Dustin was tall and bone thin, and his skin had a sickly pallor. Though he was only twenty-eight, his pale hair had begun to thin in a pattern identical to his father's.

"What do you mean . . . where have I been? I've been right here."

He alighted to the brick floor of the foyer; the clip of his bootsteps stopped before her. Quietly, Mercedes slipped into the kitchen. Drawing his hand to Isabel's unadorned black bonnet, he mused, "And you go about the house in your bonnet and cape, cousin? I think not. I saw you from my window, pausing in the garden in that thoughtful manner of yours, wishing that the flowers were still in bloom, eh?" Slowly, annoyingly, he began to circle her, his fingers linked behind him. She refused to meet his mocking gaze.

Isabel clicked her tongue, dismayed that he should have felt the need to spy on her. "Where I went is no business of yours, Dustin Emerson. You're as cocky as a two-dollar rooster and I demand that you stop strutting around me as such!"

"My uncle said that I should keep an eye on you."

"My *father*—" She deliberately emphasized her closer relationship to Grant Emerson, "didn't say that you should stand guard over me like an old warrior!"

Suddenly, Dustin laughed, pausing again in front of a fretting, frowning Isabel. Then he took her hand and held it gently. "Aren't we something, Isabel? Anyone who happened upon us about now would swear that we hated each other."

Casting off her bonnet, along with her dark mood, Isabel hugged him warmly. "Oh, Dustin, I love you . . . I truly do. Why, if you weren't my cousin, I'd fall madly in love with you—"

Dustin's moment of humor instantly faded. Stepping back, taking Isabel's hands as he did so, his gaze moved over her winter-pale, heart-shaped features. Her eyes were pale and crystalline, like her father's, the mirrors of every mood that came over her. Tall and slender, she often claimed to be terribly clumsy, but he saw her as nothing less than graceful. Removing her cape, which allowed the thick masses of her long, loose golden tresses to escape, he cast the garment aside and turned her into the wing of his arm. Dropping his hand over her shoulder, Dustin coaxed her toward the kitchen. "Come . . . I catch a whiff of hot chicory coffee and freshly baked bread."

"Horsefeathers—" Isabel had picked up the silly re-

14

tort from her mother, the beautiful Delilah Emerson of Shadows-in-the-Mist Plantation on Bayou Boeuf. Oh, how she missed her . . . and her dear father, too. "I do declare, Dustin, you are always thinking of food! How you stay so thin is a mystery to me!"

Together they moved through a corridor where the decaying plaster clinging precariously to the walls did not detract from the overall elegance of Imogen's house on Royal.

Hardly had the cousins settled into chairs at the table before great-aunt Imogen entered from another direction. Though family records would easily put her age at ninety-one, she claimed to be not a day older than seventy-nine, which, if one believed that, would have made her a child-bride of nine years about seven husbands ago. "Good morning, children," she greeted, folding her hands upon her brass and oak walking cane as she sat. Her jowls hung long and loose, like white handkerchiefs draped over a pale, veined marble bust. Her eyes were small and watery, and when she smiled, the thick rouge upon her cheeks darkened like ripe apples. She was a proud old aristocrat who had few interests outside her own family, gambling, which she very much enjoyed, and Mr. Thackeray, of whom she was extremely fond. This old house on Royal, in which she had been born, had sheltered her from the world all her life, and she did not have to leave its confines to pursue any of her interests; hardly a night went by that any manner of human beast did not rap upon the door, begging entrance to her private gambling parlor at the center of the house.

"Good morning, aunt," replied Dustin.

"I'm not your aunt!" she quickly pointed out, though the merry twinkle in her eyes lessened the severity of her protest. "I'm the great-great aunt of my

15

Isabel—" she continued, taking the younger woman's hand across the table, "the great-aunt of her beautiful mother, and the aunt of her grandfather, bless his dear, departed soul. If you want me to be your aunt, too, you'll have to pay me a worthy fee for the privilege!"

Dustin laughed. "You are a grizzled old charmer, aren't you, dear?"

Though they were not related by blood, Imogen loved the young man just as if he had been born to one of her own.

Returning her attentions to Isabel, Imogen asked, "Have you gotten over your bout of homesickness, child?"

Isabel refused to be angered by the old darling's referral to her as a child. "I know mother and father felt that I needed to get away from the plantation," she replied. Shrugging, she added, "I really can't blame them. I did take entirely too many liberties—"

"Liberties, my hiney!" snorted the ancient woman. "It was those ungodly britches you put on to go riding in . . . and that common boy who was violating you, I might add, with your encouragement! That was not a liberty, young lady. That was obscene!"

Pressing her mouth into a comical frown, Isabel thought back to that Saturday afternoon on the Boeuf. Her parents had journeyed into Alexandria and had announced that they'd be gone for the entire day. So Isabel, feeling stifled by the restrictive skirts she'd had to wear, had once again donned a pair of her younger brother's trousers. Thereafter, she had taken to the woods with one of the young men from a neighboring plantation. Having just dropped back against a summer-warmed oak, she had been on the brink of a passionate kiss when her father had sneaked upon them. She shivered to recall his fury.

16

"What are you doing, girl?" bellowed Grant Emerson, dragging her up by her elbow. "And you—" His finger dug painfully into Lawrence McCallum's shoulder, "You get the hell out of here or I'll fill your backside with buckshot!"

"But papa," Isabel had protested, furious that the cowardly young man scattered like a covey of quail. "I'm twenty-one years old and I've never even been kissed. I want to know what it's like to be with a man! You're being unreasonable—"

He had turned to her, his glare a most lethal warning. "You've taken liberties, Isabel Emerson. Look at you!" His eyes raked her up and down. "Wearing your brother's britches and carrying on with that boy like a two-bit doxie. If you want to know what a man is like, choose one that is worthy of you!"

Groaning her outrage, she had shot back disrespectfully, "You wouldn't consider a king or a prince fit for me, papa. If I leave it up to you, I'll be a shrunken old maid! I'll—why, I'll probably die a virgin!"

Grant Emerson had responded in a quiet, controlled tone, "I can think of worse things. You're going to New Orleans to Imogen, and perhaps she can make a lady out of you. God knows, your mother and I have tried everything we know—"

"What are you thinking, cousin?"

Isabel snapped from her trance, almost surprised to find herself seated at the table with Dustin and Aunt Imogen when her thoughts had carried her far, far away, to the meadow abutting Bayou Boeuf. "I was shamelessly daydreaming," she confessed, taking a sip of her cooling coffee. She had been with Aunt Imogen for almost six months, and she suspected that her father expected her to stay until she had found a suitable husband to bring back to the Boeuf.

17

A long series of raps echoed from beyond the walls. Wiping her hands on her apron, Mercedes moved into the corridor and toward the front door. Muted voices soon followed; then the door closed and Mercedes returned, carrying a letter. "It's fo' you, Mistah Dustin," she announced.

Thinking it to be one of the normal, newsy letters he received weekly from his stepmother, Ellie, Dustin quickly unfolded the pages that would yield her usual bright news from the Boeuf. But scarcely a third of the way through the top page, his brows buckled into a frown. "Dear God," he mumbled. "My mother has died in Boston."

"I'm so sorry," came Isabel's sympathetic response, even as she wondered silently why he was so affected. His father had won custody of him from the mentally unsound woman when Dustin had been only seven years old, and he had not seen her since.

"She died in the asylum and her father—my grandfather—wishes to see me. I wonder if I should go."

"What does Ellie say?"

Quietly, Dustin continued to read. "She assumes that I wish to go. My father will arrive here tomorrow to make the journey with me—"

"Uncle Aldrich is coming to New Orleans?"

"Don't you get excited," interjected Aunt Imogen. "You'll not be going with them. You still have six months to serve of your sentence in Warden Imogen's prison."

Isabel smiled for her aunt. "I don't consider being your houseguest as serving a sentence. In fact, I'll admit that I've thoroughly enjoyed the education I've received under your tutelage these past six months . . . even though you have been temperamental and domineering, you old dear!"

"I've kept the fellows out of your underthings, haven't I?"

Shock immediately registered in Isabel's features, though she had learned to expect anything from Aunt Imogen. "Really, Auntie . . . I can do that quite well for myself!" Casting an embarrassed glance at her older cousin, she continued quietly, "I do wish you'd think before you say such things, especially in the presence of Dustin."

Dustin flicked his wrist. "Don't worry, I'm not listening."

Continued Aunt Imogen, "You'd better get adept at halting roving fingers, because I've made an appointment for you for the theater tomorrow night."

"Oh, Auntie—" Isabel clicked her tongue, a habit she thought she had broken, but which Aunt Imogen had resurrected with her outrageous efforts at matchmaking. Already, she had paired Isabel with a bank teller who had discussed for two hours over dinner the amount of fertilizer and horse excrement he used on his roses, a night watchman who had fallen asleep at the theater, and a Medical College student who had offered to show her the size of his—

"What are you thinking about, girl?"

Crimson rose in Isabel's cheeks as she met Aunt Imogen's questioning gaze. "Big medical books," she responded quietly. Only then did she realize that the somber Dustin had left the kitchen. "Who is my lucky escort tomorrow night?" she asked indulgently. "And do I have the option of bowing out?"

"Actually, no. You're payment of a gambling debt. I lost last evening—"

A moment of bewilderment instantly became shock. "Auntie . . . did you have those ruffians over last evening while Dustin and I were out? I do declare—" Isabel rose so swiftly to her feet that she up-

19

set her cup of coffee. "I will not be gambling stakes. How could you? You're supposed to be taking care of me, engaging me in gentle society and, if my father would have it, introducing me to men worthy to consider as a husband!"

"I'm working on it," the old woman responded. "Don't go getting your dander up. I wouldn't wager your welfare to just any man. Mr. McCaine is quite a handsome fellow . . . and he has money."

"Some black rogue who engages in pirating and the black market, I would venture," came Isabel's smart response. "I hope he doesn't use fertilizer—"

"What did you say, girl?"

"I said, I hope he isn't a womanizer." Linking her fingers, Isabel began pacing back and forth. "Auntie, I just don't think it is in my best interest to stay at Royal with you. Perhaps I should return home—"

"It is the rainy season. You'll drown crossing the river." Without awaiting her great-grand niece's response, Imogen began chatting with Mercedes. In that moment, Isabel's thoughts wandered away, drawn into the past by something her aunt had just said. She recalled the trembling little girl she had been in 1864, sitting quietly in the shade of the gallery at Shadows-in-the-Mist and watching the glow of many lanterns moving along the Boeuf. The Yankees had burned Alexandria two days before and had moved eastward, indiscriminately burning and pillaging—her mother's adored riverboat, *Bayou Belle,* permanently moored on Bayou Boeuf, had been burned, though no one was really sure why. Soon thereafter, her four-year-old brother, Eduard, had disappeared, and many speculated that the little fellow, upset over the absence of the boat, had thought the *Bayou Belle* had merely sunk beneath the water's surface and was looking for it. The little cap he had been wearing, as well as one of his black boots, had been found on the bank of the Boeuf just a few minutes after he had been discovered missing from the gallery where he had been playing. The men had searched for two days. She had never seen her parents so distraught. Though the volunteers had given up after a week, believing Eduard to have drowned in the Boeuf, her parents had never stopped searching and had posted rewards throughout the states. Even to this day they refused to believe he was dead. Four years ago, the New Orleans *Picayune* had run an extensive story on the Emersons of Bayou Boeuf, a story that had included the disappearance of their son, Eduard. For months afterwards, many letters had arrived at either Aunt Imogen's house, or at Shadows-in-the-Mist, from young men claiming to be the lost Eduard. Each claim had been thoroughly investigated; all had been discounted. One of the letters had actually come from a girl. The only interest that had propelled these people to make such claims was the vast wealth of the Emerson family.

Instinctively, Isabel's hand rose to the gold medallion she wore around her neck, one identical to that worn by her little brother the day he had disappeared. Her sixteen-year-old brother, Paul, also wore one of the medallions.

Holding the coin that had been made into a necklace, Isabel studied the intricate details of the feminine Oriental profile, then turned it over and moved her thumb gently over the single yew tree engraved upon its side. Her mother, Delilah, enjoyed telling the story of how her father had buried a treasure of gold coins on the plantation in 1846, and then had forgotten their whereabouts after a terrible accident that same night. To this day, no one knew where Angus Wickley had gotten the gold, and no one knew where the simple-minded slave girl, aptly named Peculiar, who'd accidentally stumbled upon it some years later, had rehidden it. The gold had cost two lives, that of the slave Lathrop who had been with her father en route from New Orleans when he had drowned in the Boeuf that stormy winter night, and that of a treasure hunter who had been killed half a dozen years later in his quest for the gold. Just over four pounds of the coins had been given to the dead man's brother as small compensation for his death, and six of them had been kept by Isabel's mother. Made into pendants and hung on gold chains, each of the children of Grant and Mariah Emerson wore them. Isabel felt naked without her own, and as far as she knew, Paul was never without his. Somewhere, perhaps buried in the mud beneath the swirling waters of the Boeuf, lay the medallion her brother, Eduard, had worn.

Though neither Aunt Imogen nor Mercedes had spoken to her in several minutes and she could easily have slipped out undetected, Isabel said politely, "I think I'll go to my room and write to mother and father."

Moments later, a pouting Isabel threw herself into the wicker rocker by the veranda doors. Looking out onto the cluttered galleries across the street and the gray roofs, like overhanging brows, she found herself fretting over Aunt Imogen's declaration. Surely she had been teasing . . . surely she would not gamble her honor at the tables and allow her to be won by some unscrupulous swill? Her gaze wandered across the rooftops, toward the skyline that had turned the color of pale ash. How she wished she was back on the Boeuf, riding her mare through the meadows of Shadows-in-the-Mist. At least there she was familiar with the habits of the local men, and each knew she could take care of herself, and certainly would if compromised. But here . . . here in this dirty, cluttered city, with a guardian like Aunt Imogen, she was surprised that her virtues were still intact. The old lady had not been at all discreet or selective in choosing the men who courted her, and Isabel could hardly believe that her parents would have sent her, had they known Aunt Imogen's true nature.

Men! Men . . . was there a single decent one anywhere in the world? Isabel seriously doubted it. She had often wondered what it would be like to find a perfect man, and to enjoy a perfect marriage like the one her mother and father enjoyed. Those two dear people had come through so many trials together . . . the loss of their eldest son, the ugly war that had ravaged the plantation and left them little more than the house and the land, then the merciless carpetbaggers who had continued to infect the South long after Lee's surrender at Appomattox. As if that had not been humiliating enough for the proud men of the Confederacy, the carpetbaggers had continued to inflict further punishment by invading the governing bodies of the defeated Southern states, and assessing taxes on the planters so high that many were left bankrupt. Her family plantation, Shadows-in-the-Mist, might not have survived the war and its aftermath if her father had not kept considerable funds in his Eastern bank, an act that had left many of his neighbors doubting his loyalty to the South. Certainly, they'd had their hard times in the fourteen years since the war had ended, but Shadows-in-the-Mist was as profitable today as it had been before the war.

Shadows-in-the-Mist . . . how she wished she were there this very minute. She thought fondly of the open-air gazebo her father had built for her on her

23

sixteenth birthday . . . a gently winding garden path of handmade bricks twisting among profuse beds of miniature roses, marigolds and flowering vines, and the gazebo itself enclosed within a balustraded wall. To the left and slightly back he had planted pink and white crepe myrtle, and a tiered birdbath gleamed with fresh water. There she had gone to dream of romance and what the future might hold for her, and to stare wistfully across the gentle waters of Bayou Bouef, as though her dream lover would suddenly appear to her on the opposite side.

Oh, but how she had dreamed . . . She cared not what he might look like, only that he would have a tender, giving heart, that his hands would awaken the desires so long suppressed within the realms of her girlish innocence. But did he exist, this man she dreamed nightly of, whose touch she had felt on those warm summer afternoons at Shadows-in-the-Mist.

"I'm young," Isabel said softly, linking her fingers among the folds of her burgundy skirts. "I have so much to experience, so much to see, and so much to learn. Who will be my teacher?" Something sweet and warm and wonderful had yet to happen in her life. "Oh, Isabel, what has reduced you to talking to yourself?"

Isabel's Uncle Aldrich arrived at midmorning of the following day, and by noon he and Dustin had begun the first leg of their trip by train to Atlanta, Georgia. Now she was at the full mercy of her great-great aunt, with no Dustin around to save her. Wishing she had the nerve to destroy her parents' illusions about the dear old woman, she retired to her chamber, had Mercedes bring her meals to her, and read poetry by the veranda doors until the light had faded from the day.

With one warning rap, Mercedes entered the chamber. "Young miss, it be time that ya got ready. Mistah McCaine, he'll be comin' 'round to fetch ya mos' any time now."

Rising, flipping back her thick hair, Isabel approached the servant. "This is the last time, Mercedes. The last time I will be courted by a man of my aunt's choice. You've seen what she's invited to the house. Why, I could do better on the Boeuf. In fact, an unwashed hog caller would be improvement over these — these poor excuses for men that my aunt pairs me with!"

Raising her hand to Isabel's flustered cheek, Mercedes smiled sadly. "Now, don't you be workin' yo'self into a fret. If'n you don't wanna go tonight, then you jes' won't go. Ol' Lady jes' have to pay that hundred dollars to Mistah McCaine—"

"A hundred dollars!" bristled back a surprised Isabel. "Auntie lost that much at the table? Lord have mercy, Mercedes! Just what does this McCaine expect me to give him that is worth one hundred dollars!"

"Don't 'spect Mistah McCaine wants anything from ya but yo' company fo' the theater."

"Lord, Mercedes!" Turning away, Isabel Emerson crossed her arms, and her right foot tapped upon the highly polished planks of the floor. "Do you have any idea what kind of vermin would accept the company of a lady in payment of a gambling debt?"

"Naw'm . . . what kind o' vermin, Miss Isabel?"

Isabel turned back, her pale eyes darkening to the color of midnight. "The kind that lives under a rock, Mercedes. Lord, let me get this evening over with!"

"Mistah McCaine, he might surprise you."

25

"Nothing will surprise me, Mercedes. Nothing at all. Let's just hope and pray that he didn't miss the last step in evolution."

"Huh?"

Turning, tearing open the doors of her armoire with a mighty heave, Isabel mumbled, "Nothing, Mercedes . . . just let me know when the awful creature arrives!" Suddenly, a thought came to Isabel. "Mercedes, is Auntie retired?"

"Yas'sum, least until ten, when the fellas start arrivin'."

"Doesn't Mrs. Etienne's maid quit her duties at seven o'clock?"

"Yas'sum, sho' does." Mercedes frowned. "What you is up to, Miss Isabel?"

Isabel rushed to her writing desk and dragged stationery toward her. After she had written a quick note, she folded it and handed it to a silently waiting Mercedes. "Will you take this over to Golda right away?"

"What you is up to?" she asked again.

"You'll find out, dear. Please . . . please hurry! Time is of the essence." When Mercedes shook her head in silent acceptance, Isabel laughingly added, "You're about to find out what a clever girl I am!"

Two

Shadoe McCaine dragged his tall, well-proportioned frame into a long stretch beneath the covers of his bed. Since he had been in New Orleans, the gently dropping evening twilights had become his dawns. He enjoyed the night life in the raucous city, and had made a habit these past three months of sleeping through most of the bright hours.

Throwing off his covers, he caught the pale whiff of spice from the bath prepared by the pretty hotel maid he had befriended. She had grown accustomed to his nocturnal habits and accommodated him with more interest than she did most of the other guests at the St. Charles Hotel.

Shadoe raked back his damp, midnight-colored hair and arched his shoulders to relieve the stiffness he felt there. Then he rose, lazily traversed the expanse of rug separating him from the inviting bath and immediately caught his reflection in the cheval mirror.

"You pitiful-looking beast," he mumbled to himself, "are you even remotely human?" His pale gray eyes narrowed in a feeble attempt to focus in the half-light of the well-furnished chamber.

Looking about, he noticed that the maid, Jascena, had hung his freshly laundered shirts on the outer door of the armoire while he had slept. His boots had been cleaned and polished to a high gleam, and his wide-brimmed hat had been brushed of its lint and dust. He wondered if she performed the mundane chores because he was a man and she was a woman, or simply for the sake of the few dollars he gave her every week. Whatever the reason, he enjoyed the attention.

Shadoe had just slipped into the hot, steaming water when the door opened and Jascena entered. When she saw him at his bath, her pretty features eased into a charming hue of pink and she turned away with a sharply spoken, "Ohhh! Pardon, Mister McCaine . . . I forgot your clean towels . . ."

"Don't worry," came his deep, humorous response. "I am not the least bit shy about a woman seeing me at my bath."

"Perhaps you're not," the petite, dark-haired Jascena replied, "but I certainly am." She was not at all typical of the bold, self-centered Creole women he had encountered in his visit to the Crescent City; rather, she was charmingly timid and undemandingly delightful.

Stifling a laugh, Shadoe leaned over the side of the tub. "Why don't you back toward me with those towels?" As she began to take slow, precarious steps, he warned, "Be careful of the corner of that rug." When she was within touching distance of him, his hand moved out, and rather than taking the towels as she expected, his fingers closed firmly over her elbow and dragged her down, depositing her firmly upon her buttocks on the floor.

"Mr. McCaine!" she protested demurely, turning her eyes away once again. "What a devil of a man you are."

"But a charming one, eh?"

"For a self-confessed gambler and rogue cowboy, I suppose you are," she responded, casting him a timid glance. "Now, unhand me and allow me to go about my duties before I am dismissed. I understand you won an appointment with a lady at the tables last evening."

"Yes, an ancient, and very charming, old mariner offered her niece in lieu of the hundred dollars she had lost to me."

"And for her—" A note of jealousy eased into the soft, feminine voice, "you are going to bathe, dress in your finest, and purchase roses at the shop in the lobby, I suppose?"

"Actually—" Shadoe's fingers eased beneath the pert chin and forced her dark Creole gaze to meet his own, "I imagine if the woman can get an appointment only at the gaming tables, then she must look like a horse. Why don't you go down to the desk and . . . Gandy Cobb does get off duty at half past six, doesn't he?"

"Yes," Jascena responded.

"Go down and ask him if he'd like to earn twenty dollars this evening."

"I'm sure he'll want to know what he must do for it."

"Tell him all he has to do is pretend to be me for the evening. I'll provide him with a proper suit of clothing, two theater tickets, and a woman to dangle from his elbow."

Jascena's mood brightened. "You're going to send him in your place . . . to take the homely niece to the theater?"

"That I am, girl," he replied, sinking back into the water. "And if you can get off early, I'll take you to the theater. What do you think about that?"

With feigned indignation, the pretty maid rose to her feet. "And what makes you think, Mr. Shadoe McCaine, that a nice girl like me would want to accompany a gambler and a rogue cowboy to the theater?"

Shrugging, Shadoe replied teasingly, "Very well . . . I'll ask another pretty girl—"

"No—" She turned back, a smile brightening her pixielike features. "I'll go with you. I'm due some time off." But even as she spoke, she thought of her father, with whom she lived, and who had never—absolutely

29

never—allowed her to be with a man at night.

"What time shall I call for you?"

Perhaps her father would permit her to visit a female friend? Would he even believe such an excuse for leaving the house at night? "I'll meet you in the lobby at half past six," she answered.

"Would you like a corsage?"

"Would you have purchased one for the homely niece?"

"I imagine that I would have."

"Then I would like one, too. Now—" Dropping the towels to a chair, Jascena took small steps toward the door. "I will carry your message to Gandy."

A wink rewarded her hesitant look in his direction. Hardly had the pretty girl been gone five minutes before Gandy Cobb rapped upon the door and entered. He was about Shadoe's height of over six feet, but any similarities ended there. Whereas Shadoe was clean-shaven, the hotel desk clerk wore a strange mustache that curled up on the ends, and a goatee to hide a weak chin. His dull brown hair was heavily greased and combed starkly back from a wide, flat forehead.

Shadoe looked toward him, and when he did not speak, snapped, "Well, what about it, man?"

"You have a deal, Mr. McCaine. Twenty dollars is more than I make in a week."

"And what if the woman is a dog?"

"For twenty dollars she can also be old, toothless, and diseased. It's only the theater. I don't plan to touch her."

"Good boy!" The water was beginning to cool. Shadoe stood and dragged the clean towel around him as he stepped from the tub. "The money and theater tickets are on that table over there. You're to call for the lady at Number 124 Royal. Her name is, umm . . ." His brows crinkled in his attempt to remember. "Blast, what is—oh, yes, Emerson . . . Miss Isabel Emerson.

30

And take an extra coin to purchase a corsage."

"Certainly, Mr. McCaine."

Left alone once again, Shadoe tended to his own dressing . . . forgoing the wide-sleeved black shirt and black pants in favor of a dark blue suit and white shirt. He wore his favorite boots and a time-worn hat with a gaudy silver hat band. He'd won the hat in a poker game south of the Rio Grande, and the boots at a road ranch in Wyoming. In fact, he didn't own a thing he hadn't won in a game of chance. Even his horse, a fine black stallion, had once belonged to an Indian in the Dakota territory who had given it up begrudgingly, then had drowned his sorrow in a gallon of cheap whiskey. He had also lost on occasion, though he didn't much like thinking about that.

There wasn't a place between the Pacific and Atlantic that Shadoe hadn't visited. He'd been as far north as King George Islands in Hudson Bay and as far south as Punita Arenas in Chile. There wasn't a place anywhere around the globe he didn't plan to visit at least once in his lifetime. He wanted to see everything there was to see, and in his thirty-five years he was sure he had only touched the tip of the world's offerings. Perhaps his obsession to see everything in the years he had left stemmed from the fact that he had spent his early years on a reservation, the son of a half-breed Cheyenne renegade and a white schoolteacher. Both were gone now—his father killed by a cavalry patrol, his mother dead of cholera when he had turned eighteen. He'd been on his own ever since.

He had always been a wanderer, taking on any job that paid a few dollars, and staying only until he got bored. The longest position he'd held was as a rover on a ranch south of San Antonio. He'd left there under circumstances he still considered an injustice. He had been twenty-eight at the time, and the experience had

31

left him with a deep hatred of rich, spoiled daughters of overprotective, doting fathers who thought these demons in skirts could do no wrong.

Looking at his watch to check the time, he dropped the elaborate gold piece into an inside pocket of his jacket. Then he moved from the room and into the corridor, making his way to the hotel diner off the lobby. He needed a good meal to fill the painful hunger twisting in the pit of his stomach.

While he ate his meal in silence, he watched the comings and goings of patrons among the various and sundry shops off the hotel lobby. Occasionally, a particularly striking feminine form would catch his eye and he would watch her until she disappeared into one of the shops. Two ladies sat at an adjoining table, giggling childishly when he happened to glance in their direction. One of them dropped a handkerchief, and if it hadn't been such a ridiculously obvious ploy to get him to their table, he might have responded in a gentlemanly manner. Rather, he was terribly annoyed and pushed away from the table without his usual enjoyment of a cup of strong chicory coffee.

Thereafter he purchased a corsage from the flower shop and sat in the busy lobby to await the young lady who would accompany him to the theater. Since he had given his tickets to Gandy Cobb, he hoped Jascena would arrive shortly so that he could purchase their tickets at the window before the seats sold out. However, by quarter to eight, a very irate Shadoe McCaine realized he'd been stood up by the pretty Jascena. What to do for the first hours of the night? he wondered rising, and gallantly presented the corsage to the first lady he met in his exit of the hotel. Ah, yes . . . the niece of the spry old New Orleans matron . . . what was her name? Miss Isabel Emerson? He could still make the theater and see what manner of female atrocity he might have been paired with for the evening.

He had already formed an image in his mind: a toothless hag with hanging jowls, sagging flesh and a loud, coarse voice that could grate on the nerves of a deaf man.

Golda Dumont was at Isabel's suite at 124 Royal within minutes of completing her duties as Mrs. Etienne's maid. The ten dollars Isabel had offered to pay her was far more than she made in a week, and on her paltry salary she was not able to afford the luxury of the theater.

"But will you hate me?" entreated Isabel of the girl she had befriended, "if he is old and ugly?"

"For ten dollars, he can be anything he wants," came Golda's enthusiastic response. She held up the gown Isabel had offered to her to wear this evening, and could scarcely believe her good luck. Never in her life had she worn such a lovely dress. She was delighted by the gentle hues of the floral print with its frothy white lace framing the shoulders and edging the sleeves. Green velvet ribbon trimmed each flounce of the voluminous skirt, and Isabel had offered a black lace ornament for her to wear in her thick honey-colored hair. "It is so beautiful, Miss Isabel."

"You sits here," demanded Mercedes. "I'll fix ye'r hair jes' like I does Miss Isabel's. Would you like that, Miss Golda?"

"Is it all right?" asked Golda, looking to Isabel.

Isabel loved a well-thought-out and harmless deception; she was having a lot of fun. "You are me for the evening . . ." she replied, turning her glance to Mercedes. "Will you fix her hair the way you do mine, with the ringlets drawn to the left side of the head?"

"You mean, Miss Isabel, when you *lets* me fix it up.

33

You is one stubborn-minded woman . . . always wantin' to do everything by yo'self."

"I'm just not accustomed to being waited on. I'll have you know that back on the plantation—"

"You ain't back on the plantation," came the maid's instant reply. "Yo' old auntie wants you to be pampered, an' you one stubborn gal, fo' sho'."

"My hair?" interjected Golda. "You're going to fix it?"

In the moments that followed, the plain little maid from across Royal was transformed into a lovely lady fit for an evening at the theater. At half past seven, when the bell finally rang at the front garden, Golda accompanied Mercedes downstairs and Isabel rushed to the balcony in an effort to see the man she had rebuffed. In the overhanging darkness, she saw little more than his tall physique and the gleam of his hair. Was it silver, or merely coated with grease? Regardless, she drew a small breath of relief when, moments later, the hired cab pulled onto the street.

Now, how to spend a Friday evening? Isabel mused, turning back to her chamber. Wouldn't it be terribly amusing to see how the appointment went? Auntie was abed and wouldn't arise until close to ten, the usual hour she opened her private den of iniquity to the chosen few. Yes, yes, she would go to the theater alone, and would spy upon Golda and the greasy gambler.

Confiding her plan in Mercedes, the maid instantly argued, "Ain't decent fo' a lady to go out in public unescorted an' without a chaperone, 'specially, this time o' the night. Men 'bout N'Awleans, they be thinkin' you is a loose woman, Miss Isabel. Be thinkin' ye'r britches'll be a might easy to crawl into. Lawd, Missy, where is yo' brains?"

"Well, Mercedes," responded an undaunted Isabel, lifting her chin in a haughty air. "In a half hour my brains will be at the theater with the rest of me. Which dress shall I wear?" she continued, throwing open the armoire.

"I ain't a goin' to help you, Miss Isabel. You go out unescorted, an' you get yo'self hurt, they be liable to hang Mercedes, jes' like they did that nigrah Pauline what beat her mistress and the little white chilluns back befo' the war. Naw'm, Miss Isabel, Mercedes, she ain't even goin' to help you pick out a dress. You gets out o' this house unescorted this time o' night, you does it without no help from me."

"Very well," shrugged Isabel. "Just keep an eye out for auntie, will you?"

"Naw'm." Shaking her head, Mercedes began her retreat. "Ain't goin' to help you no way . . . *no* way. You is on your own."

Isabel simply would not have her plans thwarted by the plain and simple good reasoning of her auntie's maid. She was going to the theater, escort or no escort.

Moments later, she assessed her overall appearance, tucked up a recalcitrant lock of flaxen hair and drew a burgundy cape around her slender shoulders. Tiptoeing along the corridor so as not to awaken Aunt Imogen, she traversed the stairs and stepped upon the banquette. When Mercedes cast a disapproving glance from the parlor, a stalwart Isabel whispered, "I suppose you won't hail a cab for me either?"

"Naw'm. Onliest thing I'll do is ast you one mo' time to stay home."

"No," came Isabel's rebellious answer. "I'll hail my own cab."

At the street, Isabel raised a gloved hand, summoning the cab sitting quietly at the corner of Royal. The clip of the horse's hooves seemed overly loud, and she cast a quick glance up at Aunt Imogen's window, hoping that the noise would not awaken her. Darkness continued to prevail there, and she breathed a little sigh.

When she settled into the cab, the driver asked, "Where to, ma'am?"

"The St. Charles Theater." As the cab pulled away, Isabel realized that she'd failed to return her medallion to her neck after she'd finished her hair. "Driver—" The cab halted, and in that moment as he awaited her direction, she decided it was not worth the chance of detection to return for her necklace. "Never mind," she said, and the cab began to move once again.

Nervous energy made her palms feel damp within the confines of her gloves and she removed them, tucking them into her reticule. The night was cool and overcast, and beyond the rooflines the gentle flashes of lightning brought a distant threat of rain. Suddenly, she realized how foolish she was being. She wouldn't return from the theater until after ten, and one of her aunt's male visitors might be aware that she was to be accompanied by that snake McCaine. Suppose he should relay the encounter to Aunt Imogen and be much too quick to point out that she had returned alone? Auntie would surely have directed him to see her safely to the door.

Horsefeathers! thought a defiant Isabel. What will auntie do? Take a strap to me? Report my indiscretion to my parents? They know me well enough to expect anything! Well, she would accept the consequences of her reckless breach of accepted manners when and if the occasion should arise. For now, she wanted only to enjoy the theater and see the dreadful creature who had won her company at Auntie's gaming table.

Nothing was going as planned for Shadoe McCaine this evening. By the time he arrived at the theater a few minutes before curtain time, he found all seats sold out.

He stood upon the walkway, his thumbs tucked into the waist of his trousers, his feet apart, and his eyes sweeping up and down the street. It was much too early for the saloons, and he really wasn't sure what to do with himself. When a hired cab pulled up to the theater he gave its occupant, lost in the shadows of the dark interior, little more than a perfunctory glance.

But when a small, exposed ankle met his downcast gaze, his full attentions were upon the passenger. Though she was faced away from him and covered by a somber cape, he could tell that she was tall and slim, and the flawless hand placing a few coins in the driver's hand gave clear evidence of her youth. Then she turned, betraying her lovely oval face, patrician nose, and powder-blue eyes, and he felt his knees suddenly become as flaccid as weeds. What an expressive mouth, full, sensual and pouting . . . and he had never seen such a complexion, so soft and glowing that he could hardly believe she was not a porcelain statue. When she moved, for a moment her eyes connected to his, and he was sure the smallest smile had touched upon her rose-colored mouth. He wanted to pinch himself to make sure he was not imagining the loveliness moving quickly past him.

Then Isabel Emerson saw the sign which read Sold Out, released an indignant "Oh!" and stamped her foot. As she turned, she dragged the heavy cloak from her shoulders. "Nothing is going right this evening!" she complained.

Shadoe McCaine saw his opportunity. Turning, he removed his hat and said politely, "Same thing happened to me. I was really looking forward to seeing this play." Actually, he couldn't care less about the play. He cared only that an enchanting beauty such as he had never even imagined stood before him.

Isabel Emerson lifted her eyes to the swarthy male

features, then made eye contact. He was quite handsome, though oddly dressed in comparison to other men in and about New Orleans, and she thought he had the most remarkable, and almost exotic ash gray eyes, a halo of black encircling their gray depths. He had spoken to her and she couldn't be rude. "Yes, I shouldn't have arrived so late," she offered an answer.

Shadoe McCaine, unable to find his voice right away, felt a trifle ridiculous. He was crushing his hat to the broad expanse of his chest like a giddy schoolboy. When she suddenly swept her head to disengage a lock from the collar of her shimmering pink jacquard gown, he noticed that her thick blond hair was accented by a braid entwined with pearls. He could imagine their rich depths long and full and loose, intertwined among his caressing fingers. Crimson rushed into his bronze cheeks as his eyes met her cool blue ones once again. "Sorry, I was daydreaming—"

"At night?" came her subtle response.

Though he had immediately recognized her to be a lady, and one who would certainly exercise some discretion, Shadoe McCaine blurted out, "Do you have room in your life for a new friend?"

Isabel had thought she'd heard every line a man could use to meet a woman, but this was one she'd certainly never heard before. And it was quite a charming one at that. With a shy smile, she responded, "It would all depend on who the applicant for the position was."

Shadoe grinned. "How about me? Would you care to have coffee and we can get to know each other?"

Certainly, Isabel was more than a little interested in the handsome rogue. She had to remember, however, that she was not on the Boeuf, surrounded by young men she had grown up with and whose every planned encroachment she could predict by instinct. Though her heart longed to take the chance, her mouth very softly uttered the words, "I hardly think so, sir. I don't even know your name."

"That's easy to fix . . . my name is—" His mouth pressed into a grimace. Suppose this lovely young lady should know Isabel Emerson and was aware that she was being accompanied to the theater this evening by Shadoe McCaine? Certainly, she would wonder how he could be in two places at once. But perhaps she wouldn't know a simple hotel clerk. "Cobb . . . Gandy Cobb," he lied, offering his hand. "And you are?"

Isabel's hand slipped into his warm one, withdrawing almost instantly. "And I am—" Could she tell him the truth? Suppose he should know that gambling rogue Shadoe McCaine and that he was accompanying a woman named Isabel Emerson to the theater tonight? She couldn't be in two places at once. "I am Golda Dumont."

"Now that we are acquaintances, Miss Golda Dumont, shall we have that cup of coffee?"

What harm would it do? thought Isabel. There was a restaurant across the street, and many people within. Certainly, if this Gandy Cobb attempted to take liberties with her, any number of gentlemen would jump to her defense. Besides, she did not plan to ever see him again and he would never know of her small lie. "Very well, since we've both missed the theater." Pointing gracefully across the street, she added, "At that restaurant over there." As she took a place beside him to cross the road, Isabel mused, *I can't believe I am doing this! What would auntie think?"*

Moments later, Isabel sat across a table from him, her hand resting upon a red checkered table cloth as they waited for their coffee. She dropped her gaze from his warm gray eyes and began drumming her long, tapered fingernails upon the table. "Are you nervous?" questioned Shadoe McCaine.

39

Her gaze cut coolly to his own. "No . . . should I be?" She shuddered to imagine what he was thinking of her, a woman going to the theater with neither escort nor chaperone, then accepting the invitation of a man she had never seen before. He probably thought she was one of the "friendly" ladies of New Orleans and would be rewarded with whatever those kinds of women did in the long hours of darkness.

Shadoe McCaine was amused by the supremely elegant lady sitting across from him. He was also very much in awe, as his silent scrutiny failed to find even one tiny flaw in her. She was like a porcelain doll he had seen in a San Francisco shop window.

A somber young waiter deposited two cups of coffee on the table between them. "Cream or sugar?" he questioned.

"Not for me . . . Miss Dumont?"

"I would like both," she answered.

"Sugar rots your teeth, and cream makes you fat," said Shadoe McCaine.

Lifting her gaze to the waiter, she said, "Sugar and cream, please. I will take my chances on the long-term effects." When the waiter departed, she said to Shadoe McCaine, "Do you plan to be around long enough to watch my teeth fall out and the fat roll over my bones?"

"Can't think of anything I'd like better," he muttered, drawing his hand against his smiling mouth.

Isabel did not see the waiter approach. Thus, the tray carrying cream and sugar deposited beside her left elbow startled her. Preparing her coffee to her liking, she looked toward Shadoe McCaine, smiled, then said, "Tell me about yourself, sir."

"Better yet. Tell me about you."

She smiled prettily. "Why don't we keep the mystery in this unexpected meeting. Let's not tell each other anything about ourselves. Won't that be much more interesting . . . letting our imaginations run wild?"

He shrugged. "I'm game." *And if I'm lucky, you might be pleasant game for the evening,* he thought, cutting his gaze to the steaming black liquid in his cup. *After all, wasn't she attending the theater unescorted? Was my first impression all wrong? A well born lady would never have attempted such an indiscretion.*

"What are you thinking?" asked Isabel, cutting into his moment of silent thought.

"I was thinking that it might rain tonight," he responded, a half-cocked smile grazing his mouth. "What are you thinking?"

"Actually—" Isabel leaned a bit over the table and whispered, "I was trying to surmise what your nationality might be. Are you an Indian?"

"Quarter, actually. My father was a half-breed Cheyenne . . . my mother was white."

With sweet innocence, Isabel remarked, "I like your eyes. They're very kind . . . very mysterious."

Shadoe smiled his pleasure at the easily offered compliment. "And you . . . I have not seen another Creole woman with hair like spun gold and eyes so pale a shade of blue that the color is hardly there at all."

"I am not Creole," she responded. "I have my father's coloring—and he was born in the East." Then she added, "and I have my mother's temper, though my dear old aunt with whom I am now residing would certainly agree that my temper came directly from her."

What a shame! he thought. *The pretty thing has lost her parents and has been taken in by a caring relative.* "Is that a fair warning?" he said after a moment.

"Take it as you wish." Taking a sip of her coffee, she quickly set the cup down and grimaced. "Even with sugar, it still tastes like mud."

"You could have had tea," said Shadoe McCaine.

"You know what I would like right now?"

41

He smiled. "What is that?"

"A cab."

His disappointment was as readable as acute pain. "So soon? May I see you home?"

Alarm flashed in Isabel's pale eyes, though instantly suppressed. "No, I—" Oh, what excuse could she come up with and not be considered rude? "I work for a woman who does not approve of male companions."

"You're a maid?"

Raising a finely arched brow, Isabel asked with some indignation, "Isn't it an honorable enough profession?"

"The way you are dressed . . . I would hardly have guessed that you're in domestic service."

"Well, I am and I'm not ashamed of it. Please, won't you hail a cab for me?"

"May I see you again?"

"Perhaps."

"When?"

Isabel's gaze moved boldly over the handsome bronze features. She liked the way he looked at her in return, though it made her blush with embarrassment. "I shop at the French Market on Saturdays. Perhaps we'll bump into each other."

When she arose, Shadoe McCaine stumbled to his feet, taking her cape to drop it to her slim shoulders. Together they moved out-of-doors, and Shadoe hailed the nearest cab. As he assisted her into the seat, he entreated once again, "Are you sure I can't see you safely home?"

"I am quite certain. I cannot take the chance of my employer's disapproval." Tucking herself among the plush seats, Isabel said to the driver, "We may go now." As the cab pulled away from the curb and the tall, swarthy stranger, Isabel turned to watch him, confident that in the darkness he did not see her do so. She was so terribly attracted to him that it made her insides tie into knots. Her heart was beating oh, so quickly, and she could still feel the warmth of his hand upon her elbow as he had assisted her into the cab.

She knew, without a doubt, that she would see him again tomorrow. It pleased her immensely to think that he might tarry about the French Market all day, waiting for her. She smiled to herself. *I can find my own male companions, Auntie, thank you.*

Three

As Shadoe McCaine neared Jackson Square, he met a steady stream of people laden with baskets and bundles. Unaccustomed to the light of day, his eyes were still struggling to adjust to the glare of the sun this cool November morning. But it was a small inconvenience. He had only one purpose as he joined in the cadence of the busy-looking people, and he soon stood on the corner opposite the French Market.

The sight of the market never failed to amaze him: the strangest and most complicated mixture of races anywhere on earth, the baskets fat or delicate, adorned with ribbons or so decayed the worn ribs scarcely seemed able to carry their various and sundry produce. The stalls were deeply worn and dirty, and at the chicken repository dead poultry hung downward from the roof in grim waiting for interested buyers.

The dialects of the many fascinating residents of this strange place, the odors of dead poultry and fresh and rotting vegetables, even the endless clucking of the live chickens waiting in coops to be killed did not detract from Shadoe McCaine's search.

Above the jabbering of dark-skinned children, he listened for the sound of her voice. Ignoring the sickly smell of flat, white-headed cabbages, he ached for the aroma of her lightly perfumed skin. Beyond the thick-set women at their stands busily filling baskets for their patrons, he longed for the sight of gleaming golden hair, powder-blue eyes, and the slender form of her en-

44

folded within yards of freshly laundered calico.

He cared not a whit that he'd gotten only a couple hours of sleep that morning. He had to see the beauty who had stamped her foot at finding the theater sold out. She was all he'd thought about for the past ten hours, and he would wait all day to see her if need be.

Shadoe thought of his conversation with Gandy Cobb that morning at the hotel desk. The young man had not been overly impressed with Miss Isabel Emerson. Though she had been pretty, he had found her to be giddy, absentminded and a little strange. So absorbed had she been in the play that she had scarcely responded to the sound of her own name. The money paid him had been worth it, he had assured Shadoe, and Gandy had not considered the evening a total waste.

"Where are you, pretty lady?" muttered Shadoe McCaine, his gaze sweeping longingly over the stalls and counters of the marketplace.

Isabel had arisen early, as was her usual habit. Sitting in the kitchen with Mercedes, she nursed a cup of weak coffee between her fingers. She wasn't the least bit interested in the plate of eggs and pancakes Mercedes had placed before her, nor was she in a talkative mood. She could think of nothing but raven-colored hair, ash-gray eyes and a subtly sarcastic masculine voice nurtured by the tones of the wild West.

"Is you listenin' to me, Miss Isabel?"

Isabel's gaze lifted blankly to the pinched and worried features of the maid. "Huh?"

"Don't you 'huh!' me, Miss Isabel Emerson. I done spent the las' five minutes tellin' you that Miss Golda brung back yo' dress this mo'nin', an' I be's askin' you if 'n you had a good time at the theater las' evenin' an' you sittin' there like all the life done worked its way out 'a yo' body through yo' big toe."

"I'm sorry, Mercedes." With a weary sigh, Isabel shrugged her shoulders. "The theater was sold out. I didn't get to go."

"Oh?" A dark brow shot up and Isabel was certain that this was where the interrogation would begin. "You was gone fo' a while. Where'd you go then?"

"Well—" Dare she tell Mercedes that she'd allowed herself to be picked up by a strange man? She thought not. "I had a cup of coffee and then I just had the cabbie drive me around the city for a while."

"What fo' you do that, Miss Isabel?"

"Just didn't feel like coming straight home. Tell me, Mercedes—" she continued, in an attempt to change the subject, "did Golda say how she enjoyed the theater?"

"Says it was jes' fine but she weren't too impressed with that Mr. Shadoe McCaine. Says he was a bit absentminded an' uppity an' didn't even seem to recognize the sound of his own name. Said he was real stuffy-like. But she says it was worth it and to thank you fo' the ten dollars."

"What ten dollars is that?"

Isabel was sure her heart had skipped a beat, so startled was she by the grave texture of Aunt Imogen's voice as she entered the kitchen. Drawing a trembling hand to her throat, she quickly explained, "I lost ten dollars from my purse last evening at the theater. I was just telling Mercedes about it."

"Careless, girl. Very careless." With a smile that gave Isabel a full view of her oversized false teeth, Aunt Imogen asked spryly, "How did you like Mr. McCaine? I do hope he conducted himself as a gentleman."

"I had no complaints," she replied a little sheepishly, casting her eyes downward. If Aunt Imogen knew what

46

she'd done, she wouldn't hear the last of it for days. "I must insist, Auntie, that you stop these pesky attempts at matchmaking."

"I'm to take it then that you don't plan to see the young man again?"

"I certainly do not," she responded, allowing the softest note of indignation to affect her tone. "Your gambling debt is cleared and that is all that matters."

Mercedes mumbled something beneath her breath.

"What did you say?" growled Aunt Imogen.

"Mercedes, she ain't said nothin', seen nothin', an' knows nothin'. I's jes' cookin' this here egg fo' you, sunny side up, jes' the way you like it."

Flicking a long, bony finger, Imogen snapped, "And I don't like that burned black fringe around it either. I do hope you're using the lard and not the butter. I just hate the way the butter burns on the bottom of the egg!"

"Jes' stop that complainin'," Mercedes fussed right back at her, turning to the table with the plate, then setting it before the old woman. "If it ain't the way you like it, I'll eat it myself an' fix you another!"

Isabel smiled. Despite the bickering of the two women, they were deeply devoted to each other. Mercedes had been Aunt Imogen's slave for twenty years before the war, and afterwards she had stayed on, not the least bit interested in the paltry salary paid to her every week. She'd tucked every penny of it into her account at the Bank of New Orleans. Mercedes had told her not too long ago that the way Imogen de'Cambre went through her own funds, she was going to need the money she was saving to bury her one day.

Rising, casting the two women a loving glance, Isabel announced, "If either of you has a list for the market, I'd like to have it before ten. I thought I would go to market early today."

"You can't go without Dustin," said Aunt Imogen

firmly, waving a bony finger.

Isabel's mouth dropped open. "Don't be ridiculous. Dustin is not here, I have marketing to do for the household, and I will not, I repeat *will not* be treated like a child. Now, have your list ready or I'll go without it!"

Suddenly, Imogen de'Cambre cackled, tapping her cane heavily upon the floor several times. "Listen to that girl, will you, Mercedes? Just as spritely and hard-headed as her mama. Have you ever seen anything like it?"

Mercedes shared a look between her mistress and a grim-faced Isabel. "Naw'm, can't say as I ever have."

With a childlike quality, Imogen asked, "When's the girl going to give me my birthday gift?"

A dark eyebrow eased upward. "What makes you think she's got a gift fo' you?"

"Because I found where she hid it!" laughed Imogen.

"Shame on you!" admonished Mercedes. "You is a jes' terrible, Miz Imogen . . . jes' like a child!"

"You certainly are!" agreed Isabel.

Isabel had fidgeted more in the past two hours than she had in her lifetime. By the hour of nine she had brushed her hair to a high gleam, leaving it long and loose, then had tucked it up into combs. She had powdered her cheeks, then had scrubbed them, thinking he might like a fresh, clean face instead. She had changed her gown five times already, and really wasn't satisfied with her final choice. Should she wear the brown shoes or the black lace-up boots? Should she wear her gray wool cape or the lighter cotton one?

As she met her flustered reflection in the mirror at her dressing table, she wondered why she was bothering. She was simply going to the market, and that devilish rogue she'd met last evening had probably forgotten about her the moment the cab had pulled away from him. And why should she care anyway if she saw him again? He was just a silly man!

Oh, but who was she trying to fool? He was a devastatingly handsome male creature, and the pace of her heart quickened at the smallest thought of him.

Without warning, Mercedes' old tomcat jumped to the dressing table. Taken aback for just a moment, Isabel quickly scratched the scruffy patch of fur between his war-torn ears. "Where have you been, Mr. Washington?" she asked. "Off prowling and fighting over the girls, were you?" A long, low "merrooww" answered her question. Standing, she picked the gray tabby up and held it close. "Come on, I've got some prowling to do myself this morning."

Isabel met Mercedes in the corridor, wielding a mighty mean broom. "So! There's that beast!" she grunted. And when a startled Isabel staved off the impending blow, she continued, "That beast done took my pancake off my breakfast plate while I was fetchin' my coffee and chugged it right down in front o' my eyes!"

Clicking her tongue, Isabel elbowed her way past the maid with the purring and smugly satisfied cat clutched protectively in her arms. "I do declare, Mercedes! There was a whole plate of pancakes. Poor old Mr. Washington was hungry, that's all!"

Trailing behind Isabel, who moved spritely toward the stairs, Mercedes mumbled, "I done give him all them fish entrails this mo'nin'. That beast is a bottomless pit! Lawd, I should'a named him John Brown. Maybe he'd of already met his private li'l hangman an' saved me the misery of him!"

As Isabel began to descend the stairs, Mr. Washington spied a mouse scurrying along the baseboard in the banquette below. As he pushed himself from her arms with the might of a small army, Isabel lost her footing and suddenly found herself tumbling down the last flight of stairs. With a frantic and squealing Mercedes close behind her, Isabel sat spraddled upon the banquette, her skirts scattered about her legs and her hair dragging across her face. As tears, more of anger than of pain, flooded her eyes, she exclaimed, "Oh, that beastly puss! I think I've sprained my ankle!"

"Child, is you bad hurt? Lawd, is you bad hurt?" wailed Mercedes, dropping to one knee.

Crossing her arms, Isabel raised a pale eyebrow. "I think, Mercedes, that I sprained my ankle." At which time, an unthinking Mercedes grabbed the extended foot and gave it a mighty tug. Isabel screamed, the tears now filling her eyes of acute pain. "It might be broken now, Mercedes. Oh do help me up, will you?"

Soon Isabel was dropping into a chair at the kitchen table and drawing the swelling ankle up across her knee. Removing her shoe, she squeezed her foot, hoping the injury would not be too bad. But again, pain came to her eyes and she bit her lip. "I simply must get to the market," she said to Mercedes, who was dropping a small towel into a pot of hot water.

"Naw'm, you ain't goin' to the market today."

"But I must!" retorted Isabel.

"Well, you ain't," Mercedes spoke firmly. "I'll go today. Walk'll do these tired ol' bones some good!"

"But *I* must go. It is imperative."

"Bein' real ridiculous there, Miss Isabel. Ain't no life and death situation, goin' to the market. I'll fetch Dr. Tillman to look at yo' ankle, then I'll go to the market myself." Holding the steaming towel across a wooden spoon, Mercedes squeezed the excess water from it, approached and dropped the towel across Isabel's ankle, which was just beginning to swell. "Do you hear me, girl?"

Isabel did not answer. Her downcast gaze holding

the floor as if she expected gold to pop up in the cracks, she was thinking of a handsome rogue with coal-black hair, hanging patiently around the French Market waiting for her to arrive. The thought of disappointing him mortified her. Meeting Mercedes' now sympathetic gaze, she drew a trembling sigh and entreated, "May I confide in you, Mercedes?"

To which the maid replied, "Always could, Miss Isabel."

"I met a man last night," she quickly confessed. "I am sure he will be at the French Market today because I told him I would be there."

"So!" Shaking her head, Mercedes mumbled, "That's why you so anxious to get to the market today, is it?"

"It is. Oh, please . . . please, Mercedes." In an effort to reinforce her desperation, Isabel took her hand and held it gently. "Won't you give a message to him? Won't you let him know why I'm not there? He won't be difficult to recognize. He has gray eyes and coal-black hair—"

"Harumph!" growled Mercedes. "Jes' about all that Creole pond-scum down at the market has that black hair!"

"Oh, but he is different. He stands out in a crowd . . . tall and incredibly handsome. Please, oh, please, won't you give him a message?"

"Well—" It had always been difficult to deny Miss Isabel anything. Mercedes loved her as much as she might have her own daughter, had she been so blessed. "I reckon if I sees a man fittin' that description, it won't hurt to pass on the word."

With a smug but lovable smile, Isabel crinkled her nose. "What would I do without you, Mercedes?"

Scarcely had Mercedes left the house half an hour later before Isabel was an agonizing wreck. She limped

51

painfully back and forth in the banquette, trying desperately to think of a way that she might intercept Mercedes before she reached the market. Perhaps if she hired a cabbie to take a message to her. Perhaps Golda would leave early for the market and draw Mercedes aside. Oh, what was she to do?

She had forgotten to tell Mercedes that she had assumed Golda's identity last evening. Should Mercedes spot her Gandy Cobb at the market, relay that *Isabel Emerson,* for whom he was waiting, had twisted her ankle and wouldn't be at the market, he might possibly think she'd gone a bit daft. Her handsome rogue knew her as Golda, not Isabel. Oh, what was she to do?

Dr. Tillman arrived at the house a few minutes later, looked over Isabel's ankle, tugging it here and poking it there, and finally announced that it was, indeed, merely sprained. "Not a single broken bone," he jovially announced, giving her foot a short series of soft pats. Wrapping it in several yards of gauze, he gave instructions that she stay off it as much as possible for at least a week.

Moments later, she sat alone in the parlor, fretting over the untimely accident, cursing the beast that had caused it, worrying over the message Mercedes might relay to a very confused fellow, and wishing she had never awakened to this dreary, overcast day.

Shadoe McCaine was just as fretful as Isabel Emerson at that moment, as he paced back and forth, looking at his watch, then across the road at the gathering faces of the French Market patrons. At fifteen minutes past the hour of ten, he was beginning to think that his lovely New Orleans maid would not make the appearance she had promised. Surely she would want to get her shopping over with early and return to her domestic regimen.

Never in his life had he felt so compelled to take a lady away from such a life. He felt like the mythical knight in shining armor rescuing the maiden from the fiery dragon. He went through large sums of money as soon as he made it, and his largest holding at the moment was the value of the stallion he'd won in a poker game. What could he offer such a lady? But then again, wouldn't any way of life he offered her be preferable to working as a maid for some crotchety old Creole matron?

What was wrong with him, thinking so seriously about a woman he'd spent only a few minutes with last evening? Thinking so seriously about a woman he might never see again? Perhaps he'd had too much to drink at the club last night after he had left her and wasn't himself. Perhaps he was losing his mind!

Ah! There was a familiar face. Crossing the muddy walkway in several long leaps, Shadoe McCaine's tall, imposing frame soon loomed over the short, wide-girthed Mercedes. "Good morning, m'lady," he greeted, tipping his hat. "How is that charming old gambler you work for?"

Mercedes looked up, a smile widening her round face. "Why, Mr. Shadoe McCaine, what is you doin' out in the light o' day? Why, don't you know that Dr. Frankensense gave his monster the life in the dark? Durin' a thunderstorm at that . . . an' I think the sky's goin' to open up real soon!"

"I think that's Franken*stein.*" Shadoe McCaine took shorter steps to keep pace with the woman. "Mercedes, do you read those horror stories? I thought you had better taste."

"I do's," she calmly pointed out, selecting a firm head of cabbage and dropping it into her basket. "Don't I avoid company like yours?"

Shadoe McCaine laughed. "Then why did you slip

me a bottle of Imogen's best champagne the other night?"

Mercedes smiled. True, she liked the young fellow with the coal-black hair and gray eyes. He was— "Lawd!"

The single, sharply spoken word compelled Shadoe McCaine to inquire, "What is wrong, Mercedes?"

Her gaze swung up to take in his features as if she had never seen him before. Was this the man Isabel had hoped to see this morning? This man she had rebuffed last evening? Hadn't he attended the theater with Golda, thinking her to be Isabel? Mercedes suddenly couldn't think. "Is you by any chance hopin' to see a certain lady this mo'nin?" she asked, pinching her dark brows together in a severe frown.

Shadoe was momentarily taken aback. How could she possibly have known that? "Well, yes, as a matter of fact."

Setting her basket beside her, Mercedes raised her right hand. "Is she 'bout yay high, a lookin' like a graceful willow, with hair the color o' corn silk and eyes about the same shade as that stone on yo' finger?"

Shadoe looked down at the large topaz in his ring. "You described her perfectly."

"Well, I'll be a po' man's paramour!"

"Do you know her?" asked Shadoe, taking up the basket for her.

"Know her? She's sittin' back at that house a frettin' 'cause she done twisted her ankle an' couldn't come to the market this mo'ning. Lawd, is she a frettin'!"

"She hurt herself? How did that happen?"

As Mercedes wandered among the stalls, picking out her produce and paying for it with the coins in her apron, she related the details of the accident that had happened that morning. Then, curiosity got the best of her, and she asked, "How'd yo' evenin' with Miss Isabel go las' night?"

A sheepish grin captured Shadoe's handsome features. "I'm afraid I hired a hotel clerk to fill in for me. Wasn't nice of me, was it?" Mercedes smiled to herself, making no comment. Wasn't it ironic, two young people working so hard to avoid the other's company, meeting by accident just an hour or so later, and being so attracted to each other that they conspired to meet again? Fate. That's what it was. Somebody up yonder was determined that Shadoe McCaine and Isabel Emerson would be together. "Do you think the lady would mind if I drop by to see her?" asked Shadoe.

The images forming in her mind made Mercedes smile once again. "Don't 'spect it would hurt. You tag along with me, Mr. Shadoe McCaine, while I completes my shoppin', an' you can escort me back to Royal."

"Is that where she lives? Is she a neighbor?"

"That's where she lives, sho' 'nuff. Lawd, but is she goin' to be surprised to see you!"

"Will she lose her wages due to her incapacity?" inquired Shadoe.

"Huh? What you is talkin' about?"

"She will be unable to perform her domestic duties, won't she?"

Mercedes wondered what he meant. Isabel performed domestic duties, but only because she chose to do them. She certainly did not receive wages like an ordinary maid. There was nothing ordinary about Miss Isabel Emerson. Since she was not sure what fibs Isabel had told this young man last evening, Mercedes replied matter-of-factly. "She'll tell you all that herself, I reckon," and left it at that.

Four

Auntie had risen just long enough to receive her birthday gift from Isabel and fuss over her injured ankle. She was now holed up once again in her private suites, and Isabel curled up on the divan with a book. She enjoyed the writings of the Shelleys and was trying to get into *The Last Man,* Mary's second novel. She smiled as she remembered Mercedes' wide saucerlike eyes as she had listened to passages she'd read to her from *Frankenstein,* emphasizing the especially frightening scenes. Isabel thought it wickedly delightful that to this day Mercedes was not sure if there really had been a monster such as the fictional Dr. Frankenstein had created.

After a while, Isabel began staring absently around the large, well-furnished room, seeing everything and yet seeing nothing at all. In her mind, she was following the vision of him—her handsome knight—as he sauntered about the room. Those seductive, ghostlike gray eyes turned to hold her with sweet compliment, his mouth twisted into that wry, boyish smile again, and his low, masculine chuckle reverberated through the parlor like a magical, unseen breeze. Sighing deeply, Isabel closed her book upon her lap and let her eyelids fall heavily, as though she hadn't gotten a moment of sleep last night. She had slept, but she had also dreamed, wondrous, captivating visions that had kept her frolicking like a day old filly. Yes, she had slept last night, but, oh, how tired her dreams had made her!

"That's ridiculous. There must be a good reason why I'm so tired," she mumbled to herself, trying to drag her eyelids open but finding it physically impossible. So, she allowed sleep to capture her and draw her into its peaceful, green summertime domain. The air was sweet with new clover and wisteria, and far beyond the timberline, robins moved slowly over the meadows. She sat in the summerhouse her father had built and listened to droplets of rain begin to splash in the fountain, to a warm breeze rush along the treetops.

But there . . . moving up the banks from the gently swirling waters of Bayou Boeuf . . . who dared invade her solitude? She prepared to reprimand him, to send him back from whence he had come, to flick him off like so much dust if he became a persistent interloper.

But then she saw who it was: her black-haired knight with his ash-gray eyes, his tall, perfect male physique naked to the waist, his strong, sinewy hand slinging a crisp, white shirt across his broad shoulder. The closer he came to her, the more narrow were his eyes, the more revealing were their fathomless depths. No words were exchanged between them; their eyes said everything that needed to be said. She arose, her arms opened and he stepped into her welcoming embrace. How strong and virile he felt against her, how intoxicating the spicy, manly aroma of him . . . and she melted, like sugar in a rainstorm, against him, becoming part of him. . . .

"Kiss me, my handsome rogue," came an oh, so

far away demand from somewhere deep within her subconsciousness. "Kiss me before I might die from lack of it."

Shadoe McCaine had at first been surprised to find a mere maid relaxing in the luxury of Imogen de'Cambre's elegantly furnished parlor, but it could not nearly match the degree of surprise he felt at hearing her gently spoken demands as he hovered over her. He had entered the house on Royal Street with a softly chuckling Mercedes, who had motioned him to the parlor and immediately withdrawn toward the kitchen with her basket of plucked chickens and fresh produce.

Now, he knelt on one knee beside her, watching the rapid movements of her eyes beneath translucent eyelids indicating that she was dreaming. Who was this unseen lover she so seductively invited to share the warmth of her kiss? He had never seen such a lovely creature, her slim ankle wrapped in its yards of gauze exposed below the hem of her clean white dress with its soft gathers of crocheted lace . . . her hair was like a golden cloud upon her shoulders and her hands rested oh, so gently upon the pages of the book she had been reading. Shadoe McCaine felt at that moment that he could kneel there for the rest of his life and simply look at her. But when her mouth again parted and she whispered, "What are you waiting for, rogue?" his fingers gently entwined among the tresses of her long, loose hair and his mouth, quivering like a nervous school boy's, touched softly upon her own.

Shadoe had expected her to come fully awake, release a cry of indignation and slap him with every ounce of her feminine might. Rather, her hands scooted across the expanse of his shoulders, and her mouth responded to his bold caress with wanton abandon. While the chance was his, Shadoe savored the sweet taste of her kiss, which was like none he had ever experienced before. His flesh prickled with delightful sensation beneath the slow travels of her long, tapered fingernails and he almost wished she would never awaken, never be aware that her dream had become reality, that a mere, flesh-and-blood mortal had assumed the identity of the illusionary lover she had invited to her sensual mouth.

In the realms of her dream, Isabel Emerson was surprised that the kiss of her lover had gained such acute reality. She could still see the Boeuf across the shimmering distance, still feel the summertime breeze teasing and caressing her hair, and still feel the carpet of green splendor beneath her satin slippers . . . all that was a dream, she knew beyond a shadow of a doubt. But the man in her arms was more than a dream, more than an illusion. Slowly her eyes crept open, focused in the pale light of the parlor, and gained the depth and clarity that brought her sensual response to the kiss of her dream lover to an abrupt halt.

"Ohhh!" Isabel Emerson jerked back to the pillows upon the divan, her eyes wide and searching, her mouth parting in shock and disbelief as she met the steady, good-humored gaze of the man she had just kissed. "Wh—what are you doing here?" she asked the man she knew as Gandy Cobb. "How did you find me?"

"Mercedes brought me here," he responded, drawing slightly back and preparing for the slap she might possibly deal him. But it did not seem forthcoming and he relaxed a little. "You did not tell me you were a maid in Mrs. de'Cambre's house. She must give her domestics quite a few liberties not afforded in other households."

Despite the pain beginning to throb in her ankle, Isabel swung her feet to the floor, quickly covering them with her voluminous skirts. "You shouldn't be here," she warned, casting a look across his shoulder as she watched for her aunt. The dear woman had a habit of appearing at the most inopportune of times.

Rising from his knee, he dropped to the divan beside her. "You must be the personal maid of Mrs. de'Cambre's niece."

Her features paled. At the moment, she felt that she could literally throttle Mercedes for bringing this man here and putting her in such a situation. She had wanted her to give him a message . . . that was all . . . not drag him home like a wayward pup! How would he feel when he learned that she had lied, that she was, indeed, the niece? She simply had to find a way to get rid of him, before her aunt made a second appearance of the morning and blew her cover. "You simply must go. I am not allowed to have visitors while I am on duty."

"But you are hurt," he quietly pointed out, taking her hand. "How can you perform your domestic chores?" Then he had the forethought to realize that if Mrs. de'Cambre made an appearance, she would most certainly address him by his true identity. The lovely woman whose company he was now enjoying would then realize he had lied. Because the morning had not been a total waste—he had, after all, tasted the sweetness of her kiss—he quickly got to his feet. "Yes, yes, of course, you are right. I should not take up your time. But may I see you again?"

Before a startled Isabel could react to his unexpected need for haste, a gravelly old voice called sharply, "Isabel!" and Shadoe McCaine hopped to his feet.

Slinging her gaze heavenward, Isabel drew in a short, ragged breath, her last she was sure, as she felt the mere instinct to breathe suddenly cease. There, in the doorway, stood Aunt Imogen, hunkered over her brass and oak cane like a staunch old guard. Just before she dropped her forehead against her hand, Isabel saw her gentleman caller quickly glance around the parlor, looking for still another person. The cat, so to speak, was out of the bag.

"My boy," Imogen laughed, shuffling into the room. "You have come to see my Isabel!" Then she looked at her slumping niece and clicked her tongue. "Naughty girl . . . you told me you would not be seeing my young friend Shadoe McCaine again."

A speechless Isabel threw her head up, her gaze immediately locking to the equally stunned one Shadoe McCaine visited upon her. "You are . . . Shadoe McCaine?" she muttered disbelievingly.

"You are Isabel Emerson?" he returned the favor in an equally disbelieving tone.

The moment met all the requirements of becoming a very embarrassing situation, but they began to laugh simultaneously, and moments later, as Shadoe McCaine sank to the divan beside her, they were laughing so hard it brought tears to their eyes.

"You are . . . Shadoe McCaine!" Isabel managed to repeat, hugging her ribs.

Shadoe pointed a finger, his own laughter beginning anew. "And you are . . . Isabel Emerson—"

Aunt Imogen, shaking her head, began her retreat with a softly growled, "Youngsters! Never could figure them out!"

The pain intensifying in her midriff, an hysterical Isabel stammered, "You unconscionable beast . . . you were supposed . . . to take me . . . to the theater—"

Sinking back to the divan, Shadoe brokenly responded, "And you were supposed . . . to be . . . my companion—"

"I sent . . . the maid . . . from across the street—"

"And I sent . . . the hotel clerk—"

Without full comprehension of the moment, Shadoe and Isabel hugged each other. "Ain't we something?" she said, employing that untidy drawl she had picked up on the bayou, drawing in a breath as she attempted to still her laughter.

"We sure are," he replied.

"You kissed me, you rogue."

"Sure did."

"I hate you."

"No, you don't."

Isabel managed to recapture enough of her good senses to end the embrace she was sharing with the man she had met just last night. Their gazes met and only now did Isabel feel embarrassed by the intimacy they had shared. She wanted to be angry with him, to reprimand him for taking advantage of her while she slept. She wanted to scold him for lying to her last evening about who he was, but she had been just as guilty. She knew only that she was happy to be with this swarthy trickster. As she thought about the six months she had remaining as Aunt Imogen's guest, she thought how grand it would be to be escorted about town by a man like Shadoe McCaine. He would certainly brighten her remaining time here.

With that in mind, she asked, "Would you like to stay for lunch?"

"I would love it," he responded, favoring the pretty little niece of Imogen de'Cambre with a half-cocked smile. "Perhaps we might discuss another appointment for the theater, and we'll play ourselves this time."

"I must stay off my ankle for at least a week."

"I can wait."

Isabel and Shadoe McCaine shared a smile. Though neither knew what the other was thinking, their unspoken thoughts were the same . . . where would the future find these two unlikely acquaintances?

Shadoe McCaine forgot his passion for the gambling tables and the saloons. For now, Isabel Emerson was the only passion in his life.

Within days they had become inseparable. Shadoe had readjusted his schedule, had stayed away from the gaming tables and spent every hour of every day with Isabel. He felt protective of her. Though he knew nothing of her background, he supposed that she had been orphaned and placed in the care of the dottering old woman who adored her. Often, Shadoe had wanted to question her, but he did not know how painful her past might be to her. Only one thing mattered to him: she did not fit the mold of spoiled daughter of rich planter or rancher who might get him beaten within an inch of his life. That was the only manner of feminine beast he abhorred.

His little Isabel was everything he expected in a woman. She was thoughtful, fun-loving, intelligent . . . his tragic little flower . . . a woman who would be a perfect companion for a man and whose eyes reflected a fiery nature that might prove exquisitely delightful in the confines of the night and a man's bed. She was perfect, from the top of her flax-covered head to the tip of her gauze-wrapped foot.

"What are you thinking about?" asked Isabel, watching his gaze move blankly over the high ceiling of the kitchen. They had just breakfasted together, and Mercedes had gone about other chores around the house so that they could be alone.

Shadoe had been shamelessly daydreaming and thinking that he might like to settle down soon. But he did not make that confession to Isabel. "Actually, I was thinking about my mother and the last time I saw her in Arizona."

"Oh?" This was the first Isabel had heard about the self-confessed adventurer and gambler having roots.

"She was a schoolteacher on the Cheyenne reservation in Oklahoma when she met my father. He was young and wild, hated the reservation, and eventually became a renegade. I was only nine when he was killed by a cavalry patrol about twenty miles from the reservation."

"At least you have some roots," said Isabel, feeling a little embarrassed by the pampered life she had led, when his had apparently been hard and tragic. "And your mother? She is still in Arizona?"

He shuffled his booted feet off the chair where they had been resting and leaned across the table. "After my father's death, she took a teaching position in Phoenix. She died when I was eighteen." Then he smiled across at Isabel and said, "And because of them, you are sitting across the table from this loveable rogue now."

Stabbing absently at the cold eggs on her plate,

with no intentions of eating them, Isabel imagined Shadoe McCaine having a mother who was a schoolteacher. "And you are a loveable rogue," she eventually responded for lack of anything better. "Your parents—or rather, I'd imagine your mother—did a wonderful job of raising you." Then, "Do you remember your father?"

"Not really," replied Shadoe. "I just remember that mother was always angry with him, and I remember that they loved each other. Indians rarely show love—in an emotional way—but I remember that my father was gentle with her. That's the memory I cling to, not the fact that my father was a renegade and that he robbed and killed white people."

Isabel quietly said, "Do you know what I think, Shadoe McCaine?"

"What is that?" he chuckled his response.

"I think you're wonderful."

Shrugging, Shadoe came to his feet and arched his back. "And I hope you keep thinking that, because—" Now, he went to her back, then bent and touched his cheek with her own. "Because I like you, Miss Isabel Emerson." Forcing a smile, Shadoe continued, "For a while after my father's death, I imagined that rather than being his son, that I might be a prince or something—"

"I'd wager on the 'or something,' " laughed Isabel. The chain of her medallion became caught in the lace of her dress and she carefully removed it, disengaging it before any harm could be done to either medallion or dress. Shadoe instantly took it from her.

"This is beautiful," he said, looking over the pendant with more curiosity than Isabel thought it deserved.

So, she told him the tale of Angus Wickley's gold, embellishing it with tales of murder and mystery, secrecy and speculations as to what had become of it. "And this," she said after her long narration, smiling at him across the table where he had returned, "is just one of the six my mother kept. I've worn it all my life, though I must confess that it's been through quite a few gold chains in the past twenty or so years."

When Isabel attempted to rise, Shadoe arose, then swooped her into his arms, and held her close. "Doctor said to keep off that foot, didn't he?"

Isabel said, "Put me down, you rogue gambler." Her gentle laughter faded as her gaze held his, transfixed, the expression in his eyes demanding, lusty, and complimentary. She could feel the muscles of his back through the thick material of his shirt tighten beneath her fingers. She did not have to wonder what he was thinking as he stared into her eyes. He wanted the same thing as she, and convention forbade them to seek it.

Drawing in a deep breath, Shadoe broke his concentration. He moved from the kitchen and into the corridor, soon depositing Isabel upon the divan in the spacious parlor. He said nothing as he withdrew from her, approached the window and drew back the heavy winter drape. She was a lady, but at the moment he wished she were the most wanton hussy in all of New Orleans. It would make it so much easier to claim the prize he coveted, a prize he considered more valuable than all the gold in Colorado.

"What is wrong, Shadoe?" asked Isabel, propping her chin on the back of the divan as she watched him. "Have I said something to displease you?"

He snapped about, the medallion still clutched absently in his hand now being absently tucked into his pocket, his eyes almost angry as they connected with her own. "No . . . no, you've said nothing."

"Why are you angry with me?" As he returned his gaze to the street outside, silence settled between them. Had she unsettled his mood by asking about his past, giving him an opportunity to speak about his dead parents? "I'm sorry," said Isabel softly.

He turned once again, the anger withdrawn from his eyes. "Sorry? What on earth for?"

"For whatever has prickled your mood."

Shadoe quickly closed the distance between them, then sat on the divan beside her. Enfolding her hands between his warm ones, he said, "I have never met a woman like you, Isabel. I never even thought a woman like you could exist. I've known you for scarcely a week, but when I am apart from you, I feel empty inside. Tell me that I am a crazy man. Tell me that you find my attentions to you disagreeable and I will leave you alone."

Isabel pretended to consider his request. But when he raised a dark, questioning brow, she smiled, turning her hands about in his so that she could clasp his fingers. "How has this happened, Shadoe McCaine? From the very first moment our eyes met, we have been attracted to each other . . . and we are both frightened. Do you think that I am not confused by my feelings for you, just as you are? I cannot imagine anything that could be said or done that could burst the bubble of joy I feel just being near you. Call me crazy, if you will, Shadoe, but I lie awake at night thinking of you and wanting to be with you. Could it be that we are destined to be together?"

Shadoe looked deeply into her eyes. He saw there the innocence of youth and the wisdom that came with age. He saw there a woman who had been protected and nurtured by a doting aunt who surely must want a more suitable mate for her than he could ever be. True, the old matron had gambled her away at the tables, but it had been simply for an evening at the theater. Shadoe could not imagine Imogen de'Cambre taking any risk that would prove ultimately harmful to this beautiful young woman. With that in mind, he replied, "I'm not the kind of man who would meet with Imogen's approval beyond an evening at the theater."

"It isn't my aunt's approval you would have to earn, Shadoe McCaine. It would be my father's."

"What?" Sheer horror darkened his features.

"Are you so surprised to learn that I have a father?" Isabel queried.

He pulled his hands away as if he suddenly found her repulsive. Standing, he again withdrew to the window. When he turned once again, he harshly demanded, "Who is this father I am just now learning about?"

Cocking her head to the side, Isabel gave him a thoughtful look. Why was he acting so strangely? "Did you think that Imogen had raised me?"

"I did," he snapped.

She didn't like his tone, but she would not allow him to spoil her mood. "I was raised on Bayou Boeuf, at Shadows-in-the-Mist Plantation with my father and mother and brother. I am spending a year with Imogen, so that she may expose me to the gentle cultures of the city." She was stunned by Shadoe's attitude, as if she had unexpectedly confessed to being a murderess. "Heaven forbid, Shadoe. Why are you so surprised to learn that I have parents?"

"And what would this father of yours do if he caught you with a man like me?"

Isabel laughed, though it was a short, brittle one. Then, in an effort to dispel the tension that had settled between them, she said with a renewed note of humor, "I suppose he might take a horsewhip to you," though she knew her father would never do any such a thing.

Shadoe pivoted smartly, drew back the drape with a swish of his hand and dropped his forehead against the cool, clean window pane. A planter's daughter . . . a spoiled, pampered bitch who could snap her fingers and have a man whipped for daring to glance in her direction . . . an uppity bit of rich trash who considered herself superior to every man and who wouldn't pass up the chance to put him in his place. God! Why did she have to be the one kind of woman he abhorred, the one kind of woman he could not tolerate, no matter how beautiful she was! His shoulders quaked in absolute revulsion.

It did not matter that he had loved her company, that she had said nothing that might indicate she considered herself superior to him. Hatred pounded in his heart. He pressed his thumb and forefinger to his eyes so fiercely that pain shot through his head. He became unaware of the silence between them, of the moisture that suddenly sheened her pale blue eyes. The only thing driving within him was a compulsion to be as far away from her as possible.

Drawing in a deep, trembling breath, Shadoe McCaine straightened as he turned his back to Isabel and announced tonelessly, "I must go."

And before she could open her mouth to question him, the door in the foyer slammed resoundingly behind him. She caught a mere glimpse of him through the crack in the draperies as he rushed through the courtyard and entered the street.

She had not realized that he'd taken her gold medallion with him.

Mercedes appeared from somewhere deep within the house. "Was that Mr. McCaine a leaving?" she asked.

Isabel was almost too stunned to answer. "Yes," she whispered, surprised that even that one small sound was possible.

"What'd you do, Miss Isabel? Did you run him off?"

Dropping her gaze, Isabel quickly flicked the tears from her eyes before Mercedes could notice. Drawing in a small breath, she said with a little more strength, "I must have said something. He left in an awful huff."

One of the maid's dark brows kicked up. "He's been hanging 'round here like a lovestruck rooster for days, Miss Isabel. Surely, you must'a said somethin'—"

"I didn't say anything!" she snapped, feeling the tears refreshen in her eyes. When she looked up and saw that she had hurt the dear woman's feelings, she extended her hand. "Oh, Mercedes—" The dark, plump hand clasped her own. "Forgive me. Perhaps he remembered another engagement and did not realize how abrupt his leaving was. Perhaps it is just his way."

Mercedes feigned agreement. She could see that Isabel was sinking into an emotional state. She had no idea what had brought it on, and would be unable to offer a solution. "Why don't you read to me out o' that book 'bout that monster Mr. Frankensense done made from dead fellers, Miss Isabel?"

To which a sadly smiling Isabel responded, "That's Franken*stein*, Mercedes. Now, sit, and I'll

70

read something to you that you haven't heard yet."

"Just don't read them real skeery parts," Mercedes warned. "Or I's liable to be up all night a waitin' fer goblins."

Shadoe did not visit again that day, nor did he make an appearance the next day, or the day after that. By Saturday, Isabel was trying to walk on her ankle to build a tolerance to the pain. If Shadoe McCaine would not come to the house and explain the reason for his abrupt departure, then she would seek him out at his hotel.

She had fretted away the whole of yesterday, tearfully angry with him, but today, her anger had changed into an ugly, hostile thing that demanded an explanation. She was also fretting over the loss of her medallion and couldn't quite remember the last time she had seen it.

Tossing herself upon the divan, she bent forward and firmly clasped her still swollen ankle. "Heal, will you?" she demanded in a soft, low voice. "I have things that must be tended . . . a fellow to reason with and my necklace to find."

"I've never seen anyone talk to their ankle before."

Isabel looked up, then smiled for Golda Dumont. "What are you doing here?"

"Mrs. Etienne is resting, so I thought I would slip over to see if you have a list for the market. I know that Mercedes doesn't really like that riffraff down there."

Isabel could hardly believe it had been a full week since that darn cat had caused her to sprain her ankle. "Thank you, but Mercedes left a half hour ago."

"All right . . . is there anything I can get you

71

while I'm here?"

"Thanks, no . . ." A thought came to Isabel. "Do you think that on the way to the market you could do a small errand for me? I'll pay you."

"You want me to take a message to him, don't you?" Surprise met the pretty maid's look. "Mercedes mentioned yesterday that something had happened and that he'd not been back to visit you."

"Mercedes has a big mouth," Isabel said, pouting. "Will you take a message to him? You can leave it at the desk."

"Of course I will."

Rising, hobbling to the desk just across the room, Isabel took a piece of her personal stationery from the drawer and began writing the note. Then she folded it, tucked it into a matching envelope on which she had written Shadoe's name, and offered the missive to Golda, along with a few coins for her trouble. "I'll do a favor for you one day," Isabel promised.

Golda sauntered across the room, then turned. "I saw him from the window of Mrs. Etienne's parlor the other day. He is quite a handsome fellow." And before Isabel could respond one way or the other, she quickly resumed her retreat from the house.

Through the window, Isabel watched the cardinals scatter as Golda moved through the courtyard.

"If you don't respond to my missive, Shadoe Mc-Caine," promised a prettily pouting Isabel Emerson. "Then I shall come to you. You just see if I don't!"

Then she breathed deeply, attempting to still the mad pounding of her heart caused by the very thought of him.

What had she done to offend him?

She was so desperate to know the answer that, if he forced it, she would seek him out and demand an explanation. She wasn't the least bit timid when it came to getting what she wanted.

Wasn't that why her father had sent her away from the Boeuf?

Five

Shadoe McCaine had thought he could walk away
from One Twenty-Four Royal . . . and Isabel Emerson . . . and never think about either again. But
these past four days had felt more like four years,
and as he lay upon the massive bed in his hotel
room, his palms tucked lazily beneath his head and
his gaze darting absently over the ceiling, Isabel was
all that filled his thoughts. Damn it! Why did it
have to happen this way? Why couldn't she have
simply been a poor little waif left on the steps of an
aging relative, knowing so little of the world outside
New Orleans that her naiveté was her most charming asset? Why did she have to be a rich plantation-
owner's daughter? Why? Damn it, why? And why
couldn't he forget her!

It had been seven years since he'd nearly lost his
life because of a spoiled, vengeful rancher's daughter
in south Texas. He had tried to forget her name
. . . Venetia . . . but it was fused into his brain.
He had tried to forget the brutal pummeling of the
fists of henchmen ordered to leave little of him but
bruised flesh and broken bones, he had tried to forget the sound of her laughter — the spoiled, pampered daughter he had spurned, the demonic brat
who had torn away her clothing in a mindless
frenzy and dragged her shoulder against the tines of

a pitchfork to make it look like he had raped and beaten her.

He had tried to forget that because of her he'd been forced to run from the law for seven years. He was considered a criminal; that was the label forced upon him by the beautiful, and lethal Venetia Mendez. Venetia was the reason he could never go back to Texas, one of the few places he had really loved. She was the reason he continued to run. He had gotten more confident as the years had passed, and had taken to watching less frequently over his shoulder. Still, the danger was there, and the instinct for self-preservation kept him moving.

The door opened, cutting into his morbid concentration. There, in slim outline against the gas lights of the corridor, stood Jascena, her shoulders slumped and her mouth in a pretty, pouting, upside-down smile. He raised his wrist from the bridge of his nose just enough to study her for a moment. "You stood me up," he quietly pointed out. "And because I was late to the theater, I was unable to get a seat."

Lifting her chin, Jascena deposited clean towels on a chair. She turned, her arms moving, pausing rather like a jointed doll, then twisting together against her waist. "My father wouldn't allow me to leave the house," she responded, tears welling in her downcast eyes. "He threatened to beat me within an inch of my life."

"Why don't you get a place of your own? Women your age should not fall under the domination of a brutal father."

Only now did Jascena's gaze connect with his own rather angry one. "How old do you think I am, Shadoe McCaine?"

He swung his feet to the floor, sweeping back his

dark, unkempt hair as if he fully intended to assault it. "Twenty . . . twenty-one, I suppose."

"Sir, I am only fifteen—"

Shadoe's gaze shot to the girl in disbelief. The Southern climate, and the brutality of a dominating father, had certainly added years to the child-woman standing several feet from him. "Hell! Why didn't you tell me the other day?"

"I wasn't aware it would make a difference."

"You underestimate me, Jascena." Thinking of the reward he had intended to claim following their excursion to the theater caused a shiver to rock through Shadoe's tall frame. "Now, get on out of here," he growled. "Girls your age should be skipping ropes on sidewalks, not playing maid at hotels . . . and certainly not accepting evening invitations from strangers." The pretty maid in her dark blue dress and oversized white apron once again dropped her head. When she moved slowly toward the door, as dejected as any child he might ever have scolded, Shadoe's voice softened. "You're a pretty girl, Jascena. Somewhere there is a lucky boy who is waiting for you to enter womanhood. Wait for him and turn your dark eyes away from rakes like me."

Pausing at the door, Jascena offered him a most timid smile. "I'll consider your advice, Shadoe McCaine," she replied, then quietly opened the door. "Will you still be my friend?"

Ignoring the ugly scowl in his heart, Shadoe allowed his mouth to twist into a smile. "Sure, Jascena. You remember that I'll be here if you need me."

"Thank you," she answered. "I shall leave the door open, Shadoe McCaine, so that you will not climb back into that comfortable bed."

"I have nothing to do this morning."

She smiled, remembering a conversation she'd had just a few moments before with Gandy Cobb at the desk downstairs. "I wouldn't be so sure about that," she laughed lightly, turning into the corridor where her cart and more fresh towels waited for distribution among the hotel's eighty-seven guests.

Shadoe couldn't be bothered to rise and push the door to. He slung his booted feet back up to the coverlet and again tucked his palms beneath his head. Absently he removed the medallion from around his neck, the medallion that belonged to the pretty Isabel Emerson, and dragged it back and forth across his chest. He tried to think about mundane things—his horse munching away on corn and sweet feed at the livery down the street. He even allowed himself a few scattered thoughts of his parents who had died young. Despite his tragic beginnings, he should never have begun his wanderlust . . . never met Venetia Mendez. At eighteen he'd taken a job on a sheep ranch, but he'd hated the stink of them. He'd hated the nightly raids of enraged cattlemen vying for grazing land that had dwindled the herds to a few ragged head; he'd hated the wind and the dust and the shimmering heat of that vast open plain.

Now, Shadoe McCaine knew it was time to leave New Orleans. He'd already been here a couple of weeks too long. But before he left, he had to send the medallion back to its owner.

Shadoe liked to think he was a lot like the handsome stallion he had won in a poker game: ready to sprint into the wind at a moment's notice and discover new territories and fresh dangers . . . and certainly, avoid old ones. So what was he waiting for? An invitation out of town? A railroad track to be run out on? He knew bloody well what was holding

77

him back: her pale, porcelain skin, big, powder-blue eyes, her lush mouth aching to be kissed, and hair the color of spun gold. And, blast it, the mystery of a hundred pounds of gold coins!

Damn! He had to get out of New Orleans before the vision of her drove him insane! He hated what she was and what she stood for. He hated her seductive smiles and the soft, velvety tone of her voice. He hated the enticing swells of her youthful breasts that could make him lose his mind.

But did he, indeed, hate the beautiful Isabel Emerson, who had done absolutely nothing to him, or was it the vision of the wicked Venetia Mendez that he hated? Was it reasonable that he should compare her to Venetia simply because she had a wealthy, doting father who wanted only to protect her and ensure the best possible future for her? He had spent seven years hating such women, hating everything they stood for. And yet Isabel was holding him to New Orleans just as surely as if she had wrapped him in chains.

Damn her father! A wealthy, overprotective father would surely investigate the background of any man who showed interest in his daughter. How long would it take him to learn the terrible secret he was running from? Not long at all, he supposed. Shadoe had kept one step ahead of bounty hunters because he had an obsessive, contagious need to stay alive. He would not be able to outrun his past with a woman like Isabel Emerson at his side.

"Shadoe?"

Snapping his eyelids open, Shadoe cast a glance at Gandy Cobb. "Man, don't ever sneak up on a thinking man."

With a husky laugh, Cobb approached and allowed a bit of folded paper to drift down to him.

"This was left at the desk for you."

Digging into his pocket, Shadoe flipped a silver dollar to the young man. "Thanks." When Cobb retreated, he propped himself against the headboard and pried open the envelope with his index finger. Irritation darkened his gaze as he read the flowing feminine hand:

Shadoe, please come to 124 Royal this morning if you are not too busy. It is imperative that I speak to you. Please be warned that if you do not answer my summons, I shall come to your hotel room. If you are not there, I shall camp outside your doorway until you do return.

She had signed the missive, *Isabel E.*

Blast! It was just as well she summoned him! It would give him the opportunity to return her medallion.

Though he wasn't sure why he went to the trouble, he began to make himself look presentable. He dragged the medallion over his head and tucked it beneath the material of his shirt. He was determined to tear himself away from New Orleans and the enticing temptress who had consumed his every thought. He had seen only the beautiful, tender side of her; the urgency of her missive suggested an ugly, demanding side. Perhaps it would quell his desire for her. That would help him shake himself from Louisiana.

He combed back his hair, attempted to scrub the anger from his swarthy features with a cool washcloth, pulled on a clean jacket, and left the room just a short ten minutes later. He had tucked Isabel's letter into his vest pocket, though he wasn't sure why. Perhaps by doing so, he had unconsciously placed a bit of her against his heart.

Shadoe stopped off at the livery and visited a few minutes with his stabled horse. "You're anxious to get out and run, aren't you, *Mirlo?*" The stallion rubbed his ebony head against the shoulder of the man who had tamed him these past four years. "You are my blackbird, my *Mirlo,* and don't you worry. We will soon be flying with the wind. I've—" He chuckled without humor. "I've got to tie up a few loose ends and we'll be on our way. Then, I'll give you your head and you can take me where you will, even to the ends of the earth."

The old man who worked for the livery owner walked up on Shadoe while he spoke to the horse. When he turned, acknowledging the friendly old negro who took care of Mirlo, Shadoe asked, "Has he given you any trouble?"

"Naw, suh," replied the gentleman Shadoe knew only as Old Pecan, "But Mistah McCaine, ya saids jes' de other day that if'n I's be needin' anything . . . anything a'tall, that I jes' be astin' ya. Well, sho' 'nuff, Mistah McCaine, they's a favor Ol' Pecan be wantin' to ast ya . . . 'bout that fine ol' boy ya has der."

"He's not for sale," said Shadoe without hesitation.

"Naw, suh, din't reckon he was." Old Pecan scratched at his thick, gray hair. "Ol' Pecan, he has dis fine young mare back yon in a stable what Mistah Lomax gives me fuh my pay here at de livery when he was short o' cash las' year, an' that li'l mare, she's jes' ripe as she can be fo' a fine stallion like dat one, an'—well, Mistah McCaine—ya reckon it'll be all right wid ya if'n I turn 'em into dat pen in de back fo' a couple o' days together so dat fella can get de chance to cover my mare . . . sho' would like ta have a colt of'n dat fine stallion o' yours."

Shadoe laughed. "You know this was once an Indian pony. But if you want a wild vein in a colt, well . . . who am I to deny *Mirlo* his romp in the hay. You just take care of him and you feed him real good."

A very appreciative Old Pecan instantly grabbed the friendly young man's hand and shook it firmly. "Thanky . . . Thanky, Mistah McCaine, sho' 'nuff, I'll takes real good care o' dat stallion."

Shadoe gave the horse a final pat, tipped his hat to the old man and exited the livery. He imagined that the invitation to Isabel Emerson's house would not result in the same kind of entertainment Mirlo was about to enjoy in the small, enclosed pen.

What a damn shame!

Isabel tidied the house, more to search for her lost medallion than because it really needed it. Aunt Imogen had made one of her rare and unexpected departures from the house to visit her old friend Prudence Liliana at Magnolia Hill Plantation fifteen miles to the north of the city, and a very reluctant Mercedes had accompanied her. It had been almost two hours since Golda had delivered the message to the St. Charles Hotel, and it never entered Isabel's head that Shadoe McCaine would not respond with a visit. She had all afternoon and night, and a better part of Sunday, to extract confessions from him. She simply had to know what she had said or done to turn him so cold and distant when they had become such easy friends.

She had just changed into a rose-colored day dress and whipped her hair up into combs when she heard the rough clank of the bell at the garden en-

81

trance. Giving herself a final look in the mirror, she pinched her cheeks to add a little color to them, tugged up her bodice, and smoothed down the gathers of her voluminous skirts. Then she hurried from the room and down the stairs, slowing her footsteps only when she entered the banquette.

Opening the door, she immediately met the gaze of Shadoe McCaine. "How very nice. You've come almost at once."

He moved quickly past her and into the foyer. "Of course. I couldn't have you camped outside my hotel room, could I?" His voice was harsh, toneless, almost as if he found the visit an annoying duty. Tearing the medallion over his head, he held it out to her. "Sorry, the other day when I was looking at it, I absently dropped it into my pocket. Now, what else do you want?"

Isabel smiled as she shut the door. She would not allow him to darken her mood. "Do come in. I've made a fresh pot of coffee."

"I don't want coffee," he growled. "I just want to know why I have been whistled for. If it was for the medallion, you have it back. If for any other reason, then here I am, your obedient mutt, Miss Emerson." When he met her gaze, he saw unfeathered reserve there, and he suddenly had a dastardly need to prickle her, as her missive had prickled him. "An old colored fellow at the livery just asked me if my stallion could service his mare. Is that what *you* want, Isabel . . . service?"

Isabel had heard all manners of atrocity from men in her few years of maturity, but such a crude remark from a man who had been nothing less than a gentleman stunned her. Her face turned as pink as the gown she wore. "I guess I have misjudged your character, Shadoe McCaine," she responded, scarcely able to keep the tremble of rage and hurt out of her voice. Opening the door, she met his narrow, vicious gaze. "We have nothing more to say to each other."

Instantly, Shadoe was thinking of the things he might say to erase the unnecessary insult he had uttered. But was there anything that would take the hurt out of her eyes, that would make her full, sensual mouth cease to tremble? God! What a rotten bastard he could be at times! For want of a proper response, Shadoe took her in his arms and kissed her with the longing of a lovestruck soldier returned from war.

At first, Isabel was too stunned to react. She stiffened her arms at her sides and attempted to press her mouth into a rebellious line, but it simply would not be so restricted. Warmly, passionately, hungrily she responded to his bold kiss, even as she wanted to ball her fists and pummel him until he was black and blue and weak from the attack. Then her senses returned with full force and her palms landed full upon his chest, pushing him away with all her might. She was just about to reprimand him when a rap sounded at the front of the house. Her chin lifted defiantly as she pivoted about. Shadoe McCaine crossed his arms and waited for her to return.

After taking the mail, she slammed the door much more resoundingly than she had intended. Returning to the parlor, she threw the letters upon a side table and turned to Shadoe, preparing to take up where she left off. But one of the letters fell to the floor and overturned, immediately catching her attentions.

On the back of the envelope someone had made a pencil rubbing of a medallion like the one she wore. Beneath it was carefully printed the words, "I've been wearing this as long as I can remember."

For the moment, Shadoe McCaine ceased to exist. A very numb Isabel turned over the envelope and read the name of the addressee: *Mrs. de'Cambre on Royal Street, New Orleans, in the State of Louisiana.* Under normal circumstances, Isabel would have never considered opening mail addressed to another person, but her aunt was away, and the medallion rubbing was an irresistible puzzle. Her fingernail eased beneath the flap of the envelope and flipped it up. With trembling hands, she extracted the single sheet of paper and unfolded it.

"What is that?" asked Shadoe, a little annoyed that he was suddenly being ignored.

"I don't know . . . but I have a peculiar feeling." Slowly, she began to read and the further she read, the paler grew her features, and more trembling was her hand as it rose to her throat. Then she dropped the letter into the folds of her skirt and uttered, "Dear Lord, I don't believe it." Looking up, she handed the letter to Shadoe. "Please, read it to me. Surely my own eyes are deceiving me."

Shadoe was puzzled by her reaction to whatever she was handing him. Taking it from her he approached the window, then turned. "Dear Mrs. de-'Cambre," he read, immediately looking up. "This isn't for you, Isabel."

"Yes . . . yes, I know. Please read it."

Again, Shadoe looked down.

"I got here in my hand a copy of the *Picayune* dated June 16, 1875 that was wraped around some dishes that was shiped up from Mississippi and sat back in the store-room for the past for years or so. You don't know me, but I done read that story in their about that fella named of Emerson, and their was a piece in their about that boy of his that was drownded and that was waring a gold medallion. Well, I got a gold medallion, and the fella that raised me, he says I was wearing it when he found me. He done died last year, so I cudn't ask him if I was that boy of Mr. Emerson's, and his brother Red, he says he don't know where his brother found me. So, ma'am, I'll be wantin' to know if I could be that boy. Red, he says by ruf estim that I'm about ninteen or twenty years old, so if you cud writ me back I'd be real graitfull. I'm real sorry, ma'am, if I didnt get all the words right, but Red, he done tried real good to tech me to read and write and add up numbers and all. Please, mam, wil you writ me back? I hankering to find out who I am, who I really am, cuz I know my name aint really John C. Fremont Sewall, like I been calt for all the years I can recall."

Shadoe looked up, waved the paper as though he couldn't be more annoyed, and asked, "What does this mean?"

Instantly, Isabel felt the coolness of her medallion between her fingers. Then she looked again at the rubbing on the back of the envelope and the neat print a young man named John C. Fremont Sewall had written there. The boldness of Shadoe McCaine's captured kiss was forgotten for the moment.

Recovering from her muted shock, Isabel extended her hand, waiting for the letter to be returned to it. Shadoe was certainly confused by her frozen thought. He had just stolen the sweetest of kisses from her, and she acted as if it had never happened. All she cared about was that damn letter! If curiosity hadn't suddenly gotten the best of him, he might have stormed from the house on Royal Street without looking back. "I asked, Isabel, what is the significance of the letter?"

She looked up, a world of pain reflected in her crystalline gaze. Letters had come either to Imogen or Shadows-in-the-Mist since the story had appeared in the *Picayune,* but the careful rubbing on the back of the envelope in her hand was all the proof she needed that her dear little brother was alive . . . and, dear God, reaching out for family. Without realizing her thoughts were transgressing into words, Isabel uttered, "I don't believe it . . . after all these years—"

Despite the fury pounding inside him, Shadoe's fingers, as if possessing a mind of their own, slid gently across Isabel's slim, trembling shoulders. "Will you tell me what's going on?" he entreated on a gentle note. When she failed to answer, he continued in a stronger voice, "Are you going to tell me, or must I assume? Blast it, does this have something to do with that filthy-rich father of yours?"

Isabel, usually so quick to jump to the defense of her father, might have been listening to a report of the weather for all the response she gave. Holding the letter to her bodice, she moved into a small antechamber, returning as quickly as she had disappeared. Turning a framed photograph to Shadoe's view, she said, "This is my brother, Eduard, when he was four."

Shadoe politely took the photograph and gazed over it. "A handsome lad," he remarked. Handing the photograph back to her, he awaited some explanation.

Isabel turned away, quivering so violently that she

had to drop into the nearest chair. Clutching the photograph to her, she said softly, "He was presumed drowned in the Boeuf shortly after this was taken." She began to sob uncontrollably, while a very bewildered Shadoe McCaine tried to think clearly and to respond with compassion. What was happening? Why was she suddenly so distraught? Didn't she have the sense to know that a woman's tears tore away at his insides?

But Isabel couldn't think clearly. All she knew was that somewhere in a place called Tongue River, Montana, her brother, Eduard, was alive.

Shadoe McCaine dropped to one knee beside the chair and took Isabel's hands gently between his own. "Do you think the young man who wrote the letter could be your lost brother? Surely others have made such claims—"

"Yes." Isabel sniffed back her tears. "But no other ever sent me this . . . anything like this," she said, showing him the pencil rubbing. "This proves that he is my brother. Oh, Shadoe . . . Shadoe, what am I to do? Do you think you can help me?"

The woman so tenderly weeping before him was a rich planter's daughter, the most despicable kind of woman. But that didn't seem to matter to Shadoe at the moment. All he cared was that she was reaching out to him for help. "I don't know what I could do," he offered after a moment.

Sniffing back her tears, Isabel held out her own medallion. "My mother gave it to me," she explained. "She also gave one to each of my brothers, Eduard and Paul. We thought Eduard had drowned in the Boeuf when he was four years old," she repeated, tears again welling in her eyes, her warm hands scooting around his midriff beneath his coat. "Oh, please . . . please, you must take me to this

87

place, to this Tongue River, Montana. I've got to bring my brother home!"

Sure, and have your father fast on my tail with his henchmen! he thought. "It's a damned long trip," said Shadoe McCaine, biting back the retort that surfaced first.

"I'd go to the ends of the earth to find my brother, to bring him home to mother and father and Shadows-in-the-Mist." Pulling impudently back, she threatened, "I will go alone if you will not take me. I swear, I will go alone!" Immediately, she wondered why he would even care that she would put herself in such danger.

"You'd never make it!" he was quick to point out. Softening his tone, he added, "Suppose I should agree to take you . . . how do you propose to get away from your aunt, and do you think your parents would allow you to make such a trip with a rogue like me?"

Leaning ever so close, Isabel rushed the words, "Oh, do say you'll take me, Shadoe McCaine! I will take care of all the details! If you want money, I will pay you. I will do anything to see Eduard again."

Painfully affected by the very nearness of such a lovely woman, he growled, "And suppose I should want to carry you to your bed and have my way with you this very minute, and every night, as my payment for taking you to Montana—"

Her mouth parted, touched by the gentlest of trembles. "If that is what you want—"

"No . . . no, Isabel—" God! What was making him utter such ridiculous denials? "That is not what I want."

"You don't?" She looked a little perplexed, even hurt that he should not want her in that way. "Am not attractive enough for you?"

"You're a lady. I'm a black-hearted rogue with a half-breed renegade for a father. And . . . there are other things about me. I was only teasing you."

Still, her mouth trembled, her powder-blue gaze darting quickly over his swarthy features. "Wouldn't you like to kiss me again, Shadoe McCaine?"

He raised a dark eyebrow. "You're a bold little thing, Isabel."

"Would you?" Her palms pressed to the broad expanse of his chest.

"You don't have to seduce me, Isabel. If you want me to take you to find this man you believe to be your brother, I will do it for no other reason but the adventure of it." Suddenly, Shadoe's stomach tightened into knots. What the hell was he doing? He couldn't travel two thousand miles with Isabel Emerson on a blind search for a man she believed to be her long lost brother. If it had, indeed, been him, he could be anywhere in the world right now. When he thought about it, he realized that no one stayed at a road ranch for long. Weary travelers sought the crude accommodations of such places with the sole intent of moving on at first light. Thus, it came effortlessly as he stood, turned away with his arms crossed and growled at her, "No, damn it, I'm not going to let a woman's tears press me into doing something irrational. I can't take you to Montana. I *won't* take you! You belong here . . . or on that blasted plantation on—what did you call it—the Boeuf?"

Sucking in her emotions, Isabel shot to her feet, her hands gathering imploringly upon his shoulders. "Please . . . please, you must. I won't be any trouble. I can take care of myself and I can cook if we happen to be on the trail. But if we travel by train, it won't take more than a few—"

He turned sharply, his eyes narrowed treacher ously, a score of emotions flooding his brain. " don't ride trains. My only mode of transportation i my horse."

"I'm a good rider," she offered tearfully. "Please— Her fingers locked over the lapels of his jacket, he mouth trembling ever so slightly as it closed the dis tance to his own. "I can endure endless days in th saddle with very little to eat. And I won't complai . . . please, I swear, I won't complain—"

"No!"

Her mouth quivered as fresh tears glistened i her eyes. "I have a hundred dollars in my room Take it . . . take it and buy a good horse for me one that will keep good distance with your own. will make all the arrangements so that I will not b missed by either my parents or Aunt Imogen. Don make me beg, Shadoe, more than I have alread begged. Allow me what dignity I have left."

Shadoe drew in a deep, ragged breath, his ches rising beneath her fingers which continued to clutc his lapels. It was all he could do to keep from cap turing her trembling mouth, from taking her in hi arms and drawing her close. He wanted to sna about and withdraw from her, to reassure himsel that no force on earth could make him turn back but he knew that such a force did, indeed, exist and it was a soft, tearful, feminine one, mightie than the greatest mountain he had conquered Thus, his hands rose, gently covered her own, an his words spilled out before he could catch them.

"I have enough money to buy a horse for you. I' give you three days to make all your arrangements and then we will leave New Orleans together."

Laughing and crying in the same moment, Isabe

threw herself into his arms and hugged him tightly. "Oh, thank you, thank you. I promise you will not regret it."

I already regret it, he thought, responding instead, "I'd better go and see about that horse."

Isabel hesitated to release him from her embrace, lest he change his mind for lack of the intimacy. "We were destined to meet, Shadoe McCaine. You know that, don't you?"

He smiled without mirth. "Yes. I just hope my death isn't part of that destiny."

And before she could question such a grim declaration, he roughly pulled her arms from his neck and retreated before she could call him back.

Part Two
The Treacheries

Six

Reading Red Sewall collected the books on the small table beside his cot, preparing to return them to the shelves where he had amassed more than four thousand volumes, mostly from travelers who traded them for other goods. He loved to read, and the locals had taken to calling him "Reading" in respect of his great passion. His road ranch was the most popular on Tongue River and never a day passed that people didn't stop off, heading East after misfortunes in the West, or West after tiring of Eastern life.

Reading Red scarcely fit the description of an educated man. He dressed in garments made of deer and elk skins, and his hair was so long and unkempt that he looked ferocious. But one had only to look beneath the wild facade to see the gentleness of the man. He'd give the shirt off his back to anyone who needed it more than he did.

The boy Red's brother had named John C. Fremont, in honor of the man he had considered the greatest Union general ever to draw breath, was spending these twilight hours taking care of the horses and cleaning the stables. He was a good-hearted boy, kind to animals and humans alike, and

95

usually had a various and sundry assortment of wounded or needy creatures of both species out at the barn. Last year, he'd taken care of a young Indian boy wounded while raiding the chicken coops of a local rancher. This year he was raising kittens to give to homesteads along the river to help control the usual run of rats and mice the spring would produce. Reading Red knew it was approaching time that the boy would leave the rambling road ranch and seek his own life. That was a real lonely feeling for him, especially since his brother had died last year and he would be left alone.

In addition to his road ranch, Reading had entered every other avocation the West had to offer. He'd been a prospector and blacksmith, a horse trader and merchant. He'd never intended to settle down to run a road ranch in Montana. After the big war that had divided the nation, he and his brother had intended to prospect for gold in the Black Hills, as much to keep his brother safe from Army patrols as to make themselves rich. Reading knew little about his brother's life during the war. He knew that he'd deserted his unit somewhere in the South, because he didn't approve of the burning and looting his commander had ordered, and while making his way northwest and far away from the war, he'd come upon the little boy on the banks of a quiet bayou. All the coaxing in the world had not extracted so much as a single word from the scared child, so Red Sewall's brother had thrown him across the back of his horse and headed northwest with him, eventually reuniting with his brother and settling on Tongue River in the Montana territory.

Red knew his brother had spent the first few years on the river praying that an Army patrol wouldn't come after him as he had worked to build up the road ranch into a thriving enterprise. He had considered John his son, and his neighbors on the river were none the wiser. Now, Red looked at the boy as his nephew and he couldn't imagine life on Tongue River without him.

John had known all along he wasn't Gideon Sewall's son, and he'd been so curious about his past that Red had often lost his temper with him. Why couldn't the boy just be happy on Tongue River, and forget his roots?

The door slammed soundly, but not without allowing a cold burst of Montana wind into the large front room. John released a high-pitched, "Yeeoww, Red . . . it's colder'n a frostbit pig out there!" Hugging his thick coat firmly to him, he asked, "What's for supper, Red?"

Red gave him a long, glowering look. "Boy, you puttin' some meat on those skinny bones?"

A laughing John Sewall opened his coat to expose a quartet of quiet, bright-eyed kittens. "They looked kind'a hungry, Red, an' that ol' mama cat ain't fed 'em all day. Thought I'd give 'em some of that fresh milk I brought in this morning."

As John deposited the kittens on a chair covered in buffalo skins, Red Sewall suppressed a grin of pride he felt in the boy as he bellowed, "Hell, boy, if you ain't worryin' about your critters, you're worryin' about your next meal. Hell, critters an' eatin' . . . eatin' an'—"

"An' women!" cut in John, easing into the chair among the restrained, yet curious kittens. "That purty Jolie Ann . . . Lord, she's got some real anxious lips on her!"

"I told you, boy, to keep away from that red-headed woman. I suppose she's the reason you wanted me to order them store-bought shirts and britches for you? Skins ain't good enough for you no more, boy?"

"Just want to look nice for her. Been shavin' every day an' keepin' my hair trimmed. She didn't like it that other way, all long and grizzled, like a mangy ol' bear."

Red spooned soup into a wooden bowl and put it at the end of a long table where John always sat. "Fill your stomach, boy. You ain't goin' to have no energy to go a courtin' otherwise."

Warmed by the fire in the massive stone hearth, John threw off his coat, quickly poured milk into a bowl, and brought it to the kittens. Then he sat at the table just as Red was filling his own bowl. Taking several slices of freshly baked bread, he began breaking it into small pieces and dropping it into the bowl. "Red?"

Here it comes again! thought Red Sewall. All them dang blasted questions the boy hankered to ask. Collecting a moment of calm, and tolerance, Red dropped into his chair. "I'm listenin', boy."

John C. Fremont Sewall was the spitting image of the man he did not know existed . . . his hair as pale as sand, but his eyes golden, like his mother's. He was tall and slender, like his father, Grant Emerson. At the moment, he was thinking about the letter he had written to New Orleans two months ago, and wondering how it had been received by the old lady the newspaper had said was a relative of the Emersons. Even before he'd read that piece in the *New Orleans Picayune,* John had been fascinated by the idea of bayou country. He'd read everything he had found in Reading Red's books about Louisiana, *Gri Gri,* voodoo, and the Creoles and Cajuns. He could almost imagine himself sitting on the bank of a cool Louisiana bayou, and watching those flat-bottomed boats . . . what had they called them? piroques . . . floating lazily through the current with a man as dark as midnight guiding her gracefully among the treacherous cypress stumps. . . .

"Red?" he began again. "Could it be possible that Gideon picked me up as far south as Louisiana?"

"Doubt it," growled Red, slurping his soup. "I kinda figured you for a Yankee kid myself."

John twisted his fingers through the chain at his neck and brought the medallion out of hiding. "Where do you reckon I got this?"

"Gideon says you was wearin' it when he found you. Maybe you stole it, boy. Ever think about that?"

"But I was just a little sprite of a lad," argued John, stirring his spoon absently among the soaked pieces of bread. He hadn't told Red about the letter he'd written to the lady in New Orleans. It would only upset him. And John, of course, knew that he was grabbing at straws by even thinking he might be Eduard Emerson. A part of his heart loved Montana; the rest of it was somewhere else . . . and he wanted to know where that somewhere was. "Red?" Again, the thin, aging fellow in bulky, odorous skins lifted a gray eyebrow. "Think I might have brothers and sisters?"

"Reckon you might. Eat your soup before it gets cold."

"Red, how do you say the name, E-d-u-a-r-d—" he slowly spelled the name he'd read in the newspaper.

"That's the French way to spell it, I reckon. Same as Edward. Sure, same as Edward."

Several times John repeated the name, "Eduard," before asking, "How long you reckon it takes a letter to get, oh, say, 'bout six states south'erd?"

"You thinkin' 'bout writin' a letter, boy?" Red asked matter-of-factly.

"Naw . . . just wonderin', Red."

"I suppose if it hooked up with a train line, two weeks or so, maybe three."

"Ain't that somethin'?" With that noncommittal remark, John C. Fremont Sewall turned his full attentions to the soup Red had been nursing all day on a slow fire, adding a pinch of that and a dash of that to flavor it just so. He was thinking about bayous and cypress, friendly black folks and haunting ballads. Somewhere in the back of his mind a picture tried to form, just as if he'd seen it all before.

After dinner, Red cleaned up the dishes and John stoked up the fire, preparing for another long, cold Montana night. He could hear coyotes howling far, far across the river. He could hear the distant rumble of thunder, and a whistling through the trees that could lull a man to sleep on the most sleepless of nights. Tonight was just such a night. John couldn't imagine that he'd sleep a wink. He'd written a letter to New Orleans and it should have gotten there weeks ago. What had happened to it? Had it been cast aside, given no more attention than a blank sheet of paper? He'd worked two days on the letter and the least somebody could do at the other end was read it.

The newspaper that had been wrapped around those new dishes Red had ordered had said the Emersons were wealthy folks. But John didn't care about that. He just wanted to know who he was and if anybody still thought about him. He wanted to know if he had family, and if it was these Emerson folks down there in Louisiana. He wanted to know if it could be possible that after all these years he could be reunited with people who loved him. He'd added the pencil rubbing of his medallion to the envelope as an afterthought, hoping they might recognize it. Gideon Sewall had said he'd found him half-drowned and that he'd appeared to be about four years old. The Emerson boy had gone missing in 1864, and that was about the same time as old Gideon had found him.

"What you thinkin', boy?"

John looked up, a sheepish smile turning up his youthful masculine mouth. He didn't want to worry Red with the true direction of his thoughts. "I was just thinkin' about that purty Jolie Ann Campbell—"

"Her pa wants you to stay away from her. She's only sixteen—"

"Well, I ain't much older," argued John. "Hell, Red, she's the only purty girl within twenty miles."

"You'd better find another gal, boy. He come by the other day an' said if he caught you with his gal again, he'd shoot your kneecaps off."

"He's just full of it, Red. I like Jolie Ann, an' she likes me a lot."

Red dropped into a chair and took up his pipe. He might have been asking about the chicken feed as he mumbled, "You busted that gal, John C. Fremont Sewall?"

The boy blushed violently. "Don't reckon that's none of your business, Red—"

"Awe, hell—" Red shook his head of long, mangled gray hair. If John hadn't been with the girl . . . that way . . . he'd have quickly denied it. "You done it now, boy. Dang blast . . . that gal gits herself knocked up an' her pa'll be lynchin' you from the highest tree."

101

"Reckon that'll be before or after he shoots my kneecaps off?"

"Don't you smart-mouth me, John Sewall."

"I'm goin' to marry Jolie Ann," said John quietly. "I asked her the other night at the shindig an' she said she'd be mighty pleased to be my wife."

Rather than respond, Red lightly ordered, "You'd better go put the cows in the barn. Storm's goin' to pound down from the north tonight."

John drew himself up with youthful agility. "Sure, Red. I should have done it earlier. I seen that storm comin' in myself." Pulling on his thick wool coat, he pulled the collar up around his neck. "I'll bring in some more firewood while I'm out."

As John stepped out on the porch, the echo of horses' hooves sounded through the night. Red set down his pipe as male voices rose treacherously. "I told you, boy, to keep away from my Jolie Ann!"

Hearing Campbell's bellowing tone, Red moved with more strength than he thought he possessed. He heard John's voice, low, calming and apologetic, but by the time he got to the porch a single shot had already rang out against the howl of the wind.

John cried out, collapsing into Red's arms just as Pomeroy Campbell and his three boys reined their horses back to the West.

Red dropped to his knees with John's weight. "Dang blast it, John, I told you to stay away from that gal."

Agony masked the young man's features in the half-light of the porch. "I—I think I'm hit bad, Red."

Reading Red Sewall clasped his hand over the boy's chest, feeling the warmth of blood spread between his fingers. Tears filled his eyes. "You're goin' to be all right, boy . . . ol' Red says you gotta.

Hell! You ain't brought in that firewood yet!"

With waning strength, John removed the medallion from his neck and pressed it into Red's bloodied hand. "If somebody ever . . . comes lookin' . . . fer me, Red, will you . . . give them this?"

John closed his eyes against Red's heaving chest, and the rain began to collect in large puddles across the packed earth.

With the rush of the past three days, Isabel was surprised that she took these moments to pamper herself. She sat at her boudoir where frilly flounces dressed the windows and lavish ornamentations graced the walls. In the moments that followed, she powdered her face and added a little blackener to her long, thick lashes to better define them, a luxury she usually did not allow herself. Her father hated artificial coverings upon a woman's face—just for whores, he had said—and on the Boeuf she'd pampered herself only on those days when he was away on business.

She thought of the telegram she had sent to her cousin, Aimee Claire, in Alexandria. Her request had been simple, and one that she knew Aimee Claire, who owed her many more favors than she could ever repay, would honor. *Send a telegram to Aunt Imogen telling her that I must come home immediately. Sign father's name. A letter of explanation will soon follow.* Then she had gone to the post office and requested that all mail addressed to her be held there until she collected it. She had spent all morning yesterday writing two dozen letters to her parents, which she had given to Golda to post at the rate of one each week. That way, Imogen would think she was at home on the Boeuf, and her parents would think she was still with Imogen.

Shadoe had frowned darkly on her plan, though he had not been able to offer any alternative ones. He had become a strangely mystical beast, this man who had so attracted her from the very beginning, and these past few days Isabel had been much more curious about his past than she had been before.

Dropping her chin upon her linked fingers, Isabel met her reflection in her boudoir mirror. Then she looked beyond her reflection, into the blank depths of another world. She imagined that Shadoe stood there, dressed in his usual black attire that gave him a sensually devilish look, like the darkest and fiercest of pirates, his ash-gray eyes narrowed, his ebony hair untidy as if tossed by a sturdy Louisiana wind, his arms sweeping out to invite her into their protection. For just a moment, she closed her eyes, wishing that she could turn and that he would, indeed, be standing there. She cared not that her heavy brocade dressing gown dragged down from her arms, exposing her lacy underthings, that enough of her breasts were uncovered so as to allow no room for a man to use his imagination. She cared not that in her enticing state of undress, she could become easy prey to a man who hungered for a woman . . . in that way. She just wished that her elusive, secretive Shadoe McCaine was with her this very minute.

The telltale light knock of Mercedes echoed at the door of her suite. Isabel called, "Come in, Mercedes," then attempted to wipe her shameless thoughts from her mind. She patted her cheeks, hoping the pretty blush that had risen there would not be too noticeable to Mercedes.

"Miss Imogen, she'll be wantin' to see you at her chamber," announced a somber Mercedes. "Got a telegram this mo'nin' from yo' pappy."

Isabel forced the alarm into her pale blue eyes with the talents of the most accomplished actress. She spun from the mirror. "Oh, dear . . . nothing is wrong at home, is it?"

"Naw'm," replied Mercedes, shaking her head. "You jes' cover up that purty white bosom and go on in to yo' auntie. Yo' is one flauntin' hussy, Miss Isabel."

She took immediate offense at the untruth, then grinned smugly as she prepared to reprimand Mercedes. But was it really worth her effort? She knew that Mercedes enjoyed prickling her with her teasing remarks, and that she was simply trying to get a rise out of her. She also knew that Mercedes loved her and for that reason, such teasing should be tolerated. Didn't she tease Mercedes just as much?

Thus, Isabel rose, flipped back her thick, long hair, and drew her robe firmly about her slim figure. Soon, she stood, gently knocking, outside her aunt's suite.

"Come in, girl," called the old woman.

Isabel moved unobtrusively into the room, maneuvering through a maze of overstuffed and massive furniture, too much clutter, in fact, for the two adjoining rooms her aunt inhabited. "You sent for me, auntie?"

Imogen thrust the telegram across the coverlets toward her, nearly upsetting the breakfast tray that straddled her thin form. "You'll be going home, Isabel. Your father misses you."

Isabel raised a finely arched golden brow, her eyes cutting guiltily from her aunt's narrow scrutiny. "Indeed, auntie? Will I be coming back?"

"That'll be up to your father, I would imagine," came her throaty response.

"Well—" Isabel shrugged as if she found her auntie's information a trifle untimely. "I guess that since the rain has let up I'll be on my way tomorrow. I'll go out this afternoon and purchase a ticket at the railroad station. I believe Shadoe will visit. Surely, he won't mind accompanying me." As she arose from a well-plumped settee beside her aunt's bed, a thought came to Isabel. She turned, her finger rising to her chin to tap gently there. "Oh, by the way, auntie, about Shadoe. I thought you told me that he was wealthy. Why, he hardly has a penny to his name . . . just enough to get him from one city to the other."

"Did I say he was wealthy?" exclaimed Aunt Imogen, stirring her fork in the liquid egg yolk upon her plate. She had that sheepish, "I've been caught" look upon her wrinkled old features.

"Don't you play the innocent with me!" bristled Isabel. "I do declare! You know that you did."

"You'll be seeing him again, will you, child, after you return home?"

Isabel looked at her aging relative with a haughty air. "I hardly think so. Why, I would hope that I never see the swarthy gambling rogue again as long as I live."

As she prepared to exit the overly warm suite, her aunt informed her, "Tomorrow after you leave Mercedes and I will journey back to Magnolia Hill—" She referred to her friend's plantation to the north. "Thought we'd get out of the city until the spring."

Isabel smiled. "That'll be wonderful." Actually, things couldn't have worked out better. If Aunt Imogen and Mercedes were away from the house on Royal, then chances of her small deception being uncovered were much less likely.

Quietly, Isabel left the chamber and soon entered her own. She chose a suitable dress of dark gray wool from her armoire, then a traveling jacket and hat, and moved downstairs just as the clock in the foyer struck the hour of ten. Shadoe had said he would visit her at that hour, and he was seldom late.

As she entered the banquette, pulling on her gloves, the bell rang in the courtyard. Isabel opened the door and found herself facing Shadoe McCaine. He still wore the subtle annoyance upon his face that he had yet to give her reason for.

Before Shadoe could enter, Isabel quickly moved into the courtyard and pulled the door to behind her. "We must go out," she explained. "Auntie must think I am purchasing a train ticket."

"I would suggest that you do purchase one," he reasoned, "in case she asks you to present it. But first—" Politely, Shadoe took her elbow as they moved back toward his rented surrey. "I have something to show you."

Assisting her into the seat, Shadoe was soon flicking the reins at the black haunches of the harness mare. Isabel said nothing, but sat quietly with her hands linked upon the folds of her gown. But when, scarcely ten minutes later, he turned into the livery on Charles, she brightly exclaimed, "Oh, did you find a suitable horse for me?"

Shadoe adored the changing faces of the beauty who now offered herself into his arms and gracefully swung to the hard-packed earth. She could be so quiet and ladylike one moment, and so childlike and giddy the next. Taking her hand, Shadoe moved toward a stall where fresh hay had been added. There, quietly munching sweet feed in a bin, stood a fine sorrel mare with four white stockings. "How do you like her?" asked Shadoe.

Hugging the mare's head, Isabel rubbed her hand down the wide white blaze between her eyes. "She's beautiful. Wherever did you find her?"

"A plantation north of here . . . Magnolia Hill—"

Isabel drew in a short, deep breath. "Magnolia Hill? Dear Lord, you didn't say you were purchasing the horse for me, did you?"

Shadoe's gray-black gaze narrowed. "Would it matter if I had?"

"Dear Lord . . . they are friends of Aunt Imogene. And they know me very well—"

So lovely was her alarm, and the rush of crimson darkening her cheeks, that Shadoe drew her into his arms quite before he realized he'd made the move. "No . . . no, I said nothing," he chuckled. They were alone in the livery, except for the horses, and he found the warmth of her against him so enticing that he couldn't imagine breaking the intimacy himself. He knew he should hate her, hate everything she stood for, but half of his doubts and indecision these past few days were because he couldn't hate her. There was nothing he wanted more than to spend the next few months between here and Montana, just being with her. He was willing to take his chances. After all, it had been seven years since Venetia—

Without warning, he jerked straight up, refusing to meet Isabel's questioning gaze. Then he put her away from him. "Forgive me."

"For what?" she asked, moisture sheening her eyes. "For hugging me? I was rather enjoying it."

Shadoe ached to exhibit displeasure, to say something that would make her dislike him enough to keep her distance. But, at the moment, he could think of nothing that would fit into the moment

108

'Come—" he said after a pause. "I'll show you something even finer than the mare." Momentarily, he stood outside Mirlo's stall, and the stallion immediately turned to offer his head to Shadoe's affections. "This is my horse. Won him off an Indian about four years ago."

Isabel had never seen such a splendid animal, even among the thoroughbreds her Uncle Aldrich and Aunt Ellie raised on their horse farm on Lamourie Bayou. He was sleek and black and hard-muscled, his head small and ell-defined, and his mane thick and long. Not so much as one white hair marred the perfection of his glistening coat. 'He looks as if he's inordinately pleased with himself."

Shadoe did a double take as he suddenly burst into laughter. "I guess he should be, Miss Isabel Emerson. He has spent the past three days servicing a very willing mare."

Isabel blushed furiously. "I do declare!" she retorted, pivoting from him. "You do say such awful things!"

Shadoe wasn't sure why he was so pleased with her company this morning. He knew that he was taking a terrible chance just being with her, agreeing to accompany her all the way to Montana so that she could find a long-lost brother, but he wanted nothing more than to be with her. If he really made up his mind, he could force himself to travel by train, but . . . ah . . . therein lay the reluctance! By train they could get there in a matter of weeks, but by horseback, he could spend months with Isabel and savor every delicious moment of the wild Louisiana belle in his protection . . . and his arms. Slowly, his arms circled around her waist, and he pressed his cheek to her thick hair. When the edge of her hat grazed his temple, he said, "Why do women wear these wicked things?"

"So that we will look pretty," said Isabel, dropping her head against his mouth as if it were the most natural thing in the world. Then, quietly, she turned into his arms, and her powder-blue gaze connected with his gray-black one. She wanted to compress her lips and frown, but rather, her mouth parted, exposing straight white teeth, and unconsciously, her tongue wetted her upper lip.

"Women shouldn't do that when a man is holding them," said Shadoe in a strangely controlled tone.

"Why not?" came Isabel's sultry answer.

"A man takes it as an invitation."

"An invitation to do what?"

"This—" His head dipped and his mouth tenderly grazed her own. When she made no protest, his mouth again closed upon hers and caressed softly, then firmly and almost bruisingly, then in small, teasing nips that became wild, enduring caresses.

"Don't . . . don't—" she whispered in a half-strangled voice, attempting to withdraw from his embrace. But he held her firmly, refusing to let her go. And even as she might have continued her subtle protests, her trembling mouth lifted to be claimed again by his own. Then her hands circled his slender hips beneath his jacket and he drew her against the warmth of his body. Was it still November? Was it cold? Was she dreaming? Isabel knew only that there was nowhere else she wanted to be at that very moment. Being in his arms, the musky, manly aroma of him intoxicating her senses, seemed as natural as drawing breath.

Seven

Alighting the cab, Dustin dropped his one canvas bag to the walkway while he dug in his pockets for a few coins for the driver. He was so tired he could hardly hold his head up and wished he'd stayed over in Natchez with his father, who would visit acquaintances before journeying home to Lamourie Bayou.

The house on Royal was unusually quiet; not even the distant clatter of Mercedes' pots and pans as she prepared the evening meal. With twilight falling this late December eve, Dustin had expected to see at least one light shining from within, but there were none, not even the lamp in the parlor that was always kept burning.

As the cab pulled away, he picked up his bag, hoping to hear the gentle sound of Isabel's laughter, some small betrayal that life existed in the ancient Creole house beyond the winter-bare courtyard. But he heard no laughter at all, only the low, guttural caterwaul of the battered old tomcat that came to the gate to meet him. "Where is everyone?" asked Dustin, half-expecting a reply of some sorts. He was that tired.

He was just about to try the door when a woman's voice sounded behind him. "Dustin ... oh, Monsieur Dustin—"

The tall, slim young man from Lamourie Bayou

turned, his eyes instantly catching the spry Golda Dumont as she hoisted up her skirt to dash across the road. "Golda, what is wrong?" he asked, a little concerned by her haste.

She curtsied prettily. "Nothing is wrong, Monsieur Dustin. I was merely bringing the key. The old missus and Mercedes are visiting at Magnolia Hill. She left the key in the event you returned from Philadelphia—"

"Boston . . . I was in Boston," corrected Dustin, accepting the key. "Thank you. My cousin is also at Magnolia Hill?"

Golda was thankful for the veil of darkness and the light of the road lamp held back by the tangle of shrubbery. Dropping her eyes, she said, "Miss Isabel has gone home to Lecompte. Her father missed her." Golda very much liked her friend's older cousin, and the lie she told brought a rush of shame upon her. Turning, she prepared to put distance between them before he might interrogate her further, which would surely require more lies.

Alone once again, Dustin entered the cool, dank house. In the parlor he lit a lamp, then moved toward the kitchen, hoping something might have been left in the pantry. He missed the feigned annoyance displayed by Mercedes, he missed the old rascal who was Isabel's great-great-aunt, and he missed his beautiful young cousin—oh, how he missed her! He had so many things to tell her: about the funeral of his poor mother, mourned by very few, even her own family, about other relations in Boston he hadn't seen since his early childhood. And he wanted to tell her about Melody Granger, the woman he had met and fallen madly in love with . . . a woman whose father would allow her to visit him on Lamourie Bayou this summer, with the hope that a true romance might flourish. Though Melody was pretty, she was also stubborn, hard-headed and nearly twenty-seven years old. Her father, a charming old aristocrat from Beacon Hill, felt that Dustin was her last salvation from spinster-hood.

She was the first woman Dustin had ever met that he felt he could love more than he loved Isabel.

Dragging open cupboards, pantries and the cold cabinet, Dustin soon sat at the table with a plate of cheese and slightly stale bread. He had snatched a bottle of wine from the cabinet in the parlor in his journey and now sat back to fill his stomach and think about all the different ways his life would change.

"Isabel . . . Isabel, why aren't you here? I need you so."

But she did not answer, and the loneliness of the house was almost more than he could bear. So, he retired to the bedchamber reserved for him and slept well despite the chill permeating the room. He had been much too tired to light a fire in the hearth. The following morning, he hired a horse from the livery on St. Charles and rode out to Magnolia Hill for a required visit with Aunt Imogen.

The country air did wonders for the dear old matron. She actually seemed pleased to see him.

"Back from the East, eh, boy?" she questioned, her ruddy cheeks beaming beneath a cold December sun.

"Why are you out on the gallery, Auntie? You'll catch your death."

"Poppycock; I survived six husbands, two wars, a cholera epidemic last year and a Yankee occupation in my beloved New Orleans. I can certainly survive

113

the cold! Now, tell me why you've journeyed to Magnolia Hill?"

"To say good-bye. Golda told me Isabel is back at The Shadoes so I am going home, too."

Frowning in that familiar manner Dustin had grown to know so well, sort of a reproof, but not quite outright disapproval, Imogen reminded him, "Isabel is your cousin! You should get romantic notions out of your head! There is a law—"

"Yes, I know, you nagging old dear," Dustin cut her off sternly, as he gently took her hand, "but if you will let me continue, I did meet a lady in Boston that I am very fond of. She will be permitted to journey to Louisiana this summer—"

"Some young snip, eh, manipulated by a stern father?"

Dustin laughed lightly. "Nothing of the sort. She will be twenty-seven in March—"

"Oh?" Imogen raised a thin, pencilled-in eyebrow. "Widowed?"

"Never married."

"What's wrong with her? Why . . . by the time I was twenty-seven, I was on my third husband!"

"And they're buried in your root cellar," teased Dustin, patting her hand as he arose. "May I kiss you farewell and be on my way?"

Lifting her wrinkled cheek with childlike mischief, Imogen replied, "Do as you please. But, young man, you rest assured there isn't a place on this ancient old woman that hasn't been kissed by the best of them."

Dustin touched his mouth to the cool, dry, heavily-rouged cheek. "I love you, you old bird dog."

"Poppycock!" Imogen flicked her wrist, dismantling her heavy shawl in the move. "You're just hoping I'll name you in my will! And I'll have you

114

know—" Her thin, painted mouth widened into a smile, "that you are. But . . . I'll not tell you what I have left you. That'll be a surprise."

Squeezing her hands, Dustin said in parting, "And please, Auntie, make it a very, very long time before your will must be executed." Giving her hands a final squeeze, Dustin turned to his waiting horse. Mounting the placid beast, raising his hand in farewell, he said, "Love to all."

Throughout the day he tidied up business, purchased a train ticket, and once again packed his bags. He wanted only to be home and to see his family again. He wanted to tell Isabel about Melody.

During the stopover in Baton Rouge, Dustin deposited the small inheritance his mother had left him to his bank account there, visited with an old family acquaintance, then returned to the depot for the last leg of his journey to Lecompte. There, he planned to rent a horse from Mr. Doughty, and made a stop at Shadows-in-the-Mist on his way to Lamourie.

The churning of the train almost put him to sleep. He tried to relax beside a very large lady in the cramped passenger car, and frequently felt her well-padded elbow digging into his shoulder. He was relieved when the whistle blew and those great iron wheels began their laborious stop at the Lecompte depot.

As he stepped down to the train platform, his heart began to beat with a quicker cadence. His beloved cousin was just a mile to the east, at Shadows-in-the-Mist, surrounded by the people who loved her most, safe from all harm and danger.

As the two weary horses approached the outskirts of Natchez, Mississippi, Isabel took special precautions to hide her exhaustion from Shadoe McCaine. They were making about twenty miles per day in their travels, and Shadoe had estimated the distance to Tongue River at seventeen hundred miles. Allowing a few days here or there for problems that might arise along the way, he had set their time of arrival for the end of January, 1880.

The self-described jack-of-all-trades had become even more of a puzzle to Isabel in this past week of traveling. Though they had cleared New Orleans easily, with family and friends none the wiser, Shadoe seemed to watch constantly over his shoulder. During those long, cool nights, Isabel had slept beside him, not so much because of the dangers that might lurk outside the perimeters of their campfires, but, traitorously, simply to be near him. The musky, manly scent of him made her head swim with strange and alien sensations. A warmth would flood her body and she would long to be in his arms, beneath his blanket rather than her own. What was this wonderful, puzzling emotion that flooded her from head to toe? It was erotic, naughty, compelling, something she had never experienced with any other man, even that handsome young man on Bayou Boeuf with his dark Cajun eyes.

Sometimes at the campfires, Isabel and Shadoe would talk lightly and she would see humor skirting his eyes; at others, he seemed stern and implacable, and almost hostile in his efforts to avoid speaking to her altogether. Sometimes she saw that strange and alien warmth in the way he looked at her, as if he wanted to pounce upon her for any reason other than murder, and at others, she was sure she saw silent loathing and brutal lust. Sometimes she felt like the willing recipient of his admiration; at others, she felt like the victim of a ruthless scoundrel.

Whatever his intentions were, she would not allow him to intimidate her into aborting their trip, if, indeed, that was what he had in mind. First and foremost in her mind was the necessity of finding her brother and bringing him home. The first day of their trip, Shadoe had demanded to know exactly why she did not tell her father of the letter and let him fetch the boy home, and her explanation that she had lost favor in her father's eyes and wished to regain it had not washed well with him. Daughters *did not* lose favor, he had explained. They merely disappointed their parents. So much for her explanation. It had made sense to her; why didn't it convince him?

Isabel did not care what dangers lurked in the wild countryside between New Orleans and Montana. She tried not to think about Shadoe's stories of the brutalities of the Indians, though he was quick to admit that the lies and deceptions of the whites through many generations of encroachment into their lands had instigated the hostilities, and she tried not to think that something might happen to him that would leave her alone in hostile lands. Eduard was all that mattered. He was the reason she put on a strong facade. He was the reason she refused to admit that blisters stung her buttocks and the tender flesh of her inner thighs from sitting in the saddle from dawn till dark.

As they entered the small, bustling city of Natchez, Isabel drew her horse up in front of a drug store. "Shadoe?" His horse halted; he turned in the saddle and glared at her as if she'd rudely interrupted an important thought. "Would you mind if we stop here so that I can purchase some iodine?"

"Iodine! What the hell do you need iodine for?"

The veil of evening twilight hid the crimson flushing her pale, winter-cooled cheeks. She wanted to respond, *That's none of your concern,* but rather said saucily, "I have blisters on my fingers from holding the reins. The mare is headstrong, you know."

His eyebrow twisted sarcastically. "Want to turn back?"

"Horsefeathers!" Swiftly, she dismounted, glad of the horse separating her from Shadoe McCaine, so that he would not glimpse the pain etching her features. She felt like scalding water had been poured between her thighs.

With a grunt, Shadoe turned his horse and dismounted, then draped the reins over the hitch rail beside Isabel's. She had entered the small, dimly lit drug store and he could see her through the window, speaking to a tall, thin, bespectacled gentleman.

Shadoe was worried, not so much about an irate and irrational father who might lead a posse to rescue his daughter, but about his own rather precarious standing in the eyes of the law. Thank God, they would not have to pass through the state of Texas to get to Montana.

He was traveling with a chit of a girl who had only one thought in mind . . . finding a brother at a road ranch on a godawful place called Tongue River. He still couldn't believe he'd agreed to it. Blast! If her father sent out a posse—

Which was why he had kept one eye open, even when they slept at night. Mirlo, his stallion, had exposed a special talent soon after Shadoe had come into possession of him. If strangers approached,

Mirlo would squeal frantically and rear on his haunches, creating a frightening ruckus. Under normal circumstances, Shadoe had been able to sleep most nights, even in hostile environments, but with Isabel, he felt protective and could not bring himself to leave night guard strictly to his horse.

Shrugging off his own weariness for the moment, Shadoe entered the drugstore. When the proprietor, alarmed by Shadoe's dark, dusty appearance, seemed to edge toward something beneath the counter, Isabel, thinking he might be going for a gun, quickly said, "It's all right, sir. He's with me."

Narrowing his eyes, Shadoe irately asked, "Do you propose to shoot all strangers who come in here, mister? Wouldn't be too good for business, would it?"

The proprietor's thin lips thinned even more. "You misunderstood, sir. I was merely looking for a rag to clean the counter."

"Sure," said Shadoe rather sardonically. "What's wrong with the one in your hand?" Approaching, speaking so that only Isabel could hear, he asked, "Do I really look that bad?"

With a pretty smile, she replied, "Well . . . you haven't shaved in two days. And you could use a bath, Shadoe McCaine." Before he could utter a protest, she continued with haste, "I do hope we're going to seek lodgings at a hotel tonight. I could use a bath myself." In the next few minutes, Isabel chose a few personal items: a bar of White Soap, since hotel soaps dried her skin; hair pins; a new brush to replace her broken one, and a pair of thick wool socks to wear on nights that would grow more frigid the farther north they traveled. From the corners of her eyes she watched Shadoe saunter through the store picking up items of his own.

Soon they paid for their purchases and returned to their horses. Within a few minutes, Shadoe had spotted what he considered a suitable hotel on a small, dark street and they were standing before a dour young clerk. Leaning close to Shadoe's back, Isabel whispered harshly, "Isn't this a little seedy? We could have done better."

And the clerk, overhearing, snapped, "If you don't like it, ma'am, then go down the street!"

Without warning, Shadoe's hand shot across the span of the counter and grabbed the smaller man up by the lapels of his shirt, dragging him toward him. "You apologize for your tone of voice," he warned between tightly clenched teeth, "or you're liable to get a little dirty wallowing in the street out there."

Two thin, trembling hands gripped Shadoe's wrists, compelling him to loosen his grip. "I—I'm sorry, ma'am, didn't mean no disrespect."

Isabel was stunned by Shadoe's heated reaction. She didn't expect a little worm of a man from Mississippi to treat her with the same respect as a Louisiana gentleman. She managed a small, embarrassed smile, but said nothing.

"Do you want to stay here, Isabel?" asked Shadoe, slinging the fellow away as if he'd suddenly found him repulsive.

"As long as I—we can have a bath," she responded.

"Together?" he whispered huskily.

Her mouth pressed impetuously, her eyes berated him. "When the sky rains pigs, Shadoe McCaine. Now—" She moved from him, dropping her gaze from his humored scrutiny. "Sign us in, and don't forget to arrange to have our horses stabled for the night. They could use a little pampering—"

"I'll take care of the horses." Turning a warning gaze to the clerk, Shadoe instructed, "Give us two of your best rooms with a connecting door. And by the time I get back I want hot baths readied in both."

"You must sign in, sir."

"I'll take care of that," offered Isabel. "Don't forget to bring in our saddle bags."

Gaining momentum, Shadoe slipped his hat back onto his head, then moved toward the door. Just before he exited, he turned, his narrow gray gaze connecting with Isabel's unreadable one. Did he see fear there, or was it melancholy? Was it loathing . . or was it desire?

He didn't know how much longer he could wait before he found out for sure.

The long nights at the campfires, alone with the stunning nymph, were certainly taking their toll on his nerves . . . and his patience.

Isabel tested the temperature of the water in the tub with a carefully placed toe. Though it was a little warmer than she liked, she prepared to drop her robe and slip into the tub. Suddenly a knock sounded at the door connecting to Shadoe's room, and without awaiting her response, it opened, though he did not step in. Turning swiftly, dragging the robe around her once again, Isabel called, "Yes, what is it, Shadoe?"

"Are you decent?" he asked.

"Yes." He stepped in. Seeing her in her charming state of half-dress, the ivory swells of her breasts exposed above the lapels of her robe, Shadoe forced his gaze to rise a few inches. Her look was reprimanding at best. "I forgot to ask the fellow at the

121

livery to replace that broken girth on your saddl[e]
Just wanted to let you know I'd be gone for a fe[w]
minutes."

Pivoting smartly, Isabel replied matter-of-factl[y]
"Hurry back before your bathwater gets too col[d]
Silence. The door closed once again. "The rake
she muttered. "He was probably hoping to catch m[e]
in my altogethers." Then she cast a final look at t[he]
door, assuring herself it would not yield still anoth[er]
intrusion, then dragged off her robe and slipp[ed]
quickly into the suds. "Ah . . . this is absolu[te]
heaven, Isabel Emerson!"

The bar of soap she had purchased felt like si[lk]
between her wet palms. She rubbed the bar ov[er]
her shoulders and behind her neck beneath the ta[n]
gled fringes of her pinned-up hair. The soreness b[e]
tween her thighs began to subside, and she felt sh[e]
must have misjudged the degree of blistering on h[er]
buttocks, because the water had stung for only [a]
second. She smiled, thinking that she really hadn[']
wanted to douse her tender flesh with the ugly re[d]
stains of iodine.

The water began to cool more to her liking. Clo[s]
ing her eyes, Isabel sighed dreamily. For a mome[nt]
she felt that she must be back on the Boeuf, wit[h]
her family and her friends all around her, becaus[e]
she felt a sudden peace of mind such as she had fe[lt]
only there. Perhaps being with Shadoe McCai[n]
produced that blissful, ethereal state. She felt s[o]
protected with him always nearby, even when he in[-]
vaded her private moments. He was certainly [a]
mystery, but a mystery she very much looked fo[r]
ward to unveiling on their long trip to Tongu[e]
River. She had told him she wanted to regain he[r]
father's favor by returning with their long lost so[n]
and brother, but Isabel knew that was not her onl[y]

122

otive; she wanted to be with Shadoe McCaine, ven if he did detest her without reason that she uld see. That was why she had not protested beond the required word or two his refusal to travel y train. The trail, by horseback—even with blisrs—would give her a chance to get to know the gue, her "dark wolf," the man whose name might r might not be Shadoe McCaine.

She really wasn't sure why she distrusted him, ven to questioning whether he had given her his uthful identity. He claimed to be a gambler, a roer, a drifter . . . a lover. . . . He had questioned er unmercifully a few nights ago about the medalon she wore, then had cast off his curiosity with a areless shrug. He had wanted to know where it ad come from, then had narrowed those smoky ray eyes suspiciously when she'd said she didn't now. *Peculiar knows. Ask her!* she had replied. To hich he had replied, *Who the hell's Peculiar . . . if ot you!*

Oh, what an exasperating man he was. She had efused to remind him that Peculiar was a simpleinded slave girl who had found the gold accidenally many years ago and had stolen it away to her wn special place, promptly forgetting its location. Ie was the curious one! If the lure of gold was all nat would bring him back to Louisiana, then she ould certainly feed that curiosity!

Isabel dragged in a weary breath. Did she care nough about him to, even now, be planning to enice him back to Louisiana? Yes, she thought she id. She wanted the mysterious rogue in her life, hough she was still not sure what purpose he would erve there. She had imagined shameless acts with im in the deepest recesses of her sleep, and oftimes she had awakened, sure that he had read her face as plainly as the pages of a favorite book.

Draping her arms along the smooth sides of the tub, Isabel again sighed, though this time wistfully rather than with weariness. The soreness that had radiated throughout was subsiding, the little ache in her temple was going the way of spent words, and the nagging cramp in her right foot was nonexistent beneath the warm surface of the water. She thought of the first night she and Shadoe had camped out on the shore of Pontchartrain, and how cold the water had been when she'd washed away the day's dust. If only horses could be equipped with modern conveniences, sort of like a traveling hotel—

A rattling at the door startled Isabel. She lurched forward, her fingers gripping the sides of the tub so tightly that pain claimed her knuckles. "Who is there?" she called out timorously. "Shadoe, is that you?" No reply. Again, the door rattled, and Isabel, hopping from the tub with the agility of a spooked cat, quickly pulled on her robe.

A clink . . . then the key she had inserted in the corridor door popped out of the lock. With a small cry, she rushed for the door, but before she could traverse the rug, it creaked open. Lurching to a halt, a wide-eyed Isabel Emerson found herself facing two men, one of them the clerk from downstairs.

A lecherous grin crept across the clerk's face. The other man, a large, bony man with dark, ragged hair, stepped threateningly to the left. "What do you want?" asked Isabel as firmly as the situation would allow. Her eyes darted around the room, searching for a weapon.

The clerk held some kind of club which he slowly and deliberately pounded against the palm of his other hand. "I didn't like the way your man talked o me downstairs," he sneered, moving slightly to he right. "Me an' my friend here, well, we seen our man leave, an' I reckon it's time to teach you lesson, little lady."

"I git her first, Odell," interjected the tall, mal- dorous man.

"You just leave enough of that sweet thing for ne," said the clerk, pulling on his crotch in the ame moment he spat tobacco juice against the ;rimy wall.

Even as they moved threateningly toward her, Isa-)el's hands worked subtly, tying and retying the belt f her robe, until she was sure it would take a lock- mith to free her from the bindings once the danger ıad passed. Her heart thumping so quickly she was ure she would faint, Isabel began to back away rom the two men, her eyes darting hither and yon n search of the elusive weapon. In the absence of)ne, she quietly threatened, "My man will be right)ack. He said he'd be gone no more than ten min- ıtes."

"Little lady, that man of yours . . . I'd venture to guess he's been detained a tad by the night life of Natchez-under-the-Hill. If you're lookin' for him ıereabouts anytime soon, I wouldn't hold your)reath a-waitin'—"

Isabel wasn't sure where she found the courage to dive for the door separating her room from Shadoe's . . perhaps instinct for self-preservation, perhaps)ecause she could imagine no fate worse than the ınwanted attentions of the dastardly pair, but sud- denly she was struggling with the rusted handle with one hand and banging upon the wood with the)ther. Then a pair of brawny hands circled her waist and forced her backwards, and she began to scream and flail and kick out her feet in a desperate attempt to free herself. She was vaguely aware of her foot making contact with a particularly sensitive spot below the clerk's waistline, and from the covering of her unkempt hair that had fallen loose from its pins she saw him double to the floor. Rough hands mauled her breasts, and she felt herself falling backwards to the bed with the vile creature holding her prisoner.

"Shadoe! Shadoe!" she screamed, tears stinging her eyes and her body tensing against the vicious attack of the beast who held her down while the other regained his senses.

She felt so alone, so afraid, and so betrayed by the man she had placed such unabandoned trust in . . . a man who might have sought out a saloon and a game of cards, giving her little more than a disgruntled thought . . . a man who would allow a fate worse than death to befall her . . .

Clenching her hands into fists, Isabel continued her fight for survival once again. She had to rely on her own strength and wits.

Shadoe had deserted her.

Eight

Shadoe McCaine opened his eyes. He got a strong whiff of some substance piled close to his face that, normally, he would have taken special precautions to avoid stepping in. Something stabbed into the crease at the right corner of his lip, and he made a feeble attempt to shake the offending thing loose. Forcing himself to gain momentum, his eyes focused, and his left palm eased toward the side of his body, to be used as leverage to pick himself up.

Shadoe had only a vague recollection of entering the livery, and part of that recollection was Mirlo's warning squeal and powerful hooves beating at the sides of his stall. Scarcely had he entered the dark interior before something blunt forcefully struck the back of his head, sending him staggering into unconciousness. Now that his senses were returning, he checked his jacket and found his wallet still in its inner pocket. Apparently, the motive for the attack upon him had not been robbery. He was a stranger in Natchez; he could not possibly have made enemies. What then was the motive?

Drawing himself into a seated position, Shadoe picked bits of straw away from his face and then felt the painful knot at the back of his skull. Mirlo had freed himself from the stall and was standing over him, his soft muzzle pushing against Shadoe's temple. Lifting his hand to the stallion, Shadoe mumbled assuredly, "Don't worry, old boy. I think I'm still alive."

"Good Lord, man!"

Shadoe instinctively went for his weapon, his hand ceasing as his gaze met that of a thin, well dressed gentlemen.

"I was passing by and saw you here," said Aldrich Emerson, bending to one knee. "You've had a run-in of sorts?"

"Of sorts," replied Shadoe McCaine, attempting a half-cocked smile. "Apparently, somebody didn't like my face."

"Shall I summon a constable?" asked Aldrich, offering his hand to help Shadoe up. "Were you robbed?"

These past seven years Shadoe had made it a policy to evade anyone in law enforcement, and that included small-town constables. "No." Shadoe accepted the politely proffered hand and rose unsteadily to his feet. "No need of the law. Whoever attacked me is long gone." Shadoe turned, his finger easing into the ring of Mirlo's halter. "You must be all right, mister," continued Shadoe. "My horse didn't lift your scalp."

"Fine animal," said Aldrich, his right hand plying a fluid course over the strong muscles of Mirlo's haunch. "My wife and I raise horses. Don't think we've ever raised any finer than this." Lifting his hat slightly, Aldrich said, "Well, if you're all right, young fellow, I'd better be keeping my appointment."

Shadoe chose another stall for Mirlo, since he had left the first one in splinters. "Thanks for your help. It's reassuring that at least one resident of this town has a decent bone in his body."

Aldrich chuckled. "I'm afraid I'm not a resident. I stopped off to visit friends and to purchase a new carriage for my wife, Ellie."

Shadoe, too, laughed. "Well, so much for my impulsive assessment."

Aldrich quietly approached the stall and gave the tallion another long scrutiny. "Would you be interested in selling him?"

For just a moment, Shadoe looked stunned. Then he again smiled, his hand lifting to the stallion's powerful jaw. "I'd sell my wife first . . . if I had one." Suddenly, alarm flashed in Shadoe's eyes. Suppose the attack upon him had been for the purpose of stalling him . . . suppose Isabel was facing the real danger. Turning swiftly, Shadoe slammed the gate of the stall shut. "I've got to be going."

And before Aldrich Emerson could respond, he had emerged into the overhanging darkness of the Mississippi night.

Isabel fought with all the power that was hers. She would have screamed, but a rough hand covered her mouth. Her feet kicked out, only to be caught in a powerful grip, and she begin anew to flail her arms, breaking them free only to have them captured once again. As the taller man's hands flattened upon her shoulders, her hand suddenly found the lamp on the bedside table. With one mighty heave, she brought it crashing against the man's head and almost before he could roll off the bed, the tall man was fleeing, screaming, from the room, his oil-soaked jacket engulfed in flames.

The clerk stood at the foot of the bed as if bolted to the floor, his wide gaze transfixed to the flames that were now spreading across the bed. Isabel scooted on her belly across the planked floor and curled up in a dark corner, waiting for the clerk to flee from the fire. The weathered hotel, with its dry, clinging patches of lead-based paint and its old-fashioned wicker lamps and gas stoves, would go up like timber in a drought. Isabel wanted only to be far away from the danger, but there was no way to escape past the man who had initiated the brutal attack against her. He did not appear to be aware of her and was watching with macabre fascination as the fire spread to the carpet.

Isabel was not really sure if her heart was still beating. She felt almost lifeless, as if she really didn't have the strength to flee the fire when the chance was hers. She was separated from a window by only a few feet of floor space on the right, and on the left the door stood open, the corridor brightening with flames. Only then did she hear the final whimper of the tall man as his burning body dropped to the floor with a resounding thud somewhere in the corridor. Shuddering with horror and revulsion, she would have buried her face against her drawn-up knees, but the clerk continued to stand there, his face strange and frightening, and sharply outlined against the glow of the flames. She wanted to be aware of any move he made.

The room was suddenly filled with smoke, and that gave the clerk the incentive to flee into the corridor and away from the flames. But Isabel continued to crouch in the corner, her hands circling her shins and her eyes strangely blank of emotion. The smoke billowed outward along the ceiling and down the walls, enveloping her where she sat. The flames were close enough to touch, and yet she was not afraid. A strange, distant void surrounded her, cutting her off from reality . . . from the wall of death moving so quickly upon her that there was no place to run. Not now . . . she had waited too long—

Did she hear her name being frantically called? Or was she merely dreaming? Was it even her name? As the smoke filled her lungs and all sounds slowly drifted away, she was as devoid of fear as if she was already dead. Her mother had told her that when her grandfather Angus died, the cardinals had come to take his soul to heaven. Were they waiting just outside the billowing smoke and leaping flames, to carry her own soul to a far and distant peace—

Suddenly, her body was being dragged up and cradled in strong, masculine arms. The flames licked at her sleeves and the hem of her robe. The heat billowed within her lungs, replacing her strength and her will to live. She knew only that on the other side there were angels and guardians and loved ones who awaited her. . . .

Then something cold and brutal stung at her flesh and her backside suddenly struck a rough barrier. This was not heaven; dear Lord . . . had she been sent to hell?

Shadoe McCaine hovered over Isabel and harshly spoke her name. His hand patted her cheek so roughly that he could see the redness brightening upon her tender flesh. The robe she had been wearing dragged against the planked sidewalk and her hair was like loose golden clouds that could not be contained by mortal means. If she was alive, she gave no indication of it.

With a frantic, frightened groan, Shadoe McCaine pulled her firmly up by the shoulders and shook her limber body. Her lips were slightly parted and he could not see even the vaguest glimmer of life in her half-closed eyes. She was like a rag doll in his arms, and he himself was so weak with fright he thought he would collapse atop her.

"Isabel . . . dear, sweet Isabel . . . come back to me," he whispered with husky emotion, ignoring the people gathering about him, the clank of bells growing louder in the cold December night. Behind them the hotel burned, explosions of gas stoves and oil

131

lamps hurtling a million glowing embers, like fire-works, into the darkened sky overhead. When a fire-man jumped down from the fire engine and attempted to pry him loose, Shadoe slung out his hand. "Get away . . . get away from her. She's my woman!"

He was as unaware of the words he had uttered as he was of her state of life or death. He knew only that she was in his arms and he was powerless to help her. He knew only that she might be gone from him, and he had not told her that he had fallen in love with her that first night when she had stamped her foot indignantly and turned her cool, powder-blue eyes to him for the briefest of assessments —

Snapped from her netherworld, Isabel suddenly in-haled a long, trembling breath. Her hands balled into fists, then plummeted against Shadoe's chest before he was even aware of her movement. She felt him against her, his own body quaking, his cheek pressed so close to her own that she wasn't sure if she could continue to drag in the much-needed gulps of air. Then the familiar scent of him filled her nostrils, and her trembling arms circled his waist to hold him close. "Shadoe . . . Shadoe, I—I thought I was dead."

Relief flooded him. He cared not a whit that tears of joy stung his eyes and he was trembling like a bul-lied school boy. He knew only that Isabel was alive and in his arms . . . he cared only that he would not lose her.

Then the harsh, frantic declaration he had barked at the fireman ricocheted through him like a bullet. *Get away from her . . . she's my woman!* Had Isabel heard him speak those words? Had she been pretend-ing unconsciousness? Gritting his teeth, he put her away from her so quickly that he nearly lost his bal-ance. Then he sat back on his knees and covered his thighs with his hands. "Well, you're not dead!" he retorted harshly. "Can't you stay out of trouble, or must I watch you every minute?!"

A large man suddenly hovered over them. "Young lady, were you inside when the fire started?"

Isabel sniffed back the tears Shadoe's harsh words had caused. "Yes . . . yes, I was. It started in my room—"

Just moments ago, he had been barking orders at his firemen to forget the engulfed hotel and concentrate their efforts on the adjoining buildings. As he stooped, he turned his attentions to the shivering young woman and asked much more gently, "Young lady, do you think you can tell me how the fire started?"

When she hesitated, Shadoe snapped, "Well, can you?"

Even in her disoriented state, Isabel's feelings reeled at his unwarranted tone. She lowered her eyes for a moment, took a long, deep breath, then met the kind eyes of the fire chief. "Yes, but could we get off the street? I feel a little awkward sitting here."

While a silent, narrow-eyed Shadoe looked on, Isabel was escorted into a cafe across the street that had been emptied of human occupation. Everyone for blocks around stood on the street watching the fire. There was always something captivating about a fire, even when it destroyed property and took lives. Putting a cup of coffee in front of her, the fire chief asked, "How did the fire start?"

Isabel felt foolish, sitting in a cafe wearing only a robe, her damp hair dragging across her shoulders and back, and her feet bare. But even more important than her state of undress was what had happened in those terrifying moments before the fire had started. If she told the fire chief that two men had attacked her and that she, herself, had started the fire, would she be required to remain in Natchez for

133

some kind of hearing? Possibly, even a trial? Would she be blamed for starting the fire, regardless of the precipitous circumstances?

Drawing in another steadying breath, Isabel carefully composed her reply. "I was in my room, the clerk came to fill the lamp with oil and accidentally spilled it upon the bed. Just at that moment, a most foul man passing by in the corridor flicked a cigar butt into the room and the spilled oil caught fire." She had spoken with her eyes downcast; now she lifted her gaze in an attempt to discern the fire chief's reaction. He had drawn his finger to his chin and was slowly nodding his head. "And that is how it happened," Isabel ended on a final note.

"Well, I certainly have no cause to doubt you, young lady. That is precisely what I will write in my report. May I have your name?"

Glancing up, Isabel caught the reflection of Shadoe McCaine against the cafe window. His back was turned to her, his thumbs tucked into the pockets of his Levis. "My name is Isabel Emerson," she replied after a moment.

He arose. "Where will you be staying tonight, in the event I should have further questions?"

"I don't know. You might ask my companion, who is waiting just outside."

Just before he exited, the fire chief turned and said, "You don't seem the kind of lady who should have such a companion. The young fellow has a chip on his shoulder."

"No, not really —" Isabel cut off abruptly. She wasn't really sure why she felt obligated to defend Shadoe McCaine. After the day he had stormed from her aging relative's house on Royal Street, she had felt that chip growing ever larger, and wondering always where it had come from in the first place. They had gotten along so wonderfully at first, even though their initial meeting had resulted from lies and deceptions. Then she had said something, small as it certainly must be, and try as she might she could not reconstruct the conversation that afternoon with any degree of success. If she could, perhaps she would be able to pinpoint the source of his sudden change of attitude. Aware of the silence that had disrupted her conversation with the fire chief, Isabel looked up and quietly said, "I believe you were going to ask Mr. McCaine where we were staying tonight?"

He bowed perfunctorily and the next sound Isabel heard was his large, shuffling boots and the door being opened to the inferno of noise outside. The fire chief paused beside Shadoe McCaine, muted voices reverberated against the small, dirty windows of the cafe, and then Shadoe was entering the dining area. He stood over her for a moment, saying nothing, then slowly crossed his arms. "I told the fire chief we would stay at the hotel down the street. He says it is respectable."

"I lost all my things in the fire," she said quietly. "I lost my portfolio and all of my money. I lost —" Emotion cracked in her voice. "I lost my brother's letter." Without reply, Shadoe's hand moved to the pocket inside his jacket. Instantly, he withdrew the letter written by a young man in Montana searching for an identity. Isabel took the letter and held it endearingly to her bosom. "How . . . oh, Shadoe, how did you come to have it?"

"Do you remember a couple of nights ago when your horse slipped on the trail and the portfolio fell out of the saddle case? While you were bathing the mud from the mare's haunches, I was collecting up your portfolio. For some reason I tucked the letter into my pocket rather than returning it where it belonged."

"And thank heavens you did!" she exclaimed, managing the smallest of smiles.

Shadoe sat across from her, then pressed his palms firmly together before linking his fingers. "I heard the story you told the fire chief about how the fire started. Now, Isabel . . ." Silence, his eyes narrowed almost threateningly. "I want you to tell me the truth."

Rebellion and feigned indignation suddenly captured her pretty features. Her topaz gaze connected with his narrow gray one in a clash of wills. Could he see so clearly into her soul, and know that she had lied, or was he merely acting on a supposition? Of course, if she *had* told the truth, she would have immediately defended herself to Shadoe, and the fact that she had allowed this time to elapse was probably a pretty clear indication to him that, indeed, there was another story, one that she had chosen not to relate. She found herself in one of those rare situations in her life when she was choosing to lie, and knew beyond a shadow of a doubt that he was very aware that she was lying. But she simply could not help herself as she replied in a soft, sultry, and somewhat sarcastic tone, "My dear Shadoe . . . why the very idea that you would think I had lied to a man in authority."

"There are two dead bodies lying over there that nobody can touch until the heat dies down."

Her eyes widened in surprise, then she attempted to regain same degree of normalcy. "Two? I saw only one man consumed by the flames."

"Another one, that blasted clerk, died by a back entrance with the key still clasped in his fingers. Apparently, he was overcome by the smoke before he could escape."

Isabel shuddered. The mental image that came to her of those two despicable males mauling her, planning to perpetuate the vilest of attacks that a woman could suffer, made her stomach churn. Still, she was not happy that they were dead. The old adage, *dead men tell no tales*, came to her, even as she lifted her gaze to Shadoe's and again assured him, "I told the fire chief the truth, Shadoe. I don't know why you don't believe me."

"Actually, I do believe you. It's just that—" Shadoe shrugged as if they were two old friends trying to outdo each other with tall tales. "I was struck over the head at the livery and I thought that something might have happened to you that would have given some reason for the attack upon me. I thought—" Again, he shrugged, a smile playing lazily upon his mouth. "I'd been taken out for a little while so that you would be left unguarded."

Isabel remembered how confident the two men had been that they would not be interrupted at her room. The story that Shadoe told made sense and for a moment she was too absorbed in the premeditated acts of the two men to show her concern for the man who had reluctantly agreed to take her to Montana. Then, a tiny light went off in her brain, and her hand scooted across the table toward Shadoe's, covering it only briefly before withdrawing. "Are you hurt? Should you see a doctor?"

Shadoe's right palm carefully covered the back of his head. "Just a lump, and a bit of a headache. I think I'll live. I've suffered worse injuries."

"And I'm sure you've inflicted a few yourself."

"What the hell do you mean?"

Isabel was instantly surprised at his defensive tone. She managed a small smile as she replied, "I was teasing you, Shadoe. Besides, you're a man, and men usually find any reason to punch each other in the face. I've seen a few telltale scars on your knuckles and that little one at the corner of your eye, so don't you take that tone with me."

Of course, he had overreacted. A particularly painful moment in his past had come back so quickly that he'd allowed it to affect his response to her innocent remark. Softening his features, he managed a smile of his own. "Perhaps the scars on my knuckles did come from contact with teeth, but this one—" He raised an index finger to his eyebrow. "I was just a youngster when this happened. Another boy on the reservation was swinging a short length of fence wire around and nearly took out my eye. He sure got a walloping for that."

She wasn't really listening. Rather, she was watching Shadoe's eyes . . . beautiful eyes . . . and she remembered the first time she had met that magnetic, gray-black gaze and fallen madly in love. "Shadoe?"

He lurched immediately from his thoughts. "I'm listening."

"Do you regret agreeing to take me to Montana?"

"Yes," he replied without a moment's hesitation. And when she looked up at him, pain sheening her eyes, he continued, "You would have been safer accompanied by your father. You would have been still safer back on that rich plantation, letting your father take care of family matters that you have no business engaging in. My decision was too rash—"

"Then why did you make it? You could have said no. I would have found another way."

Instantly, Shadoe's hand dashed across the table and gently covered her own. "Because I want to be with you, Isabel. God forgive me, I want to be with you any way that I can."

"Then why do you act as though you detest me? This past week of traveling has not exactly been pleasurable for me, and it has nothing to do with the cold weather."

His features suddenly darkened. "I did not realize we were taking this trip for pleasure. I thought it was business. You do intend to pay me for my troubles, don't you?"

Her hand instantly withdrew from the cover of his own. Actually, the matter of payment had never been brought up, even when he'd agreed to make the trip with her. But if she took public transportation she would certainly have to purchase a ticket. "I lost my money in the fire," she said. "But if you will take me to Montana and see me safely home again, then of course, I will—"

His hand shot up. "Wait a minute, Isabel. I never agreed to come back south with you." That was a lie, of course; he fully intended to follow her back to the banks of her beloved Boeuf. "I agreed only to take you to Tongue River. Of course, I might be enticed—"

"Could we go to our hotel?" She absolutely would not be drawn into an argument with him. "Tomorrow morning I will wire to New Orleans for money from my account there—"

"No need. I have enough for the trip."

"And to meet my necessities, Shadoe McCaine? Ladies need things along the way, you know."

His fingers toyed playfully among her own. "Allow me to pamper you, Isabel. It's been so long since a beautiful woman has depended on me for anything that it will be a pleasure to me to take care of you."

"Heavens, Shadoe McCaine!" She lowered her voice to a harsh whisper only when the proprietor, who had been watching the fire, reentered the establishment. "One minute you are wanting assurance that you'll be paid for your trouble, and the next minute you are wanting to take care of me. I do declare, you are a most exasperating man!" Rising, she clasped her robe to her slim form, again self-conscious of her state of undress beneath. "I'm tired and I'm hungry. I have no clothing except this robe. I don't even have a hairbrush." Though she had not planned it, tears suddenly filled her eyes and rushed down her pale cheeks in steady streams. When Shadoe's arms opened, she stepped into their inviting warmth. "I really am stronger than this, Shadoe. Really I am."

"I know you are," he said soothingly. "And don't worry. Tomorrow morning I'll purchase some decent traveling clothing and boots for you, even a hairbrush."

"And a bar of soap, Shadoe?"

He chuckled lightly. "A bar of soap, too." Stepping back, he removed his jacket and drew it across her shoulders. Then he picked her up as if she were weightless. "Let's get those feet tucked underneath your robe."

"We'll look terribly foolish to the people on the street." Isabel felt the ripple of his muscles beneath her fingers, his shoulder suddenly tense against her armpit. "And what will the hotel personnel think when we walk in like this?"

"Who cares what they think? In case you haven't noticed"—His mouth brushed the tip of her nose—"you've got soot there"—his mouth touched her temple—"And there, darling"—her cheek—"and there. I think a sensible man will presume you were a guest at the hotel that burned."

"You're right," said Isabel, coyly lowering her eyes. "We shouldn't care what anyone thinks."

Dustin dismounted his rented gelding at the front gallery of Shadows-in-the-Mist. He hardly had tied off the reins and turned toward the stairs when his sister, Aimee Claire, was flinging herself into his arms. "Oh, Dustin . . . Dustin, you've come back. Oh, I did think you would meet new folk in Massachusetts and abandon our beloved South."

Dustin peeled his sister's arms from his neck and held out her hands. "Let me get a look at you. Why, I do believe you've grown a few inches, haven't you, sister?"

Aimee Claire's round, pixielike features pinched in disapproval as she flung her head of tight, dark curls. Her dear brother had always teased her unmercifully about her short stature. He had once called her a dwarf, and she had yet to forgive him for it. "Remember what they say, brother, that dynamite comes in small packages."

"You remind me constantly, Aimee . . . but you never tell me who *they* are. I'll have to ask John if you're really dynamite."

"Pooh!" With a tiny laugh, Aimee Claire lightly struck her brother's shoulder. "You leave my husband out of this. Now, why are you here?"

"I came by to see Isabel. I understand she has returned home."

Alarm flashed in the tiny woman's dark eyes. Taking her brother's hand, she coaxed him onto the drive and toward the pond. "Come, walk with me. I need to fill you in on everything that has happened."

"Isabel is all right?" He could not disguise his concern. "She has not been hurt?"

"Nothing is wrong with Isabel," assured Aimee Claire, moving onto the gallery of the long-abandoned overseer's cottage. "Isabel and her parents are having difficulties and she has journeyed to Shreveport to visit a childhood friend." Aimee Claire had become very adept at lying; she and Isabel had been forced to cover their tracks many times as they had grown up together. "You mustn't question Aunt Delilah and Uncle Grant. They are very sensitive about the subject."

Dustin had listened quietly. He could hardly believe that Isabel had been back at Shadows-in-the-

Mist for only a week and had already battled with her parents. "I have so much to tell her," he said, breaking the moment of silence. "I met a woman in Boston and—"

"You met a woman, Dustin? A woman who might interrupt this sad state of bachelorhood?"

He smiled. "Her name is Melody Granger and she will travel south this summer to visit. What do you think of that?"

"How wonderful. Shall I order a dress for the wedding?"

Again, Dustin laughed, though his thoughts were dwelling upon the missing Isabel. "Please, let me court her first. But I do believe her father approves of me."

Just at that moment, Aimee Claire's husband, John Adler, rounded the corner of the cottage, his gaze brightening as he spied his brother-in-law. Offering his hand, he said, "It's about time you returned. The family is putting dinner on the table. Join us?"

"Tell me that Mozelle prepared her catfish couvillion, and I'll break a record making it to the house."

John's arm slid across the shoulders of his much shorter wife. "Sorry . . . roast beef and potatoes. But I think if you want to remain in good standing with this family that you'd better break that record. Aunt Delilah saw you ride in, only to be whisked off by our girl here—" John's full mouth touched Aimee's temple. "You know that she favors her rogue nephew."

"Uncle Grant is here, also?"

"Working on the ledgers. Been at it all day."

"Mozelle's in a good mood?"

John laughed and the three of them began the short trek back to the main house. "Mozelle in a good mood? Was General Lee a Yankee?" The aging

142

servant had never really been friendly, except to Delilah. John had heard the stories of the way she'd tried to run Grant Emerson off when he'd first purchased the Shadows in 1856. The fact that a Yankee-doodle gambler had overrun the quiet plantation on the Boeuf had been as catastrophic in those days as the Yankee occupation some years later. But things changed. Today she would lay down her life for Grant and Delilah Emerson.

"Mozelle's roast beef," Dustin mused, rubbing his stomach as he walked beside his sister and brother-in-law. "I am famished! Hope aunt and uncle won't mind an extra mouth for dinner."

"You're not the only extra mouth," said John. "Uncle Grant has a visitor from Baton Rouge."

"Oh? An old friend?"

"Some business acquaintance actually. A rather boring fellow, talking to Uncle Grant about municipal bonds and investments."

As they moved quietly toward the house, Aimee Claire breathed a sigh of relief. The conversation had finally drifted from the elusive Isabel. She knew Dustin well enough to know that he would not bring up the subject again.

But then, her features drained of color. Suppose her aunt and uncle should bring up Isabel and ask Dustin if he'd seen her in New Orleans this past week? What would she do then? What would she do if they found out she had conspired with Isabel so that she could do whatever it was she had to do without out a family chaperone?

Oh, what to do! thought Aimee Claire, a one-word expletive bursting inside her brain. *Isabel can drag me into ill-sorts and think nothing about it!*

Nine

Shadoe placed Isabel's slim form upon the wide, spacious bed, then casually drew back from her. He had barked his and Isabel's names at the hotel clerk, demanded two rooms, and opened his hand to have the keys dropped into it. Now Isabel propped herself up on her elbows and watched him move cautiously around the larger of the two rooms he had chosen for her, checking the locks on windows and doors, and making sure every convenience was available to her, that nothing would have to be brought up later by hotel personnel. Once he had assured himself that the room was safe, he turned, crossed his arms, and gave her a narrow, scrutinizing look. "Is there anything you need before I retire to my room?"

Isabel wondered if he had somehow learned of the attack. His caution certainly indicated it. "I saw a little shop off the lobby downstairs," she responded. "Would you see if they sell hairbrushes?" Her hand rose to her mass of thick, disheveled hair. "If I don't brush it tonight, it'll be impossible in the morning."

His smile was a tad malicious. "You almost die in a fire, and all you worry about is your hair? Well, we shouldn't have to worry about tangles, should we?"

Oh, what an impossible man! Isabel's mouth

144

pinched, then widened into a somewhat hesitant smile. She would not allow him to nettle her. "Thank you for doing it so unbegrudgingly," she said with sweet, soft sarcasm. "And while you're at it, I could make good use of a meal." As he sauntered toward the door, Isabel couldn't prevent herself from asking, "Why are we always quarreling, Shadoe?"

He opened the door, then braced himself for a moment against the facing, his forehead resting against the smooth, painted wood. "Are we quarreling, Isabel?" When Isabel did not bother to comment, Shadoe pushed himself up, flicked his hat back from his forehead and pulled the door to.

Isabel sat forward, drew up her knees, then locked her arms around them. From deep within her came a melodic hum, an assurance, without words, that her relationship to Shadoe McCaine was not quite the business one he would have her believe. From somewhere deep within, she could hear his voice, wooing and winning her, and yet not hear his words at all. The mirrored image of his gray-black eyes told her everything she needed to know about him, and yet she knew little more than she'd known that first night outside a sold-out theater.

He was a mystery . . . a puzzle . . . the epitome of every masculine trait she had been warned all her life to avoid. And yet the mystery of what he was not telling her about himself was what drew her to him. He was like a book with blank pages. A single look could tell her everything, and in the same moment, keep the mystery so intact that she could become frustrated to the point of tears.

"Shadoe . . . Shadoe . . . what manner of beast are you?" she mused in the quiet of the comfortable hotel room. She looked around, the stale earth colors suddenly brightening. The square, plain items of furniture became as expressive as the elaborate furnishings of a palace; even her sooty robe and her equally sooty skin took on the luminescence of a princess in the most magnificent of jewel-encrusted ball gowns. She felt beautiful, she felt happy, and her mind was as free to dream her lovely dreams as it had been at the gazebo her father had built for her on the banks of Bayou Boeuf. Isabel sighed deeply, the horrors of the night as distant as the moon. She knew that Shadoe made her feel this blissful happiness, this desire to be with him, completely and fully —

The door opened a crack. Shadoe rapped once to make his presence known, then called, "Are you decent? I have that brush you wanted, and a few other items a lady might need."

Shades of crimson rushed upon her pale cheeks. Quickly covering her ankles, she responded, "I'm decent, Shadoe," and hoped that she might successfully disguise her prior thoughts so that he would not read them.

He stepped in, his ugly mood suddenly flown off with the night. Shortly, he deposited on the bed an ivory-handled brush and matching comb, hair pins and two lengths of blue ribbon, a white winter bed gown, a bar of soap and a brown package tied with twine. He held one hand behind his back. "I'll purchase the items to be worn above these —" he explained with a sheepish grin, "at the shop on the corner tomorrow morning."

"Do you care about me, Shadoe?" She'd blurted out the question before her good senses could exercise caution . . . before she could think about it first. But they were out now, and he was looking at her as if she'd suddenly lost her mind.

"Of course, I do," he responded, his exposed hand hanging limply at his side. "When I took on the job of escorting you to Montana, I obligated myself to take care of you—"

"That's not what I mean. Do you *care* for me! Am I special to you?"

Shadoe stood there, studying the exquisite blue-eyed beauty in her soot-covered robe, her hair like clouds of spun gold, her normally pale cheeks as pink as rosebuds. She sat upon the bed like a precocious child, looking at him with inquisitive innocence, and yet with womanly wisdom, awaiting his reply. What was he to say? Yes, I care for you . . . yes, I desire you and . . . yes, I love you—No . . . no, he could not make such confessions! It would bind him to her, and that was something he could never allow. But if he did not answer, she would form her own opinions, and they would be opinions molded to her own liking.

Thus, Shadoe assumed a bit of an arrogant stand, then slowly began sauntering toward her. Momentarily, his knee pressed upon the bed beside her slim, drawn-up form. He dropped the bag he had been holding behind his back and his hands roughly circled her arms above the elbows. "Yes, I care for you, Isabel . . . and I want you. Surely, you're not so naive you cannot recognize that I am a man, you are a woman, we will be spending a lot of time together, and that I have certain expectations—"

A very hungry Isabel tried to ignore the aroma of ham drifting up from the brown bag he had hastily deposited on the bed. Her pretty, copper-colored eyebrows delicately rose. "Expectations? What expectations?"

His mouth curled into a sneer. "You are not that

147

naive, Isabel. You know what I want. You know what any man would want from a woman as young and innocent as you?"

Of course, she knew what he meant and she could also see that he was trying to anger her, though she knew not the reason. With a comical grin, she picked up the bag and dangled it between her fingers. "Sandwiches?"

And Shadoe, who had been trying to ruffle her feathers so that she might loathe him, couldn't prevent a smile in return. "Ham and cheese, and a bottle of fresh milk." Forgetting the cat-and-mouse bantering for the moment, Shadoe took the bag and opened it, placed linen napkins which he'd gotten from the hotel dining room upon their laps, then handed one of the two sandwiches to Isabel. "I'm afraid we'll have to share the bottle of milk. I forgot to bring glasses."

Isabel did not bother to remind him that glasses sat beside the ewer on the table across the room. She liked the idea of sharing the milk with Shadoe, of her lips touching the same smooth glass his own would touch. What a lovely mouth he had, its sharp, masculine lines softened by the pale glow of the lamp, its fullness inviting her full attentions across the short spanse of space separating them. Absently, she brought the corner of her sandwich to her mouth and took a small bite, while her azure gaze studied his angular features, the recalcitrant wisp of hair invading his forehead, the dimple pulsating at the left corner of his mouth as he slowly ate his own sandwich.

He had held his gaze away from her own, but now lifted his eyes, making direct contact. "Why are you looking at me like that?"

"Like what?" inquired Isabel rather coyly, taking

another small bite of her sandwich.

"I'm really not sure," he responded. "Like you could just eat me up and . . . I'm not sure that's a compliment."

Lifting her sandwich, Isabel softly replied, "This is very fulfilling. You have nothing to worry about. Actually—" A moment of humor eased across her pretty features. "I was thinking that you're not so bad to look at, for a rogue cowboy—"

"Thanks . . . I think."

Isabel watched his expression, a strange mixture of contentment and uneasiness, perhaps a bit of caution thrown in. The two of them sat cross-legged upon the bed, eating sandwiches and sharing a bottle of milk, with no cares at the moment but filling their stomachs. Isabel could not understand the silent worry evident on his brow. Had he learned the truth about the fire that had consumed the old hotel just an hour ago? Had there been a witness to the attack upon her? Was he silently searching for a way to broach the subject? If he had somehow learned of the attack, did he think she was responsible for it? Oh, so many questions . . . so many worries and so little cooperation from the masculine rascal sitting across from her!

"Shadoe?"

"Hmmmm?"

"How is the lump on your head?"

"Still there."

"Does it hurt?"

"A little."

"How are the horses?"

"Dead."

"That's good."

Shadoe laughed. "Listen to yourself, Isabel! You're talking just to hear yourself talk and not

149

even listening to my answers. What is on your mind?"

"Just making conversation, Shadoe." Isabel watched him take the last bite of his sandwich and wash it down with a long swig of milk. Then he offered the bottle to her and hopped off the bed.

As he moved toward the door he said, "This hotel has a tank of hot water in the attic. Just pull that cord over there above the tub and you can take another bath."

"I know how to run bath water," she retorted with feigned indignation.

He grinned rakishly. "This hotel has a back-scrubber, too."

Now, this was something new. "Oh? Where?"

His palms landed, with a slap, upon his chest. "Me."

Her mouth pressed petulantly. "I can wash my own back, thank you." She flicked her wrist as one might do to a rebellious child. "Do go on about yourself, Shadoe McCaine, and allow me my privacy."

No one could see better than he that Isabel was not truly angry with him. Her voice was teasing, almost affectionate, and he stifled the desire to pounce upon her from this distance and do what came naturally. He could imagine nothing more satisfying than her slim body pinned beneath his own, her eyes narrowed, darkening with pretended loathing, and her trembling mouth rebelliously inviting the attentions of his own. He could imagine nothing more sensual than the "yes, no, maybe so" disobedience in her eyes, and her long, tapered fingernails digging into his flesh as she faintly attempted to disengage him from his intentions.

"Why are you looking at me like that, Shadoe

McCaine?" she quipped, halting the consumption of her last morsel of sandwich. "You look like a wolf stalking a lamb."

"Well, neither of us is in a mood to be looked at, are we? Believe me, love, you are hardly a lamb. But I will not deny that I could very well be a wolf. Don't you know every living soul has an animal spirit guide. Have I ever told you that the wolf is mine?"

"What manner of superstitious nonsense is that?"

"Indian nonsense. Just remember what I said."

Dabbing her mouth with the clean linen napkin, Isabel drew her knees up once again. "Now I must be on guard for still another danger," she remarked casually.

"What danger is that?"

"I might wake up early one morning on the trail between here and Montana and find a wolf hovering over me."

With teasing affection, Shadoe responded, "As long as the wolf is me."

"And suppose it was another two-legged wolf?"

"Better not be."

Isabel smiled, though she did not respond to his moment of subtle jealousy. "Good night, Shadoe. Thank you for the sandwich and milk . . . and the other things."

Shadoe moved first toward her, then pulled his wallet from his pocket and withdrew two ten-dollar bills. "A lady should never be without money," he explained, handing it to her. Then he ambled toward a chair and picked up his hat, returning at once to the door. "Thanks for having supper with me, ma'am," he drawled pleasantly. "You get some sleep because we've got a long day ahead of us tomorrow."

"I'll dash off a quick note to Golda after my bath," she said, swinging her bare feet to the floor and depositing the money he had given her in a side table. "I promised her a letter every week so that she will know how our trip is progressing."

Lightly bowing his head, Shadoe McCaine pulled the door closed.

Isabel tossed and turned, tugging at the large, comfortable bed gown Shadoe had purchased for her. Though the heavy blankets covered her, she shivered against the cold permeating the large chamber. Occasionally, the clip of horses' hooves on the road outside echoed through her sleep, and she would awaken with a start, only to fall fully asleep almost instantaneously. Cinders sparkling in the hearth seemed as loud as cannons exploding, and the night had an eerie, haunting sound like nothing she had ever heard before.

The door opened, allowing the faintest hint of light to enter the room. As though her limbs had suddenly lost all their strength, she tried to arise, but could not accomplish even that small task. There, against the light of the corridor, they stood . . . those two vile, horrendous creatures who had attacked her . . . one ghastly white, his eyes staring and yet not seeing at all, and the other, a charred and naked shell of a man. Two dead, twisted bodies began to move on a slow, deliberate course toward her—

Isabel awoke screaming. Her long, slim legs flailed beneath the covers, dislodging the mound of blankets that had been so comforting just moments before, and her palms pressed firmly to her temples.

When the door burst open and she was instantly

enveloped within strong, masculine arms, she saw only those two horrible men hovering over her. Her slim, trembling hands pummeled Shadoe's naked, fur-matted torso, even as he tried to still her against him.

"Hush . . . hush, Isabel —" soothed Shadoe McCaine, holding her so firmly she was sure she would faint from lack of air. "You have had a bad dream. Hush . . . I am with you now."

The familiar scent of him assailed her senses. She reeled against him, her trembling hands quickly spanning his slim hips, then rising to the rigid muscles of his back. "Shadoe, Shadoe, I'm so sorry —" Tears burned her eyes and traveled the soft contours of her features. "What a silly baby I am." As she spoke, her mouth rose in sweet invitation to his own, her hands pressed tightly to his back and the small bit of space separating their bodies became nonexistent. She felt his hard maleness against her, his rapid breaths against her cheek, the enticing warmth of his mouth as it moved from her cheek to her slightly parted lips. She had a faint, cold fear that something was about to happen between them, and unlike any fear she had ever before known, this one moved her within as deeply as happiness.

Her heart was all aflutter; she became so intensely aware of his half-nakedness she was sure she might clamp her eyes shut so firmly enough that they might never open again. A warm rush replaced the cold fear, enveloping her body as completely as a newly started fire. That was the effect he had on her, this virile, half-naked man who had rushed to soothe her and chase away her gruesome dream. He was on his knees, drawing her to him, his hands gently enfolded around her trembling shoulders, his breath as sweet as wine as he claimed still another kiss. Then a long finger moved over her cheek to flick away the single tear clinging there.

Against her hairline, Shadoe McCaine whispered hoarsely, "Are you all right now? Shall I leave?"

To which she softly responded, "No . . . no, Shadoe, please don't leave me."

With any other woman Shadoe McCaine would have known exactly what his next move would have been. But he had never felt about another woman the way he felt about Isabel Emerson.

"I want you, Isabel—" The words he uttered were almost a growl. He pulled her tightly against him and his mouth again brushed her own. "You had better make me leave now . . . now, before this goes much farther than you desire—" Even before she could respond, his mouth moved from hers and grazed along the slim column of her neck. His fingers dug beneath the neckline of her gown and slid the offending fabric down to bare her milk-white shoulders. There, he planted a kiss . . . and there . . . upon the soft swell of her breast . . . toward the other—

Sucking in a ragged breath, Isabel shoved him away, her mouth agape and her eyes as wide as saucers. Bracing herself on the bed, her gaze flitted over his angular features, over his firm chest and his muscular arms. Slowly, she dragged her gown up and attempted to loop the tie holding it together at her bodice. "What do you think you're doing, Shadoe?"

Damnation! Shadoe did not utter the single expletive, but it echoed inside of him like shrapnel from a bomb. "What do you mean, what do I think I'm doing? I think I'm comforting you—"

"You are not!" Her pale eyes seemed to darken to the color of midnight in the dim light of the room.

154

"You are taking unconscionable liberties with me!"

He drew up from the bed and his hands moved fluidly to his narrow hips. "I knew this flit of a girl once, name of Ruby Mae, if my recollection serves me right . . . a teasing bitch if ever I've met one—"

Her mouth drooped, trembling, so surprised was she by his cruel words. "Are you saying I'm a tease, or are you saying I'm a bitch?"

Tucking his thumbs into the waist of his trousers, Shadoe turned to the door. "Take it as you will. I am going to bed! If you change your mind, you'll know where I am."

Promptly the door shut and Isabel was not at all pleased to find herself alone. "Well, I never—" *And you never will, Isabel Emerson, if you keep chasing him off!* Sitting forward to hug her knees, Isabel suddenly thought of another man back home, who might have been her *first* if her father had not come upon them that afternoon on the Boeuf. Oh, how happy she was that he'd intercepted what might have been a disastrous liaison! If she weren't a lady, and if she didn't have so much pride, she would charge into Shadoe McCaine's hotel room right here and now and—

What would she do? Isabel sighed long and deeply. What would she do, indeed?

Shadoe threw himself atop his covers and dragged his palms beneath his dark hair. *Blasted woman!* he thought, *What am I going to do with her?* His gray-black gaze swept over the high ceiling as if he expected to find the answers there. But he found only the faint brown stain of water damage in one corner and a bit of dust clinging here and there in long, tenuous strands.

It was just past ten o'clock, an hour when the

155

night life was beginning to come fully awake, when gaming tables were surrounded by men who felt lucky, and women flaunted their wares beneath gaudy gowns of red and black.

With that in mind, Shadoe threw himself forward. He couldn't stand the silence of the hotel, the enticing vixen lying in a bed just across the hallway, holding herself away from him like a vestal virgin, and the ache of boredom crawling through his shoulders.

He had to get out; Isabel would be just fine in her self-imposed solitude. Shadoe pulled on his boots, picked out the cleanest of his dirty shirts from the tight packing of his saddle case, combed back his shiny black hair, and tried to scrub the anger from his features with a cold cloth.

Soon, he quietly pulled his door to and laid his boots carefully upon the carpeted corridor in his retreat so as not to make any noise. Entering the street, he turned to the right, toward the infamous Natchez-Under-the-River. Any of its bawdy establishments would suffice for what he had in mind.

When he paused at a street corner, trying to decide which way to go, he was immediately pounced upon by a female who could not in any way be described as a lady. Her thick, loose hair was as red as the dress she wore, her ample bosom spilled heavily over a bodice that might have better fit a woman thirty pounds lighter, and her face was frighteningly deathlike against painted black eyes, red, moist lips, and ridiculously applied circles of bronze-colored rouge upon her cheeks. He physically withdrew from the flaccid arms encircling his shoulders.

"Lookin' fer a good time, honey-pie?" a throaty voice asked enticingly.

The pure, lovely image of Isabel Emerson immediately popped into his mind. Certainly, the doxie hanging on him like fungus was unappetizing in comparison and he grasped the spongy wrists to peel her from his neck. "Leave me alone," he snapped, his gaze cutting to her hideously painted one, only then noticing the one pretty thing about her, the color of her eyes—as pale a blue against the mounds of black cosmetics as Isabel's complementing her perfectly formed oval features. And because of the color of the doxie's eyes, Shadoe softened his voice as he said, "I mean no offense. I just want to be alone."

As she withdrew, her bejeweled hand roughly patted Shadoe's shoulder. "Sure, honey, sure. If you change your mind—"

"I won't change my mind."

The woman turned, rejoining others of her kind leaning seductively against the brick facing of a saloon. He moved on southward, his footsteps slow and deliberate, pausing occasionally to get a feel of the mood. When he eventually turned into the door of a saloon, he again paused, his eyes assessing the overall appearance of the large, smoky room and the position of any male who might ultimately prove a threat. He had a way of making quick enemies in establishments like this, especially when he sat at a table where men were gambling.

Ambling over to the bar, Shadoe eased onto a stool and ordered a whiskey. His gaze swept over the tables and the ambivalence of each. He eventually picked up his drink and moved toward a dark corner. Standing slightly back, so that no man would accuse him of spying on his hand, Shadoe asked, "Could I join the game?"

A well-dressed man of about forty did not look

up from his hand as he asked, "Got any money?"

"No, I plan to wager a few chickens I have in a coop outside."

Only then did the man look up, his eyes narrow and leering, his ample mouth salivating upon an unlit cigar. His head bobbed once, motioning Shadoe to the only vacant chair. "Sure . . . I guess these fellas could use a chicken or two."

Shadoe sat so that his holster hung off the right side of the chair. If he had to use his gun, he didn't want the chair to get in the way.

Isabel was furious. If Shadoe McCaine thought she hadn't heard him sneak out, he was sadly mistaken. How dare he leave her defenseless in the Natchez hotel. She wanted to go after him and drag him back to his hotel room, but she didn't have anything to wear. Oh, how furious she was! And she wasn't going to let that stop her!

She snatched up the money Shadoe had given her, donned her robe and moved into the corridor. Turning to the left, she rapped upon the first door. A stocky, middle-aged man came to the door. "Pardon me, sir, but do you have a wife who is about my size?"

"No!" he snapped, and slammed the door.

Undaunted, Isabel moved to the next door and gently rapped. This time, a buxom woman came to the door. "Pardon me, ma'am, but would you have a daughter with you who is about my size?"

The lady looked at Isabel as if she had lost her senses. Cautiously, she replied, "Well, yes, I do . . . but why do you want to know?"

At that point, Isabel put on her most pained face, her brows drawn down at the corners and tears forced into her eyes. "I have a wicked husband who has left me alone in my hotel room, and he has taken all of my clothes." Isabel produced the money Shadoe had given her earlier in the night. "I had this tucked away, ma'am, and I would be so grateful if your daughter would allow me to purchase one of her dresses so that I might leave the hotel to seek help."

With a long, sympathetic, "Ohhhh . . . poor little thing!" Isabel found herself promptly drawn into the lady's hotel room. Momentarily, a young woman emerged from an adjoining room and her mother introduced her to Isabel, quickly relaying the outrageous story Isabel had told her.

The young woman named Samantha immediately took Isabel's hand and gave it a gentle squeeze. "You are welcome to any one of my dresses. And please . . . please, you must permit me to give it to you as a gift—"

Isabel forced the money into Samantha's hand. "Oh, I couldn't . . . you must allow me to keep some of my pride. My husband has taken so much of it away from me!" Again, Isabel forced tears to sheen her pale eyes, even as guilt ate at her insides. These two ladies were being kind to her based on the vicious lies she had told. But if she had said she merely wanted to track down her male escort, would they have offered such kindness? It wasn't as if she were taking something for nothing. Twenty dollars was an exorbitant payment for a dress.

Samantha handed back one of the bills. "Do take it. Any one of my dresses is worth no more than ten dollars. It wouldn't be right for you to pay more than it is worth."

Hesitating again, Isabel took the money. "Very well. You are very kind, Samantha."

159

Momentarily, an armoire was opened to her and the two women helped her choose one of the gowns. "This one will be perfect," said the mother, holding a cream and tan traveling gown against Isabel's slim form for sizing.

Isabel took the gown. "Thank you . . . thank you so much. I will be forever grateful."

Taking her hand to lightly pat it, the mother said, "You just take care of your business, and don't you take any guff off anyone, not even your husband."

Dropping her gaze from the two sympathetic faces, Isabel draped the dress across her arm and moved toward the door. With parting amenities at the corridor, she moved quietly to her own room.

She felt like a criminal. The first thing in the morning she would see the ladies again, return the dress and apologize for her lie.

As she closed the door to her suite, though, her primary purpose chased away all the clouds of guilt. Shadoe McCaine had gone out into the night, and she was going to find him.

But why?

As she dressed, she mused on that. Why?

He was a man, seeking the pleasures that were important to a man. It wasn't as if he had subjected her to mortal danger by slipping out into the night. As she fastened the stays of the well-fitted dress, Isabel focused on the reason and found it personally repulsive: She couldn't bear the thought of Shadoe McCaine seeking the pleasure of another woman's company.

She pressed her mouth into a thin line. No . . . no, jealousy is beneath me! There must be another reason.

Ten

Shadoe wasn't doing so well at the tables. In the first half hour, he had lost fifty dollars, and he was dangerously close to losing a hundred more. Still, he held his best hand of the evening, a pair each of sixes and tens. Gambling wasn't the reason he had sought the activities of night, so the money really didn't matter. He had wanted to get away from the boredom of his hotel room, and the temptation of Isabel Emerson, but now, other little things annoyed him; the soggy cigar between the gambler's lips that he still had not lit, the irritating laugh, akin to the snort of a rooting pig, of a patron through the smoky interior, the loud, obscene boasts of another man who had been with one of the whores that night.

He became aware of a hush falling over the saloon, of numerous masculine eyes transfixed to the same direction, and of swinging doors creaking nearby. He had laid down his losing hand and planted his palms firmly upon the table, waiting for the next hand to be dealt. But curiosity got the best of him; his eyes followed the direction of every other man's.

There she stood, her long, pale hair sitting softly upon her shoulders and flooding her back, her slim hands drawn to curvaceous hips, and her gaze

161

sweeping the smoky half-light of the saloon. "Shadoe McCaine, I am looking for you!" she suddenly blurted, drawing up one hand to wave away the smoke hanging heavily around her.

Shadoe mentally shrank. "Blast," he mumbled beneath his breath, drawing his hat down on his forehead and hoping she wouldn't see him.

But Isabel had faced the dangers of the Natchez night to track him down and he would not escape her. She moved through the tables of silent, staring men and soon stood over Shadoe McCaine. "Didn't you hear me calling you?" she asked in a sultry half-whisper.

Shadoe was suddenly embarrassed by the loud guffaws of men flooding the saloon. He pushed his chair back and slowly turned to face Isabel. So smug was she that he ground his fists against his thighs to keep from grabbing and shaking the daylights out of her. "What the hell are you doing here?" he asked.

She raised her tone to a deliberately loud pitch. "I am trying to keep you out of trouble, Shadoe McCaine! What do you think I'm doing here?"

Still, the men guffawed and at that moment, Shadoe felt he had the strength to pounce and kill each one within a matter of seconds. Gritting his teeth, he ordered, "Get back to the hotel, Isabel!"

Isabel aimed herself toward a chair that had just been vacated. Turning its back to the table, she quickly straddled it, then held up her ten dollars. "Will this buy me in?" she asked, her pale gaze cutting among the amused men remaining at the table and refusing to meet Shadoe's glaring eyes.

"For a round maybe," said the man with the cigar.

"Good! Deal the cards!" She was just about to tuck her feet around the back legs of the chair when she was suddenly grabbed up by Shadoe Mc-Caine. "Ohhhh! What are you doing, you . . . you — ?" she hissed, drawing back her hand to pummel his chest.

But before she could do so, she was unceremoniously thrown across his shoulder, which immediately drew a round of applause and renewed guffaws from the male customers. "I'm taking you home, little lady," said Shadoe, grabbing his hat, which she'd slapped from his head. "You fellows will excuse me while I make a deposit back at our hotel."

Shadoe refused to respond to their taunts as he moved among the tables with the thrashing, screaming and attacking she-cat over his shoulder. He entered the street as casually as a man with a string of butchered chickens bound for the market.

"Let me go, Shadoe!" demanded Isabel, giving his back one last thrashing with her balled hands. "I'll scream for the law . . . I'll — I'll — "

"Where the hell did you get the dress?" he demanded to know. "And the shoes! Blast, but those toes you're gouging into my midsection are sharp."

"Then put me down," she said on a softer note. "I'll be reasonable. Truly, I will."

Shadoe stood upon the planked walkway, his fingers moving deftly over the rim of his hat. He plopped Isabel back to her feet so suddenly that she nearly lost her balance, and he grabbed her roughly up by her shoulders. "You deliberately embarrassed me in there," he accused, his dark gaze penetrating her to her conscience. "And I want to know why."

Turning away and crossing her arms, Isabel dropped her gaze. "I — I thought you might be with another woman. If I'd known you were just wasting money at the tables — "

"Forget the tables." His fingers wrapped around

her arm and coaxed her back. "What if I had been with another woman? What do you care?"

Isabel again drew her hands to her hips, and her foot began to tap, tap, tap upon the planked boardwalk. "I do care, Shadoe McCaine, and the reason I do is that you might find some irresistible little nymph and forget that you promised to see me safely to Tongue River. Now, what do you think of that?"

Except for the tiniest curve at the corner of his mouth, Shadoe's features remained rather harsh. "I think you're a lying little—" He hesitated before quietly adding, "Nymph, yourself." Taking her arms roughly, his hold immediately gentled. "No matter the diversion, Miss Isabel Emerson, I will see you all the way to Montana, even if it means the death of me. For the time being, little prison warden, I would like to rejoin the game."

Fury jumped into Isabel's pale eyes, darkening them. "You would just leave me here on the street with this . . . this riffraff?"

His mouth curled into a sneer. "You came here alone through all this riffraff, so why can't you return to the hotel without an escort?"

A provocative smile chased away her moment of fury. Her fingers linking against the tight material at her waistline, she entreated with the charm of a sincere child, "Oh, do see me back to the hotel, Shadoe. I simply must be assured that you're not angry with me."

Shadoe was almost certain he heard a rattler coiling behind those sweetly spoken words. Taking her hand and tucking it into the crook of his arm, he turned in the direction of their hotel. "Little lady, you sure are resourceful. I still want to know where the hell you got the clothes?"

"Disappointed that I was able to venture out into the night?"

"A man ain't safe with you roaming the streets."

Isabel looked at his angular profile through adoring eyes. He had every right to be angry with her, but he wasn't. He had every right to hate her, but he didn't, though he worked very hard at convincing her he did. He should dump her at the train station and boot her back to New Orleans, but she knew he wouldn't do that, either. He wanted to be with her every bit as much as she wanted to be with him.

As they moved through the street abuzz with activity, Isabel bathed in the wonderful, contented silence that fell between them. Shadoe had tucked his thumbs into the waist of his trousers, flaring out his jacket, and she could feel the muscles of his arm expanding against her encircling fingers. She thought of the way he had burst, half-naked, into her hotel room that night. She envisioned what might have happened between them if she hadn't gotten frightened and chased him off. He was everything she wanted in a man, though he wasn't what her father would have chosen for her. Right now, it mattered not a whit whether it took two months, or two years to reach Montana. Her brother would be there whenever she arrived. But Shadoe . . . she feared that she might never see him again after the mission had been accomplished.

Just as they reached the entrance to an alley, a whimper caught their attentions. Shadoe turned, his eyes narrowing as they adjusted to the lack of light. Then he spied something pale and furry and moved a few feet into the darkness. He knelt and picked up a tiny puppy. Isabel moved up behind him, surprised at the gentleness and compassion with which he held the tiny life.

"An odd time of the year for puppies to be born, isn't it?" he said, not really expecting an answer. He held the puppy close enough that it licked his nose. "Lost your mama, did you, little fellow?"

Isabel knelt beside him and touched her fingers to the narrow space between the puppy's small, drooping ears. "Isn't it a shame?"

"What is that?" asked Shadoe.

"That they grow up to be nasty, smelly, vile, barking creatures."

"I take it you don't like puppies."

"I love puppies," countered Isabel. "I don't like dogs. If they could only stay small forever—"

"Everything must grow up," snapped Shadoe without feeling, coming to his feet to look around. "Even cute little girls grow up to be manipulative she-cats." Seeing a large wooden box several feet further into the alley, Shadoe moved on, soon standing over a long-haired dog nursing four other puppies like the one he held in his hand. It wagged its tail as Shadoe put the puppy down to her. "There you go, old gal. Better keep an eye on this one." Concerned for the welfare of the defenseless animals, he looked around, seeing a tin dish filled with clean water and the remains of food on another plate. Assuring himself that someone was taking care of the dogs, he pivoted about, returned to Isabel and dropped his hand to her shoulder.

Momentarily, they emerged into the light of the street and resumed their journey to the hotel. "I'm sorry if I annoyed you."

Shadoe halted instantly. "What do you mean?"

She turned to face him. "You seem a little irritated with me for not liking dogs."

Shadoe laughed, then again drew her against

166

him. "To borrow one of your favorite words . . . horsefeathers! I would hardly think that disliking dogs is going to detract from your good nature."

The gentleness of his voice and his endearing words managed with very little effort to soften her mood of the night. Turning in his arms, Isabel said, "Why don't you go on back to your card game. I'll return to the hotel and get some sleep. I suppose we'll get an early start?"

Again, he tucked her beneath his arm and moved ahead. "Forget the game. I was losing anyway."

Shortly, they turned into the lobby of the hotel and traversed the steps. When they stood together outside her room, Shadoe seemed hesitant to leave her. He supported himself with his forearm against the door frame and his knuckles resting lightly against his temple. Looking down at her, he managed the smallest of smiles. "Shall I see if there's a bogeyman in your room?" he offered. Then, before she could answer, his finger moved to trace a gentle path along the smooth curve of her cheek. "You are so beautiful, Isabel. How is it that a man hasn't snatched you from maidenhood?"

With twinkling humor in her upsweeping gaze, Isabel coyly asked, "What makes you think I am a maiden?"

"A man can always tell. There is a certain child-like quality in a woman's features before she has been with a man. Afterwards—" He paused, unsure of how to describe the way he thought a woman, afterwards, should look like. "Just take my word for it. A man can tell."

Suddenly, Isabel didn't appreciate being condemned to the same category as giddy, giggling school girls. Perhaps it was true that she had never experienced the ultimate joy her mother had once

167

told her could happen with only the right man, but she liked to think of herself as a woman nonetheless. Thus, it came with ease that she said to Shadoe McCaine, "Well, I don't believe you can tell at all. You are certainly wrong about me!" and promptly stormed into her room, closing the door behind her.

Immediately there came a sharp rap of knuckles, even as she continued to lean heavily against the slammed door. "Isabel . . . oh, Isabel—" He sang her name in his lusty, masculine voice, so enticingly that she smiled, despite the lack of his audience.

Turning about, she pressed her flushed cheek against the cool wood. Ignoring her compulsion to open the door and pull him in, she called in a sultry tone, "What do you want, Shadoe McCaine?"

"Let me in."

"Shadoe McCaine, don't be absurd. If you think for a minute I am going to open this door and let you in, you're sadly mistaken. Why, I've just about decided that you're a devil and a dog and I should send you on your way and hire a decent gentleman to take me to Montana. Why, Shadoe McCaine, I think I just—"

"Isabel?"

"What?"

"You're rambling."

Her heart was all aflutter; Isabel was sure he had pressed his own cheek to the door and that she could feel its warmth penetrate the barrier separating them. "Am I?"

"Are you going to let me in?"

"No."

"Why?"

Her hands pressed lightly to the closed door and her fingers flayed, as if waiting for his to link with

168

them. "As I said, you're a devil and a dog—" Were those her fingers turning the key in the lock and letting him in? Isabel shook her head in silent, self-reproval. Suddenly, he was there, hovering over her like the wolf he had spoken of just that night, his hand high upon the door frame and his eyes narrowed and searching, as if he were seeing her for the first time and was silently appraising her. Suddenly the exhaustion of the day's travels, of the cowardly attack of the two men and her near-death experience were as remote as the moon. The far away sounds of a busy town drifted off with the wind; she was aware only of Shadoe's steady breathing, and she found herself wanting only one thing, and that certainly was not sleep. She felt peaceful and happy and contented, just to have Shadoe looking at her like that, his mouth twisting into that familiar smirk, his hand dangling from his wrist as if it had suddenly been broken.

With no words spoken between them over the minute or so since she had opened the door, she quietly stepped into his arms and hugged him. Nothing mattered at the moment: not the perils of the night, not the long journey ahead of them . . . only that she was in Shadoe's arms, that his hands were gently folding over her shoulders and she was safe and secure.

Shadoe closed the door with his boot. "You have let me in," he murmured. "Now, what do you propose to do with me?" He had never seen her looking so relaxed and contented, her cheeks beaming as if she could imagine nothing more wonderful than being in his arms, her thick, flaxen hair like spun gold wrapped around his fingers. Her hands had gently encircled his waist and rested there in the small of his back, and he wished he did not

have the threads of his shirt separating his fles
from her feminine caress. He became so aware
her sensuality and her moment of vulnerability th.
his body stiffened against her.

How many times had he dreamed of being in h
arms, of holding and loving her, even as he ha
tried to convince himself that he hated her an
what she was? How many times had he wanted
feel her slim, womanly form molded to his ow
wanting to lift her pert chin and capture her mou
in the sweetest of kisses. Was his dream about
materialize? Was he about to experience the exqu
site joy of her body?

Isabel knew not where the boldness came from
she broke from his embrace and took his hand
Taking small steps, she backed toward her bed an
coaxed him along with her. How innocent were he
eyes as she made her silent appeal . . . how tren
bling and inviting was her mouth as it parted an
the tip of her tongue made the briefest appearanc
from the warm, moist depths he ached to explore

Shadoe halted, though he did not withdraw h
hand. "What do you want of me, Isabel? I will n
be teased and then raked out like an invading r:
before I have tasted the bait in the trap." Withou
awaiting her response, Shadoe roughly pulled h
lithe body against his own. He wanted this treasure

He knew that he should withdraw, turn his bac
and march out the door, leaving her alone and ur
touched. But he could not do that; she was almo
hot against him, her pale eyes darkening with pa:
sion as they lifted to his, her mouth parted and ser
sually inviting. Had he successfully disguised th
lust in his gaze, or was she aware that she had th
effect on him?

"I ask you again, Isabel . . . what do you want

me?"

Coyly dropping her gaze, Isabel let her hands rise to caress his taut shoulders. "Is it necessary that I tell you that?" Her gaze made bold contact with his own. "Can't you see what I want from you, Shadoe?"

She shivered; was it from the December cold, or from the anticipation heating to a full boil within her? She grew taut for the briefest of moments; was it from fear, or from passion?

An ache crawled through Shadoe's shoulders, washed through his chest and abdomen, then hardened at his groin. He wanted her now, this very minute, without prelude. He wanted to feel the soft, yielding curves of her against him; he wanted to feel her beneath his palms, beneath his body. He could feel her gentle pulse quicken against him, her heart beginning to beat as rapidly as his own. Though he remained hesitant, Shadoe knew that within moments she would belong to him completely.

Isabel suddenly found herself being lowered to the bed, Shadoe's hands at her back deftly unfastening the stays of her dress. She rose slightly, to make room for his movements, and his dark gaze connected with her own. "My little Creole hussy . . . and you would have me think you are naive and innocent in the ways of love—"

She pouted prettily, taking no offense at his teasing words. She cared only that he would not stop, that his hands, now scooting beneath the fabric of her gown, would find those places she ached to have touched and caressed. This time her father would not rush into the room and yank her from beneath the masterful rake whose body was rock-hard against her own.

A gentle flood of warmth washed over her, taking away the coolness of the evening. His ash gray gaze was spellbinding; his full, masculine mouth hovering close to her own made her ache with desire. Why did he hesitate to kiss her, why did his hands suddenly cease their movements at her back? Why did his eyes suddenly darken, as if he found her repulsive and his own actions abhorrent?

"Don't you want me, Shadoe?" she entreated softly, her fingers rising to the lock of black hair at his forehead. As she swept it back, he gently kissed the palm of her hand, then took it roughly and held it there for the longest time.

"If you have any sense at all, you'll order me from this room . . . before this goes any further."

Sweet naiveté softened her features. "But, why on earth would I do that?"

"Because, my darling Isabel, you are embarking on a journey you have never been on before. In just moments, indeed, perhaps even now, we are like two people alone on a ship, a ship lost in the middle of a vast ocean, a ship without rudders and controls, a ship that cannot be turned back, but must go on—"

"Horsefeathers!" Isabel's finely arched brows drew slightly together. "You are talking about ships and oceans and rudders and controls. I don't care about those things. I want you, Shadoe . . . and I want what a man and a woman do together when they are alone." As she watched him, he became a blur above her; she could not see his angular features, or the direction of his gaze. She could not read the expression in his eyes, nor could she assume what he might be thinking. She was aware only of the maleness of him against her thigh. She knew only that when she awakened in the predawn hours of a new day, she would no longer be the naive, innocent little Isabel he had so easily compared to a giddy schoolgirl on more than one occasion. She wanted to be a woman. "What are you thinking, Shadoe?" she asked, breaking his moment of brooding and concentration.

"I am wondering, Isabel . . . why me? Surely, there have been other men more deserving of you . . . other men who would love you and be faithful to you —"

"Do you want me?" she snapped. "And if you don't, make it known this very minute —" And with that, she cupped his face gently between her palms and coaxed his face against her own. His ample mouth brushed hers tenderly, and his hands commenced their explorations beneath the fabric of her gown. Quite before she realized it, both her shoulders had been bared and his lips were covering her ivory skin in small, teasing kisses. A naughty, wondrous pain burst through her as she anticipated the erotic moments to come . . . those moments she had always wondered about and dreamed of and longed for, though not with the urgency she now felt for this rake of a man named Shadoe McCaine.

Isabel could think of nothing more desirable than being Shadoe's prize . . . of him being her own. She wanted to be loved by him, fully and completely, to know the intensity of love that her mother Delilah had expressed with such adoring reminiscence for her father. She wanted a love like theirs was, one that would last for all the ages to come and always be the guiding force in her life, and she wanted it to commence now, with Shadoe McCaine, the only man she had ever met that she would have allowed such naughty, delicious liberties with her person.

She was under the spell of his masterful caresses. Her body was commanded by him. She would never know how she found the strength to gather her trembling fingers at his lapels and begin to unbutton his shirt. Within moments, she was drawing his shirt down his sinewy arms, and his hands were gently cupping her bare breasts.

No words were shared between them. She wanted his body to speak the language of love, and she prayed that her responses were natural, that he would not realize how inexperienced she was. Dear Lord . . . would he be gentle with her? She was suddenly frightened, but not frightened enough to cast him off . . . not now. . . .

Shadoe wanted to be free of his clothing instantly, but she seemed to enjoy, though nervously so, removing his garments herself. He had flung off his shirt when the sleeves had gathered around his wrists; now her fingers were fumbling with the buckle at his waistline.

Finally, when she seemed a little annoyed by its stubbornness, he murmured against her pale hairline, "Would you like a little help there?"

To which she softly responded, "Well, if you wouldn't mind —"

Quickly, he drew the leather through the loops, then propped himself on his elbow. The index finger of his right hand traced a circle around the pale bud of her breast. "You are so beautiful, Isabel. I hope that no other man has seen these. . . . They are so perfect . . . so delicious —"

Isabel was a little distracted. She wanted to see that which seemed to push against the tightness of his trousers, and yet she was embarrassed. Her hand moved toward the tiny buttons tracing a line between his navel and . . . and there . . . but she knew he was watching her, witnessing the crimson flush upon her cheeks . . . watching the tremble jerk through her shoulders . . .

A humorous smirk playing upon his mouth, Shadoe took her protesting hand and placed it upon his fullness. "I have nothing that will bite you, Isabel."

"But you are a wolf," she protested demurely, attempting, but without success, to withdraw her hand. "You said so yourself."

"But a wolf who is gentle as a lamb," he chuckled, holding her hand against him there. "There . . . now, do you feel teeth?"

Isabel knew that her face must be as red as the heat she felt there. She was almost relieved when his head lowered and his mouth drew in one of her breasts and teased it to peakness, then captured the other and gave it equal attention. His right hand explored a path over the flat plane of her abdomen, then eased beneath the fabric of her underthings. As she drew in a short, ragged breath of surprise, his fingers were suddenly between her thighs, gently easing them apart and fondling the intimate depths of her.

When her mouth drew into a pucker of protest, Shadoe instantly covered it, a rough and yet stimulating caress that left her no room for the little protest she had begun gathering. Wantonly, she eased her thighs apart, allowing for the deeper explorations of his fingers. Then, with a low, steady groan, he paused just long enough to free himself completely of his trousers.

Isabel had never imagined that a man could be so large . . . there . . . and just for a moment she thought she might faint. But taking another long, steady breath, she willed herself into readiness as

175

she lifted her buttocks and allowed him to sweep the remnants of her clothing away from their bodies. When his slim, naked hips eased between her thighs, she drew in a breath and caught it there, her eyes shut tightly.

For the moment, Shadoe was alarmed by the fright sitting upon her brow. His hands rose and cupped her face. "Do not worry, my Isabel . . . not yet . . . not until you are ready."

Isabel's senses suddenly came reeling back. Lord, what was she doing? Jerking her eyes open, her hands rose to his shoulders and with one swift push, she was free of him, scooting to her knees and pulling one of the pillows of her bed between them.

"What the hell is this? It's hardly the time for modesty!" barked Shadoe McCaine, his hand moving toward the corner of the pillow.

Instantly, Isabel slapped his hand away, then bristled back to attack again if the need arose. "How—how dare you seduce me!"

If the situation were not so grave, his body not paining so badly for the relief he thought was almost his, Shadoe would have laughed. Instead he growled, *"Me* seduce *you?* I think, Miss Emerson, it is the other way around!"

"I hardly think so! You . . . you did something to me . . . something despicable . . . you made me forget that I'm a lady!"

Shadoe's gaze narrowed. Drawing up and dropping his hands to his knees, he made no attempt to hide his nakedness from her. The situation called for something, but he was not sure what. He had never found himself in this predicament before and it would certainly call for original thinking.

All right! he thought. *If that's the way she wants it—*

Slowly swinging his legs off the bed, Shadoe retrieved his trousers and began to pull them on. He said nothing, nor did he watch the mixture of surprise and disbelief flash across her eyes. "What are you doing?" She rushed the words in a harsh whisper.

"What do you think I'm doing? I'm pulling my clothes on and getting out of here."

Isabel wasn't sure what she wanted, but she was very sure that she didn't want him to leave. She was surprised that he would exercise such control. Could he simply make his male lusts and desires go away with the snap of a finger? She really wasn't sure what she should do now.

Shadoe buttoned his trousers. He picked up his shirt and slung it across his shoulders. He searched beneath the edge of the bed for one of his boots that had become separated from their tangle of clothing.

And he wondered what the hell Isabel was going to do!

Eleven

Who was he trying to fool? Isabel could see that Shadoe McCaine's desire for her had not gone away, though she imagined he might possibly have willed it. He wanted to make love to her, she had no doubts about that. So, why was he playing this silly little game?

She was right, of course; he did want her. So pained was his unsated body that Shadoe McCaine found it extremely difficult to move. He lifted his chin, perched his hat atop his head and moved toward the door at a slower pace than usual.

"See you in the morning, ma'am," he drawled as politely as possible.

"You stop right there, Shadoe McCaine!" she snapped at him. "You can't just walk out of here like nothing has happened!"

He half turned, though his gaze did not connect with her own. "Nothing did happen, ma'am," he continued outrageously. "Or have you forgotten? I just don't—" His words ended abruptly as he finally turned to look at her. God! What a sensual beauty! She sat there, her knees straddled, the pillow held tightly against her slim, naked form, her hair billowing wildly over her milk-white shoulders. Her powder-blue gaze had darkened to the color of evening twilight, and he was sure he saw alarm and unsated passion burning brightly in their depths. Her mouth parted, trembled, started to lodge still another protest, then puckered rebelliously. When his bare feet began taking slow steps back to the bed, he could have kicked himself for his lack of self-discipline.

He stood so close that his knee pressed against the bed rail, watching her eyes, trying to read her mood. Would she shove him away again, or did she want him? Was she frightened, or was she toying with him? He certainly couldn't tell. So deep was he in his thoughts that he was unaware of her hand darting out, until it caught in the waist of his trousers and brought him spraddling upon the bed. His boots flew hither and yon, and he was sure one of them hit the far wall.

When he turned to his back and, surprised by her burst of strength, gave her an incredulous look, she looked down at him as one might look at a creepy, crawly thing scurrying along a baseboard. "No man sees me naked, then simply walks out until I have what I want . . . and what he wants!" she added as an afterthought.

Shadoe grinned. "Hell, woman . . . if you're strong enough to toss me on my back, then who am I to argue?"

Slowly, sensually—deliberately—Isabel let the pillow fall, revealing her soft, womanly form to his lusty gaze. Then she bent and touched her mouth to his forehead, unaware that her breasts grazed his chest until his hands rose to roughly cup them. "You will not push me away again, Isabel," he warned with husky passion. "I will not allow it."

"I plan—" Her kisses heated a path along the line of his brow, touching each eyelid, then lowering to his mouth. In between her teasing kisses, she promised, "I might possibly make you fight for me, Shadoe McCaine. Am I worth it?"

He swiftly rolled her to her back and dragged himself across her. "I plan to find that out, pretty lady . . . tonight . . ." he uttered, dragging his trousers, once again, down his long, muscled legs. Positioning himself at the apex of her thighs, he made no move to enter her.

Shadoe was certainly suspicious as to her motives as his gaze lustfully held her own soft, controlled one. His features darkened with passion; Isabel liked the way he looked at her, the way he controlled himself when she knew he was aching to possess her.

Momentarily, he drew to his knees and his ash-gray eyes swept over her lithe form: the firm, youthful breasts crested with buds the color of dark sand, a waist small enough that he could almost span it with his hands, the flat plane of her abdomen and her tight navel. His palms touched her outer thighs and traveled smoothly along them, then moved masterfully at her knees and up her inner thighs. He knew she held her breath as his palms gently covered the treasure hidden from him, and when he rubbed his manhood against her, he felt her body stiffen.

Closing her eyes lightly, Isabel wet her lips with the tip of her tongue, her fingers flexing among the covers of the bed. When he lowered himself to her, her hands rose to his neck, to pull him close, and her lips parted to accept the hungry explorations of his tongue. Betrayed by her instincts, Isabel plied her fingers through his thick, dark hair, half-gulping his kisses, her breasts heaving against his muscular chest. She tried to ignore the gentle thrusting of him between her thighs, but something warm and wonderful ached within her, something that felt empty and hungry, and she wanted him as she had never wanted anything before. Her fingers traced along his hard muscles, pressing into the small of his back, telling him wordlessly that she wanted him to fill her.

His movements below came closer to their goal. Instinctively, Isabel's thighs fell apart, her body so hot she was afraid it would melt beneath him. When he again hesitated, his hands exploring her body, his mouth teasing kisses between her mouth and her passion-sensitive breasts, Isabel boldly claimed his slim buttocks between her hands and coaxed him toward her.

When his hand lowered and gently guided himself into her, she felt a small prickle of discomfort and her eyes pressed firmly, instantly to be covered by his kisses. When she felt some degree of fullness, she breathed a small sigh of relief and her eyes slowly crept open. She had expected it to be worse than this . . . she had expected pain of an incredible magnitude, though she had expected it to be of extremely short duration.

When she smiled, Shadoe McCaine asked, "What is so amusing?"

Her eyes downcast, watching their splendid joining, she quietly responded, "I thought it would—" Then, without warning, his fingers entwined roughly through her hair and he drove his full length into her with such force that her abdomen was seized by the horrid, yet instantaneous pain of it. In that moment, his mouth covered hers, and if she made any vocal protest caused by pain, he quickly gulped her cries so that there was nothing but silence between them.

As tears filled her eyes, Shadoe washed them away with the tip of his tongue. "The next time it will be more pleasurable for you, Isabel," he promised with husky emotion. "It will be better."

Even as he spoke, the inner burning within her ached to accept him fully. She now had only the memory of the pain, so brief was its duration, and

181

she wanted only to be sated by him. Now that her fear was over, she wanted to enjoy their union . . . to be loved by him, to be satisfied by him, to sleep next to him, and to wake up in his arms in the morning.

With her fear behind her, Isabel enjoyed the rippling muscles beneath her exploring fingers, the rhythm of his narrow hips against her thighs. She enjoyed the maleness of him stroking her to ultimate heights, where a world had ceased to exist, and all that hovered about them was an ethereal silence filled only with the tiny sounds of their bodies molding together as one and the tantalizing moans they shared along with their kisses.

Shadoe was pleased with the treasure he had captured. She was his goddess, his love, the flaxen haired beauty with whom he stole the ultimate pleasure. His hips ground harder and harder still and she matched his rhythm and pace as if she were skilled in the art of lovemaking, and yet he knew beyond a doubt that she was not.

As her head of loose tresses shook madly to each side, he felt the rage of his passion building. Faster still raced his hips, until he took a final plunge and buried himself deep within the hot depths of her. Had he stopped breathing, or had it simply been lost in this wondrous joy, in the sweet receptacle of her body that continued to fold gently around him. And he felt her shudder as her body shared in the erotic culmination of their lovemaking.

As he slumped above her, his breathing returning to normal, his fingers entwined through her hair and caught there, Shadoe could not remember being happier. Isabel was the woman he wanted, the woman he would gladly spend the rest of his life with, the woman who might tame him when no other had been able to accomplish it.

But then he stopped to think about it. She had teased him unmercifully with her yes, no, maybe so ploy, and he was outraged that he hadn't simply walked out on her just moments ago. She was probably bathing in her smug self-satisfaction that he had wanted her badly enough to endure her cruel humiliation. And now, as he silently broke his union with her, he rolled instantly to his back and vindictive and vengeful thoughts raced in to replace his contentment. She had a lesson to learn, and he could think of no one who deserved to be her teacher more than he did.

Thus, he swung his bare feet to the floor and retrieved his trousers. Before pulling them on, he reached back with his right hand and patted her roughly on her still raised thigh. "Thanks. That was sweet as honey."

A surprised Isabel drew in a deep, trembling breath. "I don't like your tone. Do you think I am a whore—"

"It hadn't crossed my mind, but—" Tucking his hand into his trouser pocket, he withdrew a twenty dollar gold piece and flipped it onto her abdomen. "You were worth every penny of it."

Isabel was suddenly at his back, screaming, crying, and pummeling his head and shoulders with her tightly balled hands. Turning so that he might ward off her attack, Shadoe pushed her to her back and straddled her body. His hands, roughly pinioning her wrists to the bed, relaxed almost immediately. He could scarcely see the blue of her eyes through the thickness of tears clinging there, and he called on all of his self-discipline to keep from succumbing to her pitiful state.

"Wh-why do you treat me so?" she stammered. "I—we were together. . . . It was beautiful, wasn't it?"

A sweet, exquisite adoration suddenly flooded him. He wanted to brush his mouth against her trembling one, take her in his arms and whisper, *I love you, Isabel . . . from the very first moment* — But Venetia Mendez had seen to it that he would never have the chance to settle down in one place for very long.

So, when she had calmed down, and seemed too weak to commence her attack, Shadoe released her wrists. But they lay limply there among the covers of the bed, and her face was turned away from him, half-hidden by her disheveled blond tresses. His heart went out to her . . . and his body began to react to the sensual nearness of the sweet treasure that had been his just moments before.

Isabel, feeling the maleness of him harden against her abdomen, slowly withdrew from the cover of his body. Pulling herself up against the headboard, she hunkered like a scared child and drew the coverlet over her nakedness. "Get your clothes and get out," she ordered softly. "And don't bother to wait for me in the morning. I'll find my own way to Tongue River—"

His hand darted out and roughly grappled for her wrist. "I said I would take you. And I'll do it even if I must hogtie you and throw you across my saddle. I swear to God—" He halted in midsentence, his hand simultaneously releasing her unprotesting wrist. Then he swung his feet to the floor, swiftly drew on his trousers and gathered up his other items of clothing. Just before he opened the door to leave, he looked back at her, still cowering there, still refusing to look at him. He wanted to take her in his arms, caress away her pain, assure her of his love, and swear that he would never hurt her again. But he was not free to make commitments. He was placing her in danger just by being with her, and it didn't settle well with him.

So he left her there alone, and as he stood in the corridor just outside, he heard her gentle weeping. Quite before he realized it, tears were stinging his own eyes and invading the rough curves of his unshaven face.

Against the cool wood, he whispered hoarsely, "I love you, Isabel," then disappeared into the semidarkness of his own lonely room.

He lay upon his bed and drew his palms beneath his dark head. As the minutes stretched into hours and midnight came and went, sleep had still not overtaken him. He could think of nothing but Isabel Emerson, lying upon her own bed and tossing in her sleep. He could imagine that she might still be crying, and his heart broke.

Soon he willed himself to fall asleep. But even then he knew no peace. Nightmares plagued him. His own brutality came back to slap him in the face, and Isabel's slim, weeping form was as clear to him in the deepest recesses of his sleep as his own image in a mirror. Without awakening, he promised himself that, in the morning, he would apologize.

In the morning, he would tell her that he loved her.

Isabel had spent a sleepless night. Just after four in the morning, she arose, donned the gown the nice ladies in number twenty-two had given her, and crept into the corridor. She stood for a moment outside of Shadoe's door, listening for some sound, no matter how small, then moved toward the stairwell.

She would never forgive him for using her as easily as she would have a whore, nor for cheapening and degrading her. As far as she was concerned, he could

185

go straight to hell without an escort.

But as she stood before a young hotel clerk, sh[e]
knew she didn't really feel that way. Shadoe wa[s]
everything she wanted, and she suspected that he ha[d]
some strange motive for the way he had treated he[r]
after they'd made love. She had felt his gentlenes[s]
and his caring; she had enjoyed the exquisite joy [of]
his kisses and his caresses; and a man who did n[ot]
care for a woman would not have taken such precau[-]
tions to prepare her for their first joining. A ma[n]
who did not care would have sought only his own sa[t]
isfaction and cared nothing about her own.

"Ma'am?"

The young man's voice extracted her from her mo[-]
ment of deep thought. Crimson rushed upon he[r]
cheeks. "I am sorry, here is my hotel key. The gentle[-]
man in number nineteen has already paid the bill[.]
He took the key, checked his register, then gave her [a]
polite nod. She turned toward the door and the lin[-]
gering darkness of the predawn, then slowly turne[d]
back. "By the way, the lady and her daughter i[n]
number twenty-two—" She was about to give him [a]
hotel envelope, containing the twenty-dollar gol[d]
piece Shadoe had crudely tossed to her when th[e]
clerk suddenly laughed. "What is so amusing?" aske[d]
a blushing Isabel.

"That was no lady and her daughter. Marsha[l]
locked 'em up last night."

Isabel had felt guilty about lying to the ladies i[n]
order to get the dress that she was going to give the[m]
the twenty-dollar gold piece. But now, she discreetl[y]
tucked the envelope into her pocket and asked[.]
"Why? What did they do?"

"The law's been tryin' to get them two for nig[h]
onto two years. They been goin' all over th[e]
south. . . . That young woman, she been gettin' th[e]

men up to her room and druggin' 'em up, an' the older lady, she'd go in an' clean out their wallets when they was out cold. They had a fellow what would wait outside the back to dump the hapless victims in an alleyway on the other side of town—"

The ladies had been so kind to her that Isabel was visibly surprised by the hotel clerk's tale. "I can hardly believe they've been getting away with this for two years. Wouldn't the victims have made a report?"

"No, ma'am. The victims, they was all married men, an' they didn't want to be explainin' what they was doin' up there with that sweet young thing." Well, so much for apologizing for her small deception last evening. When Isabel turned back to the exit, the hotel clerk asked, "You ain't goin' out there without a coat, are you, ma'am? It's pokin' up to rain real fierce."

"I'll be all right," assured Isabel. "I have a canvas cape strapped to my saddle." Then she raised her hand for the briefest of moments and quickly left the lobby.

Assuming that Shadoe considered the mare he had purchased for her in New Orleans as her property, Isabel didn't think it would be wrong of her to take it with her. She planned to travel on to Monroe, and then by train to El Dorado, Arkansas. There, she would seek out Poe Hamlin, who had once worked on her father's plantation, to make the trip to Tongue River with her. He had worked as overseer at Shadows-in-the-Mist during the war, and had been very fond of her and her brothers. She felt that Poe would jump at the chance to bring Eduard back home to Louisiana. She only hoped he was still in El Dorado. She only hoped that he was still alive.

She was unaware that she had covered the short distance to the livery until the mare whinnied at her

187

over the stall door. Drawing her hand up to grip the halter, a smiling Isabel murmured, "Didn't know I could get up this early, did you, girl?"

And at that moment, a familiar masculine voice, without a discernable form that she could see in the shades of darkness, asked softly, "And I'll bet you didn't think I could get here before you, did you, Isabel?" Clothed in his usual dark attire, Shadoe Mc-Caine emerged from the shadows. "You were going to run away from me, weren't you?"

"You seem to have all the answers," she snapped. "What did you do, sneak out the back door like a thief in the night?" Approaching her, Shadoe's hand attempted to cover her own upon the mare's forehead, but Isabel quickly drew away. She felt crimson suffusing her features and turned her head. Instantly, Shadoe's fingers were beneath her chin, coaxing her to face him.

He became intimidatingly silent, and he lowered her head in an attempt to make eye contact, which she staunchly avoided. "May I apologize for the way I acted last night?" he said after a moment. "You have every right to hate me—"

Her eyes darted swiftly up. "And I exercise that privilege, here and now . . . so, why don't you go do . . . whatever it is that men like you do this time of morning?"

His hand dropped to her shoulder but she shrugged it away. "Come back to the hotel, Isabel, and I will show you what men like me do this time of the morning—"

"I am not your whore!" she lashed out at him.

Shadoe certainly felt the sting; a quiet fury darkened his dove-gray eyes. "No . . . you are not my whore, Isabel . . . you are the woman I—"

Silence. Had it not been for the intimidating

188

ength of it, Isabel would never have made eye con-
act with the rascal who had taken her virginity last
night. "I am the woman you what?" she continued in
her same venomous tone.

Shadoe had been dangerously close to saying, "The
woman I love", something he had decided last night
that he would divulge. Now, he shrank back from
making that commitment and said, rather, "The
woman I have sworn to see safely to Tongue River.
Don't you remember that you have a brother waiting
here for you?"

"It is the only thing I am prepared to remember
from this moment forward. I don't need you, Shadoe.
I will find my way to El Dorado, where I have a good
friend, and I will have him take me to Tongue
River—"

Grabbing her arms, he pulled her roughly against
him. "What man? What man are you talking about?"

A green-eyed devil had leaped into Shadoe's flashing eyes and a very pleased Isabel caught the smile
before it curled the corners of her mouth. "A tall,
handsome man who is strong and virile and brave. A
man I very much admire . . . a man I would marry if
he asked me—" As the true image of Poe Hamlin
crawled into her mind—the image of a paunchy, middle-aged, though very kind man, with thinning hair
and tobacco juice streaming down a ragged chin—Isabel dropped her gaze from Shadoe's darkened one,
lest he become aware of the lies she had told. Actually, the only attribute poor Poe had going for him
was his good heart. He had remained close to the
Emerson family, even after all the years he had been
away from Shadows-in-the-Mist, and had pledged to
always be available if one of the family needed him.

But could Isabel be content with the company of
an old family friend when the virile rake who had

made her his woman was still willing to take her to Tongue River? She loathed Shadoe for the way he had treated her after they had made love, and that she would even entertain the idea of continuing the journey with him made her shrink inside. A rebellious desire burst within her, making her want to be with him even as her good senses warned her he could never be good for her, that he would humiliate and degrade her at every turn in the trail.

"What are you thinking, Isabel?" asked Shadoe, breaking her concentration so quickly that her nerves leaped to the surface of her skin.

"I'm thinking that I should wrestle your gun away from you and shoot you in the back."

Instantly, Shadoe removed his gun from the holster and held it out to her. "Take it. Shoot me if that is what you want."

"You're not worth hanging for," she countered vehemently.

"You're too pretty to hang. Besides, ain't no jury going to hang a woman like you over a worthless scoundrel like me."

"You've probably got a price on your head somewhere. I'd probably get a reward for shooting you down."

Silence. Shadoe's hand dropped and he swiftly returned the gun to its holster, then turned back and took her hand in his. This time she did not protest. "You shoot me down, Isabel, and you could collect five thousand dollars reward from a man named Mendez in Texas. Don't ask me what I did to be so honored, because I cannot — will not tell you —"

As he had spoken, her eyes had lifted to his. She had watched his mouth move, because she could scarcely believe the words he had spoken, and had to assure herself of her sanity. But she had not heard his

190

declaration in a dream; she had heard the words spoken from his own lips. He was an outlaw, with a price on his head, and she had trusted him to take her all the way to Tongue River, Montana. Her mouth gaped in horror. She had made love to this man . . . and she knew she would make love to him again and again and again—

When she was finally able to find her voice, she asked, "Why would this man want you dead? Why would it be worth so much to him? Surely, you must have some idea—"

Silence again fell between them. Shadoe was not so sure he wanted the ugly image of Venetia Mendez to dampen the love he felt for the fiery woman whose hand rested gently within his own. When he brushed a tantalizing caress against her mouth, she did not protest, but when he attempted to imprison her mouth roughly against his own, she bristled back with fire rushing into her pale eyes.

"A kiss is small in comparison to the love we shared last night," he sulked.

Isabel lifted an index finger and shook it close enough to his face that he could have bitten it, if he'd been so inclined. "Let's get one thing straight, Shadoe McCaine. I want to go to Tongue River and find my brother. I need an escort, and thus far, you have proved reliable enough. I don't care what you did in the past and I don't care about bounties on your head or injustices you may have suffered. And let's get something else straight. What happened last night will not—I repeat *will not*—happen again! Do I make myself perfectly clear?"

"And you're one crazy lady," he chuckled, attempting to draw her close to his solid strength, "if you think for a moment that I won't try. I made you mine last night, Isabel, and that makes you mine for life.

No other man will ever touch you."

She was both frightened and pleased by the threat. She opened her mouth, but could not find the strength to utter a word. Should she condemn him for trying to take possession of her simply because they had made love . . . or should she throw herself into his arms and proclaim the depths of her own love and adoration for him? Should she take his threat as a proposal that he intended to spend the rest of his life with her . . . or should she feel like the captive embarking on a perilous, life-and-death voyage with a self-destructive kidnapper?

Because she could not find an answer, she returned her attentions to the mare who had stood in silent witness and lifted her trembling hand to the wide white blaze between her brown eyes. But Shadoe roughly took her arm above the elbow and reeled her to face him. "Do I make myself clear, Isabel?"

Her mouth puckered petulantly. "What are you saying, Shadoe? That you love me? That you want to be my husband . . . that I will be your wife? Or do you simply want a life mate, someone to warm your bed and cook your meals and bear your children? You've really not made yourself clear at all. If you would stop talking in ridiculous circles, I might be able to make some small shade of sense out of you."

"I want you, Isabel—"

"As what? Your maid?"

"No."

"As your bed mate?"

"Not just—"

"As your wife."

"Perhaps . . . no, probably—"

Tossing her head of dawn-colored hair, Isabel laughed sardonically. "Oh, am I to be flattered that you might possibly—even probably—want me for a wife? Well . . . what makes you think I would consider you for a husband?" When his grip tightened, she ordered, "Let me go!"

To which he replied harshly, "No. Now, stop being a foolish girl and let's get another couple of hours of sleep before we must resume our journey."

Isabel jerked her arm from him, then winced as she was sure his fingers had left bruises upon her tender flesh. "You just keep away from my bed, Shadoe McCaine or I'll—"

"You'll what, Isabel?" A smirk gripped his mouth and for one long, intimidating moment he drew his hands to his narrow hips and held them there. Then he again took her arm and jerked her about, half dragging her toward the livery door. When she groaned in protest, he snapped, "Do, hush, my little woman . . . you'll wake the horses!"

The merciless, unsavory philanderer! she thought, her struggle against him feeble enough that he might think she liked his bullishness. "Don't call me your little woman, Shadoe McCaine," she ordered in a light, insincere tone. "And if you'll let me go, I'll go with you willingly."

Promptly, Shadoe let her go, and when she found herself free, her foot scrambled out from beneath the hem of her gown and caught him full upon the shin. As he grabbed for the sudden pain, she took off in a dash toward the hotel, and he was too surprised to chase after her. "Blasted woman—" he mumbled, even as a smile turned up his mouth.

His fiery Isabel was going to be a handful to tame.

And Shadoe very much looked forward to being the one to accomplish the pleasant task.

Twelve

Mercedes set the two canvas bags upon the banquette and moved confidently through the rooms of the house on Royal, assessing her duties according to priority. Their three-week absence had allowed a chill to settle throughout the house, and the first priority was lighting the hearths of the downstairs rooms and the one in Imogen's suite on the second floor. When the late December chill began to dissipate, Mercedes unpacked the bags, then moved toward the kitchen, her favorite room in the house. Despite the chill lingering there due to the one small window kept open for the comings and goings of the cat, the large room was homey and inviting. It was the place where meals were prepared, where polite sitting and chatting were done, and where the laughter usually began.

But this morning there was no laughter. Isabel was back on the Boeuf, Dustin at Lamourie Bayou, and the house was morbidly silent without the two young people so dear to Mercedes' heart.

Heaving a sigh of loneliness, she set about preparing a brunch for herself and Imogen, who was now resting in her chamber. The old lady had engaged in more activities these past three weeks at Magnolia Hill than she had in the past three years at the house on Royal. Still, Mercedes smiled to herself, thinking that Imogen would open her parlor at the first opportunity to her gambling acquaintances. Just before Mercedes had left her at her chamber, Imogen had asked if "the cards were sorted out," and Mercedes had assured her they were.

The bell rang at the front courtyard. Wiping her damp hands on her apron, Mercedes shuffled toward the banquette and the unwelcome intruder. But there, smiling widely, stood Golda Dumont, and Mercedes could not help but smile herself. "I've collected your mail," said Golda, who, unbeknownst to Mercedes, was following Isabel's direction to remove any mail arriving from the Shadows.

Mercedes took the bunch and sifted through them, then tucked the letters and bills into the large pocket of her apron. "I'll bring over a few coins for your trouble," offered Mercedes. "I haven't anything on me right now."

Golda raised her palm. "No need; it was no trouble at all. Good morning, Mercedes."

Mercedes turned to reenter the house, again flipping through the items of mail. As was her habit, she separated the bills from the letters, placing them in two stacks on a hall table. Moments later, she returned to the table with Imogen's brunch tray and set the several letters that had arrived against the bud vase bearing a single white rose that had bloomed against the back wall of the house. So rare were the roses this time of the year, that when one bloomed, Mercedes took special care to see that Imogen enjoyed its short span of beauty before it withered and died. Soon Mercedes ascended the stairs and entered the suite of rooms where Imogen rested.

"See what I've brought you, ma'am," said Mercedes, placing the bed tray over Imogen's lap. "A rose done bloomed in the garden despite —"

"Despite the absence of our lovely young ones," ended Imogen, thinking of Isabel and Dustin and missing them terribly. "How good you are to me, Mercedes." Gently, Imogen placed her withered old hand over the plump hand of her longtime maid. Perching her spectacles over her nose, Imogen began sorting the letters, placing the ones from her family atop those from her friends and acquaintances. "What is this?"

"What is that, ma'am?"

"I do declare," said Imogen with sudden strength. "It is from young Paul. Why, I can't remember the last time that snip of a boy wrote his old auntie a letter."

Of the three children of Grant and Delilah Emerson, Paul, the youngest, was the one Mercedes didn't care too much for. She'd always thought he acted too mature for his age and he was, in her own carefully chosen words, a "stuffed shirt . . . he should be a banker or, God forbid, a lawyer!" "Oh?" remarked Mercedes, taking up the white linen napkin for Imogen. "What'll you reckon that boy'll be wantin'?"

"We'll just find out," said Imogen, slitting the flap of the envelope with the ivory letter opener Mercedes had placed with the mail.

When Imogen paled beyond her normal color, an alarmed Mercedes asked, "What's the matter, Miz Imogen? Somethin' done happen't up yon at the Boeuf?"

"I don't know, Mercedes." Flicking her wrist, Imogen ordered flatly, "Hurry over and fetch Golda. I must talk to that girl." When Mercedes hesitated to leave her, Imogen's voice crackled with emotion as she added, "Don't tarry. Quick, Mercedes, as quick as your legs will carry you!"

Scarcely had five minutes passed before a silent Golda Dumont, surprised to have been summoned, stood beside Imogen's bed. The letter thrust into her hand, Golda quickly read the words written in the hand of a sixteen-year-old boy from Bayou Boeuf. Then she looked up, shame reddening her pretty features, and quietly said, "Oh, my . . . I let one slip by, didn't I, Mrs. de'Cambre?"

"What do you mean?" Imogen snapped.

A trembling hand thrust forward to hand the letter back to Imogen, then drew back. Golda's fingers linked tightly together. "She asked me to intercept any letters sent from her family—"

"Who did?"

"Isabel, Mrs. de'Cambre. She had somewhere to go, and she didn't want her family to know. They—" Golda shrugged. "They believe she is still here with you."

"And where is she?"

"The only letter I have from her was posted in Natchez—"

"Natchez. Dear, dear—" Imogen shook her head with the same casualness as a tolerant young mother who had caught a child sticking his tongue in the sugar bowl. Then she puckered her mouth, crossed her arms, and lifted a sagging chin as she suddenly sized up the situation. "And I'll wager, young woman—and don't you dare deny it—that she is with my naughty young friend, Shadoe McCaine?"

As if to justify her part in Isabel's scheme, Golda responded, "Well, don't you think she is safe with him?"

Imogen shot back, "He's a man . . . of course, she isn't safe with him!" Flicking her wrist in dismissal, Imogen said more to herself than to either

197

Golda or the silently observing Mercedes, "Well, I'll just have to see what I can do to rectify this situation. Her parents would never forgive me if some calamity befell her—"

"Or if she gits with child by that black-hearted Cheyenne rake," added Mercedes, confident that her small smile was successfully hidden by the shadows of the corner where she stood.

"God forbid!" said Imogen, catching the attentions of the hastily departing Golda. "You, gal—" Golda turned, instantly facing a madly shaking finger. "I'll be talking to you again. And if you've been holding any letters from the Emersons, you bring them to me straight away."

Golda curtsied nervously and her feet leaped into a half-run along the wide corridor of Imogen's quaint old house.

Mercedes approached the bed. "You gonna fret, Miz Imogen, or is you gonna eat yo' food?"

Imogen slapped the tray, at which time Mercedes picked it up to halt any spills. "That girl!" Looking up at her faithful friend, Imogen cocked her head to the side. "Have I lived such a sinful life that I must be burdened with such a young, foolish girl as our Isabel?"

"You been through six husbands," chuckled Mercedes. "I reckon you been sinful enough." Turning in the doorway, Mercedes gently reminded her, "You know you love that gal, Imogen . . . why, I'd imagine that she's just like you was at that age.

"Harumph!" With childlike impudence, Imogen sank into the plush covers of her bed. "Go on about yourself, Mercedes. I must get my beauty sleep."

"Sho', Miz Imogen. I'll let you know when yo' Mr. Thackeray comes a callin'."

As she moved through the corridor and descended

the stairs, Mercedes attempted to swallow the humor threatening to erupt into uncontrollable laughter. She wasn't at all worried about Isabel. And that Shadoe McCaine! Why, she couldn't imagine that their precious Isabel could be in any better hands, whatever it was she was up to.

Three days before Christmas, Isabel began to have misgivings about her impulsive decision to travel with Shadoe McCaine. She wasn't sure which influenced her decision more — the growing love she felt for the moody rascal, or the soreness she was sure had taken up permanent residence in her backside.

They had left Fort Smith, Arkansas two days behind them and were moving ever forward toward Apache country. Shadoe planned to reach Wolf Creek, in the north of the state, within six days, and there they would purchase more adequate winter clothing for the forge further north.

Light snow was beginning to fall and the wind was blowing fiercely, pounding the snow horizontally against the two travelers. Occasionally a needle-sharp snow crystal would strike Isabel's delicate features and tears would pop into her eyes. She was sore and hungry. She wanted to sink into a warm, feather mattress. She wanted to eat dinner in a fancy dining room. She wanted to wear beautiful gowns. She wanted to have her brother with her and be homeward bound —

The dark wolf — as she had silently begun referring to Shadoe — moved onto a narrow trail a dozen yards ahead of her. How like a wolf — his confessed "spirit guide" — he was. His eyes, when he met a challenge, were unwavering. He could remain taut for half an hour and never twitch a muscle. He could betray no sign of weakness in the most dangerous of situations, and she often wondered if his fearlessness was a thin veneer, hiding a warm, emotional human heart beneath, or if he was, indeed, an animal that might easily be provoked into the fiercest of attacks and fight to the death.

Throughout the morning she rode silently behind Shadoe. Since the night they had made love in Natchez he had made no attempt to touch her or hint, even remotely, that he wanted to be with her intimately. These past two weeks he had treated her like a stranger, speaking to her only when it could not be avoided and then reluctantly.

Shadoe eased Mirlo onto a narrow precipice of the trail overlooking a wooded dale. When the stallion slipped, Shadoe touched his palm to the sleek muscles of his neck to calm him. Then, as if he had just remembered she was even alive, he turned and yelled back at Isabel, "Move carefully here. The trail is narrow."

"As if you'd care if I broke my neck," mumbled Isabel, her heel touching the haunches of the mare she had named Millicent. When she encouraged her on, the mare suddenly halted.

"What did you say?" asked Shadoe.

"I said 'the mare is giving me heck', but don't worry about it." Then she mumbled, "As if you would bother."

"What?"

"I said, 'I'll be glad to see my brother'."

The noon hour was approaching. As Isabel completed the precarious stretch of trail, she rounded a corner and found Shadoe sitting atop the stallion awaiting her. "Are you hungry?" he asked.

"Yes—for a steak and hot buttered potatoes and Mozelle's delicious biscuits and a great big bowl of peach cobbler fresh out of the oven."

Shadoe's hand outstretched. "How about the next best thing—beef jerky?"

Crinkling her eyebrows into a frown, Isabel whined, "When will we reach a town? Why can't we ask a kind farmer if he will put us up for the night? Why can't we take a train? Why can't we—"

"And why can't we send you packing for home?" interjected Shadoe McCaine in a vehement tone. "If you want comforts, then that's where you should be."

Shadoe had spoken as if he harbored a long-nurtured hatred; Isabel wondered if, perhaps, he didn't, and that hatred was for her. Her mouth pressed into a grim line and the frown became even more severe. When her gaze suddenly made contact with his still-outstretched hand, Isabel turned her nose up at the beef jerky. "No, thank you. I'd rather go hungry."

"So be it." Shadoe chewed off a morsel of the food she had declined, then turned his horse back to the northwest.

Isabel was furious. He didn't care if she was hungry. He didn't care if she needed to stop and rest. Suppose she had private duties to attend? Would he even care? Just because he was a man and could ignore the call of nature for hours on end didn't mean that she could, too. Thus, Isabel dismounted her horse, caring little that the black stallion did not slow its pace. As far as she was concerned, Shadoe McCaine could put two miles' distance between them and leave Indian signs for her to follow. As far as she was concerned, he could go to hell in a thorny basket!

Isabel promptly plopped herself down on a flat rock and allowed her booted feet to dangle over the shady dale. Millicent found a bit of greenery thriving, despite the bitter chill, against a rock behind her rider and busied herself digging for it. A wild array of emotions channeled through Isabel, compelling her to hate Shadoe McCaine, and to love him in the same moment, making her bite her lip with irritation, and simultaneously drag in a heavy sigh as she remembered her night in the scalawag's arms.

Shadoe had moved several hundred yards ahead, forging a safe trail for Isabel, when he suddenly discovered her missing. He doubled back, then drew Mirlo to a halt in the shade of the timberline and watched Isabel for several minutes. How indignant she looked! How infuriated! And—a wry smile twisted the corners of Shadoe's mouth—how infuriating she was to him!

She had crossed her right leg over her left, and her foot was pounding against the heady wind that had chilled them to the bone all through the night and morning. Shadoe wondered if she was thinking about the night they had spent together, and wondering why it had not happened again.

How could he tell her? It was because of Venetia . . . it was because of her father . . . it was because an innocent girl named Mary Ellen was murdered . . . and it was because of the price on his head . . .

He would never be free to love Isabel. He would have to watch constantly over his shoulder, lest some lawman clamp a heavy hand there, then bind him in irons and drag him away. The very thought of that happening in the presence of Isabel was humiliating. He could not love Isabel.

But, damn it! It was too late for that!

Tapping his heel gently against Mirlo's belly,

Shadoe eased him ahead.

As he came into view, Isabel attempted to still the mad pounding of her heart. She could have balled her hand and laid him out flat that very minute, but she could also kiss away his hurt and draw him into a loving embrace. She hated the rebellious feelings stirring within her. It was obvious that he had merely taken advantage of her vulnerability that night, and that she meant nothing more to him than a few minutes of pleasure to sate his wicked lust.

When Isabel lifted her pert, defiant chin, a low growl rippled from Shadoe's throat. What an infuriating little vixen she was, swinging that pretty, booted foot and crossing her slim arms beneath the heavy material of the leather jacket he had purchased for her. He had also purchased boy's Levis for her in Fort Smith, more to humiliate her than because they were truly practical for traveling, but she had taken to them like an otter to water. They had fit her snugly, rounding out her buttocks and outlining her curvaceous hips. Were it not for the oversized shirt she had cinched around her waist with a long beige scarf, his masculine inclinations would never survive her allure.

Dragging Mirlo to a halt about twenty feet from her, he bellowed without feeling, "What the hell is the matter with you?"

She did not look at him, but continued to gaze across the timberline as if she were on a casual nature outing. "I am hungry and I am cold and I am tired. Other than that, I am just fine."

"I offered you jerky—"

"I don't want jerky," she snapped. "I want fried chicken and Saratoga chips and a great big glass of warm milk with chocolate in it!"

203

"I thought you wanted a steak and potatoes."

"I'll take anything," she quipped, "Except that blasted jerky!"

Shadoe slowly dismounted, and Isabel attempted to make no visible response to the threatening way he sauntered toward her. His demeanor was cold enough to freeze burning coals and she found herself stifling a chuckle. When he stood within touching distance of her, he crossed his arms and said, matter-of-factly, "If you're not up by the time I count to ten, I'm going to hog-tie you over that saddle."

"You wouldn't dare!" she challenged, immediately softening her voice as she warned, "You wouldn't be able to sleep at night, because that is when I would get my revenge."

The Oklahoma countryside was dotted with homesteads. Keeping her eyes peeled toward the woods allowed her to catch the sight of the dim swirl of smoke that indicated a cabin might be nearby, perhaps a half mile or so through the woods. It was noon, the time of day when normal people ate normal meals, and with that thought in mind, she hopped to her feet. "It won't be necessary to drag me up, Shadoe McCaine," she said with the flippancy of an argumentative child. "I'm going this way through the woods, then I am going to get down on my knees and beg some kind Oklahoma folks for a hot meal."

Curling an eyebrow upward, Shadoe spied the dissipating smoke. "You'll do no such thing. That might be the campfire of outlaws—"

"Oh, criminy, Shadoe McCaine. Why must you be so—" She searched for the proper word from the many she had attached to him these past few weeks. "So infuriating," she ended on a softer note.

Actually, Isabel was only toying with him. Though she certainly wouldn't turn down a hot meal if it were to be offered, she was more than willing to content herself with the jerky he kept in supply. She didn't want to be argumentative and cause trouble for him, but she liked the look that crossed his features—dark and threatening—when she tested his endurance. Right now, she was sure that his face had become a slab of granite. His gray-black eyes were as black as pitch, and his bronze skin had darkened, giving him a wild, untameable look. That was when her mouth parted and her need to laugh would not be contained.

But at that precise moment, the heel of her boot caught in a patch of gravel, and before she could catch herself, she was sliding down the hill on the side of her thigh. It had happened so quickly that she was halfway down the hill before she opened her mouth to scream. Her long fingers attempted to catch in the brush dotting the hills, but the attempt managed only to peel away her glove and the top layer of her skin. She was only half aware of Shadoe's growl of alarm as his boots dug into the sides of the hill as he eased toward her.

Isabel finally landed with a dull thud against the massive trunk of a winter-barren oak. For a moment, she did not feel the pain of the injuries she had suffered in her tumble down the hill, but now she felt fire burning in her hand and along the length of her right thigh and leg. She felt a throbbing at her right temple and attempted to draw herself forward. Then she screamed, as the most horrible pain she had ever felt ricocheted through her chest. By the time Shadoe reached her, she was gently crying.

The pain was not nearly so intense when he

pulled her against his chest and held her close. "Are you hurt?" he murmured. "Dear God, tell me you're not hurt."

Isabel buried her face against the thick fabric of his jacket. "Would you care?" she whispered.

Rather than respond, his hand rose and gently entwined through her thick hair. Then he put space between them so that he could look at her. "Where do you hurt?" he asked.

"Here—" Isabel's trembling hand started to cover her thigh, but instantly withdrew. "And here—" Her hand at her ribs was instantly replaced by his own.

"I don't think you have a broken rib," he said, gently massaging her beneath her jacket.

"And here—" Isabel raised her scraped, bloody palm and Shadoe took her hand to hold it gently.

"I reckon ol' Doc McCaine is going to have to fetch his little black bag." Shadoe's attempt at humor extracted the smallest smile from Isabel. Then his brows drew together and he accused in a half-teasing voice, "I bet you tumbled down that hill on purpose, just so I'd worry about you."

"Did you?" Her head cocked sweetly to the side.

Rather than offer a commitment, Shadoe remarked, "I hope you still have that iodine you purchased in Natchez."

"Iodine!" Isabel's tears dried just enough to add detail to her shock. "Why, you might as well dunk me in a vat of alcohol! Thanks, but no, thanks."

Assuring himself that she had no broken bones, Shadoe picked her up with ease and cradled her in his arms. Their gazes met, locked, an unwavering challenge to each other for only a moment before the passion burned brightly between them. If she were not hurting, Shadoe knew he would have taken her, here and now, despite the bone-deep chill. Isa

206

bel knew that if she were not hurting, she would have allowed herself to be taken. Unconsciously, her mouth parted; her tongue eased toward her top lip and rested there for a moment. She could feel the heat of his breath against her own flushed features, and she wondered, cutting her gaze quickly away, if he had seen the desire in the depths of her eyes. Certainly, she had seen it in his.

Holding her close, Shadoe looked up the precarious stretch of hill where their two horses grazed. He took a moment to hope the beasts didn't take off through the woods, though he was reasonably sure that Mirlo was much more loyal to him than that. The mare would stay with the stallion. If only it could be as simple with the feisty nymph in his arms—

"What are you thinking, Shadoe?"

"How the hell I'm going to get you back up that hill."

"It's nice here. The wind is cut off by the sharp elevation of the hill. Why don't you call Mirlo to you. Millicent will follow."

Shadoe's gaze narrowed; he feigned annoyance. "I suppose you want me to build a fire and open a can of that beef I picked up in Fort Smith?"

She shrugged against him, pleased by the sheer, muscular strength of him. "Well . . . it wouldn't hurt. Perhaps a can of those potatoes, too? We could whip up a stew in your little black pot." With teasing inflection, she promised, "Perhaps I'll let you tend my wounds."

"With iodine?" he asked darkly, hinting, with a mirthless smile, that he might enjoy inflicting further pain.

"No . . . a little cold water, perhaps, and that salve you carry in your saddlebags."

"That salve's for horses."

"They won't mind sharing."

Her wide, luminous gaze softened Shadoe long enough that he reconsidered her small requests for food, fire, and medical attention. A long, shrill series of whistles stirred Mirlo into action and he immediately found a safer way down the precipice, with the mare close at his heels.

Half an hour later, Isabel sat upon a blanket, free of her jeans and wearing her one riding skirt, while Shadoe nurtured the fire into blazing warmth, then stalked off toward a wide, clear pond. Though she had spent the short, tender moments in his embrace, by the time they had made camp, his mood had turned dark and somber again. Just before he'd moved off with a makeshift fishing pole and one of the hooks from his saddle case, he'd thrown the jar of salve on the blanket beside her, ordering tersely, "Clean those wounds good. We don't want them to get infected."

While she tended her needs, she watched him through the short spanse of woods. He stood patiently at the edge of the pond, watching the water as if it were a very good book absorbing his attentions. She wondered what he was thinking in the few minutes it took him to pull in a couple of trout. As he sat upon the bank to clean and gut what would be their noonday meal, he ventured not a single glance in Isabel's direction.

"Why do you despise me so, Shadoe?" she asked softly.

Something in his past had made him a very bitter man. Isabel had no doubts that the *something* was a woman. How could she compete with a phantom?

Thirteen

Startled, the black stallion jerked back from the caress of Isabel's hand. She had left the campfire to seek a moment of solitude, but a strange sound had drawn her to the clearing where the horses grazed. Mirlo seemed much more nervous than usual, and his ears pricked to the woodline just a hundred yards or so to the northeast.

"What's the matter, old boy?" asked Isabel, rubbing his muzzle softly. Shadoe McCaine relaxed at the campfire, his hat drawn over his forehead and his wrist settled across the bridge of his nose. "How can you relax in this bitter cold?" she asked, puckering her mouth into a brief pout. But even as she silently mumbled the question, Isabel reassured herself that he was too blasted inhuman to feel something as trivial as the weather.

So absorbed was she in her thoughts, and in calming the still alarmed stallion whose nostrils continued to flare, that Isabel did not at first see the two young boys skirting the fringes of the thick woods. One was tall, slim, and dark-haired, the other a head shorter and more towheaded.

Both of the young Oklahomans had only one thing in mind — getting back to their pa's cabin with two fine looking horses.

"Whatcha think, Obie? Should we knock her in the head and take them horses while that ol' fella's a nappin'?"

x

209

The younger boy allowed a moment of thought to settle among his thickly freckled features. "I's thinkin' maybe we ought'n ta take the lady back to the cabin, too. I shore am fed up with pa's cookin'."

"You one crazy boy, Obie. Don't ya listen to nothin' pa says? Ya can always tell when a female's a good cook, 'cus she got some good plump meat on her bones. Why, look at that female! She ain't nothin' but skin 'n bones. Prob'ly poison us right off!"

"Shore is purty though, ain't she? Pa says females good for other things 'sides cookin'."

Drawing back his hand, the older boy struck a mighty blow to the younger one's head. "Ya a stupid son-of-a-bitch, Obie. Pa likes 'em plump, no matter what they's a doin'."

Obie rubbed his head. "Ya don't have to clobber me, Roy. I was jes' thinkin', that's all."

"Well, ya better start thinkin' how we's goin' ta clear out that thar female and gits them hosses out of the clearin' before that fella comes out from under that hat—"

"We could kill 'em—"

Again, Obie's head reeled from a fresh blow. "Pa says it ain't polite to kill folks. Now, you give me that sling shot and a big rock. I'll see if I can lay her flat long enough to git them hosses."

From her vantage point on the slight rise of the clearing, Isabel spied a movement in the shade of the woodline. She knew that two people hid there, and was reasonably sure that they were very young. Were they just curious, or were they plotting some childish larceny?

She had caught no glint of weapons and yet was much too smart to let down her guard. She continued to coddle the stallion, even as her ears pricked for any movement toward her. Oh, if only she could catch Sha doe's attentions. If the children were up to no good, it would certainly be advantageous to have a man about who hadn't locked himself in blissful sleep. What kind of guide and protector was he anyway?

Shadoe wasn't as relaxed as Isabel thought he was. Not only had he ascertained the presence of humans, but he had spent the last few minutes watching them and guessing that the horses were probably the prize they were after. They were much too young—he guessed that they were between ten and twelve years of age—to be interested in the beautiful woman who was his traveling companion. Feigning sleep, Shadoe watched their two heads bob among the underbrush, and when one readied a slingshot preparing to let go of a good-sized rock, Shadoe shot forward and yelled, "Duck, Isabel!"

She was much too startled by his hoarsely called warning to follow his direction. But she spun about, and the rock that would have otherwise struck her in the side of the head hit the neck of the stallion. With a long squeal, Mirlo reared back on his haunches, breaking loose of Isabel's fingers that had held his halter, and charged for the timberline. While two young fellows themselves squealed in fear and surprise, Mirlo pounded his hooves against the underbrush, sending the conspirators scooting backwards on their backsides.

By the time Shadoe reached the stallion and managed to subdue him, the boys were hugging each other in shocked silence against the trunk of an oak. Shadoe bent and grabbed the slingshot from the bigger of the boys. Shaking it in their faces, he growled, "How would you like it if I loaded a rock into this thing and shot at you?"

Then he slung the offending weapon far into the woods, let go of the stallion, and grabbed a leg of each of the boys to drag them into the clearing.

"Don't kill us, mister," howled Obie. "We jes' wanted

211

to take the horses home to our pa."

"Confound it, boys, those are our horses. Are you sayin' you were going to steal them?"

Roy was the older and braver of the two. Pressing his mouth in youthful rebellion and defiance, he blurted out, "Shore was, mister! Whatcha goin' ta do about it?"

Shadoe stifled a grin, the situation was much too serious to show any humor. He remembered himself at the age of these boys and the lesson his mother had taught him when he'd attempted to steal a coveted colt from a neighboring rancher. It had worked then; and he had no doubt it would work now.

When Isabel silently approached, Shadoe said, "Get me the rope off my saddle, Isabel. These young fellas were going to steal our horses, so I think we got to hang 'em."

Obie started yelling and attempting to free the leg that Shadoe held. "Don't' hang us, mister. We won't do it again."

And Roy, the defiant one, tersely ordered, "Shut up Obie . . . he's jes' tryin' to skeer us."

Isabel felt that she'd seen enough gentleness in Shadoe to know that he had no intentions of hanging two young boys. Thus, she took up her role with the talent of a true actress and quietly said, "I'll get the rope, Shadoe. But since one of those horses is mine, I think I should get to hang the little one."

"All right, then. I guess it's only fair since I got to hang that boy near Fort Smith last week."

Seeing the fear in Obie's face contagiously wash over into the older one's, Isabel pivoted sharply away lest they see the humor easing into the corners of her mouth. As she moved toward the saddles, she heard Shadoe's terse tone adding emphasis to the punishment he planned to inflict on the boys. As she bent and pretended to be untying the rope from Shadoe's saddle she heard him suddenly yell, "Hell, the big one's go

212

away! Come back here, boy! Quick, Isabel, saddle the horses! The little one got away, too." And Isabel turned, seeing only a blur of the two boys scatting into the woodline.

When he was sure the boys had covered the distance of half a mile in the few seconds since they'd "escaped," Shadoe turned and laughed, "I don't think those two will be planning to steal any more horses." But when he saw the tenderness reflecting in Isabel's quiet gaze, his eyes darkened and the softness left his swarthy features. "Night is approaching. Let's add some more logs to the fire and get a good night's sleep. We lost half a day of travel due to your foolishness, and we have to make up the time."

As he attempted to pass by her, Isabel's hand landed upon his arm, halting him. "Why are you so afraid, Shadoe?"

His head turned slowly, his eyes narrowing as her gaze connected to his own. A tic jerked beneath his left eye and his eyes narrowed even more in his attempt to control it. "What do you mean, what am I afraid of? Do I look afraid to you?"

"You're afraid of me, Shadoe. Every time you let your guard down and act a little human, you immediately turn nasty and mean. Why do you do that?"

Without warning, Shadoe roughly gripped her arms and drew her firmly against him. "I'm a mean, nasty man, Isabel. Haven't you been with me long enough to know that?"

A smirk played at the corner of her mouth. "I've been with you long enough to know that you're full of bull, Shadoe McCaine. You can't bear the fact that I see beneath that rough-and-ready exterior. You can't bear it that I might see a gentle, loving man who is trying desperately to scratch through the barrier of hate and bitterness he has built around himself. You can tell me you're mean and you can tell me you're nasty; you can

213

even tell me you're a self-centered bastard if you want
to. But I know the truth. I know who you are, Shadoe
McCaine, and you're none of those things. So—" Only
now did she allow a small smile to invade her pretty features "—Why don't you kiss me and tell me how happy
you are to be with me?"

Shadoe felt an overpowering need to meet her challenge, to take from her the hottest of kisses, to claim her
for his own, confess his love, and swear that he would
never leave her. He wanted to feel her sensual, naked
ivory flesh molded against his own and take from her
the sweetest of treasures. But . . . God . . . wouldn't
she like that? Wouldn't she be pleased with herself . .
this high-and-mighty daughter of a rich Southern
planter . . . this coy Southern belle who felt that her
personal pedestal could never be high enough. If she
wanted him to adore her and revere her and pinch himself to make sure he wasn't imagining that she'd given
him the prize of her virginity, well, she could wait til
the heavens opened.

He would not—could not—give up the game of cat-
and-mouse that made his every waking minute—and
some of his sleeping ones—the most thrilling moments
in his life. Thus, he drew in a long, ragged breath and
briefly reabsorbed some of her remarks. Tipping his
hat with perfunctory indifference, he released her arm
and casually walked away.

Dustin eased the gelding into a gentle lope as he
crossed the meadow and soon skirted Bayou Boeuf.
This time of the year the water was stained the color of
tea, and the terrain was sluggish and muddy, a perfect
concentration of muck to grab the shod hooves of the
horse and drag them under. An irritating sucking
sound interrupted Dustin's train of thought, and he
moved the gelding off the trail and onto the firmer

ground of the woods.

Soon, he crossed a quiet stream overhung with Spanish moss and coaxed the gelding into a faster lope. The rooftop of Shadows-in-the-Mist loomed over the treeline and when he entered the east pasture, he skirted the cemetery, then drew the gelding to a halt.

His gaze swept over the ethereal setting, and over the many graves, some bearing elaborate tombstones, some simple wooden crosses and others mere indentations in the ground above the remains of those known only to God. There in a corner of the cemetery lay old Philo, who had served Shadows-in-the-Mist both as a slave and as a free man of wages. Beneath a towering oak were Delilah's parents, Angus and Irene Wickley, and to the right of them stood a towering memorial that had been erected for Delilah's lost son, Eduard, who had drowned in the Boeuf more than fifteen years ago. Dustin only vaguely remembered Eduard. He remembered that his hair had been pale, like his father's, and his eyes the color of gold, like his mother's. Regrettable that Eduard's body had never been found and that he hadn't been lain to rest among those who had gone before and after him.

When he saw his uncle emerge from the stable, Dustin coaxed the gelding ahead and soon entered the clearing where Grant Emerson saddled his horse. The older man grinned his pleasure at Dustin's unexpected visit. "What brings you out this way, nephew?" asked Grant.

"Business for mother. She has a couple of new mares you might be interested in. And—" Dustin untied a small wooden box from the back of his saddle. "This was with our mail. It's addressed to you and Aunt Delilah."

Grant took the box and his pale blue eyes swept over the large lettering bearing *Mr. and Mrs. Grant Emerson, Shadows-in-the-Mist Plantation, Lecomte, Louisiana.* Sitting upon a small stool—the very one old Philo had worn smooth in his many years on the plantation—Grant unbuckled the pair of leather straps, opened the box, then lifted and unfolded the letter on top of its contents and began to read. Shortly, he mumbled, "Good Lord—"

Dustin, settling comfortably on a bench across from him, asked, "What is wrong, Uncle Grant?"

Grant quickly read the letter, then folded it and dropped it back into the box. "You remember Philo?"

"Sure, Uncle Grant . . . I just stopped at the cemetery where he is buried."

"The letter is from a man in a place called Stillwater, Oklahoma, and it's about Philbus, who was Philo's son. He left Shadows-in-the-Mist a long, long time ago."

"I remember hearing you talk about Philbus. He was Mozelle's first husband, wasn't he?"

"Sure was. I guess I'd better go in and give Mozelle the news. She'll want to know."

His aunt Delilah emerged from the gallery of The Shadows and moved spritely toward the stables. "It's good to see you, Dustin." She hugged him briefly, then moved to Grant's side. Seeing the frown upon his pale brow, she asked, "What is wrong? You two aren't quarreling, are you?"

Grant withdrew the letter and handed it to her. "Bad news about Philbus," he replied, handing it to her.

Pain settled upon Delilah's pretty features as she read the letter. "He was a good friend," she said after a moment.

While Delilah and Grant shared a few reminiscences of the past, Dustin took a moment to study his aunt and uncle. He could hardly believe his uncle was in his mid-fifties, his aunt in her early forties. They were both youthful, slim and healthy. His uncle's hair was thick and pale, with only a scattering of gray at his temples. His aunt was as beautiful as the day he'd first seen her as a seven-year-old boy climbing down from a train in

216

Alexandria to begin a new life with a father he had never known. Dustin smiled to himself; he knew beyond a shadow of a doubt that their happiness and their love kept them young, and he prayed that he would be as happy with the woman he ultimately chose. If things went according to plan, he would have that love before year's end.

Momentarily, Delilah looked up and said quietly, "I do apologize, Dustin. Here we are reminiscing on the early days of the plantation as if you weren't even here. Won't you stay for supper?"

"As long as Mozelle's in a good mood."

Standing, Grant added his thoughts. "I think she's in a fair good mood."

"Oh, you two," interjected Delilah. "You're both being mean." But they weren't. Whenever Mozelle had a bone to pick with any member of the family — and it was usually the youthful Paul — she deliberately over-salted the first meal following the altercation. for that reason, everyone tried to remain on Mozelle's good side, since she was otherwise the best cook on the Boeuf. Slipping her arm around Dustin's waist, Delilah coaxed him toward the house. "I'll tell you what. We'll wait until after supper to tell Mozelle about Philbus . . . just in case it puts her in a bad mood." Over her shoulder, she called to Grant, "Don't be too long at Wellswood, dear." As she and Dustin moved toward the house, Delilah mentioned, "I'm surprised I didn't get a letter from Isabel this week."

Aimee Claire had forbidden Dustin to bring up the subject of Isabel in Grant's and Delilah's presence, since, in his young sister's words, "They were rightly concerned about their Isabel and emotional over the issue." But now, his aunt brought her up as easily as she might have brought up baking a cake, and she sounded not the least bit emotional or concerned. "How is my cousin doing, Aunt Dee?" he asked, moving with her

217

onto the steps of the gallery.

"Her letters are a trifle vague. Each seems to be exactly the same, except for a word or two. I had hoped Aunt Imogen would have kept her entertained."

"Imogen!" Dustin halted in place. "What do you mean? Isabel is in Shreveport, isn't she?"

Turning, Delilah gave her nephew a small laugh. "Wherever did you get such an idea?"

Dustin thought about it; until he knew what was going on it was best not to implicate Aimee Claire, from whom he had gotten his most recent information on Isabel. "I thought she was in Shreveport. I am mistaken, Aunt Dee."

"Well, of course, she isn't . . . unless she's left Imogen's house in New Orleans. Surely, Imogen would have let me know."

With a flourish, Dustin slapped his forehead with the palm of his hand. "Lordie me, Aunt, it's not Isabel I'm thinking about . . . I was just remembering that Miss Alice, who lives next door to Aimee Claire, has journeyed to Shreveport."

"I see . . ." Delilah grinned. "You must have that pretty girl you met in Boston on your mind."

"I must." Dustin let the matter rest. It was best not to alarm his aunt and uncle until he investigated the matter himself. He had promised his parents he would stay around and help them with the ledgers since half the Emerson herd of thoroughbreds would be sent to the auctions in the east by late April, but now, Dustin knew he would have to return to New Orleans. Grant and Delilah Emerson believed their daughter was still with Imogen — and his own little sister, Aimee Claire, had outright lied to him. Now Dustin would have to find out the truth for himself.

Good God, what was his impudent young cousin up to now? And where the hell was she?

No matter how deeply she burrowed into her sleeping bag, Isabel could not get away from the cold. A dark, foggy haze enveloped the clearing where she and Shadoe slept, and the fire was now little more than a few glowing embers against the darkness.

At least she wasn't hungry. Shadoe had purchased a piece of beef and two potatoes from a friendly Kiowa just before nightfall and had cooked it over the fire. Despite the lack of seasonings, Isabel could not remember ever having eaten such a good meal, and the water Shadoe had fetched from an underground stream had been clean and pure and cold. She'd saved a canteen of the water and had made them a cup of tea from the last dregs of the loose tea she had bought in Fort Smith.

Occasionally, a moonbeam would defy the overhanging fog of darkness and light the clearing, and Isabel would take the opportunity to look across at Shadoe. She knew he wasn't sleeping soundly — he never did — but there was no movement in his features to indicate he was awake. His black eyelashes fluttered only slightly, the cold wind tossed the single lock of hair that insisted on resting against his forehead, and the fingers of his right hand twitched like those of a man itching to go for his gun.

Despite his roughness and his many shortcomings, Isabel wanted nothing more at that moment than to be in his arms, to be sharing his bed roll with him and feeling the warmth of his breath evenly against her temple. She wanted to feel the taut strength of him against her palm, to touch the coarse mat of hair across the broad expanse of his chest. She wanted to become one with him, as she had that night in Natchez —

A single shot rang out. Simultaneously, Shadoe and Isabel shot forward in their bedrolls and Shadoe's hand instinctively went for his gun. But the shot echoed . . . echoed . . . echoed . . . until nothing was left but a dim thud through the region. Shadoe relaxed, sure that the shot had been fired at least five miles away.

But now he was awake. Looking across at Isabel, he drew up his knees, then dropped his wrists across them. He said nothing, but she knew he watched her like a hungry old wolf staking out its next meal . . . and it wasn't at all a flattering thought.

Thus, she growled, "Don't you look at me like that, Shadoe McCaine. I'm causing you no trouble, and you've no need to be distressed with me. So—" Turning her back to him, she eased down into her bedroll once again. "Good night!"

With stolid indifference, he replied, "And good night to you."

Shadoe made no attempt whatsoever to return to his slumber. His gaze cut across the darkness to where the horses grazed, only the mare tethered. Occasionally, Mirlo nickered into the gloomy darkness, almost a taunt to any threat toward the mare he circled and protected. Twice he had trotted up to where Shadoe had slept and had nuzzled his master's face. He returned to Shadoe now, lowering his head to have it rubbed.

As Mirlo withdrew to the clearing, Shadoe's attention was once again drawn to Isabel. She had dragged in a short, deep breath and he saw her slim form grow taut beneath the thick fabric of the bedroll. She was suddenly so still she might have been made of marble, and Shadoe wondered if a nightmare had captured her renewed moment of sleep. He was genuinely concerned.

Across the short expanse of space separating him, he asked, "Are you all right, Isabel?"

She did not reply. Shadoe shrugged; she must be asleep.

Though numb with fear, Isabel couldn't help but notice that the creature was beautiful. Its red-brown back stripe rippled as it coiled; the dark stripes behind its

220

small eyes were almost alive by themselves. The loosely interlocking segments of its rattle produced a low buzzing noise, and as it coiled more tightly and lifted its rattle higher into the air, Isabel slowly opened her mouth and attempted to speak.

She had heard Shadoe ask her if she was all right. *Of course, I'm not all right,* she had thought. *There's a blasted rattlesnake in my bedroll!* But all she could do was stiffen her body and try ever so hard not to move.

Between her narrowly parted lips she whispered harshly, "Shadoe . . . Shadoe—" but received no answer. When the wide head of the snake pivoted slowly to the right and its beady eyes turned toward her left hand, she attempted to ease her right from its perch atop her hip. If only she could jab against the back of her bedroll, Shadoe might see that something was wrong.

But he apparently noticed none of her jabbing, since he did not jump to her rescue, and now the deadly creature was rolling across her elbow as if it belonged there. Isabel became so tense she was sure her bones would never again unlock at their joints. She tried again to call "Shadoe . . . Shadoe—" but managed only an indistinguishable whisper.

Then the creature began moving toward the opening of her bedroll, and when its forked tongue was mere inches from her cheek, she said a small prayer. *This is it . . . I am about to die . . . and, blast it, with a man who is supposed to be protecting me not ten feet away!* The deepest kind of fear tunneled through her, as she realized her death was very close at hand.

Even as she might inwardly have cursed him, Shadoe had very cautiously slid from his bedroll and was moving toward Isabel. When he stood just behind her, his ebony gaze adjusting to the deeper darkness of her bedroll, he spied the snake. As his heart pounded fiercely, he eased to his knees and his right hand moved stealthily across Isabel's shoulder. In one swift dash he had pinched the rattler's lowered head firmly between his thumb and index finger and slung the deadly beast as far as his might would allow.

Instantly, Isabel shot from the bedroll and performed what might, under normal circumstances, have been viewed as a rather comical dance. But Shadoe saw the pallor of fear in her wide-eyed stare, and the hysteria with which she raked her hands through the midnight darkness. As he held her tightly to him, her senses reeled back like a mighty blow and she screamed against the fabric of his shirt, the screams instantly becoming sobs which wracked her body.

Then, when she was calm, when Shadoe's hand was gently caressing her back beneath her coat, when his breath was sweet and warm against her cheek, she stood back from him as if nothing had happened. The softness in her eyes did not match the cold detachment in her voice as she quietly said, "I'm all right now." And by way of explanation, "I just don't like snakes."

"As well you shouldn't," Shadoe responded evenly. "That could have been a very deadly encounter."

Isabel turned away, then tucked her hands into the pockets of her jacket. "Thank you . . . it seems you are always rescuing me."

Shadoe approached, his hands moving up to enfold her shoulders. Brushing his mouth against her pale hairline, he murmured huskily, "Let's call a truce, Isabel. No more tense moments. No more looking at each other as though we wanted to kill. We're together for a very long trip and we could make it pleasant, couldn't we?"

Isabel sighed deeply. Of course, she wondered how sincere were his words. He was the one who had been tense, unpredictable, and indifferent. She'd tried every way she could these past few weeks to draw him out of that deplorable shell he had tucked himself into. She thought she had accomplished that the night they'd made love in Natchez, and though it had been wonderful for her, he had treated it as one forgettable encounter in many. Her feelings had been hurt—were hurt—and she was not sure she could simply overlook the past weeks and go on as though everything was smooth and wonderful between them.

But—again, she sighed—she would like nothing better. Turning, managing the smallest of smiles, she stepped into his arms. "We'll give it a try, Shadoe. And one day . . . one day perhaps . . . you will trust me and believe in me. Perhaps one day you will see that I'm a normal, red-blooded woman who wants to be treated like a human being. I have never set myself up on a pedestal, and I hope you will stop treating me like someone you deplore. I'm just a simple girl with simple needs, who wants to bring her brother home to the Boeuf where he belongs. Yes . . . we'll try to make this trip pleasant."

Shadoe had listened very intently. How well she had read him these past weeks of traveling. Had his inner turmoil been like a mirror to her? Had she seen everything? Involuntarily, he shuddered, and when she looked up cautiously, he said, "It's blasted cold. How about if you pull your bedroll over near mine and we'll keep a watch out for those blasted snakes together?"

Drawing slightly away, Isabel hesitated to break physical contact. "All right."

Shadoe watched her move the few feet away and cautiously pick up the corner of her bedroll, then shake it vigorously.

He made a silent vow to himself. He would try to put his past where it belonged, far behind him, and go on with the future. He wanted Isabel in that future, and he had treated her deplorably these many days they had been together. Tonight would be a new beginning.

Tonight, the conflict was over, and they would go forward together. Shadoe groaned inwardly. He had done something he had sworn seven years ago he would never do. He had fallen in love.

Fourteen

Isabel threw herself full upon the bed, caring little about the dust that gusted up and then resettled slowly about her. They had found the small, recently abandoned cabin up the bank from the Cimarron River in southern Kansas, and Shadoe had promised a two-day rest stop before they resumed their journey northward toward Montana. Of all the luxuries she could imagine enjoying, none pleased her more than being able to wear lady's clothing for two whole days. She silently swore that when she returned home to the Boeuf she would never again wish to wear men's trousers, regardless of their practicality. If she learned nothing else from the trip, she had at least learned to enjoy her femininity.

Despite the change for the better in Shadoe's disposition, this past week had been especially lonely, since the week between Christmas Eve and New Year's Eve were very happy times for the Emerson family. Isabel was sure that boxes of gifts had been sent to New Orleans . . . which she hoped Golda had successfully intercepted . . . and her own gifts, purchased the day before she and Shadoe had left New Orleans, should have reached her family by Christmas Day. Though she and Shadoe had mended their difficulties before Christmas, he had made no mention of the holiday, and her efforts to draw him into reminiscences of Christmases past for both of them had proved quite futile. He was still reluctant to speak of a past with a half-breed renegade father, but surely there must have been happy Christmases with his mother. He had spoken so fondly of her on the rare occasions he had mentioned her. There was his adult past, too, that he was secretive about; Isabel still held out hope that one day he would trust her enough to confide in her.

Christmas was behind them now, and tomorrow was the beginning of a new year. Isabel was reasonably sure that it would prove to be the best year in her life, and in the lives of the Emerson family. Bathing in the warmth of her hopes and dreams, she returned her attentions to the activities of her dark-clothed companion and lover.

By fall of night, Shadoe had stoked up a healthy fire in the brick grate, and delightful warmth permeated the cabin. When Isabel began flicking a cloth over the few items of dusty furniture that had been left behind by the previous occupants, a laughing Shadoe exclaimed, "We're not setting up house, Isabel, and I believe we can tolerate the dust for a couple of days." Then he had swooped her into his arms, disengaging the bit of cloth from her fingers, and growled against her cheek, "How about plasterin' them purty lips right here—" With playful teasing, Shadoe eased his mouth into an exaggerated pucker.

Sharing in his laughter and his teasing affection, Isabel touched her mouth to his, then flit from his arms like an excited wood sprite. "Shadoe McCaine, don't you get feisty . . . and don't you get any ideas. Why—" Touching her palm gently to her almost-healed right thigh, she forced a most pained look upon her oval features, "my leg is still awfully sore from that fall I took down the hill."

Shadoe threw himself heavily onto a divan, instantly protesting the exposed spring that raked against his leg. Then he dropped his head back and peered at her from beneath the fringes of his thick, dark lashes. "Well, ma'am . . . I saw that purty leg just yesterday and as I recall, it looked just fine to me."

Recalling the sport they'd been engaged in when he had seen her thigh, crimson flushed Isabel's cheeks and she dropped to the divan beside Shadoe. Her hand gently caressed his chest beneath the fabric of his shirt. "Shadoe, these past few days have been delightful. *You* have been delightful," she emphasized, touching her index finger to the cleft in his chin. "Sometimes I think you're two different people —"

"Oh —" A dark eyebrow shot upwards. "And which one of them do you like best?"

Snow was again beginning to fall beyond the one small window looking out toward the south. Lurching up, Isabel shot to the window, and her fingers clamped over the thin board upon which the window closed. "Oh, look, Shadoe . . . 'little snowflakes from above/fall upon this land we love —' "

Shadoe chuckled. "You're going to recite poetry, eh, little one?" Rising, his slow, methodical footsteps closed the distance between them. When he stood behind her, his hands rose to caress a path down her arms, and in their final ascent embraced and massaged her shoulders. "Well, I can recite poetry, too. 'Tonight, I might be happy, love/for a moment, maybe two/if I can look around, my love/and catch a glimpse of you/A single glance, a moment, love/could take me through each day/when thoughts of

love and happiness/might carry me away. . . .' "
Slowly, Shadoe turned Isabel to him. His voice became a husky, adoring whisper. " 'And just a glance of me, my love/I hope that it might seem/that in this moment, you might share, my momentary dream.' "

Tears flooded Isabel's eyes, and rather than allow emotion to spoil their tender gathering, she sank into his embrace. "What are you saying, Shadoe? That you love me? That you want me to share your life?"

Shadoe dragged in a long, ragged sigh, his hands rising to caress her back. He wanted to make a commitment . . . and a confession . . . but he felt it was too soon. Thus, he collected his thoughts, then replied, "I was simply reciting poetry, Isabel . . . very bad poetry, at that," and in an effort to maintain the euphoria existing between them, he vowed softly, "but when I let down that blasted barrier you say I've built around myself, you will be the woman I allow inside."

"And no other, Shadoe?" she murmured. Pressing her cheek lightly against the fullness of his mouth, Isabel instantly felt the most gentle of kisses.

"My God, Isabel . . ." He stepped back and smiled devilishly. "You mean, there *are* other women in the world? I thought they'd all ceased to exist." Taking still another step back, Shadoe pivoted toward his saddle case. "By the way, my Southern belle, do you know what tomorrow is?"

She smiled. "It is the first day of the New Year . . . 1880 . . . the last year of another decade in our lives."

He fumbled a moment in the case, then returned to her with a small, brightly wrapped package. "Since I didn't get you anything for Christmas, I give you a New Year's gift to bring you good luck."

With childlike charm, Isabel took the package he held out. "For me, Shadoe? Oh, but I didn't get anything for you!"

"That is because—" His smile broadened, "you had only a little money, and you spent that on necessities for the trip."

Flinging her head to disengage her hair from the collar of her white blouse, Isabel dropped to the edge of the bed. "What is it, Shadoe? It's too beautifully wrapped to open. When did you purchase it? I didn't see you—"

Instantly, Shadoe's finger pressed to her mouth to halt her chattering, then he sat beside her and draped his arm across her shoulder. Though he had paid to have it wrapped at the trading post near Wolf Creek, he would not spoil the mood by confessing that the brooch was booty won in a poker game back in New Orleans. He'd been carrying it, carefully wrapped in paper, in a deep compartment of his wallet. "It was wrapped to be opened, and if you don't open it, I'm not telling you what it is."

Hesitating only enough to emphasize her pleasure, Isabel began to unwrap the small package, carefully removing a small satin bow and unfolding the tissue-thin paper. Soon a small box of rose-colored velvet rested in her palm, and she looked briefly into Shadoe's dark eyes before she returned her gaze to the gift. When she finally opened the box, she breathed a long sigh and her fingers began to tremble as she took up the exquisite piece of jewelry it contained.

"Shadoe . . . Shadoe, how could anyone afford something like this?" Her gaze picked across the basket-shaped brooch of diamonds and rubies set in silver and gold, its stylized blooms and leafage obvi-

229

ously of a seventeenth-century origin. The larger diamonds and rubies were rose-cut and sparkled, she was sure, as magnificently as the delight in her eyes. "It's so expensive . . . it's so old—" Then she threw herself into Shadoe's arms and hugged him tightly. "Dare I accept it?"

"Dare you crush my feelings by refusing it?" he responded in return. "Just don't wear it in front of grizzled old fellas who might want to snatch it off you. I'd break the arms of each and every one if they so much as touched you—"

"Why, Shadoe McCaine," she teased, drawing back so that her pale gaze could dance for his dark one, "I do believe that green monster named jealousy has grabbed you up again—"

In one swift move, Shadoe rose, took Isabel's hand and pulled her against him. Then his hand went behind her skirts at the knees and he swept her into his arms. "I've given you a gift," he murmured huskily, taking the brooch and tossing it to the divan behind him, "now it is time for you to give me mine."

Without prelude, without those teasing moments they enjoyed undressing each other, Shadoe and Isabel lay naked in each other's arms. With unrestrained passion, her dark wolf dragged her across his body, then turned and joined to her in a mixture of impatience and intoxicating skill. The cabin had become almost hot, and as Shadoe's hands gently cupped Isabel's cool features, he felt that he himself had reached the same fevered pitch. He had not moved within her, but enjoyed the warmth of her womanhood surrounding him.

"God . . . what a woman you are!" he growled, beginning a series of teasing kisses at her mouth and over the soft curves of her lovely features. Then

230

his caresses became hungry and demanding, and she responded with equal intensity. When he began to move within her, slowly at first, she arched her hips to accept the complete and abandoned fullness of him. Nuzzling against his mouth, trailing her own sweet kisses over his passion-dampened flesh, she entwined her slim legs among his firm, muscular ones.

"Do you love me, Shadoe?" she whispered, nipping playfully at his earlobe.

"What do you think?"

"I think that you do."

"Then think as you will. I will deny nothing."

Though vaguely noncommittal, Isabel did, indeed, read his reply as her heart wished, and she savored every delicious moment of his erotic movements against her, within her, his gentle palms bathing every inch of her passion-warmed flesh and arousing it to wondrous frenzy. She loved the way his eyes raked her lustfully, admiringly, then connected to her own gaze, the mirrors of his love and adoration—equal, she was sure, to that which she felt for him. He could speak with calm detachment, but she knew he loved her; he could growl his noncommitments, but she heard his heart. She wanted only to enjoy the erotic torment of his body against the delicate spread of her hips . . . a kittenish moan escaped her mouth at each near-exit, a groan of sweet, wicked delight at each pounding of his loins at the juncture of her thighs.

When at last, he lay exhausted above her, his strength robbed from him by the fever of his quest . . . only then did he feel the violent quaking of her own body against their joining, and he looked up and grinned.

"I believe this might have been the best ever," he

teased. "I do believe I'm good for you, Isabel—"

"You are wonderful for me," she murmured in her own sweet exhaustion, her fingers rising limply to the recalcitrant lock to sweep it back. "I cannot imagine spending the long hours of night without you—"

He forced a most severe darkness over his features. "Oh? Is that all you want from me? A good tumble beneath the sheets?" Laughing, Isabel flexed her intimate muscles over the evidence of his still-hardened manhood. He groaned in delicious torment. "Hell, woman . . . what are you trying to do to me?" and he instantly withdrew, lest she choose to continue her torture. Propping himself on his side, Shadoe's finger drew a circle around her damp navel, then moved teasingly over the flat plane of her belly, and back up, to circle her breasts before he gave each one a brief kiss. "You are so beautiful, Isabel . . . the most beautiful woman I have ever seen free of the restrictions of clothing."

"And I suppose you've seen many?" she asked with a note of jealousy.

"Hundreds . . . thousands . . ." he said, and when her features pinched to add emphasis to her jealousy, he laughed: "No . . . tens of thousands."

"Well—" Isabel shrugged as if it didn't matter one way or the other. "If you admitted to having seen only one or two others, then it would not be such a compliment that you consider me the prettiest. But, since it might have been tens of thousands"—Only now did she allow the graveness to leave her features—"then . . . my goodness . . . what a compliment you have bestowed on me!"

One of those familiar little mischiefs crept to the corner of Shadoe's ample mouth. Slowly, erotically his hand lowered to cover her belly. "What would

232

you do, Isabel . . . if a child began to grow here."

Did he think she hadn't considered it? Isabel raised a pale eyebrow. "I suppose I'd have to polish up on mothering duties," she responded, undaunted by the possibility that her firm, youthful figure might bloom. "And I would certainly hope that the rascal who planted his seed would not abandon me."

"I would not," Shadoe responded, the sweetest reminiscences softening his features as he imagined himself a father. "I would hope the child would be a daughter — a pretty, pale-haired child like her mother. I would insist that she wear lace and frills and flounces . . . and yet she would have to be a good horsewoman. She would be able to defeat a man with her feminine wiles . . . and lay him out flat with a good punch if he took liberties —"

Isabel laughed softly. "Listen to yourself, Shadoe. Why, you'd think I *was* with child. You'd think you were even now waiting outside the birthing chamber for your blessed event to be placed in your arms. Why, Shadoe McCaine, you're nothing but a softie!"

He grinned, his fingers moving up to gently pinch her chin. "Can't a man dream? Can't he wish for the very best that life has to offer?" Then, strangely, a bitter line etched along Shadoe's sharp jawline, and his eyes narrowed. "But dare I dream of enjoying the blessing of a son or daughter?" he asked with husky anger.

"Whatever do you mean?"

"I'd imagine that by the time your father got finshed with me I wouldn't be in a condition to enjoy iving, much less fatherhood."

Suddenly, all the moments of the past came rushng back at her: the moments when they had enoyed each other's company and he had become nean and nasty without provocation; that day in

233

the parlor of Aunt Imogen's house on Royal, when he had abruptly departed, giving no explanation. "Is that what is troubling you, Shadoe? The fact that I have a father who cares about me?" When her hand rose to his cheek, he roughly took it and pressed it to his heart. "Is that it, Shadoe? Have you suffered a brutal encounter with another woman's father at some point in your past?"

Dragging up the one blanket to cover their bodies, Shadoe began to speak in a low, graveled tone. "Her name was Venetia Mendez. I worked on her father's ranch in West Texas, and she was everything evil, everything wicked, and everything a man should avoid." When Isabel's mouth parted and he thought she would interrupt, Shadoe quickly drew his index finger to his mouth to hush her. "And I did avoid her, Isabel. I avoided her like a man avoiding the black plague, but she tormented me like a dagger with a soul of its own. No matter where I turned she was there, taunting me, attempting to seduce me, . . . throwing her charms at me until I thought I would be sick at the very sight of her. One morning I was saddling my horse in the stables, preparing to join the other men who were bringing in stragglers. And she was there—beautiful, dark-haired, dark-eyed Venetia, emerging from the darkness of the stable, dragging up her skirts to show me that she wore nothing underneath . . . and with her other hand she caressed her own breasts beneath a blouse as thin as gauze. When I ignored her she became like an enraged animal, tearing at me—tearing at herself. When I attempted to mount my horse she screamed—screamed like a woman being brutally murdered and I attempted to stop the horrid pitch of her screams with the palm of my hand." Raising his hand for Isabel to see, he said, "See that mark? That is where she sank her perfect white teeth into me. The only way I could get her off me was to strike her: the first—and last—time I have struck a woman. I was finally able to mount my horse and I rode out of there as fast as I could hightail it. I figured she'd run to her old man with stories, so I was going to wait till he calmed down enough that I could tell him the truth. Hell, I didn't know what Venetia was capable of then—" Shadoe shrugged, disengaging the blanket covering his shoulder. "But I learned."

When he hesitated, and his thick eyebrows furrowed thoughtfully, Isabel asked, "Did she cause you trouble after that?"

Shadoe laughed sardonically, and his hand came up to gently massage her shoulder when she turned to face him. "Did she ever. After I rode out—and I heard this from one of the young fellows—she ran into her father's house with her clothing ripped from her and related to him how I had attacked her in the stable and raped her."

"My God. Is that why you have a reward on your head?"

"A private reward, but a reward nonetheless, and one that many men would give their eyeteeth to collect." Closing his eyes for the briefest of moments, he continued, "The fellow named Chaps, who had been with Mendez that morning, immediately rode out to the range to tell me what had happened. Mendez was in a seething rage and he had gotten a few of the men together. They were going to hang me out there. But I rode out as fast as my horse could scat, and the next I heard, Mendez had put a private bounty of five thousand dollars on my head . . . dead or alive." Grinning without mirth, Shadoe mused, "That's quite a price on the head of a man who didn't do a damn thing, isn't it? And this is quite a tale, huh, little woman?"

"It's a horrid tale, Shadoe," Isabel pouted, snuggling against her dark wolf's naked chest. "That Venetia Mendez should be horsewhipped! It is no wonder you hate rich girls . . . and their rich fathers."

"It wasn't just what she did to get me run off her father's ranch. There was—" He hesitated, his eyebrows pinching together as he gained a moment of calm. "I was sweet on a girl named Mary Ellen, whose pa had a small spread just east of the Mendez place. Two days after the incident with Venetia in the barn—and while I was still hiding out—Mary Ellen was found dead in a small pond. Sheriff said she drowned, but . . . I know Venetia killed her. There were marks on her neck. Sheriff said it was caused by the necklace she wore. I say it was Venetia's hands." He forced a smile, but it was one without feeling. "So, now you know why I'm leery of rich girls." Shadoe touched his mouth in a gentle kiss to Isabel's forehead. "But I am no longer leery of you, Isabel, and I certainly don't hate you."

"But you did for a while," she argued without feeling.

"For a while. I still expect your father's going to be none too pleased with me when he finds out what you—what we've done," he quickly amended.

Isabel smiled in gentle reminiscence. "He's going to love you, Shadoe, when our Eduard is back at Shadows-in-the-Mist and he has you to thank for it. A thought came to Isabel and she looked into Shadoe's dark, warm eyes. "If you have a price on your head, then . . . can I assume that Shadoe Mc Caine is not your name?"

"Bold as a cockade I am. Refused to change m"

name, even if it meant my life." Shadoe smiled broadly. "But if I did have another name, what do you reckon it would be?"

"I don't know . . . ummm, how about, Jerico Jenkins?"

He chuckled, attempting to put the vicious image of Venetia Mendez out of his mind. "Nah. How about Clarence Mayhew?"

She playfully slapped his chest. "Doesn't suit you!"

"Mortimer Sootyfoos."

Then she looked deeply into those sensuous eyes and moved her fingers in a gentle caress over his relaxed features. "You look like a Shadoe McCaine to me."

"I *am* Shadoe McCaine. And . . . I want you."

"Horsefeathers! You have me!"

"No—" Gently, he took her hand and placed it over his hard loins. "I *want* you, Isabel. Now . . . again—" And when she smiled, her own lusty gaze giving him all the confession he needed that she wanted him as much, he raked off the offending blanket and positioned himself between her hot, willing thighs.

With expertise and masculine endurance, he spent the better part of an hour bringing his wild winter flower to the ultimate pinnacle of pleasure and fantasy.

When the two travelers eventually rode away from the cabin, Isabel wished that she could box it up and take it with her. She'd spent the best two days of her life in the simple, rustic cabin beside the Cimarron, and she wished she could relive them over and over again. Her hands resting lightly over the pommel of her saddle, she watched the weath-

237

ered structure disappear into the distance behind her. With a whimsical sigh, she tucked the cherished memories deep into her heart, to borrow for reassurance in the future should Shadoe's mood become dark and grim.

A crisp layer of snow blanketed the forest and gray, overcast day hinted that more might be on its way. But Isabel did not plan to feel the chill and the bitter cold of the Kansas winter. Her love for Shadoe McCaine — her dark wolf — warmed her through and through.

For many days they traveled, leaving town after town, meeting the strangest array of people Isabel had ever imagined. She hadn't realized how protected she had been in her Louisiana environment, exposed to the gentle life of the plantation and the rollicking life of New Orleans with a doting old aunt as her tutor and chaperone.

As the days stretched into weeks, and they began to travel a section of the old Mormon trail that paralleled a Platte River tributary called Lodgepole Creek, Isabel began to feel the tightness of anticipation as she realized her brother was just one state away. Shadoe attempted to divert her often melancholy thoughts by giving her a history of the area and pointing out the weathered residue of the Mormons' terrible journey toward Utah, but the only thing that could get a deep hold was her beloved little brother. Soon she would see him; that was all that mattered.

But was it, indeed? Something else mattered very much to Isabel. She wanted Shadoe McCaine. She wanted his confession of love and his commitment to be her life mate; she wanted to take him back to Shadows-in-the-Mist and say to her father, "This is the man I love and I insist that you accept him."

But would it ever happen? These past weeks of traveling had gone too smoothly. Could she hope to accomplish her mission, find her brother at the road ranch on Tongue River and return to the Shadows, unscathed by the long journey, and with Shadoe McCaine still at her side? It all seemed too simple, too pat; she couldn't imagine an uneventful trip and accomplishing all her ends without some degree of difficulty.

"Look over there—" Startled from her deep thoughts, Isabel followed the direction of Shadoe's outstretched arm, her gaze locking to the remains of what appeared to be several weathered and broken down carts of some kind. "Some years ago, several thousand Mormon emigrants came this way," he told her, "pushing their baggage in those handcarts. They were too poor to afford wagons and draft animals."

"How dreadful," said Isabel, who could not shake her thoughts away from her lost brother and the narrowing distance between them.

"Blizzards paralyzed them and disease ravaged their exhausted bodies," Shadoe continued. "Those broken carts are evidence of the repeated Indian attacks they suffered."

"How do you know all this?" asked Isabel.

"I read a lot," he admitted. "Bet you didn't know that?" Turning in his saddle, Shadoe grinned pleasantly. "But you're not in a mood for a history lesson, are you, little woman?"

She shrugged, casting her eyes downward. "I am a bit preoccupied," she admitted.

Drawing up his horse, Shadoe quickly dismounted, then put his hands up to help her down. A cold north wind was blowing, and she had to catch her long scarf before the wind whipped it from her head. But her gloved hands felt frozen in place and she could scarcely manage to move them at all. Taking her hand, Shadoe moved with her onto a trail of the forest, and scarcely a hundred yards farther they entered a wide ravine. Here, the wind did not blow. It was not nearly so cold, and Isabel welcomed the fire that Shadoe spent only a few minutes putting together.

Sinking to her knees, Isabel waved her gloved hands over the golden flames. "When we return to Louisiana, I don't plan to ever leave again," she said, looking across at Shadoe, who was warming his own hands. "I've never spent so many days being frozen through to the bone in all my life. Why—" Apparently, she did not see the dark, thoughtful look that passed over Shadoe's face. "Do you know that during a typical Louisiana winter, we might have less than a week of truly cold days? And then . . . they are nothing like this!"

Dropping his hands to his thighs, Shadoe became thoughtful for a moment. Isabel was so sure he would return to Louisiana with her. Did he dare believe he deserved the love of such a beautiful, sensual woman as his Isabel? Shadoe liked to think his luck might be changing.

They were surrounded by a great stand of Ponderosa pine, and Shadoe decided it would be a good place to spend the approaching night. He remembered seeing a stream just before they entered the ravine, and now he rose to his feet, took his and Isabel's canteens from their saddles, and moved off to fill them with fresh water. Just before he exited the ravine, he turned. He watched Isabel for a moment as she warmed her hands over the flames, then again began to put distance between them. He couldn't worry about the future, nor whether he de

MORE PASSION AND ADVENTURE AWAIT... YOUR TRIP TO A BIG ADVENTUROUS WORLD BEGINS WHEN YOU ACCEPT YOUR FIRST 4 NOVELS ABSOLUTELY *FREE* (AN $18.00 VALUE)

Accept your Free gift and start to experience more of the passion and adventure you like in a historical romance novel. Each Zebra novel is filled with proud men, spirited women and tempetuous love that you'll remember long after you turn the last page

Zebra Historical Romances are the finest novels of their kind. They are written by authors who really know how to weave tales of romance and adventure in the historical settings you love. You'll feel like you've actually gone back in time with the thrilling stories that each Zebra novel offers.

GET YOUR FREE GIFT WITH THE START OF YOUR HOME SUBSCRIPTION

Our readers tell us that these books sell out very fast in book stores and often they miss the newest titles. So Zebra has made arrangements for you to receive the four newest novels published each month.

You'll be guaranteed that you'll never miss a title, and home delivery is so convenient. And to show you just how easy it is to get Zebra Historical Romances, we'll send you your first 4 books absolutely FREE! Our gift to you just for trying our home subscription service.

BIG SAVINGS AND FREE HOME DELIVERY

Each month, you'll receive the four newest titles as soon as they are published. You'll probably receive them even before the bookstores do. What's more, you may preview these exciting novels free for 10 days. If you like them as much as we think you will, just pay the low preferred subscriber's price of just $3.75 each. *You'll save $3.00 each month off the publisher's price.* AND, your savings are even greater because there are never any shipping, handling or other hidden charges—FREE Home Delivery. Of course you can return any shipment within 10 days for full credit, no questions asked. There is no minimum number of books you must buy.

4 FREE BOOKS

TO GET YOUR 4 FREE BOOKS WORTH $18.00 — MAIL IN THE FREE BOOK CERTIFICATE T O D A Y

Fill in the Free Book Certificate below, and we'll send your FREE BOOKS to you as soon as we receive it.

If the certificate is missing below, write to: Zebra Home Subscription Service, Inc., P.O. Box 5214, 120 Brighton Road, Clifton, New Jersey 07015-5214.

FREE BOOK CERTIFICATE

4 FREE BOOKS

ZEBRA HOME SUBSCRIPTION SERVICE, INC.

YES! Please start my subscription to Zebra Historical Romances and send me my first 4 books absolutely FREE. I understand that each month I may preview four new Zebra Historical Romances free for 10 days. If I'm not satisfied with them, I may return the four books within 10 days and owe nothing. Otherwise, I will pay the low preferred subscriber's price of just $3.75 each; a total of $15.00, *a savings off the publisher's price of $3.00.* I may return any shipment and I may cancel this subscription at any time. There is no obligation to buy any shipment and there are no shipping, handling or other hidden charges. Regardless of what I decide, the four free books are mine to keep.

NAME

ADDRESS _____ APT

CITY _____ STATE ___ ZIP

( )
TELEPHONE

SIGNATURE _____ (if under 18, parent or guardian must sign)

Terms, offer and prices subject to change without notice. Subscription subject to acceptance by Zebra Books. Zebra Books reserves the right to reject any order or cancel any subscription.

ZB0693

erved Isabel. He wanted to enjoy each day he
pent with her and let destiny take them where it
nay.

When he returned to their hastily chosen camp
ome minutes later, he found that Isabel had erected
 lean-to out of some gathered tree limbs and two
f their blankets. She also had sliced a sausage and
vo potatoes in their only cooking utensil and was
poking it over the fire. The sausage sizzled in the
an, and the aroma of the food, which he'd pur-
hased some days ago, wafted up to greet him as he
ropped to his knees.

"Damn, that smells good!" he remarked, bending
ver to take a slice of the sausage and immediately
aving his hand slapped with the wooden spoon.

"It's still frozen, Shadoe McCaine. Exercise a
ttle patience, will you?" She had spoken sharply,
ut with underlying softness, and when he stuck the
lapped finger in his mouth, she smiled prettily.
Oh, now I didn't hit it that hard, you big baby!"

Dropping to his knees, Shadoe sat there for a
noment, staring at Isabel as if he'd never seen her
efore. When she cast him a questioning glance, he
xplained, "I was thinking how good you've been on
his trip. Despite the cold, you have not com-
lained. When meals are scarce, you say you are
ot hungry. I just never expected you to have such
ndurance, to be so good to travel with—"

"And . . ." With a small laugh, Isabel shook a
nger toward him, "I've been an enjoyable compan-
on . . . especially at night."

He grinned. "That you have, my little Creole.
Iell, you can heat up a night faster than those
ames there."

Returning her attentions to the sausage and pota-
oes, she warned, "Don't you tease me, Shadoe Mc-

Caine . . . or you're liable to get burned."

"Promise?"

With a small sigh, Isabel put their playful bantering aside, and her features grew serious. "We're behind schedule, aren't we, Shadoe? You thought we would be at Tongue River by now."

"I should have allowed for the weather," he responded regretfully. "Yes, we're about four weeks behind schedule. I imagine it'll take that long to cross the mountain ranges of Wyoming. And if we get hemmed in by a blizzard, Isabel . . . Well, I just don't want to think about that."

"Hopefully, what happened to George Donner and his party in the Sierra Nevadas will not happen to us. And, if it does—" Scooting on her knees around the fire toward him, she bent forward and promised, "I won't gobble you up if you die and leave me snowbound."

With feigned seriousness, he responded, "Drat, and I was counting on it." A husky whisper entered his voice as though they were surrounded by people and he wanted only her to hear him say, "I love being inside you."

Dropping the frying pan noisily to the ground, Isabel allowed herself to be dragged into Shadoe's strong arms. Then his mouth made arousing contact with her own, and for the moment, the sausage and potatoes were forgotten.

Fifteen

Shadoe quickly drew his Isabel into a vortex of happiness—so deeply that she forgot the anxiety that had held her captive these past few days. His love and warmth chased away the fear that she might reach Tongue River and learn that the young man who had lured her away from Louisiana had pulled the cruelest of jokes and wasn't her brother at all. The physical evidence—the pencil rubbing of the old medallion—had temporarily lost its persuasiveness, and she worried that she had done something her parents could never condone. If she did not have a long, lost brother to show the family, how could she expect her parents to ever trust her again?

At the moment, Shadoe was concerned only with the hunger pangs in his stomach. He had taken their two plates from his saddle case and was preparing to divide the potatoes and sausage equally between them when a crackle echoed through the ravine. Shooting up from his knees, Shadoe swiftly drew his weapon, his palm resting on the cock for rapid fire.

Isabel stood slightly behind him, hugging her thick coat. A figure began to emerge from the darkness beyond the perimeters of their camp fire, and a pair of arms shot into the air. A gruff voice called out, "Don't shoot, mister . . . just hungry. You got enough of food?"

Isabel had thought that a man was approaching,

243

but as the figure stepped into the light emitting from their campfire, Isabel faced a large-boned woman clad in a rabbit-skin robe. She looked like a statue of dark marble, whose rough, sharply chiseled features had not been rounded and softened by the sculptor's tools. A few wisps of straight, black hair escaped the confines of a tattered scarf, and her massive hands strained against the fabric of her equally tattered gloves. Though she was an unprepossessing figure, she looked harmless, and Isabel quietly said, "If she's hungry, Shadoe, we should share."

Shadoe certainly didn't mind sharing food with a hungry person, but he remained on his guard. After all, what was she doing in the middle of nowhere, alone. When he hesitated, the big-boned woman drew up the fringes of her rabbit-skin robe, exclaiming, "Look, mister, no gun," then turned, showing him her back. Shadoe relaxed, but kept his guard, and the woman again asked, "You got enough of tha food?"

Isabel smiled hesitantly, then stepped to Shadoe's side. "If there isn't enough, we will cook up some more."

"How much you got?" the woman asked briskly.

"We have plenty—" Cutting Isabel off, the woman turned and gave a shrill whistle through her teeth. Instantly, a half-dozen children, the oldest about eight, rushed up to hug the woman's skirt and pee shyly at Isabel and Shadoe. "Oh, dear," said Isabel softly to Shadoe, "do we have *that* much food?"

"I think we can scratch up enough," said Shadoe.

And the woman, hearing him, peeled a dead rab bit from the loose tie of her skirt and threw it acros to Shadoe. "You cook this up, mister. Still fresh; bo caught today but nothing to build fire."

Isabel outstretched her arm. "Please . . . brin your children close to the fire."

Despite her massive build, hard features, and rough demeanor, the woman was gentle with the children. A softness came to her brusque voice as she said, "Go on, children . . . the white people be kind." While the quiet, reserved children warmed their hands, Isabel collected napkins from her saddlebag, since they didn't have enough plates and began to share the sausage and potatoes seven ways. The woman quickly raised her hand. "Divide six ways. Woman wait."

"When is the last time you've eaten?" asked Isabel, following the woman's direction.

"Two days ago abouts. Just before knocked old man in head and run off with babies."

"Oh?" Alarm flashed in Isabel's eyes and she asked with noticeable hesitation, "Did you kill him?"

"No kill," said the woman without malice, squatting beside the fire and watching her children eat. "Old man, he say trade for new squaw. I go back to father's house."

"You're Indian?"

"Paiute . . . born and took to wife in California. Old man, he white."

"A blue-eyed white," observed Isabel, looking at the faces of two blue-eyed children among the dark-eyed ones. Then she looked across at a silent Shadoe, keeping on his guard as he cleaned and gutted the rabbit, before returning her attentions to the Indian woman. "What is your name?" she asked.

"Name don't matter. Husband call me Squaw Woman. It good enough. But little ones—" Her face softened with pride. "Boy, oldest one, he Autumn, he youngest one, he August, and girls, they be Spring, Winter, Summer, April." Then she grinned pleasantly at Isabel and asked, "You like names?"

"I like them very much. Your children are beautiful."

"Good children," said the woman, nodding. "Boy, he catch rabbit. Wait long time over rabbit hole and when rabbit peer out—" The woman made a rather dramatic wrenching motion with her hands. Then she bluntly asked, "What your name? What your old man's name? He Indian, too, huh?"

Isabel smiled, cutting her gaze across to her traveling companion. "Part Indian, actually. My old man's name—" She deliberately and humorously raised her voice, "is Shadoe McCaine. My name is Isabel."

"Isabel. That nice name. Where you and old man go?"

"We're going to Montana."

"Cold Montana."

Isabel laughed softly. "It's cold here."

"Where you come from?"

"Louisiana."

"Never been there." Nodding toward Shadoe, she asked, "Your man . . . what tribe Indian he?"

Isabel cut a look toward Shadoe. "He's part Cheyenne. But he's lived as a white man."

"He too handsome be white man," argued the woman. "He good hump-hump? Why you no children?"

If Isabel had been eating, she was sure she would have choked on her food. A pretty crimson rushed into her features as she gathered her thoughts enough to say, "We've only been together a few months."

"He good hump-hump?" the woman persisted, showing a ragged line of rotting teeth as she smiled.

Isabel dropped her gaze, refusing to meet Shadoe's humored, smiling features as he awaited her answer. She had always thought that Indian women were quiet, subdued, submissive, and subservient, but the woman sitting across from her was as bold as crimson taffeta at a christening. She opened her mouth,

er mind revolving quickly to find a subject that
might divert the woman's interest from the subject of
Shadoe's sexual prowess, when Shadoe approached
the fire with the rabbit skewered on a sturdy stick.

"Well, ladies . . . have the little ones filled their
stomachs?"

The look Isabel gave him was a mixture of repro-
al, for his unnecessary delay, and of thanks. A smile
of relief swept over her pretty mouth. Looking across
at the little ones, she noticed that all but the older
boy had finished eating and were huddled peacefully
by the fire. "I believe that Autumn—that is his name,
isn't it?" she asked the woman.

"Said it was, didn't I?" came her blunt response
that was not meant to be offensive.

"He might want some of the rabbit when it is
cooked. I've got more potatoes and sausage cooking,"
she said, slightly lifting the pan.

"I'll tell you what"—Shadoe took up a fork and began stabbing at some of the slices of sausage—"we'll
stuff these in the rabbit to give it flavor. In the mean-
time—" Shadoe smiled pleasantly, "why don't you
dish some of that food up for the children's mother?"
When the woman who considered herself undeserv-
ing of a name met his look, surprised that he would
be concerned about her, he added, "I know you
haven't eaten for a while, and I don't like to see anyone hungry."

Without cutting her gaze from Shadoe, the woman
said to Isabel, "Your old man have kind heart. My
old man, he not care if woman hungry, if children
hungry. He eat first, and if he not eat all, then we
eat. If he eat all, then we not eat."

"That's horrible," responded Isabel, who could not
imagine such callousness by a man toward his wife
and children. "That's not the way things should be."

Dark, stern eyebrows suddenly shot up. "It not

247

that way in your Louisiana?"

"Certainly not!" Isabel remembered hearing stories of a poor family about eight miles south of Shadows-in-the-Mist who fed the five sons first, and then the three daughters were allowed to eat whatever might be left. She had thought it deplorable, but this woman's tale made that awful practice seem pale in comparison.

Much later, after they had eaten supper, and the woman and her children were snuggled beneath her rabbit-skin cape and some blankets Shadoe had given her, he and Isabel walked together in the deep ravine to discuss this unexpected development. "We can just leave them to fend for themselves," said Isabel. "They are going a very long way and they have no horses and no food. They would never make it."

"I agree," said Shadoe. "But the only thing I could suggest would cause a delay in getting to Montana

Despite the overcast night and the lack of a moon the snow was blinding enough to light their way through the ravine. She could not prevent the shade of disappointment easing across her face, a disappointment she knew he had noticed. "I imagine that you want to journey back to the south and connect with the railroad. Well, we can't just leave them to fend for themselves, so we have no recourse."

"So you don't mind?"

"In view of the circumstances, to do so would be extremely selfish." When Shadoe paused, then drew her into his arms, she said, "And I'm really not that kind of person, Shadoe. I hope you realize that by now."

"Of course, I do. I could never fall in love with a selfish woman."

He had spoken so nonchalantly that Isabel was taken aback for a moment. It was important that Shadoe love her. She had given herself fully and com

248

letely to him, and love was very important. But did he speak idly, or had he spoken from his heart? "Do you love me, Shadoe?" she asked following a moment of silence.

Putting a breath of space between them, then dropping his wrists over her slim shoulders, he smiled a little ruefully. "As hard as I might have tried not to . . . yes, Isabel, I love you with all my heart. I love you enough—" Darkness pinched his brows together, "I love you enough," he began again, "to take whatever your father has to dish out when we return to Louisiana."

Placing herself within the circle of his protective arms, Isabel sighed happily. "He will love you as I do, Shadoe. How happy you have made me tonight—"

"Why tonight?" he asked, scarcely able to suppress his rueful tone. He had fully understood how important a confession of love was to her, if that, indeed, was why she was especially happy.

"You know why—" she replied noncommittally. Isabel closed her eyes against Shadoe's taut chest. Though they were away from the fire, she felt warm, protected, secure in his arms. He was her life, her future, everything she wanted, and she was content to enjoy the tenderness of him.

Then, without warning, a sudden gust of wind played among the strands of Isabel's hair escaping below the fringes of her scarf. She looked up at Shadoe's relaxed features, but he apparently had not noticed. Strangely, it was not a cold wind . . . but a warm one, and she looked northward into the blackness of the ravine.

Drawing in an almost imperceptible gasp, Isabel stiffened in Shadoe's arms, but if he noticed, he made no indication of it. There in the blackness stood the form of a man, a large, barrel-chested

black man, his tan shirt rolled up to the elbows as i
he'd just come home after a day's work on a warn
summer day. She was mesmerized by the sight o
him, but strangely, not afraid. Then she heard hin
softly say, "Your man must be careful, Isabel," and
like a spectral mist, the human form slowly faded
into blackness once again. Tears stinging her eyes, Is
abel buried her face against Shadoe's shirt and asked
in a trembling voice, "Did you hear him . . . did you
see him?"

"Hear what," asked Shadoe. "See what?"

"Nothing . . . nothing but the night wind," she
murmured, quaking visibly against him.

"What is wrong?" he asked.

"Nothing—" Was she going mad, she wondered?
She ventured a look toward the ravine but saw only
blackness. Was the viciously cold weather and the
many long days they had spent on the trail, often
without meeting a single soul, affecting her mind?
Nothing was there in the darkness, nothing at all . .
and so as not to alarm Shadoe with tales of spectra
beings and thus renew his speculations that she was
not strong enough for the trip, she calmly replied, "I
guess I am very tired. We should return to the camp
fire and get some sleep." She was afraid. Had a warning been passed to her from beyond life's door that
Shadoe was in danger?

Slowly, they turned together toward the campfire.
They had company now in their journeys. Shadoe
was thinking of the human ones, a mother and her
brood of children. Isabel . . . the figment of her
imagination that seemed all too real.

Sleep was all they would share that night.

Nightmares would plague Isabel.

And so the following morning, Shadoe, Isabel, and

he woman who had finally confessed a given Christian name of Annie, began the precarious trek on foot while the six little ones lumbered along on the two horses.

Three days later, frozen through to the bone and low on supplies, they entered the village of Greeley, Colorado on the Platte River. In the afternoon, Annie and her children were put aboard a westbound Union Pacific — at Shadoe's expense — which would change lines near Salt Lake City for the final leg of their journey to California.

Isabel hated to see Annie go; over the past three days they had become fast friends, and both had promised to keep in touch. Annie had admitted to only a small knowledge of reading and writing, and Isabel wondered if she would, indeed, hear from her when she returned to Louisiana. They had exchanged addresses and promises and only the future would tell.

At Isabel's pitiful entreaties, Shadoe agreed to take a room in the only boarding house in Greeley just long enough for Isabel to get the chill out of her bones, take a dozen hot baths, and sleep on a real feather mattress.

The boarding house matron, a dowdy, large-busted woman who introduced herself as Mrs. Crenshaw, immediately and rather haughtily advised that more than one hot bath per day would cost a dollar each. Placing ten dollars in her hand, Shadoe growled, "Keep the hot water coming, and we'll want the full ten dollars worth."

When they were at last alone in a large, comfortable room with a fire crackling in the hearth, Isabel threw herself into the mound of covers upon the bed she would share with Shadoe. "I do believe I'm in heaven," she sighed, taking one of the pillows to drag it across her face. Peering at Shadoe from beneath its inviting fullness, she flexed her index finger at him and whispered enticingly, "Why don't you drop them thar saddlebags, cowboy, and drop here—" Her hand gently patted the bed, "by yore little filly."

Shadoe couldn't help but grin. She'd been so moody these past three days of traveling away from her destination that he'd worried about her. Now, she was the Isabel he remembered, the Isabel who could turn around the bleakest of setbacks and smile winningly, as she was now doing. Slowly, Shadoe turned toward her, and as he moved across the broad expanse of floor, he unbuckled his gun belt and let it drop to the floor with a dull thud.

For a moment, he stood at the edge of the bed looking down at her. "What do you have on yore mind, little filly?" he asked playfully, dragging his knee up to the bed beside her. "Some good hump hump, eh?" Instantly, Isabel's fingers walked toward his knee and then began to ascend his muscular thigh. When it reached a particularly vulnerable area of his anatomy, he took her hand and, with a growl, fell across her. Tossing off the pillow, he dragged his palms up to her humored features. "You sure are frisky, Isabel, for a woman who wanted nothing but a hot bath."

"Mrs. Crenshaw is boiling water for the first bath. I imagine it'll take a while—"

"Not as long as you think!" said the woman in question, pushing open the door without knocking. She smiled as Shadoe jerked off the bed in one swift move. "Didn't mean to startle you," she added, dragging in a wooden cart upon which sat a black pot of steaming water.

"You could have knocked," said Shadoe with a boyishly charming pout.

"Then I wouldn't have the pleasure," she chuckled good-naturedly, "of seeing your face turn the color of a harlot's underbritches." Isabel propped herself on her elbows as an embarrassed Shadoe assisted Mrs. Crenshaw in pouring the water into the tub that already contained cool water. Then, in departing, Mrs. Crenshaw said, "I must go now. I have a difficult boarder who requires immediate attention." Sharing a smile between Shadoe and Isabel, she ended, "Let me know when you're ready for the next bath."

Isabel stifled the laugh tickling at her throat until Mrs. Crenshaw had closed the door behind her. Then a slump-shouldered Shadoe moved to the door and turned the key in the lock. "Blast. It takes a lot to embarrass me, and that little woman managed it!"

Isabel scooted off the bed and began shedding several layers of clothing until only her underthings hid her nakedness from him. "I get the first bath," she insisted, "since gentlemen always allow the ladies to go first —"

Grabbing her elbow, Shadoe pulled her roughly to him. "Who the hell said I'm a gentleman? Let's get married, Isabel." He had spoken both sentences as if they were one, without a pause for thought in between. When Isabel's full, feminine mouth parted in surprise, he growled, "Well, how about it?"

"Married, Shadoe . . . you want to get married?"

"Is that so unreasonable? I'm ready to settle down."

"But . . . Venetia . . . her father . . . I thought you were afraid of the past catching up to you. Suppose —" She slumped against him, her eyes taking on a pained look. "You should feel threatened and you should just up and leave me. I couldn't bear it. I couldn't bear to lose you —"

His mouth brushed intoxicatingly against her own as he murmured, "I will never leave you. Not in a thousand years. We will have children and grandchildren. We will grow old together. And blast Venetia. Her wickedness is out of my life forever —"

* * *

Mrs. Crenshaw's difficult guest was pacing the floor like a caged cougar. Covered from head to toe in her black mourning clothes, the beautiful, pouting, dark-haired woman cursed inwardly. She had been wearing this dreadful color for two long weeks—since the husband who was fifty years her senior had died suddenly at their home in Springfield, Illinois—and she wondered how much longer she was expected to mourn the old bastard. As his widow and sole survivor she had what she wanted—the half-million in assets that he was worth—and now it was time to go on with her life. Oh, if only her father didn't insist that she carry on with this ridiculous facade of grief!

Down the hall from the room shared by Shadoe and Isabel, Mrs. Crenshaw rapped lightly at the door. Immediately, it was jerked open by the irate young woman. "Where the hell have you been, old woman? I paid you well to fetch me some headache powder!"

With a smirk covering her round face, Mrs. Crenshaw held out a small brown bottle. "And here it is, Mrs. Wainwright. In case you've forgotten, I do have other guests to attend." Since the reason the despicable young woman and her entourage had been put off the westbound train had traveled through Greeley faster than cholera, Mrs. Crenshaw took special pleasure in adding, "Don't blame me for your troubles, Mrs. Wainwright. Blame yourself!"

"Grabbing the woman's arm, Mrs. Wainwright hissed, "You keep your dirty mouth shut, do you hear me . . . boarding house madam! You don't know anything!"

As calmly as she might peel an orange, Mrs. Crenshaw removed the woman's hand from her arm.

254

With a silent sneer, she turned in the corridor, nearly bumping into the young Spanish woman who was Mrs. Wainwright's personal maid. Giving the girl a brief, sympathetic look, Mrs. Crenshaw hurried past her and down the stairs but did not descend fast enough to miss the brutal slap the Wainwright woman dealt the maid.

"I told you to come right back, you stupid, foolish girl!" snarled the black-clothed woman, taking the girl's arm to yank her into the room. "Did you find him?"

"I'm sorry, Mrs. Wainwright. I—I couldn't find him . . . I went all over town, but . . . I couldn't find him!"

An inner ugliness twisted upon what might otherwise have been a beautiful face. More to herself than to the maid, she said, "I went to a lot of trouble to make a scene and have myself put off the train in this godforsaken place. He promised he'd be here!"

The girl choked up with tears. "I tried to find him—"

"You cease those tears, or I'll slap your face until it bleeds!"

A knock sounded at the door. Without awaiting an answer, a tall, broad-shouldered man of about fifty stepped into the room. "You're making more noise than a rabid bull. What is wrong with you, Venetia?"

Her suddenly wistful mood belied her cunning. Settling her features into the sweetest of countenances, Venetia Mendez Wainwright tucked her fingers around the lapels of her father's jacket and prayed to God he had not heard the words she had spoken to her maid. "Oh, papa . . . papa, you know how grieved I am for poor Roger—"

"And bulls have feathers," said her father, removing the groping fingers of the daughter he loved despite her many shortcomings. "You might be able to fool

255

most men, but not the papa who raised you. You did not love Roger Wainwright; you loved his money. Now, you have it, and you go home with your papa." Turning, barking at the maid, "Get out," he said to his daughter after her departure, "Now, I want the truth, Venetia. Were you responsible for Roger's death?"

The dark, bronze-skinned beauty forced the comeliest of pouts. "Papa, what kind of woman do you think I am? Why, dear old Roger—" As she thought of the grunting and slobbering of the seventy-five-year-old man atop her in those few moments before he had died, she gave a small shudder of revulsion. Then she began again, "Poor old Roger was so happy that you came to Springfield for the wedding. And your little Venetia . . . she thinks her papa is special, too." She simply had to throw the protective old warrior off his guard. She was planning to run off to San Francisco with her handsome young lover, and when he eventually made his show, as he had promised, she did not want her father to intercept her getaway. It was imperative that he trust her implicitly, and that he be sound asleep in his room when Carl came for her. "Now—" With a sticky, insincere smile, Venetia turned her father toward the door. "Go on back to your room, papa. You must rest up so that we can catch the stage tomorrow."

He turned, eyeing his daughter suspiciously. "You seem anxious to be rid of me, Venetia. Are you up to something?"

"Why, papa," she pouted, coyly dropping her dark brown eyes but unable to control the instinctive fire in them, "Don't you trust me?"

"I once thought you were a sweet, innocent girl, Venetia, and every word you uttered I took as gospel truth. Now, I know you are nothing but a predator. I would be a fool to trust you." A matter that had been

256

troubling him for many years suddenly popped into his mind. Perhaps that familiar wildness in Venetia's eyes . . . yes, that was it, that was the look that always managed to dredge up the ugly past. "Daughter, do you remember the morning that you came running into the house, and you told your papa that you had been raped by one of the ranch hands—"

A short, startled breath escaped her. "What made you think of that?" she thundered with unrestrained passion.

"I think of it often. Tell me, Venetia, tell me the truth—did he rape you?"

"I said that he did! Of course, he did!" Her hands began to flail wildly, not so much because her father had brought the offensive matter up, or even that he doubted her, but because she was still enraged by the rejection of a poor ranch hand whose attentions she had craved. She would never forget him, and if she ever saw him again, if her father would not kill him, then she would! But first, she wanted to lie in his arms; she wanted to take what he had denied her. No man who had rebuffed her should be allowed to live!

When tears of fury, which Mendez mistook for tears of pain and disappointment, flooded Venetia's eyes, he took his recently widowed daughter in his arms and attempted to console her. "Of course, my passionate beauty, my beloved one. Of course, I believe you—"

"And if you ever see him again, papa, you will kill him, won't you?"

Felix Mendez sighed deeply. "He was a dark one, tormented by his personal demons. I do not think he is alive after all these years—"

"But if he is, papa . . . you will not let him live."

"That is something I will consider if and when the matter ever again arises. I cannot help but remember all of the times you have lied to me to have your own way. I don't know why I have put up with you, but . . ." He shrugged. "A papa must love his daughter. The heart dictates it."

"You will always make me happy . . . yes, papa?" she uttered with childlike innocence. Then she lifted her full, pouting mouth and kissed him in a way that a decent daughter would — should — never kiss her father.

Part Three

Partings

Sixteen

Dustin had been gone from the Boeuf only two weeks when he sent the rather urgent missive to the Shadows. When Delilah read the terse words, "Aunt Dee, please come to New Orleans. A problem has arisen with Isabel," she wasted no time in packing for a short trip and catching the first train out of the Lecompte depot. She had assured her worried husband, who was busy preparing the fields for the planting season, that whatever had arisen with their rebellious daughter, she would be able to handle it. Delilah, however, had not realized the full extent of the problem with Isabel until she reached her great-aunt's house on Royal.

"What do you mean, she is gone? Gone where?" Delilah's golden-brown eyes flashed in an attractive mixture of anger and concern, and she almost slung off her nephew's hands when they landed comfortingly on her arms.

"Now, Aunt Dee," said Dustin in a calm drawl. "If you'll take off your coat and let Mercedes bring you a cup of hot tea —" Looking past his aunt's shoulder, he nodded to the waiting servant, "I'll go across the street and fetch Golda Dumont. Then we'll fill you in on everything we know."

So within ten minutes a family council opened in Aunt Imogen's parlor. The old matron sat in her favorite wingback chair, her ankles crossed, her hands resting on the head of an elaborately carved wooden cane, and her mouth pressed in a petulant pout. Delilah paced the Oriental rug, Golda sat at one end of the divan, her eyes downcast and her hands fidgeting among the folds of her crisp white apron, and Dustin sat at the other end, his booted foot drawn up to his knee and his fingers playing among the limp strands of a mustache he was attempting to grow. All three waited for Delilah to speak, and she seemed hesitant to do so.

"Well?" demanded Imogen, "Say what you have to say so that I can go back to my rest."

The rich brown tendrils of Delilah's hair had been drawn up and loosely pinned. Her aunt's somewhat complacent order caused her to pivot so quickly that any order to her hairdo was lost in the move. She began flipping back the recalcitrant strands. "What do you mean, say what I have to say? I have a missing daughter—a daughter, I might add, I trusted to your care. I think the three—no, two"—she amended, since Dustin had been away in the east and was not responsible for the dilemma, "had better start relating every detail of the circumstances surrounding Isabel's disappearance—"

"Poof!" smarted the ancient matriarch. "Isabel is in safe hands! Don't you know I would have summoned you immediately had I believed otherwise?"

"Aunt Dee, don't get angry—"

Now, a properly outraged Delilah pivoted toward her nephew. "I have every right to be angry, Dustin. I should be frightened and hurt and very, very disappointed"—A scathing glance cut to her old aunt—"that certain members of my family have withheld vital information from me. Now, someone had better start telling me where my daughter is, and who she is with."

Dustin's gaze cut to the silent Golda. "Well? You're the one who entered into this conspiracy with my dear cousin. Don't you think it is your place to inform her mother of her whereabouts?"

Golda glanced up slowly, so much shame in her youthful gaze that tears suddenly became its companion. "The last letter I received from her was postmarked in Denver, Colorado."

"Colorado!" Delilah was unable to mute her shock. "What on earth is she doing in Colorado?" Extending her hand, she ordered, "Give me the letter."

A tearful Golda ventured a glance toward Isabel's beautiful, youthful mother. "Mrs. Emerson, I have given all the letters to Dustin," she advised the woman who appeared to be on the brink of explosion, so dark and angry were her eyes.

Rising, Dustin took from his jacket pocket the small packet of letters Golda had received from Isabel in the past weeks, then handed them to his aunt. "The one postmarked in Denver should be on the top," he said wearily. "I've kept them in order according to date."

Feeling that she might faint with fear for her daughter, Delilah dropped into the nearest chair. Slipping the letter from its envelope, she hastily read the words Isabel had written to Golda Dumont. Then she looked up and quietly asked her aunt, "Who is this man Shadoe McCaine she has mentioned?"

"He's a dear young fellow, a dear, dear young fellow," said Imogen with the pride of a mother speaking of a saintly son. "You needn't worry about him. He'll bring our Isabel back safely."

Drawing in a small, trembling sigh, Delilah looked around at the faces, old and young, sharing the large, overly warm room with her. "Do any of you know why my Isabel has taken this journey with a man I do not know and who"—Her glance narrowed as it returned to her aunt—"is a man that my Isabel could not have known too terribly long herself?"

"I have no idea," spoke up Dustin.

"Nor I," added Golda. "She told me that she was going away with him, but she never told me why. She said only that it was important, and that when she returned to Louisiana, all of your lives would be the better for it."

"And what did she mean by that?" asked Delilah.

Golda shrugged. "I have no idea, ma'am. But—" In an attempt to downplay the severity of the entire situation, and to ease a mother's worrying, she added, "But the letter from Denver is very cheerful, Mrs. Emerson. It isn't the letter of a woman who is in trouble. Your Isabel must have had a very good reason for leaving with Mr. McCaine. And"—Her eyes brightened as she managed the most timorous of smiles—"I met him and I found him very likeable—"

"The blackest of rogues can be likeable," said Delilah on a slightly sarcastic note. Absently folding the letter and returning it to the envelope, she added, "I really don't know what to do about this . . . but wait."

Dustin hopped lithely to his feet. "I am not going to wait. Before the day is out I will be on a train."

"Where do you think you're going, boy?" barked Imogen, tapping her cane rather loudly on the planked floor.

"I am going to Denver."

Delilah had been flipping through the letters. Momentarily, she began to read from the postmarks, "Natchez, Little Rock, Tulsa, Enid, Pueblo . . . four states, Dustin . . . she is moving steadily to the northwest with this Shadoe McCaine. She is probably long gone from Denver even now. It'll be like digging for a thread of gold in a wheat field." Then, on a note of finality, she rose to her feet and said, "No, you will stay here in New Orleans."

"And what will you do?"

"What can I do?" came Delilah Emerson's immediate reply. "I will return to my husband at the Boeuf and together we will wait for word on our Isabel." As if to justify the stand she had taken quite on the spur of the moment, Delilah quietly added, "I have to remember that Isabel is no longer a child. She is twenty-two years old and she should have the good sense to stay out of trouble. If she felt the trip important enough to conspire—" Delilah's gaze darted to Golda, but did not linger, "and to deceive her family, then she should get the adventure out of her heart. When she returns to the Boeuf, perhaps she will settle down, find a good husband and raise a family. Until then—" Delilah absently dug at the voluminous skirts of her velvet traveling gown and when she did not find a pocket, held the letters protectively to her, "we must carry on as usual."

Dustin, thinking that tears stung his aunt's eyes, moved toward her. Instantly, her hand shot up to halt him and he entreated softly, "Don't be upset, Aunt Dee. You know I cannot bear it when one of the women of my family is upset."

"You don't care if *I'm* upset, young pup!" shot Imogen, her hand raking the air to summon Mercedes to her. "Help me up, will you?" And when she leaned against the caring servant, she managed a cracking smile. "Our girl will be fine, Missy—" She had always referred to Delilah by the pet name given to the little girl she had once been, "and I'm sure she'll return unscathed." Just before she turned, Aunt Imogen shook a bony finger and declared, "But I scarce believe, Missy, knowing my Mr. McCaine as I do, that she'll return a virgin."

Delilah pressed her mouth, and had not Imogen instantly made her escape from the parlor, she was sure she'd have chewed right through her lip. Well, losing one's virginity would certainly not prove fatal and Delilah hoped that if her daughter chose to do so, she would at least love the man, as she herself had loved Grant Emerson at that same age enough to be with him fully and completely.

As Golda Dumont made a hasty departure, and Dustin, making some idle remark about brewing a pot of tea, moved toward the kitchen, Delilah dropped again into the chair.

Isabel . . . Isabel . . . what am I to do with so stubborn and rebellious a daughter?

"You must have been hell for your parents to raise!" Shadoe laughed as he uttered the words, then roughly dug his fingers among the loose, disheveled masses of her hair. His body lay hard upon hers. His eyes narrowed with teasing humor, hers with the sweet ecstasy of the love they had just made. When her mouth puckered with feigned indignation, his voice softened to baby talk. "What's the matter with my little girl? Big old mean man teasing her?"

Softly tickling her fingernails along his sides, Isabel grinned at his shuddering withdrawal from her torture. "Unmercifully, you rogue cowboy and gambler. My parents warned me about men like you."

"Obviously, my darling," he muttered, "you didn't listen."

"If I'd listened . . . and obeyed . . . my parents would have been suspicious. We can't have suspicious parents, can we?"

Darkness suddenly settled upon Shadoe's brow and he removed himself from her, dragging the covers across their bodies. He lay there, staring at the ceiling of their room, his hand moving slowly to the back of his head. "What are the chances that your parents know about this little trip we've taken?"

Turning to her side, Isabel rested her head against her drawn up palm. "I'm sure I planned it without a hitch. Aunt Imogen thinks I went home to the Boeuf, mother and father believe I am in New Orleans, and Golda will intercept any mail that arrives. I can't imagine how they could possibly find out."

"What about that cousin of yours . . . Dustin, isn't it?"

Isabel raised a pale eyebrow. "What about him?"

"You said he was very protective of you."

"Dustin's in the east. I told you his mother died—"

"But that was four months ago. What do you think he's doing, hovering over his mother's grave until the cherry blossoms bloom?"

"Of course, not." Isabel drew back to the pillow and, with a wistful sigh, continued, "He has family in the east, a grandmother and grandfather. Surely, he will want to visit with these people he has not seen since he was knee-high to a grasshopper. When we spoke that morning before his departure, he seemed very interested in spending time with his mother's family and seeing some of the country where he'd been born." Isabel scooted from beneath the covers and her feet touched the floor. Drawing on a loose dress, she searched for her slippers among the covers they had tossed off the bed.

"Where are you going?" asked Shadoe as she moved toward the door.

She turned her head, her mouth easing into a smile. "I'm ready for the next bath. I'm going to find Mrs.—what was the lady's name?"

"Crenshaw," replied Shadoe. "I never forget a lady's name."

"I'll bet you don't. Now—" Again, Isabel smiled. "You'd better get dressed before Mrs. Crenshaw comes up with the water." Isabel moved into the corridor and quietly closed the door.

She had just turned toward a darkened stairwell when a sharp feminine voice yelled, "You, there . . . come here this instance."

Isabel turned, and though she narrowed her eyes she was scarcely able to make out a dark-clothed woman standing down the corridor, her hands drawn to her hips and her toe tapping upon the floorboards. "Me?" asked Isabel, her finger resting gently upon the small indenture between her collar bones.

"Yes, you, girl!" snapped Venetia Wainwright, swaggering toward her. "I want you to tell that crotchety Mrs. Crenshaw who employs you that I need fresh logs in my fireplace." When Isabel arched her eyebrow Venetia snapped, "Well . . . don't dawdle! Be on your way!"

Isabel's gaze raked boldly over the bronze-skinned features of the dark-haired, darkly frowning woman who thought she was a servant of the boarding house. Perhaps she had made her spontaneous assessment because of the careless manner in which Isabel had dressed. Lifting her chin, Isabel replied saucily, "Tell her yourself!" at which time Venetia's hand clamped tightly over Isabel's shoulder.

"What did you say?" she sneered between tightly clenched teeth. "What did you say to me, girl?"

What a thoroughly unlikable tart, thought Isabel, drawing her own hands to her slim hips. She felt her mouth curling into a sneer, a veiled hood of anger and revulsion creeping down over her brows. She remembered a moment when she'd been twelve that she'd gotten into a ruckus with a girl on the Boeuf, and the way she was feeling right now was identical to the way she had felt then. Unconsciously, her hands balled into fists and her body became so taut she was afraid that a shrill whistle would cause it to break apart, like fine crystal before a soprano's high C. "Lady," she said in a low casual voice, "you get your hand off my shoulder or I'm going to twist it off your arm and leave a bloody stump."

A surprised Venetia instantly withdrew her hand and the surprise instantly became fury. "How dare you threaten me, you . . . you *puta!* How dare you."

Isabel knew only a few basics in Spanish, but she had heard this word used by her father's Mexican visitor last year, when he had taken offense at one of Mozelle's casual insults. "What did you call me?" asked Isabel.

"Are you deaf . . . or just stupid? I called you a

268

ita!"

And before she quite realized she'd even moved, Isabel's hands were wrapped snugly through the woman's coal black hair and she was atop her on the floor, banging her head against the planked floor. "When you call me a whore, you overstuffed snoot, I'd suggest you take off running for your life!"

So shocked was she by the physical attack that Venetia could only scream in short spurts. She could feel her hair being torn out in wads and try as she might she could not loosen the outraged Isabel's fingers. She was like a wild creature tearing apart its prey; even her pale eyes had darkened to the color of onyx and her mouth had curled into a snarl. Then, almost as quickly as the assault had begun, Venetia suddenly found herself free of the attacker's demure weight.

Dragging a trembling hand across her face to disengage what was left of her hair, Venetia could see only the vague outline of the man holding the sneering she-cat at bay. As she turned to her side, so that she might use her hand for leverage in getting up, she whimpered emotionally, "Thank you, sir . . . thank you for coming to my assistance."

The shudder wrenching through Shadoe McCaine's body was strong enough to halt the beat of his heart. He held a struggling Isabel firmly against him, fighting to control her arms as she fought to free them from his powerful grip. Her slippered feet pummeling his shins caused no pain, and even if they had, he would not have cut his narrowed gaze from the shadowy female figure struggling to gain its footing. Then, when Isabel's muttered curses might have stirred him into action, she was facing him . . . that despicable monster whose image had dogged him these past seven years. He was not sure who was more shocked, she or him, but he was the first one to allow his senses to reel back like a mighty blow. Only then did he realize an audience was gathering. Only then did he realize his

state of undress, as he'd had only enough time to pu
on his trousers. Now, gritting his teeth so firmly he wa
sure his jaws would break, he withdrew into the bed
chamber with an exhausted Isabel.

He kicked the door closed with his bare foot, hi
hands still roughly holding Isabel. "Lock the door," h
ordered.

At which time, she wrenched herself free and turne
to him with a scathing look. "What are you expectin
. . . that . . . that Spanish bitch to come after me? Sh
is too much a coward and she—" Isabel became sud
denly aware of his uncharacteristic pallor. "What i
wrong with you, Shadoe? You look as though you'v
seen a ghost." When he pivoted, Isabel could see tha
his muscles were so tight he surely must feel pain. Ap
proaching, placing her hands over his shoulders, sh
immediately felt them shrugged off. "For heaven's sake
Shadoe! What is wrong with you?"

"Get dressed and pack our things. We're leaving."

"What?" Shock fringed the single word. "What d
you mean, we're leaving. It's the middle of the nigh
and it's colder than—"

He swung back, the darkness now veiling his fea
tures macabre against the glow of dying embers in th
hearth. "I said get ready to leave! Blast it, why mus
you always argue?"

Isabel drew her hands to her hips. "Well, I'm no
moving until you offer some explanations. You're a
unpredictable as a rattlesnake, Shadoe McCaine. I d
declare—"

Instantly, Shadoe's hands circled her upper arm
and she was drawn firmly against him. His eyes wer
mere slits. "You want an explanation? Well, here'
one. That bitch you just tangled with was Veneti
Mendez. And wherever she is, her father will be, also.
Slinging her away, Shadoe half-turned, his palm risin
and pressing firmly to his forehead. "Blast! Who woul
have believed I'd run into that vicious predator in

270

godawful place like Greeley? Damn, what luck I've got!"

Isabel's features paled. Too many times she'd heard Shadoe's horror and revulsion and fear when he'd spoken the name Venetia Mendez. She turned toward the chair where they'd placed their bags. But no . . . no, this wasn't right! With newfound rebellion, she snapped around. "All right, Shadoe, so it is Venetia Mendez. You are an innocent man. I simply cannot see why we must leave. Let *her* leave. Or—" Her mouth pressed as she looked for the strength to continue under his angry scrutiny. "Are you afraid of her father, Shadoe? Is that it?" When he refused to answer, she quipped, "Or is it Venetia herself? Do you think she might pull a little derringer from her garter and shoot you dead?"

Shadoe broke eye contact, dragged his hands to his hips and breathed deeply, attempting to still the fury he felt. Then he turned, calm regained, and approached Isabel. Placing his hands gently upon her shoulders, he said, "Do not argue with me, Isabel. I have been running for seven years, because of the bounty on my head. I don't want to die now, but even more important to me, I don't want you to die. Did you forget about Mary Ellen? She was alive once, and I cared for her. Then Venetia found out . . . and Mary Ellen was dead. Get ready to leave, Isabel, or so help me God, I'll throw you over my shoulder and carry you to your horse." With a mirthless grin, he ended, "Do I make myself clear?"

Without hesitation, she responded, "Yes . . . yes, of course. We must go."

Shadoe busied himself dressing and watching Isabel, hoping it wasn't too late. He didn't like the idea of a showdown with Felix Mendez, but he would face him if it came to that. But he could not bear the thought of harm coming to Isabel. God! Her father would come after him, for sure, and he couldn't say he would

271

blame him. The man was too damned blind to know what a cunning little liar his daughter was.

Venetia had rushed immediately to her father's room. He would have sought out Shadoe . . . and possibly asked for explanations that would surely have contradicted Venetia's claim of rape . . . but it wasn't hard for her to convince him to go to the marshal's office instead. With luck, Carl, the deputy marshal, had returned by now, and Venetia did not doubt the young man's love for her. After all, hadn't he provided the poison with which she had ended the life of her stuffy old husband?

She had met Carl Weatherstone during her journey east to marry Mr. Wainwright when their train on the Santa Fe had been derailed in the middle of an Oklahoma prairie by a herd of longhorn cattle that had eluded the control of the drivers. While the carcasses of eighty or so cows had rotted, the male passengers, drovers, and crew had spent two long days restoring the train to the tracks. During the long hours of boredom, she had found a friend in the amiable Carl, who had been returning to Greeley following his half-brother's funeral in San Antonio. They spent the long nights that followed entwined in lustful embraces, lovers in the narrow berth of an otherwise vacant sleeping car. Thereafter, he had ridden all the way to Kansas City with her, his attraction for Venetia unnoticed by her father. When he'd been unable to make her change her mind about marrying the rich old Easterner, he had given her a small vial of arsenic and instructions on how to administer it. They had kept in touch by telegram, and when the evil deed had been accomplished, he had promised to be awaiting her when she arrived in Greeley.

Now, where was he, the black-hearted bastard? Her father had returned to the boarding house with a mar-

hal who had refused to take Shadoe into custody without proper papers. And had criminal charges ever
been filed in the State of Texas? No! Though Venetia
had promptly presented a poster offering a five thou-
and dollar reward beneath the likeness of her rapist,
he had indulgently explained, "It is a privately offered
reward, Mrs. Wainwright. I cannot take in this man
. . this Shadoe McCaine."

"And why the bloody hell not!" she had immediately
countered, and when her father had attempted to re-
train her, she had slung off his effort with a viciously
snapped, "Where is your deputy marshal, Mr.
Weatherstone?"

"Weatherstone is out at the mines, Mrs.
Wainwright. If you know him at all, you'll know he's a
part-time deputy. Spends half of the month down there
at Leadville. He's due back in the morning."

Venetia's thoughts revolved at an incredible speed.
That bastard—that spurner of her feminine charms—
that Shadoe McCaine, had fled once, and she had no
doubt that he would flee again. He had once rebuffed
her desire for him, and that still stirred the rage inside
her enough that she wanted to see him punished. And
there was only one way to do that. She had seen the
way he had pulled the pale-haired doxie off her, the
way he had held her closely and intimately while she
had righted herself. If the marshal would not take the
man into custody, then—

"I wish to bring charges against a woman in his
boarding house," said Venetia, and when her father
opened his mouth to speak, her dark eyes immediately
cut him off. "The woman attacked me, ripped my hair
and thrashed me. See—" Venetia showed him the
scrapes and bruises she had suffered at Isabel's hands.
"I do hope that assault and battery is a crime in
Greeley?"

"It is . . . but, do you have any witnesses?"

"Every boarder on the floor of this despicable estab-

lishment witnessed the attack. I insist that you take he
into custody."

"You are formally bringing charges?"

Venetia pressed her mouth in a hateful smirk. "I am
And I will remain in Greeley to testify against her at
trial."

Pat Crocker studied the young woman for a mo
ment. She was feisty and vindictive. He imagined tha
she might have instigated such an attack hersel
though it was not up to him to judge her as the culpri
If she brought formal charges, he, as a public servant
would have to act upon them. "I'll need you to com
down to the office and swear out a complaint."

"Then you will take her into custody?"

"Won't have any choice, Mrs. Wainwright." Turning
Pat Crocker gave the silent father of this woman a per
functory bow. "I'm sorry for the trouble you've had i
Greeley," he said.

When he had departed, Felix Mendez crossed hi
arms, his voice strangely vacant as he said to hi
daughter, "Is there any place in the world you can g
that you don't cause trouble?"

Venetia looked properly indignant. "I suppose yo
are blaming me because that awful woman attacke
me?"

"I can't imagine any woman attacking another fo
no reason at all."

"Well! That is exactly what she had . . . no reason a
all." Venetia stomped toward the door, turning to he
father with a deliberate pout. "Will you accompany m
to the marshal's office, or must I go alone this time o
the night?"

Felix Mendez shrugged wearily. "This could wai
until the morning, Venetia."

"It cannot wait. He . . . I mean, she will get away

"By all means—" Venetia's father approached, hi
hand moving upwards on the door, above the head o
the petite woman. "We must apprehend this vile crimi

274

nal before she gets away." His sarcasm was as thick as syrup. Pressing her mouth to keep from being disrespectful to her father—again—Venetia ducked beneath his arm and moved into the corridor. The door closed with a dull thud. In the corridor she slowed her pace as she moved past the door where *they* were—that attacking she-cat and the despicable man who had rejected her.

She turned onto the stairs to begin her descent, confident that he would not leave once the woman had been jailed. And tomorrow, when her adoring, spineless Carl Weatherstone returned to Greeley, he would do what she demanded with the man.

If he wanted her, he had better!

Seventeen

Carl Weatherstone went deeper into the Argonaut mine, located ten thousand feet high in the Rockies near a settlement called Leadville. Carl brought those prisoners who were given suspended sentences by the court in Greeley to work the lode. His reasoning was that they had "beat the system" and deserved to be punished. He had recruited help in a number of ways. Occasionally he had taken a drunk off the streets, and at other times he did "favors" for men who wanted to get rid of a rival or a husband; into the mine they went, to work until they died. A federal marshal who'd gotten too curious about the condition of the men working the Argonaut lode was now one of his slaves.

Carl and his partner personally owned the mine, and all of the silver that came out of it went into their own bank accounts. Neither the courts, nor Marshal Pat Crocker, for whom he worked as a deputy two weeks out of every month solely for the purpose of lining up workers for the mine, knew where Carl got the men to work the Argonaut. He and Greech could be in big trouble if anybody ever found out. For that reason there was no way out for the men Carl kidnapped except wrapped in canvas and ready for the grave.

"Did you find the bastard?" called the burly, pock faced Greech, who was his partner in business and in crime.

276

"No. Did you check the other tunnels?"

"I still got one more to check, Carl. You want him killed, don't you?"

"He's a troublemaker," quickly responded Carl. "What do you think? And that other bastard, you tear him up real good for cutting his father's chains."

"Why not kill him, too?"

"He's young. We can get a lot more work out of him before he's ready for the boneyard." Adjusting his rifle beneath his right arm, Carl turned from his partner. "Hell, let's get this over with. I've got to get back to Greeley."

Laughing coarsely, Greech pulled at his groin. "Got somethin' hot to crawl into back there, eh, Carl? That little Spanish bit you met on the train . . . reckon she'll wait for you?"

Carl cast a grin over his shoulder. "She better be waitin', Greech. If she cuts out on me, I'll wring her pretty neck."

The two men went in separate directions. Carl Weatherstone couldn't help but admire the interior of his mine, scrutinizing the framework to make sure it was solid, admiring the veins of black throughout the lode that still had to be brought out; even the sand coating the floor of the mine was black with silver. The three thousand dollars in silver per ton he had first mined had become four thousand per ton, and he'd even brought out a little gold, though not enough to satisfy Carl's greed for wealth. He hoped to deplete the minerals in the mine within five years by breaking the backs of the men whose lives he had taken away. Then he would go to work on the lesser-grade ore the assayer had estimated at approximately eighty-nine tons.

Mining was his first love; Venetia his second. She had hinted indiscreetly that her father might prove a problem, but Carl knew how to deal with men who got in his way. She was in Greeley now, awaiting him. Blast that stinkin' Californian who'd broken from the chain gang and secreted himself in the mine.

Greech let out a holler, and Carl turned swiftly. By the time he reached the tunnel where Greech stood, the thin, pitiful, half-naked man who had escaped had been beaten into near unconsciousness by the butt of Greech's gun. Dragging back his thick brown hair, Carl dropped his palms to his narrow hips. "Hell, Greech, I didn't say to torture him. I said to kill him." When Greech raised his rifle, Carl cut his eyes from the frightened, cowering prisoner and ordered, "Not that—you'll bring the timbers down."

When Breech removed from his scabbard his Bowie knife, still red with the blood of its last victim, the cowering man began to sob. "Don't kill me. I won't run again."

And Carl, dragging a cigar from his jacket pocket to tuck between his lips, responded blandly, "I know you won't," then nodded to Greech, who wrapped his hand through the wild, unkempt hair of the man and cut his throat in one swift move.

As the blood gargled through his cut windpipe, and the flailing arms quietly dropped in death, Carl threw his head back and laughed. "Make sure his son sees him before you have him buried," he ordered, turning away as casually as he might from the last dance of the evening. "I'm headed out to Greeley."

"Why not wait until mornin', Carl? Storm's a brewin' out there."

"I gotta be in Greeley by the morning," replied Carl, tipping his hat back from his head as he stepped over the corpse.

"Hey, Carl." The younger man turned back. "Bring back some whiskey, will ya?"

"Always do." Carl lightly tipped his hat. "See you

278

in two weeks, Greech. I got me a wild thing to tame."

Isabel had bundled up against the cold. She couldn't believe she and Shadoe were leaving Greeley in the middle of the night, with nothing but memories of the south and a cold wind from the north to keep them company. As black as his mood was, he certainly would not prove a pleasant companion, and for the first time since leaving New Orleans Isabel regretted the impulsive decision she had made.

That Texas tart—she wished she'd ripped out every strand of her coal-black hair while she'd had the chance. If Shadoe had not plucked her off Venetia Wainwright, she might have gouged out her eyes.

Isabel dropped to a sitting position on a small stool and her right hand absently caressed the small canvas bag carrying the few worldly possessions she'd collected during the journey. Across the semidarkness of the livery, Shadoe solemnly saddled their horses. Mirlo laid back his ears and occasionally his back hoof would make a dig at Shadoe. Isabel imagined that the stallion did not appreciate being dragged from the warmth and comfort of his stall in the middle of the night. Her own mare, possessing the mentality of a snail, couldn't have cared less.

When Shadoe turned with the readied horses and handed her the reins, she asked, "Will we travel all night?"

"If you don't mind," he responded dryly. "We can stop to rest when we've put Greeley . . . and that witch . . . thirty miles or so behind us."

"There's a blizzard rolling in."

"We'll have to weather it." Only then did he recognize the hesitation in her voice as she had spoken. Turning, he pulled her roughly into his arms and whispered against her hairline, "I am an inconsider-

279

ate bastard, Isabel. Why do you put up with me?"

"Because I adore you, Shadoe. I love you. If you're in trouble, then I'm in trouble. When you're unhappy, I am unhappy, and when you need me, I will be here for you."

Putting a breath of space between them, Shadoe favored her with a half-cocked and rather sad smile. "I never thought any woman would come into my life and give me reason to want to live. But you, Isabel, you have accomplished what I had thought impossible."

"Well, pardner—" she drawled pleasantly, returning his smile. "We'd better be gittin' the hell out of Dodge before that posse comes after us."

Shadoe gave her a brief, warm hug, and in that moment she knew that he loved her and would protect her, that one day, Shadoe would return to the Boeuf with her and boldly make his claim to her father. A fleeting memory of her father's reaction warmed her though, and for a moment the dank, winter coldness left her.

Shadoe helped her tie down their possessions, then assisted her into the saddle. After he had mounted his own horse, he nudged up beside her, took her hand and gave it a soft squeeze. Reassuringly, he promised her, "I'll never let anything happen to you, Isabel. I will always take care of you. Never forget that."

"I wouldn't be with you if I didn't trust you," she responded sadly. Then she extracted her hand, drew up the collar of her thick wool coat, and turned toward the exit. "No time to waste. Let's get out of here."

As they cleared the livery, a light snow began to fall. Turning their horses, so that they might retrace the tracks that had brought them into Greeley, the two young people prepared to enter the dark country to the north. But scarcely had their horses edged a few feet forward before a crisp feminine voice cried out, "There, that is the one. That is the woman who attacked me!"

Shadoe and Isabel, finding their path blocked by a tall, barrel-chested man and the willowy, dark-clothed Venetia, immediately halted. The man asked, "Is your name Isabel Emerson?"

And Shadoe asked in return, "Is there a problem?"

The man responded in a voice thick with annoyance, "I'm afraid charges have been brought against the lady. She'll have to come with me."

In the semidarkness, Shadoe saw Isabel's hands close firmly over the pommel of her saddle. "What charges?" asked Shadoe, ignoring the silent, gloating features of the woman he had spent seven years hating.

"Assault and battery. Please . . ." Patience eased into the marshal's voice. "Why don't you come with me to the office and we'll get this straightened out."

Shadoe asked, "Do you have a warrant?"

Marshal Crocker held it out. "A duly sworn complaint, and a warrant signed by the Justice of the Peace. It's all nice and legal-like."

Said Isabel quietly to Shadoe, "Perhaps we can just pay a fine and be on our way."

"Perhaps," he responded, hesitating to dismount his horse. When he offered his hands to Isabel, she trustingly moved into them and soon stood in the protection of his arms.

The marshal outstretched his arm as he said, "I'm sorry—"

Venetia rudely interrupted. "Don't tell them you're sorry! Just do your duty!"

Marshal Pat Crocker wished the woman's father had remained with them. Unable to sway his daughter's vindictive intentions to file the charges, he had stormed back to their boarding house, leaving her to fend for herself. He couldn't say that he blamed him. He had easily seen the mental impressions of the woman's delicate shoes all over the father. Attempting to quell the annoyance he felt, Crocker said to Venetia Wainwright, "You're no longer needed, Mrs. Wainwright."

She released a short burst of sarcastic giggles. "Oh, but I insist in seeing that she is properly locked up." She cut a narrow glance at Shadoe McCaine, but he would not give her the satisfaction. He kept his eyes downcast, so that Isabel's features were all he saw. When Marshal Crocker suddenly seized Venetia's arm, his eyes narrowing lethally as they cut straight through her own arrogant stare, she jerked herself loose, picked up her skirts and moved swiftly into the darkness toward the boarding house in an echo of mumbled curses.

"Thanks," said Shadoe.

Pat Crocker chose that moment to inform Shadoe, "You're the one she wanted picked up, mister. When she and her father could produce nothing but a private poster offering a reward, she turned on your little lady there. I'll be wanting to talk to you about the events leading to that reward."

"And I'd like to tell you about that," answered Shadoe. "It just might clear up a lot of this."

Soon, they entered a small, dimly lit office on Greeley's main street. It was neat; even the posters on a large bulletin board were tacked in a straight line. "Are you going to lock me up?" asked Isabel as she shucked off her coat.

"Only if you want me to, missy," replied the sheriff. "Why don't you sit over there for the time being," he offered, pointing to a narrow bench against the front wall. "We'll do a little talking." Scarcely had he sat and drawn his booted feet up to his uncluttered desk before he asked, "Did you rape that little lady back in Texas?"

"Never even kissed her," Shadoe offered, taking a seat beside Isabel and enveloping her hand between his own. "I worked on her father's place and all I was interested in was doing my job and getting paid at the end of every week. You know—" Shadoe looked up. "I believe if you talked to her father without her in the room, he would admit that he didn't believe I'd do something like that."

Marshal Crocker argued without feeling, "When she was trying to persuade me to pick you up, she said you tore her clothes off her and mussed her up real good."

"She's lying." He dropped his eyes, thinking that the marshal didn't believe him. "What are you going to do about the charges against Isabel?"

The front legs of the chair, which the marshal had drawn up from the floor, now touched down with a dull thud. "Not much I can do. I'll have to hold her until the circuit judge comes through in three days."

"You're going to keep me in jail for three days?" The thought of being locked up like a common criminal horrified Isabel. "Couldn't we just pay a fine?"

Marshal Crocker shrugged, coming to his feet. "The judge sets the fines."

"A bond . . . couldn't I post a bond?"

"Normally you could. But you being strangers to Greeley, well, how do I know you won't take off the minute you're out of here."

"You have my word," offered Shadoe.

"Mister—" The marshal's drawl stretched into patience. "You're just a stranger passing through, I don't know who you are. Hell, you could have killed all the fellas been goin' missin' from these parts for the past few years. Why the hell do you think I'd take your word?"

"Then lock me up instead of Miss Emerson. She won't leave Greeley without me."

Crocker laughed goodnaturedly. "Ain't nothin' in the law books says I can do that, mister. Naw, you just sit there and let me think about this. I sure don't want to lock up the little lady, but I got to do my job, too. You understand?" Shadoe shrugged. Wearily, Isabel dropped her head to Shadoe's shoulder and closed her eyes. When the marshal offered, "Why don't you go back to that first cell and lay down, little lady," her eyes flew open. Seeing the fear in her wide, pale gaze, he again laughed. "Don't worry, I won't lock the door. Your man can go with you. Ain't nothing in the books says I can lock him up, so the keys will stay right there on that peg." When she hesitated, cutting her beautiful gaze between Shadoe and the marshal, the tall, barrel-chested man said, "Go on, I can see you're tired."

"Thank you," said a grateful Isabel.

"Yes, thanks," repeated Shadoe.

A thought came to the good-hearted marshal of Greeley, Colorado. Picking up his hat, he said, "Go on and rest. I got a little errand to run. Young fellow, if anyone comes in looking for me, tell them I'll be back in about half an hour."

"Sure," replied Shadoe.

As Isabel moved into the dank area of the cells, she said, "He's being terribly kind. I think he hates this as much as we do."

"Does seem that way," Shadoe agreed, opening a door to a large cell where two cots formed an "L" in the far corner. The darkness prevented either of them from seeing into the other cells, but loud, masculine snoring could be heard from the far end. Coaxing Isabel down to one of the cots, he said, "I'll take the horses back to the livery and bed them down." When she took his hand and held it tightly, he thought how childlike and vulnerable she seemed in that moment, her pale eyes wide with fright, the slightest tremble settling upon her full mouth.

"You'll come right back, won't you, Shadoe?" she implored in a low, quivering voice. "I don't like it here."

"I know. It won't be long." He hesitated to part from her, held there by his love for her, and by her need for him, a need that was like a beacon in her eyes. It made him proud that a woman like Isabel Emerson trusted him and loved him and looked to him for support. He didn't want to leave her, but he couldn't leave their horses standing in the bitter cold of a Colorado night. When he bent and touched his mouth gently to her forehead, she placed her hands over his own. When he whispered with husky emotion, "Forgive me," she drew back as if she'd been physically struck.

"Whatever for?"

"Because Venetia did this not to hurt you but to hurt me. It is my fault—"

Isabel shot to her feet, an immediate reprimand, though one of love, flashing in her powder-blue eyes. "Horsefeathers, Shadoe McCaine! It is fate. For some reason we were not meant to ride out tonight. I believe in fate . . . dear Lord, call it backwoods superstition, if you will, but I do. Had we been allowed to ride out, something terrible might have happened to us. No . . . please—" Her head nuzzled gently against his chest. "Don't blame yourself. That wicked woman is a foe we shall vanquish together . . . you and I."

Her conviction gave him the courage to break physical contact. Slowly, he backed toward the door, then slung it wide open. "You needn't feel confined," he assured her. "I don't believe the marshal has any notions of locking you up. Frankly, I don't believe he knows what to do with you, because he knows you don't belong here."

She smiled. "Go on and take care of our horses. I'll be all right."

He moved into the semidarkness outside the cell, and when he stepped into the circle of light emitted from the office, he turned, gave her a long, searching look, assuring himself of her well-being, and disappeared from her sight. She heard the door open, then the dull thud of his boots on the planked sidewalk outside echoing into silence.

She was weary. They had backtracked to put Annie and her children aboard a train, an exhausting trip through vile weather such as she had never seen in her lovely Louisiana; they had needed sleep already when that wicked Spanish woman made her appearance. Isabel wanted to keep her eyes open and her mind awake, but it seemed an almost impossible chore. Her body was protesting the stress the events had placed upon it, and she found herself slumping to the narrow cot. When her cheek touched a cool, flat pillow, she instinctively drew up her feet, then fumbled about for the dark green blanket pressing against her back.

She felt like a child searching for sleep after a busy, exciting day. But she also felt like a woman, missing her man's presence beside her. In her state of half-sleep she dragged in a slow breath of cool air, then exhaled it just as slowly. She did that several times, and she felt herself being drawn into the deepest recesses of slumber. There, in that enchanting world, there were no Venetias, no cold, blistering wind beating against her tender flesh, no hard saddle rubbing against her thighs. There, in a world where ugliness could be forgotten, grew the hazy vision of the gentle meadows and the lazy current of Bayou Boeuf . . . yes, there walked her father and mother, and her brother Paul, and they were smiling and talking and telling her how happy they were to see her.

And in her sleep, she smiled, because they were close enough to touch, her dear family and all her friends at Shadows-in-the-Mist. She didn't want to leave this netherworld of dreams and pleasant visions, where the troubles of the moment did not exist.

"Ya jes' sleep there, Missy," echoed a deep, masculine voice that she couldn't help but compare to the soft flutter of a buttercup in a Louisiana wind. Again she smiled, mumbled an inaudible reply, then sank deeper into the realms of her sleep.

She was no longer on the Boeuf, but back in the small cell, lying on the narrow, lumpy cot. There in the darkness, he sat, a kind, barrel-chested man, his mouth smiling, his cheeks so black they shone like ebony. He wore cowboy boots, a tan shirt and a gray, well-worn hat pitched back from the short tight, gray curls covering his head. She had seen him before . . . in a ravine just across the border into Wyoming, and she felt so peaceful and contented that it didn't occur to her to question his presence in the cell where she slept.

But was she sleeping, indeed? Slowly, her eyes came open — she was sure that they did — and he still sat there, as staid as a guardian angel; her mother had said that every living human being had one.

In a strangely soft tone — she was not sure that she had even spoken — she asked him, "Why are you here?"

He replied, "Ya's goin' ta need some takin' care of, Missy. Ya be careful an' ya tell dat man what yo' love he be's in danger. Ya tells him, Missy, he needs ta be careful, too. Ya don' need ta be alone so fer from where ya's been safe."

As if in a trance, Isabel replied, "But I am the one

287

in trouble. Not him."

"Ya tell him, Missy . . . ya tell him to watch over his shoulder. Ya warn him."

"All right." Slowly, Isabel closed her eyes, then drew her hand up to her warm cheek. "I'll tell him."

When he began to hum, his deep, masculine voice echoed the sentiments of Shadows-in-the-Mist in its gentleness, and she vaguely remembered how old Philo had hummed a tune very similar to the one now being hummed by this man. She remembered the many times she had sat on one of the cabin porches listening to the haunting ballads that could not be accomplished with the same degree of beauty and melancholy as the negroes who had carried the verses from their own unhappy pasts. Here he was, this kind, gentle man, lulling her to sleep in haunting harmony, and watching over her as if she meant everything in the world to him. She felt so peaceful.

Thus, when masculine footfalls echoed slowly into the darkness and the humming stopped, the biting reprimand sitting on the edge of Isabel's tongue brought her to full wakefulness. She swung her feet quickly to the floor and swept back the thick locks of her hair. When Shadoe's tall, dark-clothed form stood before her, she rushed the words, "Don't be angry with him, Shadoe. He was merely looking out for me while you were gone."

Shadoe's dark eyebrows met in a puzzled frown. "Who are you talking about?"

A moment of annoyance rushed upon her sleepy features. "The black man—surely, you must have seen him when you came in."

His hands gently outspread. "I saw no one, not even on the street."

Calming the irritation she felt, Isabel shrugged slightly. "I guess there must be a back entrance." When she met Shadoe's strange look, she continued

288

with haste, "Well, he was here, and I would like to know who he is so that I can thank him for his concern."

With gentle warning, Shadoe replied, "Just because you were raised back there in the South with men you would trust your life to doesn't mean that you can trust every man, Isabel . . . regardless of whether he's black or white. Exercise caution when you encounter strangers."

She didn't like being treated like a child. But before she could protest, the front door opened and a larger, heavier pair of masculine boots moved toward them. Momentarily, Marshal Pat Crocker smiled down on them. "It's all settled, little lady. I just got through deputizing my wife, and you'll be stayin' at my house until the circuit judge comes through."

Shadoe instantly grasped his hand. "Thank you . . . thank you a lot for not making her stay here."

Isabel was smiling. "You deputized your wife?"

"Sure did. Now, why don't you collect up your things and I'll take you to the house." Withdrawing his hand, he said to Shadoe, "Sorry I can't let you stay, too, but the wife don't like strange men in the house."

"It's all right," said Shadoe. "As long as Isabel is comfortable."

Isabel rose and began taking up the few things Shadoe had brought in from her saddle. Shortly, they moved into the office and Isabel turned into Shadoe's arms. "I don't want to be separated from you. You'll wait for me, won't you?"

For a moment, he looked a little offended by her query. "Of course. I'd never leave you, Isabel. I'll be close by and will keep in touch with the marshal. Just you don't worry."

As they moved into the heavy darkness and the bitter cold outside, Isabel allowed her arm to be gently taken by the marshal. Shadoe halted at the end of the planked walkway and tucked his thumb into the waist of his trousers.

He watched Isabel and the marshal until they were swallowed up by the night.

Eighteen

Carl had been hunkered down in the ravine for the past fourteen hours, waiting for the blizzard to pass. He could scarcely see his horse standing with its back to the whipping wind, and just beyond the ravine, the firs, heavily ladened with the snow that had fallen during the night, bent in arches toward the blinding white blanket stretching as far as the eye could see. Dawn had come and gone, and at midmorning he had managed to dig out of the snow that had buried his canvas covering. His horse, knee deep in snow, whinnied as he made his sudden appearance, then began pulling its feet loose of the cold tethers.

"Hold on, boy," yelled Carl, fearing the horse, whose reins had unwound from the sapling, would panic and make a run for it. He eased out of the protection of the tarpaulin and moved slowly toward the beast that could mean the difference between life and death for him.

The pale sunlight, ignoring the barriers of dark clouds and the winter-thin firs to dapple the ravine, was a mere mockery of warmth. He could scarcely feel his feet through their layers of socks and the thick leather of his boots. The wind tore at features so cold that a mere touch was agony, and he felt as if his fingers would break off at the joints when he chanced to flex them. He cursed inwardly, wishing he'd listened to Greech and waited for the storm to

pass before leaving the mine. He usually shrugged o
Greech's suggestions, but this time he should hav
made an exception.

It took him a full hour to free himself and h
horse from the confines of the ravine, but once h
got back on the road eastward, time and distanc
passed quickly. By late afternoon, he was a few mil
out of Greeley, and though neither he nor his hors
had eaten since the previous evening, he did not sto
at a road ranch that served the best steak in the mic
west. His mind conjured up the delicate scent of lila
water, and the beautiful, darkly rebellious features c
his murderous Venetia materialized before his eyes.

He felt an ache in his groin that had nothing to d
with the frigid weather.

A seething Venetia paced her room at the boardin
house, wringing her hands so tightly the bones bega
to pop against the brittle assault. The shadows of th
late afternoon laboriously penetrated the thin gauz
of the undercurtains at the one long window an
speckled a worn, faded rug that might once hav
been rich colors of rose and gold. She found herse
impatiently stomping on the pale circles of light i
her busy flight up and down the room. *Damn Car*
she thought, *Damn him to hell!* He had promised to b
here yesterday, and her father was growing restless i
his desire to leave Greeley on the next train south
ward. She had spent ten years trying to escape he
father's obsessive grasp—even agreeing, to accomplis
that means, to marry that antique old business ac
quaintance from the East—and Carl had promise
faithfully to play the role of gallant knight.

Venetia was attracted to Carl in a way she ha
never been attracted to another man, even the on
whose name was Shadoe McCaine. She had becom

obsessed with him because he had not wanted her, but Carl was different. Carl was like her, their evils paralleled, their mutual greed commingled and complemented each other. Venetia ached for his rough possession and the impatience with which he claimed her, body and soul. She wanted the heated, passion-filled nights, the welts and bruises he left on her body in the throes of lust that only intensified her own naked, abandoned response; she wanted to feel the blood oozing beneath her long, razor-sharp nails as they raked down the sinewy muscles of his back.

So, where was he, this rascal, this bastard, this man who made her body pain with want of him? She would make him pay for this delay; she would make him beg for a full five minutes before she gave him the pleasures of her—

"Venetia!"

She turned sharply, annoyed by her father's voice at the door. "What do you want?" she asked with vicious annoyance. "I am resting!" The door burst open. Venetia, accustomed to a submissive, idolizing father, felt her mouth part in surprise. "What do you think you're doing?"

Extracting and looking at his watch, he said, "There is a train leaving in half an hour. If you're not on it, then you get left behind, Venetia. Your personal maid has had enough of your cruelties also, and will return to Texas with me."

"Then I guess—" Flippantly, she crossed her arms, her eyes like black-clothed rebels glaring down her nose at him, so pitched back was her head in her need to defy him. "That I am left behind!" she ended between tightly clenched teeth.

He was just about to launch into an argument when a short series of raps sounded at the door behind him. He pivoted about, stunned to see Shadoe McCaine hovering in the doorway. "I need to speak to your daughter, Mr. Mendez," Shadoe somberly announced.

"My daughter does not wish to—"

"Of course, I do!" Venetia instantly cut off her father's reply. Her hands rose, instinctively, to tuck up any locks of her hair not in their proper places. Swaggering around her father, Venetia sucked in her breath, then expelled it dramatically. "And what do you want . . . *Shadoe McCaine?*"

"I want you to drop the charges against Miss Emerson."

Venetia released a series of irritating giggles. "Why? Doesn't she like her accommodations?"

"I am sure her accommodations are fine," Shadoe replied quietly, choosing not to inform her of the sheriff's arrangement for Isabel. Before he could collect his thoughts, he turned full to Mendez and said, "I wish you had died at birth."

Taken aback, Mendez asked, without any anger, "Why is that?"

"So this creature you call a daughter had never been born."

Sometimes I share your sentiments, Mendez wanted to reply, saying instead, "The past cannot be changed. Please—" The older man stretched out his hand, "say to my daughter what you have to say."

Shadoe's fingers moved nervously over the brim of his hat, which he held between him and the vindictive witch with dancing devils in her eyes. "Will you drop the charges?" he again asked.

The sneer settling over Venetia's features diminished her physical beauty instantly, but she was the only one unaware of it. She would rather die than do something to make this common ranch hand happy, and yet she kept in mind that the situation could ultimately be beneficial to her, and might even restore her credibility in her father's eyes. In the moment of intimidating silence since he had spoken, Venetia gloried in the full control she enjoyed. "I will drop the charges if—" The smile only magnified her ugly sneer. "If you will admit to my father that seven years ago you tore my clothes off me and brutally raped me. Admit that to him and I will drop the charges against your Miss Emerson!"

"I'd die first!"

She turned away, vague and flippant again. "Very well. Have it your way. It doesn't matter to me if your Miss Emerson languishes in a women's prison somewhere." Clicking her tongue, Venetia continued with feigned woefulness, "Pity, pity, poor Miss Emerson. Why, even if she gets off with a suspended sentence, the court ordeal is going to be horrid for her. Just horrid!"

She turned, pleased with herself, ignoring the darkness hanging over Shadoe's handsome features, a darkness that could become murderous at any moment. But her poor old father stood there, almost between them; he was protection of sorts from the black rascal so patiently pleading for the woman he apparently loved. Venetia's mouth pressed in a grim line; what did the pale-haired woman have that she didn't have?

Indeed, Shadoe wanted to pounce and kill this woman whose image had haunted him, but he kept in mind that a show of temper would only be an added obstacle for Isabel to overcome. It became a moment for him when he had to consider which was more important . . . Isabel, or his own pride. He knew the answer to that one.

Dropping his hands, Shadoe attempted to still the lethal pounding of his heart. He knew that rage darkened his features, but he fought to keep it in control. He would do anything for Isabel. Thus, he drew in a surprisingly calm breath, turned his gray-black eyes to the silent Felix Mendez and said, "Seven years ago, I tore your daughter's clothes off her and viciously raped her." And while Mendez stood there, dumbfounded by the unexpected confession, Shadoe turned back to Venetia, growling, "Now, I expect you to keep your word."

"Of course—" She could not contain her smug grin as her eyes cut between the two men. "I'll see to it within the hour."

Shadoe grabbed her arm, the smile turning up his mouth fed by the pain reflecting in her eyes. "You'll come now!"

Venetia tore her arm from him. "I said within the hour!"

So that he would not act on another of his impulses, Shadoe moved quickly into the hallway and toward the stairs. His hand had just touched down upon the bannister when the gruff voice of Felix Mendez called out, "Wait!" Shadoe drew in a breath his fingers tightening over the grainy wood as he fully expected the older man to pull his sidearm and shoot him. He kept his eyes downcast to the darkness at the bottom of the stairs as Felix approached and stood within touching distance of him. Momentarily a large, fleshy hand fell to Shadoe's shoulder and he started, despite his resolve to show strength. "Seven years ago, when you worked on my ranch, did you hurt my daughter?"

The man whose hand now rested upon his shoulder had once placed a bounty on his head. The memory of it caused a shudder to travel the length of Shadoe's spine and settle in his legs. He didn't like the way this man brought back such painful memories. In a quiet, but firm tone, Shadoe replied, "No," though he did not expect the man to believe him.

"Then why? Why did you give her the satisfaction?"

Shadoe turned his eyes then, his gaze picking over the ruddy, emotional features. He was surprised enough by the man's reply that his knees weakened with relief, threatening his equilibrium. "I would do anything for Isabel," he replied after a moment.

The large, bejeweled hand dropped dejectedly from Shadoe's shoulder. "You must love her very much."

"I would die for her."

Again, Felix Mendez grasped Shadoe's shoulder, but this time there was a quiet desperation in the way he held it. "Then I would suggest that you collect your little lady and leave, before you have to do just that."

"How do I know your daughter will keep her word?"

"When Venetia says she will do something, then she will do it. You must remember that she said she would see you dead."

With sudden anger, Shadoe asked, "Why can't you control her? You're her father! I've lived for seven long years with that private bounty you offered hanging over my head. Hell, you placed a five thousand dollar bounty on me! I suspect that you knew I'd done nothing to your daughter. God! My life has been a nightmare. And, blast it, you knew all along that I was innocent!"

"That is not true," argued Mendez. "I believed everything my daughter told me."

"Then what has changed you? Why do you believe me now, when seven years ago you vowed to see me dead?"

"Venetia was a child then, only seventeen. I have since seen what she is capable of."

"Damn you . . . damn you!" hissed Shadoe. "You ruined my life, and for seven years I have been trying to recover it! I believe she killed Mary Ellen, too. Do you remember her . . . *Senor* Mendez?"

The only response Felix Mendez had was, "I'm sorry," before he turned and left Shadoe standing alone at the head of the stairs.

Mrs. Crenshaw appeared on the platform below. "Did you find the book you had left?" she asked.

Shadoe had fibbed to her about forgetting a book, so that he would not have to explain the reason for his visit. With the same smoothness, he again fibbed, "No, I must have lost it. Thanks for letting me look," then slowly descended the stairs.

Marshal Pat Crocker had indicated that he would permit Shadoe to sleep in the jail, away from the boarding house and Venetia Wainwright. Shadoe now headed in that direction to inform the marshal that Venetia would drop the charges. He was amazed by the control he had exhibited in the presence of the Spanish witch. Before Isabel had entered his life, he wouldn't have thought twice about wrapping his fingers around her long, slim neck and letting her think that he would choke the life out of her.

Isabel was a calming influence. It made him feel great to admit that she was good for him.

Carl Weatherstone spurred the horse into Greeley, then sat for a moment, watching the afternoon train chug away from the station. There weren't many things he'd let delay his reunion with the lovely Venetia, but since boyhood he had been fascinated by the great, black, smoking dragons. Soon he nudged his weary beast toward the livery, where he was greeted by Potter Barnes. Polite small talk was exchanged, then an equally weary Carl moved toward the marshal's office to check in with Pat Crocker. As he stepped up to the planked walkway, almost losing his footing in a sheet of ice, he steadied himself by instinctively grabbing the arm of the man passing in front of him. He looked up at the strange face, but Shadoe McCaine said politely, "You all right, fella?"

Carl grunted. He released Shadoe's arm and lightly tipped his hat. When both men turned into the doorway of the marshal's office, Carl stepped aside.

Shadoe's enthusiasm was silenced when the marshal emerged from the darkness of the cell area and immediately greeted the man he referred to as Carl. In the few moments of conversation, Shadoe learned that he was the part-time deputy Pat Crocker had mentioned the night before, and when proper introductions were made, he politely proffered his hand.

The necessary amenities ended, Carl asked, "Mind if I don't come in till the morning, Pat? I was up all night and got caught in a blizzard west of here. I'm real tuckered."

"Sure," responded Pat. "Old Potter's going to take the night stretch in the office. See you at five."

Shadoe had been nervously twisting his hat, waiting for the younger man to leave so that he could give Pat Crocker his news. Scarcely had the door closed behind Carl Weatherstone before Shadoe said with mustered calm, "Mrs. Wainwright is going to drop the charges against Isabel. Will you release her immediately?"

Pat Crocker laughed. "Well, I don't know, young fellow. My wife's really took to that sweet, little gal of yours an', hell, if Bonnie wasn't such a lady, I'd of got a real cussin' for allowin' the charges to have been brought against her to begin with." Before Shadoe could make a response, Pat Crocker continued, "Bonnie feels real bad about keeping you two apart. I just came from the house and she says if you want to visit, well, you just go on up. The last house on the right at the end of the street. Bonnie can't bear seeing your gal brood for you."

Shadoe took the marshal's hand and shook it firmly. "Thanks." When he reached the door, preparing to leave, he turned back and said, "You've been real kind. I'll repay you for it one day."

Pat Crocker pivoted, then began fumbling among papers on his usually neat desk. "Better go on up the road and see your little gal. I'll let you know when that *Wainwright* woman has dropped the charges." He spoke Venetia's short-lived married name as if he found it just as repugnant as Shadoe did. Pity the poor bastard that had married her!

As Shadoe stepped into the brittle cold of the March afternoon, he felt a new lease on life, a warmth flooded him that came from deep within the core of his heart. He imagined that the deceptive sunlight filtering through the rolling black clouds across the outline of humble buildings had actually managed to bring color to his cheeks. He had felt wan and poor and unhealthy since the unexpected meeting with Venetia and Isabel's being taken into custody, but now he moved at a brisk pace, his boots clipping the planked walkway, then merging into a dull thud upon the muddy roadway. He greeted a pretty lady clutching the hand of a screaming boy, said "good morning" to a merchant sweeping outside his store, then patted a path alongside the firm, fine lines of a carriage horse awaiting its passenger outside the one hotel. He began to hum, this dark, brooding, mysterious man who rarely let his feelings show, and anyone who met him surely saw the contentment in his smiling features. When he took the steps two at a time and stood outside a mahogany door with a full-length beveled panel of glass, he could almost feel the warmth and beauty of his beloved Isabel on the other side. He rapped once, then twice, and almost immediately a plump, middle-aged woman with pale, beautiful features smiled in response to Shadoe's own.

"You are Miss Isabel's gentleman. Please—" She stood aside, outstretching her hand, "do come in. We were just having tea in the parlor." She was just about to whisper, *You're precisely as I thought you'd be,* when Isabel rushed into the foyer.

Bonnie Crocker stood aside, beaming widely as the two young lovers embraced. In an attempt to excuse herself from their private moment, she softly said, "I'll fetch another cup and saucer from the kitchen," and moved toward the back of the house.

After a moment, Shadoe took Isabel's hands and outstretched them, his eyes gazing over her from head to toe, over the velvet dress as pale a shade of blue as her eyes, and the ecru lace encircling her neck and wrists. "You look beautiful," he explained. "I like the dress."

"It is one of Mrs. Crocker's daughter's. She's away at school in the east."

Taking Shadoe's hand, Isabel drew him into a neat, well-furnished parlor. As she started to sit, Shadoe again drew her into his arms. "I have good news," he murmured, his mouth grazing her cheek for just a moment as he anticipated the return of Mrs. Crocker. "Venetia is going to drop the charges."

Isabel drew back, surprise darkening her eyes. "Drop them? Why ever would she do that?"

"I gave her what she wanted," Shadoe replied.

A pale, copper-colored eyebrow eased upward. "Indeed? And what is it that she wanted?"

Shadoe chuckled. "Well it isn't what *you* think. I merely gave her the confession—though a false one, I assure you—that she wanted. I told her father that I assaulted and raped her."

"But . . . but—" Fear paled Isabel's features, and for the moment, she thought she might burst into flames, so suddenly hot was the hearth across the

301

room. "Her father. He will—"

"He knew I was lying," Shadoe cut her off. "He will pose no problems for me."

Isabel gently tucked herself into his embrace. "Then we are safe. We can resume our journey to Tongue River and find my brother. Oh, Shadoe, Shadoe, everything works out, doesn't it?"

"Always. Didn't I say I would always take care of you?"

"Yes."

"I love you, Isabel. I want you to be my wife."

Closing her eyes, she felt the warmth of tears burn behind her lashes. "Your wife?" she echoed, as if she could scarcely believe his declaration. "You want me, Shadoe?"

"Yes. I'll return to Louisiana with you."

"And my father?"

Again, he chuckled. "Hell," he whispered, scarcely able to restrain his own happy emotions. "I'll make him like me so much he'll name me in his will."

Bonnie Crocker had entered the parlor, but seeing the young people so warmly embracing, she began a quiet retreat. But rather than allow it, a laughing Isabel parted from Shadoe, took her new friend's hand and drew her into the parlor. "We're going to be married," she said, the delight like a song fringing her voice. "Shadoe and I are going to be married when we return to Louisiana."

Bonnie beamed as proudly as if Isabel were her own daughter. "I'm so happy for you. So very happy." Then, picking up her cup, she winked at Shadoe and began a second withdrawal. "You two young people need some time alone to discuss your plans." Turning in the doorway, she spoke directly to Isabel: "Now don't you escape Deputy Bonnie."

And a happy Isabel replied, "I won't. I'll be right here—" Looking up at Shadoe, she ended quietly, "with my man."

"Where the hell have you been, you bastard?"

Ignoring the viciousness in her voice, Carl pulled
the dark-clothed Venetia into his arms and held her
roughly. "Now, is that any way to talk to the man you
love, my Spanish flower?" If her eyes had been raw-
hide, he was sure his face would have been ripped to
shreds, but their fury only amused him. "Come on,
come on, Venetia, where's a sweet kiss for your
man?"

She flung her face back and forth, impishly refusing to allow his mouth to make contact with her own.
"You said you'd be back yesterday. I demand to know
where you've been!"

Her anger aroused him, her tightly pinched mouth
made him more determined to claim it, and his body
responded to the erotic nearness of her. When her
long, blood-red fingernails dug into his shoulders
through the fabric of his shirt, he pulled her even
harder against him. "Go on, get real mad, Venetia. I
like it when you're real mad."

Venetia growled in a low, seductive tone and continued to fight him as he moved toward the bed, ignoring her feet between his boots dragging in protest.
When he threw her down and began fumbling with
her skirts with one hand and his belt and trousers
with the other, she gave him an incredulous look and
attempted to scoot from beneath him. But he was
much too powerful for her, and before she could open
her mouth to utter a protest, her underthings were
rudely shredded and he was within her, roughly
grabbing her thighs to pull her fully over him.

"You like that, don't you, baby?" he muttered, his
half-cocked grin widening as he saw the dark, familiar passion wash over her rebellious features.

303

Her buttocks were scarcely on the bed, her skirts were tossed over her bodice and he was grinding selfishly against the apex of her thighs. She wanted to hate him, to draw back her foot and kick him in the groin, but yes, God yes, she was enjoying it. Easing her full mouth into a wry grin, she propped herself on her elbows and watched their joining. "I promise not to castrate you, Carl Weatherstone, in exchange for a favor which you cannot refuse—"

"Anything," he grumbled, dropping to her and tearing down the bodice of her low-cut velvet gown. "You need only ask it, baby, and it's yours."

Venetia threw back her head and laughed, an evil, wicked laugh that made even a man like Carl shudder. For a moment, he ceased his movements against her, and his hands, cupping her hot breasts, drew slightly away. "Hell, Venetia, I hope you don't want me to shoot myself."

Grabbing his lapels, Venetia drew him down to her. "You just take what I've got to offer, Carl, and I'll tell you what I want when you're weak and helpless in my arms."

A devilish smile distorted his mouth. In one swift move, he disengaged himself from his trousers and boots as if they were all one garment, tore his shirt down his arms and scooted Venetia upward on the bed. He was glad of the front buttons holding her gown together, buttons that easily ripped apart beneath his frenzied attack. Picking up her limp hands, he attempted to ease them to his back. "Come on, baby, come on, you know you want old Carl. I promise I'll give you anything you want, but, be good to old Carl."

With a high-pitched laugh, Venetia threw up her legs, then wrapped them around Carl's narrow hips. Her fingers walked to the back of his neck and over the taut muscles of his back. Then, pressing her mouth into an ugly grimace, her razor-sharp nails tore down his back and down his sides. He growled, pain etching his face as it dropped to her own, his teeth grabbing her bottom lip to gently chew it. She knew he liked pain, and she felt the evidence of it now, as that part of him joined to her swelled and pounded so that she could scarcely keep up with his cadence.

Venetia died a thousand wonderful deaths as she anticipated her reward, as her body ground against his own, accepting him, claiming him, teasing him until she knew that he was her prisoner, her slave. Blood oozed from the cuts her fingernails had made down his back, and she touched the warm blood to her mouth, enjoying the bitter taste of it. Despite the coolness in the room, perspiration coated both their bodies, and she felt herself slipping toward the edge of the bed beneath the frenzied slamming of his body.

When at last he filled her with the seed of his manhood and collapsed atop her, Venetia released a deliberately pensive sigh, then covered a feigned yawn. Carl breathed heavily, his straight, sinewy body heavy upon her, and when he could find the strength to speak, he muttered, "All right. What is your payment, baby?"

"Remember, you promised . . . anything," she whispered with throaty lust. "Whatever I ask, it is mine." With a pained grimace, Carl withdrew from her, then dropped to her side and drew her into his arms. With his strength returning, he roughly pulled her atop his body. "I will have to pay that old bag extra for the bloody sheets!" Venetia declared hotly. "You could have the common decency to clean yourself up a bit."

"Hell with the sheets," he said. "The old bag is my mother."

Venetia drew back in surprise. "But she . . . he name is Crenshaw."

"Yeah, I'm from her first marriage. She's put thre husbands in the grave already. I imagine she'll pu another down eventually." His hands at her back re laxed into a gentle embrace and he did not physicall respond to the sharpness of her elbows digging int his shoulders as she drew back to give him a hu mored look. "Now, tell old Carl what you want."

Venetia drew back in surprise. "But she . . ." It made no difference.

Yet to the Crockers and nearby Giles put

Nineteen

Although he had assured her, many times over, that the charges would be dropped, Shadoe saw the fear in the depths of Isabel's eyes. "Her father will see that it is done," Shadoe responded to her worried questioning. If Shadoe had known that Felix Mendez had left on the afternoon train, just half an hour after hearing the false confession, he would not have been so sure Venetia would keep her promise.

When night fell early over this icy evening and the marshal still had not brought word to the large, comfortable house east of Greeley that the charges had, indeed, been dropped, Shadoe decided to return to the marshal's office. He was just about to leave Isabel with Bonnie Crocker when the man he had met earlier rapped at the front entrance.

Bonnie answered the call, and muted voices could be heard. Then the lady of the house moved to the door of the parlor, where Shadoe was preparing to depart from Isabel. "It is young Weatherstone. He wants to know if the big black horse at the livery belongs to you."

"Yes," responded Shadoe, anticipating, by way of past experience, the reason for the inquiry. "But he's not for sale."

Hearing this, Carl Weatherstone approached the parlor. "It's not that, Mr. McCaine. The horse is down and Old Potter can't get him up. He's real worried that you might think he did something to him

"God," muttered Shadoe quietly, his hand instinctively closing over Isabel's as alarm enveloped him He was fond of Mirlo; if anything happened to him he felt he would lose a good friend.

"Go on and see to him," encouraged an equally distressed Isabel. "Perhaps he merely ate too much sweet feed."

Quietly, Shadoe departed, moving out onto the porch without collecting his coat, which he'd dropped across a chair in Bonnie's parlor. Carl Weatherstone fell in beside him and kept pace with the taller man "I hope your horse is all right," said Carl. "He's a real fine animal."

A grim line attacked Shadoe's mouth; he did no respond. Five minutes later he entered the livery where their horses were boarded, surprised to find i virtually unlit, except for the pale haze of moonligh filtering in through the cracks of the weathered sid walls. He had expected the old man, Potter, to b holding a silent vigil over his ailing horse until he arrived, but nowhere did he see him. Except for the occasional movements of horses in their stalls, the livery was strangely silent.

Pausing a moment, allowing his eyesight to achieve some degree of clarity in the overhanging darkness Shadoe began to ease across the hay littered dir floor. When he approached Mirlo's stall, expecting to find him down, he was surprised when the powerfu stallion began to squeal and run himself against the barrier separating him from his master.

"What the hell?" mumbled Shadoe, attempting to grab Mirlo's halter and quiet him. The stallion would not be restrained, and Shadoe, jerked off the floor over and over by his agitated mount, half-turned preparing to ask Carl Weatherstone if he would step outside until he could be soothed. As he turned, hi gaze caught the rushing shadows of four men and the side of his head caught the butt of a rifle with such force that Mirlo's frenzied screaming instantly merged into the silence of the night.

He felt something black and coarse covering his head and strangling him, but it was as if it were happening to someone else. He could feel the men around him, smothering him, wrenching back his arms and binding them, but he was powerless to act. He felt a fist like a battering ram in the small of his back, but he did not feel pain. He was aware of a man's vicious, grinding voice, a voice belonging to the one with the brutally attacking fists, but he could not hear the words.

He was sure he died then and his last thought was of his beloved Isabel.

Worried to near desperation, Isabel wiped at her tears so firmly she was sure she would also remove the top layer of her flesh. Mrs. Crocker's assurances did nothing to ease her fear, and in the two hours since Shadoe had left the house she became even more convinced Mirlo had died and he was brooding somewhere alone. When Pat Crocker finally entered the parlor with the news that Venetia had dropped the charges, Isabel wasted no time in offering her gratitude for their kindnesses toward her. The moment she entered the dark night, she edged into a half-run toward the livery.

When she entered, she was surprised to see the old man relaxing in a corner and sorting horse shoe nails. Mirlo turned nervously in his stall. She looked about, expecting to see Shadoe, and when she did not, approached Mr. Potter. "I thought the stallion was down," she said.

Potter did not look up from his labors. "Was down,

miss. He must've ate too much and got a bellyache."

"Where's Mr. McCaine?"

Still, the man did not look up. "I sent for him when I thought the horse was sick, but he didn't come. Guess he didn't care too much."

"That's not true!" But rather than argue with the man, Isabel turned to move toward the stallion. When she put her hand up to rub Mirlo's muzzle, he drew back and half reared on his haunches. Startled by his reaction, when she was the only other person he would allow on his back, and the visible trembling of the powerful beast, Isabel drew slightly back. "What is wrong with you, Mirlo?" Her voice had an instant and soothing effect on the stallion; he approached, then nuzzled her shoulder.

Isabel ran her fingers along his neck, feeling the trembling withdrawal of his thick muscles. Behind her, the old man called, "The stallion all right, miss?"

To which Isabel, controlling the anger she felt, responded, "No, he's not all right. Something has upset him." Without turning back, she accused, "I think you know something that you're not telling me."

Potter Barnes did not respond. With an imperceptible smile, he eased the bony fingers of his right hand toward the small pouch of gold dust Carl Weatherstone had paid him for his cooperation that evening. Carl had told him the man calling himself Shadoe McCaine brutalized women; Potter felt sorry for the little lady standing before the black stallion, but she was better off without the snake who had ridden him in.

Isabel certainly wouldn't have agreed. Something had delayed him and she would not leave the livery until he showed up.

She began to pace, occasionally pausing to soothe the tremors of the stallion, ignoring the apparent lack of concern of the old man, and refusing to acknowl-

310

edge the bitter cold hanging within the livery's damp, dank interior and chilling her to the bone. The clink of nails being dropped into an assortment of canning jars began to grate on her nerves. She clasped her hands, continuing her journey up and down the livery until a trail had been forged through the scatterings of hay.

"Where are you, Shadoe?" she quietly asked herself, her sudden shiver having nothing to do with the iciness penetrating the shawl the kind Mrs. Crocker had given her. "I will not leave here until—"

Until when? she wondered grimly. She had a terrible feeling about tonight. Something had happened, something that kept Shadoe away from the stallion he frequently referred to as his "second best pal." *You're my first best pal,* he would teasingly whisper to Isabel when she questioned *who he cared the most for* in those childishly jealous moments of affection they had so frequently shared.

When midnight approached and Potter Barnes informed her that he was going to bed, Isabel refused to leave until he threatened to lock her in. Finding herself out on the street, she heard lively dance hall music drifting from a nearby saloon and wondered if Shadoe McCaine might be there, enjoying himself. The mere idea—as far-fetched as it was—infuriated her. Slowly she moved toward the planked walkway and approached the wide, dirty window. She saw painted women in gaudy gowns of yellow and blue and red, all trimmed in black lace, men pawing at them or pulling them down to their laps, while other men relaxed against bars and sipped whiskey. She looked toward the tables where men gambled, but she did not see Shadoe. Deep in her heart, she really hadn't expected to. Then a group of cowboys exited the saloon, and when she was suddenly subjected to their jeers and catcalls Isabel broke into a run toward the marshal's office. When she rushed into the small dimly lit office, gasping for breath, Carl Weather stone jumped immediately to his feet.

"Something wrong, little lady?" he asked.

Isabel thought there was something too pat and planned in the way he swept up from his chair, as if he had expected her. Drawing her hair back with a trembling hand, she looked up, scarcely able to see the deputy marshal through the haze of tears welling in her eyes. "Is Marshal Crocker here?" asked Isabel surprised at the weak tremor in her voice.

Carl had thought Venetia Wainwright the most beautiful female on the face of the earth, but she paled in comparison to the blond, blue-eyed goddess standing before him now. His eyes became rude in the way they raked over her. "The marshal's retired for the night. Can I help you?"

Sniffing back her tears, Isabel met Carl's gaze. Though she didn't know why, she felt a moment of dread and apprehension shoot through her like an iron poker. Worried that she might collapse, she quickly dropped onto what appeared to be a deacon's bench. Dropping her gaze, she reminded him, "You came to the marshal's house and told my companion that his horse was down."

"He was, miss. That fine beast didn't die, did he?"

"No, I—I'm—" Venturing a look toward him, she asked, "Did you go to the livery with Shadoe?"

"No, miss, I just delivered the message."

"He never showed up there," she quietly pointed out.

"Didn't he, miss?"

Isabel was sure she heard muted sarcasm in the few words the deputy marshal had spoken. "No, he didn't. I'd like to file a missing person's report."

Carl Weatherstone laughed. Tucking his thumb into the waist of his Levis, he dropped onto the mar

312

shal's desk and began drumming his heels against the scarred wood. "Miss Emerson, you're talking about a man in a town with saloons and gambling and women. I'd suggest you go on to bed and I'll bet you he shows up by the morning."

"But this isn't like him. He was waiting for charges to be dropped against me, and he was worried about his horse, and we have a long journey ahead of us and no time to waste. He simply wouldn't have left me, not this evening." She knew she was chattering endlessly, but she couldn't help herself. She was as repulsed by Carl Weatherstone as she was drawn to Shadoe McCaine.

When Carl hopped down, closed the distance between them and clamped his fingers over Isabel's shoulder, she felt the immediate urge to withdraw, so strong was the panic and repugnance she felt inside. She didn't like this man. She didn't like his looks, his demeanor, his voice, and certainly not his touch. When she could no longer fight her urge, she scooted from beneath his hand and stood up. "Perhaps you're right." But when she turned toward the door, she remembered that she'd left all of her things, including the little money she had, at Bonnie Crocker's house. She was in Greeley, Colorado, in the middle of the night, without Shadoe and without money. Where could she go?

She had no choice. Shadoe had paid for two nights at Mrs. Crenshaw's boarding house, and they had not even remained through the first one. Though she couldn't bear the thought of being under the same roof as that Wainwright woman, perhaps the widow would allow her to stay there tonight and, hopefully, Shadoe would show up in the morning. Oh, but she was going to give him a piece of her mind!

Folding her hand over the door handle, Isabel turned. With a shaky smile, she said, "Thanks for at

313

least talking to me," then reentered the darkness of the street and moved toward the boarding house.

Images of Venetia Wainwright made her shudder, but in view of the circumstances, she had no choice but to seek lodging at Mrs. Crenshaw's. Keeping the money Shadoe had given her for the extra night would be unjust enrichment, and Mrs. Crenshaw didn't seem the type to turn her out in the street. Thus, so sure she had not misjudged Mrs. Crenshaw's character, Isabel moved at a much livelier pace.

She was worried sick about Shadoe. She imagined every manner of atrocity that might be keeping him from her, except that he might have left her. She smiled to herself, though it was not a smile of the heart. Not only would he not leave her, but he certainly wouldn't leave his valuable stallion as well.

"Do you think she saw me?" asked Venetia Wainwright as she emerged from the darkness of the cell area.

"Naw, I don't think so," replied Carl. "Just be glad we saw her coming."

She rebuffed Carl's attempts to draw her into a rough embrace. "Do you think she suspects anything?" Crossing her arms as she sauntered toward the window and cautiously looked out, she said, "You should have gotten rid of his horse as I asked you to. Then she would have thought he ran out on her."

"She wouldn't have thought that," Carl argued without feeling, approaching, his hands closing, vise-like, over her shoulders. "Now, forget it. He's taken care of, just like you wanted."

Venetia turned sharply, her arms circling Carl's waist. "Is he already dead?"

"Not yet."

She pouted demurely, "I want him dead. You promised, Carl. Before this night is out, I want the breath snuffed out of him. Make it a hideous, horrible death, and make sure the Emerson woman knows all the gory details!"

"It is already being accomplished." Carl chuckled, a pang of jealousy pressing his eyelids into a thin line. "What is this man to you, that you hate him enough to want him dead?"

"What are you implying, Carl? That if I hate him so much I must once have loved him?" She threw her head back and laughed — a laugh so malicious Carl withdrew, wary of her next move. Almost instantly her features grew blank, and her piercing gaze traced the sharp outlines of Carl's masculine good looks. Then her finger arose to trace the same path her eyes had taken. "Forget that black-hearted bastard, Carl. As you have said, he is being taken care of. There is a nice, hard cot in the back there and . . ." A teasing smile embraced her full, moist mouth, "Lordy me, Carl . . . I forgot to put on my underthings."

With a malevolent grin, Carl stepped around her and quietly slid the inside bolt of the front door.

Mrs. Crenshaw not only accommodated Isabel, but gave her a room at the back of the kitchen so that she would not be boarded near Venetia Wainwright. "I am very worried about my companion," said Isabel, turning in the doorway. "If I cannot sleep, would it be all right if I make myself a cup of tea?"

Mrs. Crenshaw posed a rather comical figure, her nightcap ballooning out to three times the size of her head, and the large bow at the end of her plaited hair matching the dozen or so carefully sewn in a straight line across the material covering her ample bosom. "Of course," replied the woman. "And there

315

are a few supper leftovers in the cold box. If you get hungry, help yourself."

Isabel cracked a tiny smile. "Thank you," she said.

Mrs. Crenshaw set down the lamp for Isabel's use and hastily departed.

During the predawn hours, Isabel accomplished little more than nervous pacing, drinking several cups of tea, wringing her hands in desperation, and even mumbling a few unladylike expletives beneath her breath—an attempt, she supposed later, to keep from crying. If she could be angry with Shadoe, imagining that he was enjoying himself in one of the saloons, winning big at the gaming tables, or passed out somewhere drunk, it would make time pass quicker. But, she stopped to think about it; she had seldom seen him drink anything harder than beer, and then only one or two during the course of an evening. No, she would have to rule out drunken insensibility.

When she finally fell asleep, somewhere around four o'clock in the morning, nothing short of a gunshot fired next to her ear would have awakened her, and possibly not even that. Since the incident with Venetia Wainwright, she had not caught more than an hour's sleep at any one time.

She awoke early, made her rounds of Greeley inquiring of Shadoe, and was rewarded only with disappointment after disappointment. When she finally returned to the boarding house just after sunset, she realized she hadn't eaten all day. With Mrs. Crenshaw's dining room closed down for the night, she raided the cold box in the kitchen and finally put together the makings of a sandwich. Filling her stomach, she closed herself off in her room and attempted to get still another night of sleep without knowing the whereabouts of Shadoe. She had thought she would find him today, and now, as she faced another long night without him, she felt tears flooding her eyes and burning her through and through. She wasn't sure how she fell asleep, but when she did, she slept soundly.

She did not awaken until eight, and she felt guilty about that. When she finally dressed—she had slept in her underthings for lack of something more comfortable—and entered the dining room where Mrs. Crenshaw had a breakfast buffet set up, she was more aware of the nervous mutterings than she was of the faces of boarders surrounding a large, rectangular table. Smiling timidly in acknowledgement, she was relieved to note the absence of Venetia Wainwright.

Mrs. Crenshaw took her elbow and coaxed her toward the stack of plates at the buffet. "Come, you must eat, dear. You look—"

"Who do you reckon he was, Mrs. Crenshaw?" interrupted a young male boarder, appearing to be about Isabel's age.

Mrs. Crenshaw answered curtly, "Let's not talk about that now. Miss Emerson hasn't had her breakfast." Leaning toward Isabel, Mrs. Wainwright continued on a quieter note, "We had a bit of excitement this morning. You didn't hear the fire bells?"

Isabel shrugged lightly as she began to fill her breakfast plate. "Nothing could have awakened me once I fell asleep," she replied, not really interested. All she cared about was filling a painfully hungry spot in her stomach and going out in search of Shadoe.

Despite Mrs. Crenshaw's warning glances, the male boarders continued their speculations of the predawn events. Isabel couldn't help but catch bits and pieces enough of their conversation and to piece together what had happened. There had been a fire at a vacant farmstead two miles north of Greeley, and the unrecognizable remains of a man had been dis-

317

covered by the firemen. "A transient," they speculated, "or one of the drunks common to Greeley who must have stopped to sleep it off and knocked over a lantern."

She was sorry for the unfortunate victim, but could not shake her worry for Shadoe, a worry that made it almost impossible for her to eat her breakfast. She sat there, the only female boarder at a table surrounded by men, listening to grisly chat about a fire and a corpse, and feeling so sick to her stomach she thought she might faint. She stabbed absently at scrambled eggs but did not eat them and managed only to swallow a few morsels of a pancake.

She was just about to push herself away from the table when a familiar masculine voice — though not the one she longed for — echoed from the front foyer of the boarding house. Presently, Marshal Pat Crocker, holding his hat to his chest, entered the dining room, acknowledged a few of the men he recognized, then turned his gaze toward Isabel. She didn't like the uncharacteristic set of his features, almost as if he felt great pity for her.

"Miss Emerson, I thought I'd walk with you up to the house to collect your things."

Was that truly the reason for his visit? She dropped her eyes, pressed her mouth, and tried to still the violent pounding of her heart. Gaining a moment, she pushed herself from the table and came to her feet. "That is very kind of you." She gathered Bonnie Crocker's comfortable shawl about her slim shoulders, and soon stood at the marshal's side.

The cold Colorado wind assailed her the moment she stepped into the morning. When she had quickly traversed the steps, attempting to keep up with Pat Crocker's long strides, she asked, "Did your deputy tell you that I was searching for my companion?"

"He did."

She hesitated to ask, "Any word of him?"

Pat Crocker drew in a deep breath, then expelled it, its warmth, intermingled with the bitter-cold air, giving him the appearance of a ranting bull. "Now, don't worry about that right now, little lady. Come along. Bonnie has a pot of tea brewing."

Isabel's heart sank, and though her feet continued to move, she knew not from whence the strength came to power them on. Dread settled about her like fog.

When she entered Bonnie Crocker's overly warm parlor, she could not remember the short trip down the street, coming up the steps, and entering the foyer that would deposit her there. If Pat Crocker had attempted to speak beyond his first few words, she did not remember them. She knew only that she was suffocatingly surrounded by an overstuffed settee, having a cup of tea she did not want forced into her hands, and that two people, acting very oddly and with pitifully drawn faces, were looking down at her.

Taking a sip of her tea, she looked from man to woman with gathered calm. "One of you should tell me what is going on," she said after a moment. "If it is about Shadoe, I would ask you not to hesitate. It is cruel."

A tearful Bonnie, fighting to control her emotions, instantly sat beside Isabel, relieved her of the cup and saucer to place on a side table. Gently she took her hands. "My dear, you know that Pat and I will do everything possible to help you—"

"I have Shadoe," came her instant reply, withdrawing her hands and tucking them within the folds of her gown. "But, thank you, anyway."

"Dear girl—" Bonnie Crocker instantly pressed her mouth, then looked up at her husband. "Tell her, Pat. Tell her what she must know."

319

Pat had hoped his wife would tell the poor little thing. Digging into his pocket, he pulled a chair up before the settee and lowered his large frame into it. Then he dropped the object he had taken from his pocket into Isabel's hand.

It was misshapened, but easily recognizable. How many times had Shadoe compared the topaz in his ring to the color of her eyes? Closing her fingers over the ring, Isabel shut her eyes briefly, dragging a now trembling hand, curled over its treasure, into a quiet embrace against her chest. "Shadoe must have lost it. He will be so pleased that it has been found. Thank you."

"I thought it was the ring your Mr. McCaine was wearing, but I wanted you to confirm it." Pat Crocker visibly flinched beneath her full, trusting gaze. At times like these, he wished he hadn't taken the job of town marshal. He hated being the bearer of bad news more than he hated sauerkraut. If Carl didn't devote the larger share of his time to the mine at Leadville, he would turn the job over to him. "Miss Emerson, what I'm trying to say is that—"

Giving no warning, Isabel darted to her feet, simultaneously unwrapping Bonnie's shawl from her shoulders. Handing it to her, she said, "I do thank you for the use of the shawl and for your hospitality. I must collect my things so that I can return to the boarding house and await Shadoe."

When Bonnie began to cry quietly, Pat reached across and gently covered her hands with one of his large ones. "Miss Emerson, Shadoe McCaine was killed last night in a fire north of town—"

"Horsefeathers!" abruptly interrupted Isabel. "That is the most preposterous thing I've ever heard! He'll come for me. He'll come for his horse. He—he's just been delayed—"

Astonished by her firm declarations, Pat Crocker

320

rose, his hands moving up to cover hips that seemed much too narrow for so large a man. He was almost angry as he looked toward Isabel, who should be venting her emotions and her feminine hysteria, but who seemed so perfectly in control he expected her to lift a haughty chin and calmly argue with him. What he did not know was that her body had grown so rigid she could not move her legs, her heart was beating so fiercely she was sure it could be seen moving against the bodice of her dress, and a fog of fear had temporarily blinded her.

Isabel's control was only a facade, for as quickly as her body had grown rigid, she now felt like a winter-killed weed fluttering in a harsh wind. She knew there had to be a very good reason why Shadoe had so mysteriously disappeared. In her heart, she wanted to believe he was alive, but her good sense warned her that he was gone and she would never see him again.

Had Pat Crocker not been perceptive enough to see that she was near collapse, she would have crumpled to the floor. As it was, she found herself slumping against him, then his hands eased behind her skirts at the knees to take her up into his arms. Momentarily, she was lain gently upon the wide, floral divan, hearing soothing feminine words, masculine concerns being voiced behind her, and a cool, damp cloth dabbing at her forehead. Her eyes were open, but she still could not see. Her hands were clenched, but she could not open them. And her heart continued to drum against the interior walls of her chest.

Shadoe is dead. Shadoe, my heart, my companion, my lover, is dead. The truth sank deeply. She felt like a ship whose bow had been ripped open, and yet she could not cry. She felt empty; she felt the loss of the one man in all the world who had taken her heart and nurtured it gently against his own. She remembered the moments they had lain together, loving, teasing, affectionate, treating the world as if it existed purely for their own happiness . . . moments they would never share again . . . and she could not believe it was possible. He was her future; without him, there was nothing.

The voices of concern slowly drifted away. Reason drifted away. She believed in fate . . . in destiny . . . and she believed in Shadoe. Nothing would keep him away from her forever. He would not allow anything—even death—to interfere in the love they had nurtured, and would continue to nurture until the end of time.

In that moment, she reversed the processes that had worked frantically within her. Her vision returned, her thoughts gathered, and the voices of Bonnie and Pat slowly drifted back to her. Strength flooded her in one swift wave, and resisting Bonnie's effort to force her down, she swung her feet to the floor.

"I'm all right," she said in a small, feeble voice. "I must collect my things. Shadoe will be looking for me."

Bonnie whispered sadly, "Dear girl, it will take time to adjust to life without him. Won't you stay with us until after the funeral?" Casting a brief look at her silent husband, she continued, "Our Estelle has a black dress you can wear—"

"I don't wear black and I don't attend the funerals of strangers," Isabel replied. "Are my things still in the room I slept in?"

"They're in the foyer, Isabel. But I do wish you'd stay with us."

"I really can't." Meeting the marshal's quiet gaze, Isabel asked, "Is there any law against my inquiring about Shadoe in town?"

There was no arguing with a woman when she had

her mind made up. Pat Crocker responded huskily, "No."

"In the event that it takes a while to find him, I'll need money to pay my expenses. Do you know of anyone in town who might have a job to offer?"

"Can you sew?"

"Yes."

"Sarah McFadden is looking to hire a seamstress for her dress shop."

"Where might I find her?"

"The little place beside Smith's General Store. Her name's on the door."

Bonnie ceased her sniffling, sharing a look of disapproval between Isabel and her husband. What was Pat doing? It seemed to her that he was feeding a young woman's delusions and ultimately it would backfire on him. But she kept the small spark of irritation under guard and offered nothing further.

Isabel moved toward the foyer and when she began to collect her few possessions, Pat Crocker offered, "Here, let me take that bag for you." To Bonnie he said, "I'll see you at dinner."

Only now did Bonnie arise and join Isabel and Pat in the foyer. "Would you take dinner with us, Isabel? There's plenty enough—"

"No—" Smiling timidly, Isabel took Bonnie's hand and gave it a gentle squeeze. "You've been so kind, but I need to make my own way and not take advantage of that kindness. I'll be all right."

Then she turned, and with her head held high, moved into the brisk morning toward Mrs. Crenshaw's boarding house.

She didn't care how long she had to stay in Greeley. She would not leave until Shadoe was by her side. He was everything she had ever wanted in a man, and she would not be deprived of him because she was too impatient to await him. She would be here when he decided to return. And when he did—

She smiled more to herself than to the residents of Greeley she met along her walk. Yes . . . when he returned she would give him a good piece of her mind!

Twenty

The night deepened, eerily soundless, across the bayou. Even the frogs were silent, although April was normally the time of their raucous mating rituals. Though the night was cool, Delilah had left the house without her shawl, her hand tucked into her husband's for all the warmth she needed, or wanted. She felt only the radiance of him, and heard only the gentle sigh that was his breathing. They were both worried. Grant let it show; Delilah nurtured her dread deep inside, allowing only her bubbling enthusiasm to surface in an attempt to ease her husband's worry.

The weekly letters from their daughter had suddenly stopped coming last month. Golda, who had forwarded the letters on to her and Grant, had written them earlier that week, advising that she had lost contact with Isabel.

"She's dead. I fear she's dead."

So softly spoken were Grant's words that Delilah was not at all sure she had heard him correctly. Then the moonlight, grazing the surface of a quietly rolling bayou, touched upon his masculine features, and she knew by the moisture sheening his pale eyes that he had voiced his deepest, innermost fear . . . a fear she tried desperately not to share with him. "No, Grant. She's going to return."

"How could she do this to us?"

A lump swelled in Delilah's throat. Had a big

bullfrog not suddenly jumped from one lily pad to another at the edge of the bayou, startling her, she might have released her own frustrations in hysterical sobbing. Rather, the moment in which her heart had skipped a beat, gave her, also, the necessary time to collect her calm. With a small laugh, she replied, "Despite our Isabel's age, I think she needs to be dragged across your knee when she shows up at the Shadows. She's—" Delilah swung around to face Grant, standing between him and the bayou that seemed to hold his attentions. Isabel was Grant's favorite child; he'd never insulted his wife's intelligence by denying it, and their son Paul seemed to feel that a father's favoritism toward a daughter was as natural as breathing. Secure in the fact that Grant loved him every bit as much as he loved their wayward Isabel, he'd never felt slighted in the least.

Dropping against a wisteria-wrapped pine, Grant pulled Delilah to a sitting position beside him. When her head dropped to his chest, his hand rose to absently entwine among the strands of her sable-colored tresses. They had been together twenty-four years, and Grant couldn't remember her being more beautiful than she was this minute, her rich hair untouched by the passage of time, her feminine form as slim and lovely as the first time he had seen her, her skin so smooth and flawless that he was still chided by locals for "robbing the cradle." He and Delilah had shared many adventures early in their relationship, and she had been quite a handful—every bit as arrogant and rebellious as the first child born of their love . . . their missing Isabel.

Grant had lost a son, and Delilah knew beyond a shadow of a doubt that losing a second child would destroy him. Even to this day, he clung to the hope that a miracle might have happened, that Bayou Boeuf had not claimed the life of their son and that he would appear, hat crushed to his chest, and say, *Father, it is I . . . your son, Eduard.*

"What are you thinking, Grant?"

He took in a deep breath. "How fortunate we are that we have the children, and being thankful for the few short years Eduard was with us."

"Oh." She didn't like thinking about her lost son. Lost . . . yes, because she still could not believe the bayou had taken him away from them. Though it had been a long, long time ago, it was still as fresh in her mind as if it had happened yesterday. In a loving tone, she said, "Not only do we have the children, but we have each other—"

Pulling her gently to him, his endearing reply was abruptly cut off by the fast-moving carriage entering from the roadway. A hoarse, masculine voice yelled, "Uncle Grant . . . Aunt Dee—" and as Grant recognized Dustin's voice, he hopped to his feet, pulling Delilah up beside him.

"What the hell?" mumbled Grant, a little annoyed that their solitude, and the stillness of the night, had been so thoughtlessly interrupted.

As they rounded the pond and half-ran past the long-abandoned overseer's cottage, their ears caught the echo of Dustin's bootfalls on the gallery, the door being slammed, then his immediate return to the moon-bathed clearing. By then, some of the workers, responding to the urgency in Dustin's voice, had left their quarters and were lingering about.

Catching sight of his aunt and uncle, Dustin puffed up as proudly as a victorious fighting cock and met them halfway across the clearing. Thrusting out his hand, he announced, "A letter from Isabel . . ." his face immediately widening into a smile of relief.

With trembling fingers, Grant slit open the envelope, and with Delilah close beside him, moved into the light of the gallery. When he began reading the letter in silence, Delilah requested, "Please, read it aloud, husband."

Clearing his throat, Grant dragged back the emotion resting there, so that his first words were uncharacteristically coarse.

Dear Papa and Mother, I imagine that you know by now what I've done and that when I return to the Boeuf, you might be tempted to put me across your knee and whale the daylights out of me. I know what I have done is irresponsible and deceitful, and I would ask that you not place blame on anyone, except me. When I return home, you will know why it was so important that I take this journey. I have suffered a temporary setback by misplacing my traveling companion, but when I find him, I will continue my journey to Montana. I love you dearly, and though I hope it really isn't necessary, I must remind you that I am almost twenty-three years old. For that reason, I would ask you to trust my judgment. In return, I will trust your judgment not to come after me, and will assure you that I am safe and well in Greeley, Colorado. I have made good friends here who have been very helpful and very kind.

Please trust me, papa and mother. When I return home, I will bring only happiness, and you will both be very glad that you have, indeed, trusted me.

I love you dearly, and I will be home, though I cannot tell you precisely when.

Your loving and devoted daughter, Isabel

Dropping the letter onto his lap, Grant said, "I am going after her."

At which time, Delilah's fingers closed firmly over his wrist. "No, Grant. Whatever has taken her away is very important to her. If you go after her, it will completely destroy her trust in us . . . a trust that time will not be able to mend." Cutting her glance to Dustin, she saw him nod his agreement, though he said nothing. "Grant, we must give her this time. We must let her see that we trust her, and that we consider her an adult."

"But this . . . this man she calls a companion. What kind of rogue would take away an unmarried southern lady without an escort and then simply allow himself to be—" He laughed sardonically, ending, "misplaced!"

Leaning ever so closely, she whispered, "The same kind of rogue I married. When you purchased this plantation, and asked me, an unmarried southern lady, to stay on, did you care that I had no escort?"

With mute surprise he responded, "That is different. Isabel is my daughter."

"And a daughter begging to be trusted."

Dustin, embarrassed to be eavesdropping on a tender moment between his aunt and uncle, politely withdrew to the house. Then Mozelle's son, called Little Jim despite his enormous size, approached the gallery. "Pardon, Mistah Grant, but Miz Isabel, she be all right? Folks at de quarters, dey really be worryin'."

Grant replied, "You take word that Isabel will be

home soon."

"Yassuh—".

Little Jim withdrew, and within moments, the clearing was empty of human habitation. His arm moving across Delilah's slim shoulders, Grant drew her close. "I'll go into Alexandria tomorrow and wire some money to Isabel, since Imogen said she hasn't touched her account in New Orleans."

"That's a good idea," replied Delilah. "But since you're busy in the fields, I'll go in. I have some dresses to pick up, and I'll talk to Hewe Penrod about that acreage across the bayou being sold at sheriff's sale."

"Ask him what the bank will bid, and let him know we'll bid a dollar more."

"Very well." Dropping her head against Grant's shoulder, she asked, "What do you think our Isabel is up to? What could she possibly be looking for in Montana?"

"A husband, maybe?" laughed Grant, though deep inside, he was still worried about Isabel. He was willing to trust her, but when she returned, she'd better have a damned good explanation.

A rustling drew their attentions across the lawn, and within seconds, a raccoon emerged from the darkness. Mozelle had made a habit of throwing scraps out the kitchen door for the dogs, and several raccoons usually showed up for a share of the spoils. They ate anything the dogs didn't eat, and Delilah enjoyed watching them sit up on their back legs and washing their feet and faces. They'd gotten so accustomed to the presence of humans that the large one passing by the gallery now gave them little more than an obligatory glance.

"Bold little thing," said Delilah.

"That's the one Mozelle calls Izzie—"

Delilah chuckled, "Because it's as bold and rebellious as our Isabel. Yes, I know."

"Promise you'll keep me in restraints."

Delilah shot a puzzled glance toward her husband's handsome profile. "What do you mean?"

"When she comes off that road, if you don't stop me, I'm going to whale the dickens out of that girl."

"No, you won't, and you know it. You'll hug her so tightly, you'll smother her against your shoulder." He grinned boyishly. "Perhaps you're right."

Isabel excused herself from the table and moved out onto the porch of Mrs. Crenshaw's boarding house. The lights along Greeley's main street spilled into the darkness of the night, and she looked that way, expecting—though not really—to see a tall, dark-clothed figure taking lanky strides toward her. Rather, the men who loitered about were the usual run of cowboys and miners taking a break from their labors of the day.

These past few weeks had managed to destroy the greater part of her confidence that Shadoe was alive. Although she still clung to a small spark of hope, the passage of each day had managed to diminish it a certain degree. She enjoyed working for Sarah McFadden, an experience she had never imagined would be part of her life, and at times, she couldn't imagine what all the big fuss was about among women back home who had been required to work for a living. The little that Sarah paid her was just enough to pay her board, Mirlo's livery fee, and keep her in necessities. To finance the remainder of her journey to Montana and to purchase clothing for the gently warming weather, she had sold her mare to the banker, content with the knowledge that Millicent, purchased for the enjoyment of his granddaughter, would be well cared for. Though her hope that Shadoe would return was now almost nonexistent, she knew she would never be able to sell Mirlo. On Sundays, the one day of the week she did not work for Mrs. McFadden, she would take Mirlo out for a run in the countryside.

Deep in her thoughts, Isabel was not aware that a man had approached until a familiar and irritating voice cut into the silence. She started, her eyes searching the darkness below the steps for the presence of Carl Weatherstone. Realizing that he had greeted her cordially, she responded in a hesitant voice, "It's still rather cool, I think." Then, "What brings you here?" She still felt uncomfortable around him, especially since she had learned of his relationship with Venetia Wainwright. The Spanish vixen had moved into his ranch house just south of Greeley, and occasionally journeyed into town to seek her out for all too frequent moments of deliberate needling.

"I just thought you'd like to know the town sprang for a tombstone for your Mr. McCaine."

"The town sprang for a tombstone for a vagrant," she countered unhesitatingly. "My Mr. McCaine will be back. It is only a matter of time." The darkness successfully veiled his evil grin as Isabel continued, "If that's all you came to tell me, then consider your time wasted."

"You're a bit uppity, miss, for a mere seamstress, ain't you?" When she turned to reenter the house Carl hastily ascended the steps and his finger clamped over her arm, detaining her. He was physically attracted to her, but these past few weeks she had treated him like dirt beneath her shoes. So, he had grown to despise her, even though he wanted her and—he gloated inwardly—he *would* have he

332

eventually.

At the moment, however, she was giving him one of those cool, threatening looks he had grown accustomed to, though he remained unscathed. "Why don't you get out of Greeley. There ain't nothing holding you here. Your man's dead. I guarantee you that!"

When her bottom lip began to tremble, she drew it between her teeth, biting down so hard she might have drawn blood. "You can't possibly know he's dead . . . not unless you killed him."

His eyes cutting to the darkness, then all about them, he immediately returned his gaze to her own. "Now that the subject's come up, Miss Emerson, I did kill him. Want to know how I did it?" Her eyes widened in shock, and she felt that she'd suddenly been impaled by the naked truth, though her heart fought to deny it. When she failed to respond, Carl continued between clenched teeth, "Me and a couple of my boys tied him up real good and we took him out to the old Hooper ranch house. Tied him down in a chair and then we set fire to the place. You know, Little Uppity Bit, we could see through that doorway . . . the flesh sizzling off his bones, and his screams—" He grinned, betraying cramped, crooked teeth. "Hell, if you ever thought he was a real man, you ought to have heard him screamin' and beggin' for his life."

Isabel visibly shuddered. This was not the first altercation she'd had with the despicable deputy marshal. She imagined that Venetia Wainwright had put him up to intimidating her to keep her wondering what they would come up with next. Like those times before, she refused to believe Carl was anything other than a vicious, lying boaster. Pulling her arm from his painful grip, she reentered the

333

boarding house.

She couldn't deny, however, that his graphic description had unnerved her much more so than his previous comments and insinuations. Tears stung her eyes and the tremble in her mouth traveled through her tightly restricted jaws. She waited until she heard the heaviness of Carl's retreating bootsteps, then cautiously reopened the door. She wasn't sure what drew her out into the night once again, but almost as if her feet possessed a mind of their own, she found herself on a deliberate course toward the cemetery. Shortly, she stood before the grave the town had decided was Shadoe McCaine's, and her eyes scanned the plain stone bearing his name and the date on which he had died. Though she felt eerie and frightened, she somehow managed to whisper, "I know you're not in there, Shadoe. I don't know who is, but I know it's not you." Then, sniffing back her tears, her voice became a harsh undertone. "Oh, I hate you, Shadoe, I hate you for disappearing, I hate you for not returning to me. You promised, Shadoe . . . You promised that you would not leave me, that we would go to Montana, find my brother, and that the three of us would return to the Shadows. You promised that we would be married, and that we would be together forever. I was a fool to trust you." Her thoughts whirled together, creating a torrent that threatened to bring her to her knees, not in prayer, but so that she would be nearer to the earth . . . near enough to pummel him with her curled fists and punish him for leaving her. Then she sighed deeply. What would be the use? It wasn't Shadoe McCaine lying there beneath the earth. No one could convince her that it was: not the kind, concerned Pat and Bonnie Crocker; not the blindingly vicious Carl Weather stone or his paramour; not a simple piece of smooth stone bearing the indentation of Shadoe's name.

The night was cool and pleasant, and she did not want to return to the boarding house, which Mrs. Crenshaw kept much too warm to be comfortable. Slowly, she sank to her knees, then began smoothing the dirt around the newly erected stone. When she began to speak again, her voice was reminiscent, free of the anger and hostility she felt toward Shadoe. "I wrote to mother and father a few weeks ago," she said quietly. "I'm sure that they must have found out I was not in New Orleans and certainly I was foolish to believe they wouldn't. But you know, Shadoe—" She began to tug at a particularly stubborn root embedded in the freshly turned dirt. "I know my parents trust me, though God only knows why they should. They will leave me alone and let me come back home on my own volition, and as much as my father might want to come after me, I know he won't." With a small, mirthless laugh, she continued, "And if he does want to come to Greeley, mother will keep him at home. You'll like my mother; father says that except for my coloring I am the spitting image of her when she was my age. Oh, Shadoe, don't you want to see the Shadows? Don't you want to meet my parents?" She sighed deeply. "Don't you want to marry me and be the father of my children? Oh, Shadoe . . . don't you love me?"

"Corpses don't love anyone!"

Though the movements of her hands ceased, Isabel did not turn to face her tormenter. In a small voice, she ordered, "Leave me alone, Venetia."

In response, Venetia grumbled, "I wanted to see the bastard's name on the stone."

She would not allow the Spanish woman to needle her into a confrontation. "Then see it and be on your way." In the moment of silence that followed, Isabel became aware of the soft movements of the horse Venetia had ridden to the cemetery. The chestnut mare, standing less than a dozen feet away with her reins trailing, dug at a patch of grass with her left hoof. Venetia approached, then halted close enough that Isabel could have touched her dark skirts. "You've seen it . . . now go."

Rather than retreat, Venetia tucked her hand into the small of her back and circled Isabel, halting just behind the newly erected head stone. Isabel felt her dark eyes connect intimidatingly to her features. "You don't seem too terribly choked up about poor old—now, what was his name, Shadoe? No, you don't seem too choked up about his death," Venetia pointed out with a quiet laugh. "Why, I would almost have to believe you're glad to be rid of him."

Isabel bit her lip, her fingers curling into the softly turned dirt with the intent of slinging it into Venetia's gloating face. But, no, she would expect something like that, and Isabel was almost certain she was even then prepared to duck. So she smiled into the darkness, then, with a shrill scream, shot so suddenly to her feet that not only did Venetia jump back a pace or two, but the skittery mare reared back, then shot down the hill from the cemetery in a stirring of dust and clods of dirt.

Seeing her hightailing mare merge into the darkness, Venetia hissed, "You bitch! Now I will have to walk!"

If anything could have amused Isabel at that moment, it was the look of dark fury in Venetia's eyes. She might not have responded to her observation

336

a shot ringing out in the night had not interrupted her thoughts. "I do hope you wore comfortable shoes," snipped Isabel, turning toward Greeley.

Venetia visited a scathing look upon the pale-haired woman, though it was wasted on her retreating back. She could wait there all evening in the darkness of the cemetery, but she knew her mare would not return out of any sense of loyalty. Venetia's heels had too often dug into the sensitive sides, and her riding quirt had just as often been felt across the sleek muscles of her haunches. No, she would have to walk, and, blast it, she *hadn't* worn comfortable boots! She had worn the cramped black laceups, designed to show off both her slim ankles and her tiny shoe size.

Isabel hurried into Greeley, her frustrations flared anew, quickly traversed the street and entered Mrs. Crenshaw's boarding house. She imagined that Venetia would go straight to Carl, whining about the way she'd been treated at the cemetery. Carl might, in turn, seek her out for one of his stern warnings. Thus, not wishing a second confrontation with Carl that night, she hurried to her room, exchanged her dress for a comfortable bed gown and tucked herself into the thick, plush covers. Mrs. Crenshaw would not disturb her sleep, not even to answer a summons by her son, the deputy marshal. Isabel had the feeling, anyway, that Mrs. Crenshaw really didn't like her only surviving son all that much.

When she closed her eyes, she was aware of the rapid beating of her heart, as though it echoed within an empty cavity. Only now did she realize how horrifying was the idea that her beloved Shadoe's name was engraved on a tombstone. It had been four weeks since she had last seen him, four

337

weeks that seemed more like four years, and she really wasn't sure why she clung to hope.

Minutes passed. She thought she heard a door open far down the corridor and at the bottom of the stairs. Though she heard a masculine voice commingled with a much quieter feminine one, nothing followed that would have remotely hinted she was the subject of the visit. Soon, she began to drift off to sleep and subconsciously attempted to fight it. She wanted to be awake and lucid and to try to decide what she was going to do in the days ahead. She had saved enough money to continue her journey alone to Montana, but was she brave enough to face the perils alone?

She wasn't sure. Her eyes closed, darkness veiled her thoughts, and all sounds of the night began to drift off with the gentle wind flowing through the gossamer curtains at the open window.

Her eyes fluttered open, all too briefly, to notice that the gauze had ballooned out, capturing the air between its threads and veiling the darkness beyond. A yawn stretched her sleepy features while her long, slender fingers closed over the edges of the coverlet pulled neck-high. In that last lucid moment, she wondered if sleep tonight would be her friend or her enemy.

But the vortex in which she found herself seemed friendly enough. Beyond the foggy haze that was her spirit, she saw the gentle currents of the Boeuf. Upon the slight rise of the hill, from which drifted the delicate fragrance of lavender and white roses, stood the gazebo her father had built for her. Floating serenely toward her was the hauntingly sad hymn sung in a deep baritone voice, and beyond came the high-pitched trill of the cardinals dotting the woodline.

In those first euphoric moments of sleep, she left the Boeuf and began her journey with Shadoe, a journey marred by violence, a journey touched by love. He merged onto the trail ahead of her own gentle, lumbering mare, his forearm resting lazily across the pommel of his saddle, his broad, dark-clothed shoulders unmoving, the cold wind rustling his ebony hair. There, against the backdrop of strange and unknown woods pranced the spirited black stallion, its hooves pacing nervously, then only briefly touching the bare earth.

In her dream, she felt the delicious torment of his body pressed to her own. Had they left the trail? She couldn't remember. They were surrounded by the rough walls of a small cabin, his hands were gently caressing her shoulders, and as she allowed herself to mold to him, like liquid gold, she felt the edge of a mattress press against the back of her knee. Then she was lying upon it, and Shadoe, her beloved Shadoe, rested above her, his mouth curled in a teasing smile, his forefinger entwining a lock of her hair over and over and over until she felt it tangle in his roughly grasping fingers and prick her scalp. All the while, his other hand caressed the smooth mounds of her breasts beneath the fabric of her blouse, and her body, wonderfully aroused, rose against him —

Isabel lurched from the dimensions of her sleep, and as her gaze connected to one that seemed satanically crimson, like orbs of fire, she started to scream, instantly feeling the brutal force of a hand across her mouth. His hand tore at the fabric of her bedgown and she attempted frantically to bring her knee up between his thighs. But he pressed harder upon her, clawing at her, saliva dripping from the corner of his mouth as it lowered to replace the hand covering her attempts to scream.

"You think you're so godalmighty better than me, Little Uppity Bit," an obviously drunken Carl Weatherstone slurred against her hairline. "What you need is a man to bring you down a few notches!"

Isabel was paralyzed with fear. For a moment, she could not find the strength to fight him. She felt the blindness of panic easing across her once again. . . .

That horrid moment in Natchez, when two brutal men had attacked her, came flooding back. Dear Lord . . . was this to be her fate? To die at those brutal hands? Or worse?

Then, like a terrifying moment of history repeating itself, fire leaped into the air behind Carl, magnifying the brutal lust stinging at his eyes, causing the saliva at the corners of his mouth to glisten, and her strength, like a receding flood, left her helpless beneath him.

Twenty-one

Greech felt his way cautiously into the portal of Argonaut's new shaft. The clays beyond the protection of the timbers, were unstable. He was at the fifteen-hundred-foot level of the mine, and even though the night was cold above ground, here the temperature was just over a hundred. As he inspected the day's work in the new shaft, he wiped perspiration from his forehead.

He was hoping that when Carl returned at the end of the week, he would be able to announce the discovery of a new mother lode. In this recently dug shaft, the ore was buried so shallow that he was able to scuff it up with his boots.

An echo rippled through the tunnel. Looking behind him he saw his night foreman, rifle slung across his shoulder, escorting in the men who would work the shaft. The candles and lamps burning along the tunnel betrayed the sweat glistening on shackled, half-naked bodies, some wearing only breechcloths or long johns cut off at mid-thigh.

The last man on the chain had refused to wear a breechcloth and Greech couldn't help but admire his rebellion, both against the heat and against his forced confinement at the fifteen-hundred foot level of the mine. Though paled by the weeks he had spent in darkness, the man had a superbly muscular form a sculptor would be delighted to duplicate in marble. Greech remembered the day he had been brought down in the cage, barely conscious, and shackled to seven other men. The two who had brought him in had requested the body of the man Greech had killed two days before, and Greech had wondered about that until Carl returned two weeks later.

Soon, seven of the prisoners were put to work with pick and shovel, delving into the shaft that was expected to yield a great mass of wealth. The one who continued to hold Greech's attention wielded a sledge hammer and a varied assortment of drill bits. The muscles of his naked torso became taut in their strength and Greech felt another uncontrollable grab of admiration for that particular prisoner.

Shadoe McCaine didn't like the way the man Greech was looking at him. Unlike the others to whom he was chained, Shadoe had not felt the sting of the whip or the butt of Greech's rifle. The man chained beside Shadoe, who had identified himself as a deputy U.S. marshal kidnapped in the mountains, had hinted to him that Greech enjoyed men "the same way men enjoyed women," and that those who cooperated were treated better, fed better and lived longer. Shadoe had already decided that he'd rather be dead.

The strength Shadoe portrayed was merely a facade; sheer force of will made it possible for him to drag the heavy sledge hammer upward. He wasn't sure how long he had been in the mine, since at this depth there was no distinction between day and night, but by counting the shifts, ten hours on and two hours off, during which they'd had to eat and sleep, he had roughly estimated that he'd been in he Argonaut for twenty-nine days. And every one of those twenty-nine days, he and the others had been driven like pieces of machinery. Except for the marshal, all the other men on the chain when he'd arrived had died and been replaced. Considering the marshal's hoarseness and the blood he had coughed up just hours before, Shadoe wasn't sure how much longer the fellow would last.

Two things drove Shadoe onward—the hope of seeing his beloved Isabel again, and the hope of snuffing the life out of Carl Weatherstone with his bare hands.

Something touched the shackle circling his left ankle. The gray tabby tomcat that had free run of the mine rubbed its head against Shadoe's leg. Normally, he wouldn't have minded, but the shackle had rubbed his right leg raw and even the softness of the cat's fur caused him pain.

"Get away from there, Hannibal!" Greech lowered his rifle and moved toward Shadoe. But before he could bend and scoop up the beast, it took a running start and landed easily upon the cage hanging six feet above the floor. Hannibal certainly had not fled in fear; Greech had never been anything but kind to the cat and had claimed ownership of him in the three years he and Carl had worked the Argonaut. It had never occurred to him that the free-spirited cat might consider that the Argonaut belonged to him, and that he shared it with the man-beasts. Before Greech moved away, he growled at Shadoe, "You weren't goin' to club my cat, were you, boy?"

"No, Boss," mumbled Shadoe reluctantly.

The rifle dug into the small of Shadoe's back. "That weren't a disrespectful tone I heard there, was it, boy?"

"No, Boss." Shadoe gritted his teeth, the line of his jaw becoming so razor sharp he felt pain. The rifle drew slightly up. *Go ahead, you bastard!* thought Shadoe. *Go ahead, give me a reason to kill you, too when I get loose. Give me a reason.*

"What you thinkin', boy?"

"Nothin', Boss," mumbled Shadoe. He hated calling Greech and the foreman "Boss," but he'd seen other men beaten senseless when they'd omitted the title. Picking up a drill bit, he began studying the rock for the perfect place to put the blasting hole.

Greech could see that the slim, muscular man mining the Argonaut against his will was concentrating on his work so that he would be less aware of man and rifle. Greech felt a sense of pride that his mere presence had such an effect on this particular son of a bitch, and he turned from him, giving him the freedom to do his work.

The men were preparing to set the sixteen blasts necessary to open the tunnel. Fifty pounds of giant powder sat at the ready and nine holes had been loaded so far. The Argonaut didn't use dynamite and machinery to drive the holes like other mines, but the other mines also didn't use kidnapped men and forced labor, which were a hell of a lot cheaper than the modern methods available.

Shadoe worked mechanically, ignoring the heat and the pain in his ankle, thinking about Isabel and wondering where she was right now. Had she remained in Greeley to look for him, or had she managed to go on to Montana to find the young man she believed to be her brother? He remembered that last moment at Pat Crocker's house . . . the despair in her pale blue eyes, the trembling of her lovely mouth, the way she had held him and begged him not to leave her. What must she be

344

thinking now—that he had deserted her? He couldn't bear the thought that she might think he was that cold and uncaring!

And why had Carl Weatherstone chosen him for this illegal imprisonment? How had he chosen any of them? These poor, unfortunate men—all of them—must have been taken from families or friends or someone who would surely miss them. How could so many disappearances be explained?

"What you thinkin', boy?"

Shadoe's flesh instinctively withdrew from the rifle digging into his back. "Nothin', boss—"

"Well, you better be concentratin' on your work or you're liable to blow these men to kingdom come."

Before he could catch his words, he mumbled, "They'd be better off."

Had he not been handling the highly explosive powder, Greech would have laid the butt of his rifle across his head. He didn't like being talked back to by the tunnel worms Carl brought him. He demanded respect, and any man who didn't give it to him would get something he didn't like. Tapping the barrel of the rifle against Shadoe's shoulder, Greech growled, "You an' me, boy . . . we're goin' to have a private little chat when this shift ends."

Shadoe visibly shuddered. The idea of tamping the hole hard enough to prematurely set off the powder went through his mind. Being torn and mangled beyond recognition, with pieces of his body scattered all along the tunnel, was a fate he preferred over a "private" chat with Greech. But the idea quickly disintegrated inside him; there were seven other men who possibly might not be willing to share his fate.

Thus, the minutes began to pass . . . an hour

. . . two . . . three . . . and in a ten minute break, during which the men were given water, bread, and meat, Greech took a small book from his back pocket, opened to a page and sarcastically began to entertain them with ballads of the miners.

For the mine is a tragic house, it is the worst
 of prisons—
In bitter stone excavated, In barren depths
 located—
Where there is no free breath, With a
 machine they give you air—
By you always burns a lamp, And your body
 struggles with the stone—
Hands work, never do they stop, And
 your chest sorrowfully heaves,
For it is full of poisoned smoke, From
 gelatin's powder white.
We, miners, sons of sorrowing mothers,
 Look like men from the wastelands.
In our faces is no blood, As there is in
 other youth.
Many poor souls their dark days shorten.
Many poor souls with their heads do pay.
There is no priest or holy man, To chant
 the final rites.

As Greech ended the lament, he dropped down the wall, and his rifle tapped what was left of Shadoe's boot. "What you think about that, McCaine? Want to hear another?"

Actually, I was thinking how amazing it is a bastard like you can read. Greech was vile and malevolent; Shadoe had decided weeks ago that he deserved to die. *You'll need final rites,* he added to his thoughts, replying instead to Greech's inquiry, "It's fine, boss."

Greech grinned, betraying black spikes that might once have been teeth. He spat tobacco juice, and the ugly brown stain dripped off the toe of Shadoe's boot. "Tell me, McCaine . . . why did Carl bring *you* here? You ain't like these other fellas, 'cept—" He grinned in the U.S. marshal's direction, "that bastard. Know why he's here?"

"No, boss," answered Shadoe dutifully, his only purpose to deter repercussions.

"Mr. U.S. deputy marshal there . . . he got a little too curious about the men workin' the Argonaut. He was goin' to cause some trouble . . . weren't you, Mr. U.S. deputy marshal?" When he did not answer, but continued to slump against the wall, the bread and meat on his plate still untouched, Greech warned, "You answer me, boy."

Shadoe looked to his side, noticing something that Greech hadn't: a line of fresh blood trickling down the man's chin. His eyes were downcast, glazed, and there was no sign of breathing. Reaching over, Shadoe's fingers circled his cool, dry wrist, then lifted to press against the side of his neck beneath his right ear. "He's dead."

The butt of Greech's rifle struck a brutal blow to Shadoe's shoulder. "He's dead . . . *Boss!*"

Shadoe gritted his teeth, refusing to react to the pain ricocheting through his shoulder and arm. When Greech drew back to strike him again, Shadoe mumbled, "Boss," and hoped his reluctance wasn't too evident.

Greech crawled to his feet, the tobacco juice dribbling down his chin settling among the scant whiskers attempting to cover a scarred, ragged chin. Dragging a large key out of the back pocket of his trousers, he threw it at Shadoe's foot. "Take off your shackle, McCaine, and Mr. U.S. Deputy Marshal's.

347

You're goin' to load him into the cage."

Shadoe cut a scathing look toward Greech, even as his fingers moved to obey his orders. Perhaps if he was free of the shackle, he would be able to make a run for it.

Yeah . . . sure, and where would he run to? He was fifteen hundred feet below the surface of the earth. The only way up was the cage, and that was manipulated from the top following a series of orders yelled upward through the floors of timbers until it reached the ears of the operator. Sure, he could run . . . but there was no place to run to.

Shadoe felt the instant relief of the iron falling away from his raw, swollen ankle. When he removed the shackle from the dead man's leg, he got to his feet, Greech's eyes following his every movement and his rifle at the ready. Easing beneath the weight of the man, Shadoe loaded him onto his shoulders. The men still on the line watched him move past them, limping on the painful ankle. As he neared the cage, he was all too aware of Greech close behind him, preparing to take him down if he gave him even the slightest provocation.

Suddenly, there came a scream from among the men in the new shaft. In the moments that seemed more like a thousand hours that it took both Greech and Shadoe to turn around, the first man on the chain had taken up the sledge hammer, charged toward the wall, dragging the other men from their seated positions, and with a final, maniacal scream, brought the iron weight down on the last charge Shadoe had set.

The charge exploded, setting off all the powder that had not been used. In the ensuing melee, the torn and mangled bodies of six men flew in every direction. Shadoe had just dropped the corpse from

348

his shoulders when the body of one man hit the roof, then fell at his feet, a horribly mangled mass of human flesh.

Razor-sharp particles of silica dust, granite and quartz flew through the tunnel with such force that Shadoe was rammed into the wall. Greech, attempting to maintain his weapon between his fingers, saw it suddenly fly off, his right hand, severed by a large slice of quartz, still attached to gun, his finger at the trigger. He dropped to his knees, already dead, the same piece of quartz embedded in his heart like a tight, swollen cork in a bottle. There was no blood . . . only the surprise of death dragging down his ugly features. The timbers began to sway and sag, bringing the weight down to crush his head like a melon.

As the timbers scattered like a fistful of dropped toothpicks, Shadoe thought of his beloved Isabel. Though he threw up his arms, he could not brace off the attack of the collapsing tunnel and its man-made support. He knew only that the weight of the mine was closing in on him, and in those last few seconds he became acutely aware of the odor of water-soaked timbers and of blood and pieces of flesh trickling down the walls.

There was nothing else after that: no fear, no dread, nothing but the darkness that surely came with death . . . and an unspoken, and final, farewell to Isabel—

Isabel screamed with all her might. She flailed her arms, hoping to disengage the horrid, odorous body of Carl Weatherstone, but all she met was the emptiness of the dark. Surprised, she fought off the covers, her eyes flinging open. There, standing

349

against the semidarkness of the corridor was Mrs
Crenshaw, holding a lamp whose flame seemed un
usually high. Though her eyes darted frantically
around the darkness of the room, they beheld n
other intruder.

Mrs. Crenshaw set the lamp aside, then sat o
the bed and drew Isabel against her. "Hush . .
hush, girl . . . you've had a nightmare—"

"N-no . . . no!" she sobbed. "He was here.
swear, I—I—and the room was on fire—"

"It was no such thing!" scolded Mrs. Crensha
who then turned and flicked her left wrist at th
other boarders who were gathered at the doorwa
"Go on back to your beds!" she ordered. "She's ju
had a spell."

Isabel immediately felt foolish. The dream ha
seemed so real that she could hardly believe it ha
been a natural product of restless sleep. Then sh
realized she must have dragged the small towel sh
had dropped to the pillow earlier across her mout
causing the illusion of a hand smothering her breat
and her screams. The heavy quilts had given the i
lusion of a man's weight, and her own frantic flai
ing within the realms of her sleep had caused th
small tear in the bodice of her gown. But what ha
given depth to the nauseating smell of drunkennes
of a man's unwashed body? Subconsciously, sh
drew in a short breath, and was rewarded with onl
the nearly nonexistent aroma of the lavender wate
in which she had bathed earlier in the day.

Drawing back from Mrs. Crenshaw so that sh
could give her an apologetic smile, Isabel explaine
"Weeks ago, when Shadoe and I were in Natche
two men attacked me in my hotel room. A lam
was knocked over and the hotel burned. Both of th
men died . . . and—" Gently, Isabel shrugged,

uess it affected me more than I had thought. Per-
aps it is because Shadoe is not with me. He does
ive me such courage."

Though she spoke lightly, she still felt the blind-
ess of panic bubbling from deep within her. She
ill suffered the loneliness of losing Shadoe, and the
oubts and insecurities of an uncertain future. She
as thankful for the friendship of people like Mrs.
renshaw, Sarah McFadden, and the Crockers.
Vithout them she wasn't sure if she'd have survived
ese last few weeks.

"Well, Isabel —" Mrs. Crenshaw gave her hand an
ffectionate pat. "Now that the whole household is
wake, there is bound to be one or two of the men
ho'll be raiding the kitchen." She had not fussed;
erely made a statement. "If you're all right
ow — ?"

"Yes, thank you," responded Isabel, dragging the
mp, heavy strands of her hair back from her face.
wouldn't blame you if you put me out on the
reet."

Again, the plump hand patted Isabel's. "Now, I
ouldn't be doing that. You're good about paying
our bill, which is more than I can say for some of
e men who drag in from the mines."

Isabel was glad she'd not told Mrs. Crenshaw that
er ruthless son had been the subject of her night-
aare. The dear lady had enough worries, trying to
upport herself in a man's world, without the added
urden of her son having such an unpleasant effect
pon one of her boarders. So, Isabel said nothing,
erely smiling her gratitude as the older woman
egan her withdrawal from the large, stifling cham-
er.

When the door closed her in that dreary dark-

ness, Isabel fell back to her pillow and pulled t
covers up. She had so much on her mind that
seemed to be a senseless mumble echoing throug
her head. Though she closed her eyes and drew
deep breath, she could not still the panic she co
tinued to feel, or shake the vision of Carl Weathe
stone's smiling mouth, with its trickle of sali
gathering at its corners. The dream had seemed
real; she could almost feel the bruises he'd left up
her tender flesh, though she knew there were non
Sometimes she worried that her mind was faili
her.

"See what you've done to me, Shadoe?" she mur
bled, feeling tears instantly begin to gather. Patch
of shade skittered across the high ceiling; fro
somewhere beyond the window, beyond the absolu
darkness, the sounds of muted conversation a
music from the saloons gained in clarity. As she l
there, attempting to still her tremor, she forc
away the voices and the music and the songs
gaudy dance hall girls, so that she became aware
the sounds within the boarding house. Even th
clock on the mantel ticked as loud as a drum cor
within a boiler factory. Tick . . . tick . . . tick .
"Oh, stop it! Stop it!" she ground out, turning
her side, simultaneously drawing the extra pill
over her exposed ear and pressing hard upon it.

She was afraid to try to recapture sleep, afra
she might succumb once again to nightmares. Pe
haps if she knew why Carl Weatherstone despis
her so deeply . . . was it because of Venetia . .
was she ordering the intimidation now that Shad
was gone and he could not be her victim? Was Ca
just mean, always having to pick on someone a
make another life miserable? Had she somehow wo
that honor? A sardonic laugh echoed within he

Well, she wished he'd go elsewhere for his entertainment.

Again, she closed her eyes, the ticking of the clock now an almost indistinguishable series of dull thuds beyond the downy thickness of the pillow. She wished that Shadoe were beside her, drawing her into his arms and awakening her passions. She ached to hear the huskiness of his voice when he made his claim to her. She wanted to lie in his protective embrace, to feel his hot flesh molding to her own . . . and because her deepest, most intimate desires were far, far out of her reach, she felt her sobs begin to choke into the fabric of the pillow.

She wished she could face the prospect that he was gone, but her heart wouldn't allow it. Some horrible fate must surely have befallen him, but she was not convinced that he had died in the fire Marshal Crocker—and that despicable Carl Weatherstone—would have her believe. There was only one explanation—he was being held somewhere against his will and was trying to return to her. He had professed to love her, and a man who loved a woman would not leave her, alone and defenseless, so far from her homeland. He had vowed to protect her, to see her safely to Montana, and whatever had taken him from her had been an overpowering outside force. She had to believe that, to maintain the conviction that he was alive somewhere and being kept deliberately from her. It was the only thing that kept her in Greeley, the only hope that prevented her from returning to the Boeuf, and to the mothering protection of mother and father, Cousin Justin, and a battle array of friends, acquaintances and unsolicited pity.

Somehow, in the moments to follow, as she continued to press the pillow to her ear, sleep rolled upon her as peacefully as clouds tumbling over each other in a dove-gray sky. If she dreamed she was unaware of it. If a nightmare plagued her, she brought no memories of it from the realms of her sleep. She knew only that when the dawn sent its scant reminder of rebirth through the gossamer curtains, she felt vivacious and alive . . . and determined that today would be the day her beloved Shadoe returned to her.

She bathed in the cool water left over from the day before, then donned the cream-colored gown, unclaimed by the patron who had ordered it, that Sarah McFadden had allowed her to purchase for pennies above the cost of the fabric and notions.

Since she had promised Sarah she would come in early to finish the final gown for Rebecca Corbin's wedding trousseau, Isabel made a pass through the dining room, claimed one unbuttered roll, which she wrapped in a napkin, and exchanged quick pleasantries with the other boarders.

She entered the cool morning and half skipped across the porch, her small feet touching each step lightly enough that it might not have been touched at all. She was just descending to the ground when there suddenly loomed before her a tall, slightly built man with a hat crushed to his chest. He smiled pleasantly as she caught his arm to keep from running into him.

"Do pardon me," said Isabel. "I shouldn't be in such a rush."

Wayland Macy had not expected a woman so tall, slim and graceful. He would have stepped aside but considering himself a clumsy man, feared making a fool of himself. As Isabel politely moved to step around him, he found his voice. "Miss, do yo know a lady named Emerson who's supposed to be staying here?"

A smile touched Isabel's mouth. "My name is Emerson."

"Oh—"

When he failed to produce further sound, Isabel asked, "Am I the one you're looking for?"

"You got a man named McCaine?"

Isabel maintained her strength, even as she felt it rush from her in one fell swoop. "Well, he's not in Greeley right now—"

"You work for Sarah McFadden, don't you?" When she nodded, he continued with haste, "Mind if I walk along with you?"

"If you would like." A strange feeling crawled through Isabel's shoulders. The man obviously had something to say, and it had to do with Shadoe. She didn't want to hear again that Shadoe was dead. She hadn't believed it the first time, and she certainly wouldn't believe it now.

"Ma'am, I've been in Greeley about a week, and been hearin' some stories here an' there about your man—"

"About Shadoe? What did you hear?"

Reaching the planked boardwalk, Macy stood aside while she stepped up, his arm extended in preparation of a stumble or missed step. Soon, he fell in beside her once again and half ran to keep up with her brisk pace. "Well, ma'am," he began, responding to her inquiry, "I heard that he might have been killed in a fire last month, but—"

"But what?"

"Well, I've been piecin' together some things, and once I heard that you don't believe he's dead, I'd like to tell you what I been puttin' together."

Isabel halted, pivoted so quickly that Macy almost collided with her, then drew her hands up to her narrow hips. They were in front of Perkins' Mercantile. Approaching, dropping to a narrow bench, Isabel's hand outstretched. "Please, sit down and tell me what's on your mind."

He sat, his booted feet apart, and his hat dangling between his knees. When he put his finger into its band and started twirling it, Isabel's hand clamped over his own, stilling the movement. He gave her a small smile. "I've been minin' for nigh onto ten years, ma'am. The Comstock in Nevada, the Klondike, Gold Bottom Creek, the Black Hills, the Winter Quarters mine in Utah, the Silver King and the Santa Rita, but hell, ma'am—pardon, ma'am—but I ain't never heard nothin' like what I heard at Leadville."

"I gather that what you've heard has something to do with my Mr. McCaine?"

"Well, ma'am, I'm just sayin' that after what I've been piecin' together this past week, there might be another reason why your man left like he did."

"The marshal believes he's dead," Isabel reminded him. "What have you got to say that would give me hope? Have you seen a man fitting Shadoe's description?"

"No, ma'am—" Instantly, a shade of disappointment passed over the lovely feminine features facing him. "But there's been rumors circulatin' at Leadville that a couple of men are working a mine called the Argonaut with slave labor . . . and most of those men have been snatched off the streets of Greeley."

"And you think Shadoe might have been one of those men? But he was with the deputy marshal the same night he disappeared—"

"Carl Weatherstone?" Isabel nodded. "Ma'am

356

Carl Weatherstone . . . he's one of the owners of the Argonaut. When I was in Leadville, I heard about men being taken down there and shackled and forced to work until they dropped dead. I heard there's a pit on the first level of the mine where the bodies are buried, three and sometimes four deep, in the same hole." When Isabel shuddered visibly, Macy continued, "Sorry, ma'am, but when I heard about your man disappearin', and him bein' with Weatherstone that night, well, I just put two and two together, and I believe he might be in the Argonaut. I even talked to the undertaker here in Greeley, and he said that when that burned up fella was brought in — if the marshal hadn't told him he suspected it was Mr. McCaine — that he'd have thought it an older man . . . an' dead long before he was burned up in that place."

"Why are you so interested in this?"

Macy thought it a reasonable question. Placing his hat upon his knee, he replied, "I'm real tired of minin', Miss Emerson, an' my lungs bein' full of silica dust. I got this cousin back east who's a private investigator, an' he said if I could solve an unsolvable case, he'd make me a partner. Well, I figure that if I could solve the case of your missing Mr. McCaine, and uncover a slave operation run by a legitimate deputy marshal, well, my cousin would have to take me on. I got a wife and two young'uns back in California, an' I don't aim to leave my Becky a widow an' my young'uns without a pa."

Isabel only then noticed the huskiness of emotion seeping into his voice. Moving gracefully to her feet, she turned, her gaze holding his own. "Why don't you and me go talk to the marshal."

"I done tried that, Miss. He got real mad an' he says his deputy ain't done nothin' to cast no suspicion on hisself, and without proof, well . . . he just don't want to hear suppositions. An' . . . he warned me not to be bringin' this up to you either. He'll be right mad."

"Then, we'll just have to convince him that it needs to be checked out, won't we?"

"Ma'am, if you'd be so kind, I'd appreciate it if you don't say nothin' to him about me. An' don't tell him that I told you all this. He's liable to shoot me dead fer bein' a troublemaker."

"I won't mention that we've talked," agreed Isabel, and in parting, "Thank you, Mr. Macy, for giving me some hope. I'll talk to the marshal right away."

With a dutiful smile, Isabel nodded her appreciation, then turned in the direction of Marshal Crocker's office.

Twenty-two

Hoping that Sarah McFadden wouldn't mind if [s]he was a little late, Isabel charged into the mar[s]hal's office. She stood there, fairly quaking, her [e]yes connecting first to Pat Crocker's, then sweeping [t]oward a side table where Carl Weatherstone poured [c]offee. He had just taken up two cups and turned [t]oward the desk when Isabel hotly demanded, "Do [y]ou have Shadoe imprisoned at the Argonaut?"

Not only did Carl's right boot miss a step, but [b]oth cups of coffee tipped, spilling their entire con[te]nts on an otherwise spotless floor. Before an obvi[ou]sly shocked Carl could find the moment to [re]spond, Pat shot to his feet. "Now, Miss Isabel . . . [yo]u're not on about Mr. McCaine still being alive, [ar]e you?"

Though she meant no disrespect, Isabel did not [ag]ain glance in Pat Crocker's direction. Her gaze [co]ntinued to hold that of Carl Weatherstone, and [sh]e couldn't help but notice the sudden drain of his [no]rmally swarthy face. A ghastly pallor evened out [hi]s features, giving them a strange flatness, like an [am]ateurishly painted portrait. When Isabel saw that [he] did not plan to respond, she demanded, "Well, is [h]e at the Argonaut, Weatherstone?" He didn't have [to] answer her; the truth was as plain as the scar [acr]oss the flat plane of his right cheek. "So . . . he [is] there! And how many others?" she continued in

359

the same demanding tone. "How many men have you kidnapped and forced to dig out the gold and silver you line your pockets with? How many men to dig out the gold you make into gaudy baubles for that Spanish trollop you have living in your house?"

That his deputy was imprisoning men at his mine was too preposterous for Pat Crocker to believe. But the Spanish woman living in Carl's house? That was *not* impossible to believe! His eyes cut to Carl's in his moment of surprise. "Carl . . . does Mrs. Wainwright live at your house?" It was important that Carl maintain the integrity required of a law enforcement agent, and living with a woman who was not his wife—especially a woman like Venetia Wainwright—did not uphold that unspoken requirement for discretion and high standard.

"For Christ's sake!" Carl was angry enough at that moment to strangle the Southern woman. Rather he turned slowly toward the window looking out on Greeley, and his hand rose to cover the tremor of his heart that he feared might be visible against the material of his shirt. "The woman's crazy, Pat," he responded dryly. "Obsessed with McCaine and refusing to believe he's dead. You've heard the talk around town . . . talk that she should get herself back down South where she belongs."

Pat immediately countered, "I ain't heard no such thing, Carl. Everybody here an' abouts—" He cut softened gaze toward Isabel, "is real fond of Miss Emerson. You know—" Instinctively, Pat looked past Carl, toward the wall of Perkins' Mercantile where the remnants of several privately printed posters still hung . . . posters listing the names of missing men, and one or two, placed there by grieving wives and mothers, offering modest re

360

wards. "You know, Carl," Pat continued, "Maybe me an' the federal marshal from Denver ought to be takin' a look at the operation of your mine."

Carl pivoted so swiftly he almost lost his balance. "What the hell for? You're going to listen to the ravings of a mad, obsessed woman?"

"If you ain't got nothin' to hide, Carl, why are you so riled up?"

"I ain't riled up," he argued, casting Isabel a murderous glare. "I just don't like suspicion thrown on me by—"

"By what?" interjected Isabel. "The truth?"

Pat Crocker's tone became patronizing. "Now, Miss Isabel. Why don't you go on over to Sarah's and let me take care of this."

Her mouth pressed into a petulant smirk. "You should keep Carl in sight until then. He'll send a warning down to Leadville and the Argonaut will be set up to look like a legitimate operation." She hesitated to add, "There's no telling what will become of the men being imprisoned there—"

"There are no men imprisoned!" Carl countered vehemently, his hands, subconsciously, curling into tight fists.

"I don't think that's necessary, Miss Isabel. Besides—" Pat shot a sidewise glance toward his deputy. "Me an' Carl, we'll be busy most of the day checkin' out some of the nearby ranches for rustled cattle. Won't we, Carl?"

"Yeah," he reluctantly agreed. "We'll be damn busy."

An abrupt fall of silence prickled Isabel's skin. She lowered her glance for a moment, her moist palms easing among the folds of her gown. In a quiet, childlike tone, she said, "When you ride to

361

the Argonaut, Marshal Crocker, I'd like to go with you."

Pat Crocker said, "A mine ain't no place for a lady."

"Or a troublemaker," added Carl Weatherstone in a slightly sarcastic tone. "And I don't like the trouble you're trying to cause for me and the legitimate workings of the Argonaut."

"We'll just see how legitimate it is," countered Isabel bravely. "I would imagine that you're going to require a search warrant when the marshals visit your mine?"

"Hell—" He'd been about to respond, *yes,* but on second thought, requiring a search warrant would certainly cause suspicion. Thus, he bit his tongue and tonelessly ended, "No. Any man who wants to look over the operations of the mine is welcome." A smile of feigned indulgence broke the angry set of his features. "And you don't need an invitation if you'd like to tag along, Miss Emerson." To Pat he said, "You just let me know when you plan to go down to Leadville."

"I'll go in the morning," replied Pat. "The U.S. marshal's in Greeley to attend a trial day after tomorrow. I don't reckon he'll mind takin' a ride down to Leadville to pass the time."

"That's fine with me. But when you get back to Greeley, I'll be expecting an apology."

"If it's due, I'll make it tomorrow," countered Pat, returning to the chair at his desk. "You'll be ridin' down with us. And—" He hesitated to reprimand Carl in front of the young lady. "You'd better be gettin' Mrs. Wainwright out of your house, Carl. I don't want any ugly rumors circulatin'. Elections'll be comin' around soon."

Priding herself on her victory, Isabel made all

haste in extricating herself from the marshal's office and from beneath the threatening glare of Carl Weatherstone. She worried that he might follow her down the street, jerk her into an alley and beat her senseless, perhaps even kill her. For that reason, she moved off the planked boardwalk, crossed the street and hurried toward Sarah's shop by way of the road.

She knew she could not wait until the morning, when Pat Crocker would ride to Leadville, and so made her apologies to Sarah and requested that she be given the day off from her duties. Reluctantly, Sarah agreed; she understood how important Shadoe was to Isabel.

Isabel made haste. The last thing Wayland Macy had told her was that he was staying at the Exchange Hotel, and she felt confident that he would accompany her to Leadville. It was important that they leave right away. If Carl was employing forced labor in the mine, he might even then be sending one of his local henchman southward. She didn't want him to have enough time to transfer Shadoe and any other men kept in slavery and replace them long enough to present a legitimate operation to Pat and the U.S. marshal.

Isabel's heart fluttered excitedly; she felt hope again . . . hope that Shadoe was alive. Though she couldn't bear the thought of him being held in captivity in Carl Weatherstone's mine, it was far better than the captivity of a coffin. She directed purposeful steps toward the hotel where Mr. Macy was staying. Please, please, let him be in.

He was, indeed. Venetia Wainwright stomped up and down the length of the room while Wayland relaxed on the bed, his boots crossed and his palms tucked behind his head. They had just made love the way she liked it, she completely clothed except for her pantaloons, the man flat on his back beneath her. "What the hell are you so nervous about, Venetia? I told you, the Emerson woman went straight to the marshal's office. If you want to get rid of old Carl, I don't know any better way than this. Once Crocker finds out that his deputy is guilty of kidnapping, mayhem, and murder, he'll be swingin' from the gallows." Wayland eased his feet off the bed and arose, humorously aware of Venetia's silent, lethal scrutiny. Approaching, he took her arms above the elbows and willed her protesting form against his own. "Why you actin' like this? Why don't you spread out on the bed and let me do it the man's way—"

"I don't want anything to go wrong," Venetia pouted, half-heartedly attempting to extricate herself from Wayland's grip. She really didn't want to be saddled with this simpleton ranch hand—certainly she didn't want him pawing at her again so soon— and planned to be rid of him once the overly possessive Carl was out of the way. But she had to maintain the facade of adoration, and show some sincerity that she would keep her promises, or Wayland wouldn't do her bidding. Thus, she tucked herself back into his embrace and gently lay her head against his chest. "I hope you understand, Wayland, how very much I adore you. I don't love Carl, and I certainly can never trust him again. I asked him to do one small thing for me and he claimed to have done it. Now—" She gritted her teeth, furious again that Shadoe McCaine was still alive and being worked in the Argonaut. "Now," she began again, "I learn that he lied to me. Blatantly, uncon-

scionably lied! And that is unforgivable!" Her tone
became sticky sweet and entreating. "But you'll kill
him for me, won't you, Wayland? When the mine is
investigated and the men are set free, you will kill
McCaine, won't you?"

"Sure, honey." Actually, he had no intentions of
killing anyone he didn't have a personal grudge
against. He had done just about anything for
women, but he wouldn't kill. He'd rough him up a
bit and run him out of the territory, but if Venetia
wanted him killed, she'd have to do it herself. "Just
don't forget, honey, that you've promised me half
that money in Carl's safe."

"Of course . . . I *always* keep my word." Actually,
she had no intentions of giving this bumpkin half of
the hundred thousand dollars in cash Carl kept in
the safe. She planned to be rid of Wayland once
Carl was gone and he had taken care of Shadoe
McCaine. Who, learning that a poor, tragic little
woman had fired her derringer straight into the
heart of this bastard, wouldn't believe she was de-
fending herself against the most hideous of crimes
perpetrated against the gentler sex? She had killed
twice—that blasted woman, Mary Ellen, back in
Texas, that old husband of hers—and she could certainly do it again. I *have to take care of myself,* she
mused. *And men are good for nothing . . . absolutely
nothing!*

"Venetia, honey, why don't you—"

A rap sounded at the door, interrupting Venetia's
thoughts as rudely as had the boringly droning
voice of Wayland Macy and his uncompleted request. "Now, who is that?" she demanded in a rude
hiss, moving into a recess where she would not be
seen by the intruder.

Tucking in his shirt, Wayland moved to open the

door. Surprised to see Isabel standing there, he quickly pulled the door to, explaining, "Don't want you to see the way a man like me lives, Miss Emerson. I ain't very neat."

She couldn't have cared less how untidy he was. "I want you to take me to Leadville right now. I'll pay you for your trouble."

"Wh—now?"

"Is there a problem? You said you weren't presently working." Isabel did not feel the same easiness she'd felt with Wayland Macy earlier that morning. But she was desperate to get to the Argonaut before Carl could act, and there was no one else whose aid she could solicit on such short notice. When he hesitated to respond, she prompted him with a curt, "Well?"

"Miss Emerson, I—" He was at a loss. If he took her to the Argonaut, the warning to the other partner could ruin their plans to be rid of Carl. It could also endanger both of their lives, since the man, Greech, whose reputation for self-preservation had traveled far enough to make most men cautious, wouldn't hesitate to kill them both and protect the operation. "Didn't the marshal believe your story?"

"He's going to take a U.S. marshal down there in the morning to check it out. But Carl was in the office, and I'm afraid he'll send a warning to Leadville. If Shadoe is imprisoned in the mine, I'm afraid he'll get rid of him . . . and the other men being held against their will, before Marshal Crocker arrives."

Wayland Macy thought fast. He really had no choice but to agree to take her to the Argonaut, or she would become suspicious. But did it really matter after the fact? She had planted the seed of doubt

366

in the mind of Marshal Pat Crocker about the operations of his deputy's mine at Leadville, and he would check it out whether or not he took the lady southward. Digging his fingers into the area of his stomach, he said to Isabel, "Would you excuse me a minute? I got a sour stomach and had the desk clerk send up a glass of milk."

"Of course."

Wayland opened the door and stepped back into the room, giving Isabel a small smile. Closing the barrier between them brought him face to face with a darkly frowning Venetia Wainwright. "What the hell am I supposed to do?" Wayland asked in a tone so quiet even Venetia caught only a word or two, though enough to give an answer.

"Agree to take her," she whispered. "But . . . get lost or something. Delay her long enough to allow the marshal to get there first."

He nodded, otherwise unresponsive. When he returned to the corridor, Isabel was slowly pacing. "There, that's better," he said, patting his stomach as he reinforced the lame excuse he'd used to return to the room. "All right, Miss Emerson, I'll take you to Leadville."

Quickly divulging her plans for immediate departure, Isabel returned to the boarding house, and donned the comfortable Levis that Shadoe had purchased for her in Fort Smith. She added a feminine touch with a blouse whose collar and cuffs were fringed with lace, pulled on her boots, and left the house by a back entrance. She didn't want Mrs. Crenshaw to see her, and possibly to mention to her son that she'd seen her ready for riding.

Half an hour later, with Mirlo's powerful muscles quivering beneath her, she and Wayland Macy eased into a gentle lope along the southbound road toward Leadville. One vision—that of the man she affectionately called her "dark wolf"—filled her mind, hope filled her heart, and a renewed determination ricocheted through her. Shadoe had saved her from countless perils since the night they'd left New Orleans. It was time to return the favor. Yes, she was afraid, but love was deeper than the fear she felt for her own life.

She saw nothing of the passing landscape, of the gentle transition of spring, nor felt the chill rush against her already rosy features. Wayland Macy had said very little, contenting himself to merely keep up with the nervous pace of the stallion she rode, and she was free to think her thoughts and make her silent speculations.

Now that she thought about it, that flouncy barracuda providing Carl's mattress work-outs probably had something to do with all of this. She had been furious that Marshal Crocker had refused to act on her ridiculous seven-year-old complaint of rape, furious enough, in fact, that she'd filed assault charges against Isabel simply to delay their departure from Greeley. It seemed a reasonable assumption that she and Carl were in it together. *Blast! Blast!* she thought. *Why didn't Wayland Macy come to me sooner? My poor, dear, beloved Shadoe! What horrors has he been subjected to these past four weeks?*

"Miss Emerson, hold up." Isabel instantly dragged Mirlo to a halt, and on command, he pranced about in a half-circle. "I believe my horse has picked up a rock," explained Wayland.

Isabel lithely jumped down from Mirlo's saddle, unaware of Wayland Macy scrutinizing the area of her buttocks enclosed within the tight denim fabric. When she turned toward him, he quickly looked down, then dragged up the front hoof of the sorrel mare. Isabel moved off the road, then dropped to a sitting position upon a fallen branch. Mirlo rubbed his head briskly against her left shoulder, almost disengaging her from her relaxation.

"Hold on, old boy," she chuckled lightly. "We'll be there soon. You'll see him again soon. I promise you."

Then she sighed deeply, her eyes only half-heartedly returning to the crouched form of Wayland Macy as he dug into the hoof with a small knife he'd removed from his back pocket. Had she not been so worried about Shadoe, she might have doubted her sudden decision to travel alone with a man she had met only that morning.

But Shadoe was all that she cared about. And she would see him again. She was sure of that.

In the three years he'd lived in the Argonaut, Hannibal had never before seen the walls come tumbling down. Though a large rock had crashed close enough to his long, gray-and-black-striped form to remove a path of fur along his back leg, he was otherwise unscathed. For the first few minutes after the rumble fell silent, the trembling feline sat at the corner of the cage and caterwauled. Then, as the dust began to clear, he started looking for escape routes, finding too many mazes among the timbers that had scattered across the fifteen-hundred-foot level of the mine.

Then he caught the distant echo of a low human moan and pounced upon the nearest of the fallen boulders.

At Shadoe's left hand lay the body of the deputy U.S. marshal, at his right lay the rifle with Greech's severed hand still attached. He tried to focus his eyes, but could see little more than the veil of dust beginning to thin as it settled about him, and the foggy outline of the rubble and mounds of timbers and boulders. Even in his pain, he was amazed to see a single carbide lamp still burning. He could hear no human sounds beyond his own and knew that none of the other men, so close to the blast when it exploded, could possibly have survived. He lay there for a moment, trying to still his own moans, trying to force himself to breathe the air that was heavy with silica dust and minute particles of shattered rock and quartz, and he hoped that his body, strangely numb right now, might give him some hint that it was still alive. Then he felt a painful throb in his left ankle and became aware of the boulder pinning it down.

Dropping his sweat-drenched forehead onto his forearm, he closed his eyes for a moment, listening through the dreadful silence, for the echo of human voices somewhere above. He took a moment to pray that the rumble of the explosion might have drifted toward the nearest mine, half a mile away.

He didn't want to die, and certainly didn't want to do it alone. When he felt the nudge of the familiar old tomcat, and the purr that was almost raucous against his ear, he put his hand up to the soft patch of fur between its ears. "Why is it everywhere I go there's a damn cat hanging around?" Then on a softer note, "You won't let me die alone, will you Hannibal?" asked Shadoe in a husky, half-strangled voice. "Not that I want you to join in on the chore," he amended in the same tone. "Just show me how the hell I'm going to get out of here!"

The boulder at his ankle shifted slightly away and Shadoe took advantage of the freedom to turn to his side. Quietly, he studied the frame of timber above him and the heavy rocks pressing upon them. One timber support was cracked almost through, and if it broke he'd be crushed by the load it precariously held back. Forcing all thoughts from his mind except those of self-preservation, he carefully extracted his ankles, then used his elbows to ease from beneath the mass of rock and water-soaked timber. When at last he pressed his back against what seemed to be a secure boulder, he drew up his knees and gently grasped the throbbing ankle. He cried out, feeling the sharpness of bone against his palm, and then the blood running down the planes of his raised hand and along the protruding vein of his wrist. The tomcat sat nearby, still purring, watching Shadoe with its battle-torn ears flicking at the air.

Shadoe knew that for the time being he was safe. But what about ten minutes from now, or even one minute, if the earth shifted? How many tons of earth rested between his temporary sanctuary and the warmth of sunshine?

An exhausted Shadoe dropped his head back, his body lurching as a boulder across the littered tunnel shifted. The owners of this mine would undoubtedly prefer no survivor of this disaster escaped to tell his tale; if, despite their intentions, a rescue operation began, Shadoe feared that it might be days or even weeks before they dug or blasted their way through the collapsed tunnel. They would have to timber it as they went in to ensure the safety of their own lives. Then a new fear eased into Shadoe's heart . . . suppose the water, only inches deep along the tunnel floor, should rise and drown him?

Shadoe tried to laugh; no sound manifested itself, but stuck dryly and uncomfortably in his throat. Did it really matter if he died an hour from now, or ten days from now? Greech was dead, as were many of the men imprisoned in the mine, and Carl wouldn't bring in volunteers, for fear of his nefarious operation being uncovered, to dig out any survivors. Shadoe knew he was a dead man, even though he continued to draw breath. But even a dead man had to keep hope alive. Thus, he lightly closed his eyes and tried not to think, finding, rather, a million separate and yet indistinguishable thoughts flooding through his brain. He lay there, unmoving, unaware of the creaking of precariously perched timbers somewhere beyond the mounds of rubble closing him in, unaware of the cat patiently, endlessly stroking its fur with its rough tongue. An hour may have passed, or a thousand years, for all he knew. Somewhere beyond the realms of indistinguishable time, he thought he heard the sounds of a rescue party working toward him. A vicious teasing in his mind tried to convince him men were blasting through the huge pieces of rock . . . he even thought he felt the concussion of an extra heavy shot ricocheting through the rubble and reaching his body, and yet when he ventured to force open his eyelids, everything was still and deathly, even the darkness beyond the crumbled walls echoed with the sounds of silence.

Had an hour passed . . . a day . . . a week? The painful gnawing in his stomach would indicate the latter, though he knew it was not possible. Did time really matter? At least, he wouldn't die alone. The cat remained close by in the darkness, now made absolute by the draining of the one light. Hearing Hannibal chewing through the bones of a rat or some other hapless creature, Shadoe became hungry enough that he'd have gladly accepted half of the cat's feast.

But then a grim thought came to him. Perhaps the cat, as trapped in the tunnel as he was, had found the remains of one of the—

Christ! Shadoe lurched up, pressing his palms so heavily against his temples that he thought his head would snap beneath the pressure. He felt sick at his stomach. His sodden clothing was rubbing his skin, and he felt that his flesh was softening, becoming so loose that it might slip and crawl over the bone and muscle beneath. Though he couldn't see his hand in front of him, and feared the temperament of the loose timber surrounding him on all sides, he began to feel along the damp lines of the nearest boulders, hoping to find a higher, dryer place.

He became aware of the cramped aching through his body as he tried to move, and feeling an even deeper pain in his ankle, he eased his palms down his leg, immediately flinching from the raw, festering wound. He didn't have to see it to know it was broken and infected. If he didn't get out of the mine soon—and if he didn't die first—he'd lose the bottom half of his leg to gangrene. With that gruesome thought in mind, he decided not to sit still and wait for rescuers who would never come. If it was at all possible, he had to get out of the mine, employing his own willpower, reserve, determination, and strength.

The high-pitched cry of the cat, who had been startled by the sudden movement of his human companion, pierced through Shadoe's oversensitive hearing and plastered his head in pain. When he tried to growl, "Shut up, Hannibal," he found his voice gone and nothing but a pained, swollen hiss escaping from his mouth. All the while he moved carefully over the mounds of boulders in the impenetrable darkness he kept hearing the blasting charges of rescuers who were not there, the inaudible mutterings of men ricocheting through the rock of the lode. He knew it wasn't real—that his imagination had gone haywire and his hopes were feeding him the illusions of freedom. What was real was the stench of death and decay. He thought he knew what a snake must feel like, slithering along on its belly; even when he felt headroom above, he didn't have the strength to take advantage of the space. He'd lost his boots in the blast, and his one good foot felt that it had been dipped in scalding water.

Why couldn't he find the courage to just lie back and die? It was going to happen eventually, so why fight it? But every time he closed his eyes, he saw Isabel's sweetly smiling features. Every time his heart beat so fiercely against the cavity of his chest, he knew it was beating for her. Somewhere, beyond the rock and timber and darkness, his precious Isabel waited for him. He couldn't let her down. He owed her too much. These past four weeks, when defeat would have crushed him, the hard, grueling work would have sapped the strength from his body and his hopes might otherwise have been dashed by the imprisoning darkness, Isabel had kept him going.

As the days passed, like minutes dragging forward into time and distance, he drifted in and out of consciousness, unaware of days turning into nights and nights into days. Was this how it would be when he died, feeling the painful and absolute loss, not of life, but of Isabel?

Twenty-three

A tall, cadaverous man, wearing a long black
[c]loak, had politely boarded Isabel in a small cham-
[b]er to the right of the large building covering the
[A]rgonaut's shaft head and hoisting works. "It's not a
[p]roper place for a lady," he had said the afternoon
[h]e had arrived to find the Argonaut collapsed and
[te]ams of half-naked men digging for survivors. Isa-
[b]el rightly assumed he'd been attempting to per-
[su]ade her to return to Greeley and wait.

But persistence had won out and she had stayed,
[a] comely distraction to the men who, in four days'
[ti]me, had found only one survivor among the
[m]ackled corpses littering the first three levels of the
[m]ine. Denying herself sleep, she had seen men de-
[sc]end into the hissing, hot rushes of steam sinking
[to] the heart of the main shaft, and return hours
[la]ter, exhausted, sweat streaming through half-inch
[la]yers of soot. They had little to offer but a prayer
[fo]r the unfortunate men who might still be trapped
[be]low, but were polite enough to offer her a tired
[sm]ile of hope.

[A] small safe hidden among the hoisting works
[ha]d yielded evidence enough to send Carl and
[Le]ech, if he survived the cave-in, to the gallows.
[Un]fortunately, when news had reached Greeley that
[the] Argonaut had blown, Carl had disappeared into

the Colorado night. Warrants had immediately been issued, roadblocks set up on main thoroughfares, and posses, composed mainly of outraged miners and volunteers, had dispersed through the countryside in search of the hideous monster who had kidnapped and killed innocent men for personal greed.

The safe had also yielded an incriminating book, with several pages torn out, listing the names of some of those imprisoned in the mine — the dates they had been taken, the dates they had died, or been killed — and had also yielded personal effects: wallets, tokens and good luck pieces, pictures of loved ones, jewelry, watches, contents of saddlebags, the badge of a deputy U.S. marshal. Among the effects, which Marshal Crocker had allowed Isabel to look through, had lain the familiar black leather wallet bearing Shadoe's initials, with over two thousand dollars still tucked carefully inside. That, along with Shadoe's name in the black book — and no record of death, thank God! — gave Isabel hope that he might yet be alive.

So, in the last three days representatives of families who'd had male members disappear came to the Argonaut to look through the box, hoping — and yet not hoping — that some small token might yield the fate of their loved ones. Isabel had seen sobbing women leaving with a familiar item clutched to their breasts, and others mumbling prayers of thanks that the same box had yielded nothing. She'd done what she could to give comfort, and had felt so inadequate at times. All the while, her own heart sobbed for the fate of the man — her beloved Shadoe — whom she knew to be in the pit of death deep in the bowels of the mountain.

Every time one of the rescuers emerged from the darkness below ground, she hoped he might be

clutching the exhausted form of a familiar man—
her dark wolf—her life, her companion, her lover.
Every time a scarcely recognizable human face
sliced a look in her direction, and a head slowly
shook—the only answer to her silent inquiry—she
felt the painful, sinking feeling of hope being lost.
Still, she continued to feel the warmth and radiance
of his nearness, and she could not believe that he
might be lost. If he were, surely, her heart would
feel it.

"Miss?"

Sitting silently upon a half keg, Isabel started at
the softly spoken words, and looked up. The cadaverous man, Mr. Jones, stood over her with a cup.
"Oh, do forgive me. I . . . I was deep in thought."

"Name's Jerico Jones."

His introduction brought a sweet, reminiscent
smile to Isabel, as she remembered how, on the trail
one night, she had jokingly asked Shadoe how he'd
like to be named Jerico Jenkins.

Mr. Jones took no offense at her unexplained
smile. "I have brought you a cup of coffee, Miss
Emerson," he said, his voice a deep, throaty growl
that did not match the kindness of his words.

"And word?" She met his gaze expectantly. "Is
there any word of Mr. McCaine—" She hesitated to
add, "one way or the other?"

Jerico Jones shook his head slowly. "Not yet,
Miss, but—" He smiled with his lips pressed tightly
together. "I wouldn't give up hope, if I were you."

With an imperceptible nod of gratitude, Isabel
took the coffee. "It's been three—almost four days.
How long could he last without food and water?
How long could any of them last?"

"There's water below. It may not be the best, but
it'll keep any survivors going. If—when—" he

quickly amended, "he comes up, he'll be as hungry as a possum treed by a bear."

"If I remember my nature studies rightly, I don't believe possums are native to this area. You must not be from here?"

"No, miss. I came up from Arkansas in '75. I've been preaching a little, mining a little, and I taught English at a public school in Denver for a few months in between."

"You're an educated man, then?" Isabel observed, more to make conversation than to solicit an answer.

Jerico Jones slowly sank to a narrow bench, linked his fingers, and pressed his elbows upon his parted knees. A sadness reflected in his downcast gaze and, instinctively, Isabel leaned across and closed her fingers over the fabric of his oversized coat. He looked up, a little surprised. "Didn't mean to be rude, Miss Emerson." Isabel politely withdrew her fingers. "I'm an educated man, sure enough, but teaching isn't an avocation I was seeking when I headed north. I wanted to get away from all that, but—" He shrugged his skeletal shoulders. "I ran out of money in Denver and I took a job at the local school. I don't really like to be around young'uns that much. I'm just not good for them."

"You seem a very kind man to me," observed Isabel, meeting the gaze of his small, sunken eyes. "I'd imagine you'd be a wonderful teacher." He'd been so good to sit and talk to her these past few days, giving her hope and keeping her up-to-date on the rescue operation. Now, he seemed to need a listener, and Isabel could think of no better way to repay his kindness than to lend a patient ear. Smiling a lovely smile, she prompted, "I'd like to hear about your teaching days, Mr. Jones."

He was just about to begin a recitation of sorts when someone from the hoisting room yelled, "We got a survivor here!"

With a small cry, Isabel shot to her feet. Instantly, Jerico Jones laid his hand on her wrist. "Now, Miss, remember, it might not be your Mr. McCaine—"

"But it could be!" she replied in a breathless rush, extracting her wrist and moving toward the door of the hoisting room. She cried out in horror as the soot-blackened form of a man with bandaged eyes, brought up in a gurney, was carefully placed on the hard floor and immediately surrounded by a dozen men and the caring old physician who'd become a fixture of late. Strands of limp black hair escaped from the gauze wrappings around the rescued miner's head, and Isabel felt her body become almost too limp to stand erect. She wasn't sure if the trembling hand she raised to her face was really her own.

Dear Lord, let it be my beloved Shadoe, her heart cried in a mixed seizure of panic that it might not be, and hope that it was. *Please, please, let it be Shadoe!*

Through the screams of her numb mind, she heard the men surrounding him begin to mumble. What were they saying? Who are you? What is your name? *Dear Lord, answer them, Shadoe . . . tell them who you are—*

"Sha—Sha—"

Dear Lord it is!

"Shannon . . . Peter Shannon—"

No, no . . . no, dear God . . . no, no . . . No!

The mutterings of the men slowly drifted away. That strained, struggling, masculine voice—the same that had whispered his identity—slowly drifted

379

off. A hand seemed to reach beneath Isabel's skin, tearing out her strength, and her slim form folded gently to the floor.

A lucid moment passed over Shadoe like a glimmer of early morning light. He reached for it, feeling it cluster around him and give strength. He forced himself into a sitting position against the damp smoothness of a boulder and passed his hands before his eyes. He could see them. Dear God, he could see them! Had he died and entered an ethereal plane, the tentacles of darkness reluctantly letting him walk into the light of a higher world?

Shadoe studied his hand as if he'd never seen it before. Light filtered between his fingers, so vague and shimmering that he felt no pain despite his many weeks in the Argonaut's darkness. "I am dead," he mumbled. "So why does my leg continue to hurt? Hell . . . why do I hurt all over?"

A low chuckle echoed through the fallen rocks, and Shadoe felt his body jerk. There, against the pale light that was almost a fog, sat a man as big as any Shadoe had ever seen, a man whose flesh was as dark as coal and who smiled as casually as a man sitting peacefully on a river bank fishing for bream. "You ain't dead, man," he replied. "Good thing, too, what with ya callin' on Hell like that."

Shadoe whispered hoarsely, "Who are you?" then grabbed at the dry pain in his throat. "How did you get in here?"

"It don' matter who I is, or how I got in here, now does it, Mr. McCaine? What matters is how we's goin' ta git ya out."

"How do you know my name?"

"That don't matter nohow, neither." He stood, a towering, broad-chested man with an astonishing grace. "Now, why don't ya come with me, Mr. Mc-Caine. I'll show ya the way out."

"I can't walk on my left ankle."

"I s'pect you'll manage, 'specially when ya knows who be's waitin' up yonder fo' ya."

Shadoe cocked a dark eyebrow. "Isabel? Is she here?"

The twinkle in his dark eyes matched the sincerity of his smile. "You come on now, Mr. McCaine."

Shadoe eased upward, taking a moment to adjust to the move, then supported his weight on his right ankle. "The cat. We can't leave without the cat." Shadoe was surprised to find his voice slowly returning.

"I 'spect he'll come right along." As though he'd understood, the scruffy beast caterwauled an answer.

"Be careful of the loose timbers," warned Shadoe, the last of his strength threatening to abandon him.

"I 'spect I'll be all right. Don't dawdle. I ain't got all day ta be wastin' on ya."

A thought came to Shadoe. "Say . . . are you the man Isabel met in Greeley?"

"I s'pect I am. Now, I tol' ya, man, I ain't got all day."

Shadoe gritted his teeth against the pain, managing to crawl along at a pace that kept him close to his rescuer. Once his feet got caught in gumbo — the sticky, wet clay prevalent throughout the lode — and he was surprised to find the cross-cut, a mine tunnel used for ventilation and communication, still standing. But his guide moved past the cross-cut, which Shadoe had assumed would be their mode of rescue, and entered still another tunnel that had been blasted through hard rock. All the while he moved, following the man who seemed unimpeded by the rubble littering the mine, he kept trying to see where the source of foggy light was coming from. But it seemed to surround the black man, who occasionally looked back to see if Shadoe was following.

To make conversation, Shadoe asked, "Are you a toplander? I've never seen you before."

"Don't work above ground . . . don't work underground," replied the man. "Jes' keepin' a promise I made—"

"A promise to who?" Shadoe halted his laborious movements to keep pace with the black man. He looked suspiciously toward him, his eyes narrowing in an attempt to add clarity to features made indistinct by the heaviness of the air. "Man, you're real spooky. Do you know that?"

"Don' mean ta be."

Shadoe became aware of the cat at his feet. He flinched, thinking that it might rub its head against his wounded ankle. But it merely ambled past him, then jumped lithely to a boulder and lay down on its side. "Good idea, Hannibal; I need a rest, too." Dropping his forehead into his palms, he mumbled, "I don't know how you intend to get us out of here, man. Sunlight's a good quarter-mile above us."

"Ain't no such a thing."

Because the voice of his rescuer faded so eerily, Shadoe's head snapped up. *Damn!* he thought. *For a big man, he sure can disappear fast.* Shadoe started to call to his unseen rescuer when a pinpoint of light painfully etched across his sensitive eyes. His palms flew upward in an effort to press away the agony flooding his head. He could hear no diggers coming through the wall, no machinery, no mumbling of male voices. Only the light screamed at him. He moved his hand, readying himself to adjust to the bright intruder, but again, the pain was unbearable.

Then, tightly closing his eyes, he reached blindly down and tore off a long, narrow piece of his shredded trousers, which he carefully tied around his head.

The brightness faded behind the denim threads. He sat very still, drawing deep breaths, ignoring the pain in his ankle, the pin pricks crawling through his weakened body, the odor of murky dampness. He wasn't sure how long he sat there, whether a minute or two or ten or thirty, but he could almost feel his pupils shrinking to accept the light. After a while, he ventured from behind the scrap of denim, closed his eyes and felt that warm, radiating light tickle across his eyelids. The pain slowly subsided; he opened his eyes.

As boulders and timbers took shape, and his thoughts took on tone he had not felt in weeks, he realized he was sitting below a winze, a passageway connecting two tunnels at different levels. But he could see debris blocking the passageway, and the light did not come from there. Rather, it came from a wall scarcely twenty-five feet from where he sat. At his feet lay a length of board, needle sharp at one end. Breaking off the tip, he eased the flat end of the board beneath his left armpit and forced himself to his feet. The makeshift crutch was a little short, so he slumped to meet its height. Every single one of the twenty-five or so steps he took was agony, but within minutes he stood at the source of the light, which was nothing more than a hole, no larger than the size of his index finger, in the side of the mountain. But as he began to dig, he realized the wall was more muck and earth than it was rock. Within minutes he had dug the hole out for a foot and a half, plunged the length of his arm into it, and felt sunlight upon his palm. And though he was a grown man, tears stung his eyes.

He stood there for a long time, his face pressed against the earthen wall, his arm extended to accept the warmth of blessed sunshine, his body flooded with a strength having no visible source. He couldn't ignore the wild pounding of his heart. At the end of his arm was the warmth of sun. He would not die. He would see Isabel again.

He looked around, thinking the black man would reappear. Had he heard another human voice and gone off to check for other survivors? Well, he had gotten into the tunnel. He surely had the good sense to get out again.

All at once, Shadoe became frantic to escape the confines of what might have been his crypt. Yanking his arm back, he raised the board he had been using as a crutch and began to stab at the loose, fragile rocks held there by the muck and earth separating him from life . . . from the sun . . . from Isabel.

He had done what had seemed impossible less than an hour ago; he had poked a hole to the world outside, the world where Isabel awaited him. His sworn oath to kill Carl temporarily eluded him; he could think only of Isabel's sensual smile, pale eyes adoringly gazing into his own, of arms wrapped around him. That vision had kept him alive.

Darkness washed over him like a wave, remaining only for a moment. Hunger made his thoughts hazy, the wound and the fever he knew must possess his body threatened to bring him to his knees. But he was so close. . . . So close . . . it didn't occur to him that the tunnel, created by the fall of rocks, might bring him onto a steep precipice of the mountain, with no way to get either up or down.

When he had looked through the hole, he had seen earth, but it had been a valley away.

Isabel lay still upon the cot, her eyes moving watchfully around the small room. A doctor had diagnosed her as suffering from fatigue and too little nourishment, then had left Jerico Jones in the room to make sure she rested for a few hours. The tall, bony man sat in a straightback chair, reading from the Bible, his bespectacled gaze occasionally flitting to where she lay.

She felt a trifle foolish for reacting so dramatically. Certainly, she was glad of Mr. Shannon's rescue from the mine, but she'd been so sure the man had been Shadoe that it had simply been too much for her to hear another man's name. She imagined that she was becoming somewhat of a pest to the men who were working the disaster, and when one of them entered the room on his way to the changing room, she thought she saw annoyance in brief glances toward her. But she couldn't leave! Shadoe would need her when he was rescued.

Patiently guarded by Mr. Jones, she did not react when one of the men yelled out, "There's a man on the mountainside! Get a rope!"

Rather, she asked, "Do you think one of the men fell?"

Jerico looked up just long enough to respond, "I reckon so, but you don't need to be worrying about that."

Turning to her side, she pouted, "I just can't lie here, doing nothing." Aware that he was avoiding her pale eyes, pouting every bit as much as was her mouth, she released a short, brittle, "Oh! Men!" then started to rise. But his scathing look halted her

385

move. "Why do they always think they have to protect women?"

"Wouldn't have to watch over you, Miss Emerson," Jerico pointed out calmly, "if you ate properly, and rested properly, and took care of yourself. You've brought this on yourself."

His observation seemed reasonable enough. Isabel folded her arm beneath her head and watched him thoughtfully. He still had not told her why he didn't enjoy teaching, and she was a little curious, a curiosity she nurtured to help take her mind off Shadoe. But he had avoided conversation these past few minutes, claiming that she "had to rest," so this would not be a good time to bring up the topic. She lowered her gaze to her fingers lightly drumming upon the mattress and listened to the sounds of men and machinery beyond the rough timbers of the wall.

The rush of excitement, mixed with masculine voices and the dull thud of the machines, had died down. She felt her eyes closing and try as she might, they would not open. Though she deliberately willed herself not to fall asleep, she felt relaxed, and the tension began to move through her body from head to toe, leaving it limp and numb. Her traitorous body sought the sleep that her mind had denied it.

She did not hear the door open, did not hear Jerico Jones slowly rise and begin to lightly back from the room. The world of dreams was very close upon her and she reached for it, feeling its warmth filter between her fingers.

Shadoe stood in the doorway, supporting himself upon the crutch one of the men had given him. He needed a doctor, food and a hundred hours of sleep, but first . . . he needed Isabel.

And there she lay, the vision that had kept him alive through the greatest trial of his life . . . his lovely Southern lady, his companion, his lover, the woman he wanted to spend eternity with. He knew that men waited just outside, anxious to determine the extent of his injuries and do for him what was necessary, but Shadoe couldn't imagine that anyone could do more for him than Isabel could, simply by whispering against his hairline, *I love you.*

Momentarily, his feet began to move, and though the pain in his ankle was agonizing, he wanted only to be near her, beside her, touching his trembling fingers to the small pulse in her temple, feeling the strands of her golden hair against his palm, seeing her pale, moisture-sheened eyes as their gazes met. His heart was pounding so quickly he thought he might pass out, like a man who'd had too much to drink, so intoxicating was her beauty.

She gave a small sigh as he knelt beside her, straining to keep the lines of pain from his face. He wanted her to see strength, not agony, when their gazes met. Shadoe hadn't realized how violently he was trembling until his fingers moved toward her rose-tinted cheek; instantly, he balled his fist, attempting to will control into it. *Isabel, Isabel, I am here* — the words echoed softly inside him but would not form upon his lips. Were it not for her, he knew he would collapse.

Watching the gentle movements of her sleeping features, he pressed his fist against his teeth. He could feel his expression tightening, fighting for control, trying to halt the nervous tick at the corner of his eye, and the quiver traveling from his mouth into his taut jawline.

"I love you . . . Shadoe . . . I love you, my dark wolf—"

Had she truly spoken, echoing her hidden dreams, or had he imagined it? But no, her mouth was still parted, her eyes darting quickly beneath the translucence of her eyelids. She was dreaming sweet dreams of him, of their love . . . she had spoken his name and she had said, *I love you*.

His dark eyes glistening with tears, he dropped his forehead against her pale, warm temple. "I am here, Isabel," he whispered hoarsely. "Awaken, my sleeping angel—"

A warm, beautiful panic seized Isabel's insides. Her dream—like none she'd had before—gave dimensions of substance and reality to her vision of him. She could feel his breath against her hairline, his voice, strangled by hoarseness, as close as the next minute.

Her eyes crept open, slowly focusing on the glistening darkness of tired, but loving eyes, like pools of India ink, on his soot-covered features and masculine mouth that quivered slightly. With a strange calmness, she whispered, "Shadoe?"

He responded emotionally, "Yes, it is me . . . your dark wolf."

Bewilderment pressed upon her brow. Had she merely dreamed that she'd awakened? Not one soul except her beloved Shadoe, knew that she called him that. With poignant calm, she whispered again "Shadoe?" Her breath, so easily drawn before, now caught in her throat, a lump as large as a boulder "Am I still dreaming?"

Rather than respond, his trembling mouth, damp with his own tears, touched gently upon her own At first, she did not respond and, had she not immediately caught herself, she would have withdrawn

388

Then her hands scooted across the shoulders of her dream and held him tightly. "Oh, please, please—" she whispered, "don't let Mr. Jones awaken me."

"But you are awake, Isabel." He attempted a small laugh, but the effort tightened without materializing. "You're choking the devil out of me."

Once again Isabel felt a swell in her throat. She wanted so much to be with Shadoe that she was imagining him, embraced in her arms, smelling like a horse and needing a bath, half-naked and altogether indecent. She could feel the tightness of familiar muscles beneath her trembling hands, and yet she knew she was dreaming; it was a cruel hoax that would hurt her when she awakened. With gulping sobs, she whispered, "I want to die. Let me die right here in my dream so that I can stay with you. Oh, Shadoe, Shadoe, hold me. Don't let me wake up. If you truly love me—"

All at once, Shadoe grabbed her arms and shook her lightly. "Isabel, you're not dreaming. I *am* here." When she pressed her eyes tightly, flinging her pale tresses from side to side, he shook her again, and more roughly.

His tight grip was hurting her, and it occurred to Isabel that there was solid weight to the presence before her.

"Dear Lord." The two words were so softly spoken she was not sure they'd even taken form. Her fingers rose to his soot-covered cheek, feeling its masculine curve, slowly traveling to his mouth to gently touch it. And the tears came, uncontrolled, mixed with her smile and her emotional laughter, as she drew him into her arms and held him for a long while. "You're alive, thank God, you're alive. I love you, Shadoe. With all my heart and all my soul."

"And I love you, Isabel Emerson," he whispered

in return. "You kept me alive down there. Without you . . ." Emotion would not allow him to go on. He contented himself to hold her, to feel the warmth of her against him, the softness of her hairline pressing upon his cheek. Then he smiled; he knew now that she loved him; she had not uttered a single complaint that he smelled like a horse.

That *was* love.

Twenty-four

He felt like a disgruntled old man, whiling away the last days of his life in a creaking, antiquated rocking chair. Drawing in a breath heavy with boredom, Shadoe watched the roadway from the porch of Bonnie Crocker's house for the appearance of Isabel. She had gone to see Dr. Riley, a kindly, white-haired country doctor, who had hinted that today he might pronounce Shadoe ready to travel.

When Isabel finally made her appearance and he saw that she was running as if a cougar was on her heels, he jumped up from the chair, adjusted the crutch beneath his arm, and hobbled toward the steps to meet her.

"What is the matter, Isabel?" He had never seen her brows pressed into such a frown.

She paused and drew in short, rapid breaths in an attempt to still the rapid pace of her heart. "Horrid news, Shadoe," she rushed the words in a whisper. "Whew! I must have run a good quarter of a mile."

Pressing his fingers to her elbow, Shadoe coaxed her onto the porch. Bonnie Crocker, who had caught a glimpse of the rushing Isabel from the parlor window, met her on the porch. Molding himself to her ankle as she walked was the Argonaut, Hannibal, whom Bonnie had agreed to give a home. "What has happened, Isabel? Did you say 'horrid news'?"

She did not immediately respond. She was thinking of the morning she and Wayland Macy had left for Leadville, the way he had purposely delayed their arrival, claiming phantom rocks picked up by his horse, grasping an ailing stomach, saying that he'd taken the wrong road. She remembered how he'd suddenly disappeared when they'd reached the mine to find that a cave-in had occurred and Pa Crocker and the U.S. Marshal who'd accompanied him were already there. Seeing her to her destination, Wayland had very mysteriously disappeared. She hadn't known why then; but she knew now. "Venetia is dead," she announced all of a sudden.

Shadoe's brows rose in surprise. "What?"

"Dear Lord—" mumbled Mrs. Crocker, hiding her mouth behind the handkerchief she'd brought out with her.

"It is all speculation. Her father, returning on the evening train, caught Venetia and Wayland Macy together at Mrs. Crenshaw's boarding house. You remember, Shadoe, that I told you about him. Mr. Mendez killed them both, then turned the gun on himself."

"He's dead?" asked Shadoe, dropping down into the rocking chair. "Felix Mendez is dead?"

"Yes. Mrs. Crenshaw is terribly upset that it happened in her house."

"Well, I would imagine so," interjected a concerned Mrs. Crocker. "After all, she is still recovering from Carl's death."

Neither Isabel nor Shadoe felt the inclination to remind Bonnie that Mrs. Crenshaw had not been too fond of her son. When the news of his death on Colorado's border with Utah had first reached

Greeley, she had merely shrugged her shoulders and proclaimed that, "I hope the miners who lynched him plan to bury him. I'll not be spending a penny of my hard-earned money to put him under." There would be no period of mourning in Mrs. Crenshaw's household, not for the evil, malicious, and murderous Carl Weatherstone, who had happened to be her son.

"Mrs. Crenshaw is a strong woman," said Shadoe solemnly, feeling no personal regret over the death of Venetia Wainwright. "She'll survive this latest tragedy." At that point, Mrs. Crocker, clicking her tongue and mumbling something about baking a pie for the poor woman, reentered the house. Taking Isabel's hand, Shadoe asked, "Is Dr. Riley going to be along pretty soon?"

"He's presently engaged in a post mortem at the coroner's office. I imagine it'll be early afternoon before he visits." Settling onto a comfortable wicker settee across from Shadoe, Isabel took his hand. "I just saw Pat, too. Now that an accounting has been completed of the holdings of Carl and Greech, he tells me that the widows and families of the men who died there will each receive shares in excess of twenty-thousand dollars. Isn't that wonderful?"

Though he grinned his pleasure, an involuntary shudder, not visible to the naked eye, crawled beneath Shadoe's skin. In the three years that Carl Weatherstone and the man, known only as Greech, had operated their slave ring in the Argonaut, two hundred and twenty men had been killed. Brothers, fathers and sons, boys whose chins had not yet sprouted peach fuzz, had lost their lives so that those two bastards could line their pockets with gold. After the rescue operation that had lasted nine days, less than thirty men had been brought out alive. The Argonaut, shut down by men who swore never to open it again, was now a grave for those who had perished. It seemed unfair that Greech lay there with decent men, and Shadoe chose to believe that he screamed in hell, while his innocent victims did not.

"What are you thinking, Shadoe?"

He lurched, his head snapping up as if he'd just realized he wasn't alone. "Nothing . . . nothing at all." Squeezing her hand, he gave her a genuine smile. "I'm ready to get the hell out of Dodge, find your brother and—" He feigned a shudder, "face that father of yours. I suspect he's going to lay me in the dirt scarcely before my feet touch down."

"He will not."

"I would," argued Shadoe, "were you my daughter with a man like me." A mischievous arch affected his left brow. "Know what I want?"

"What is that," she said, smiling for him.

"To make love to you."

"Not in Bonnie's house," she responded, lowering her eyes as she smiled coyly. "It wouldn't be proper."

"We could take a room at the hotel—"

"And they'd know—" came her immediate retort. "They'd know why we wanted to be alone!"

Again, a dark eyebrow eased upward. "So?" Leaning back and drawing his fingers to his clean-shaven chin, Shadoe raked his eyes over the dove-gray dress hugging her slim figure. The bodice was low, enticingly so, and the sleeves mere poufs, exposing her long, ivory arms. Only then did he notice the bracelet he had not seen before. A finger pointed toward it. "Where did you get that?"

Isabel leaned close and showed him the delicate item of jewelry, a chain of gold with a tiny ruby welded into every other link. "Sarah McFadden was

394

a little short of cash when it came to paying me for my last week of work. She offered the bracelet in payment and I accepted." Her eyes brightened as she studied it, then lifted smilingly to Shadoe.

A chord of guilt struck him inside. She had worn men's denims since they'd left Fort Smith, months ago, and despite the tales she'd told him of her rebellion against traditional women's clothing as she'd grown up, he could see that she was very much enjoying being a lady again. "Know what I think," Shadoe said softly, taking her fingers to hold them tenderly between his own. "I think I'd rather not see you in men's clothing again. Let's find something pretty and feminine for you to ride in—"

"But I don't mind," immediately argued Isabel. "The denims are much more practical for traveling. You said so yourself."

"Well, I was wrong." Shadoe drew slightly back, his mouth pressing into a fine line. "I like seeing you like this, Isabel, wearing dresses and jewelry—" His fingers rose, "and your hair being loose and free. Besides—" he continued, for lack of a better argument, "would you want your brother to see you wearing men's clothing? I think not!"

A quiet mood suddenly fell over Isabel. When her eyes continued to gaze absently into the folds of her gown, Shadoe's fingers moved beneath her chin. Only then did she look up and say, "Now that Venetia is behind you, Shadoe, are there any more secrets in your past that might come between us?"

"The only secret," immediately responded Shadoe, smiling, "is who I was in my last incarnation. I might have been a pirate or a prince, I might even have been a royal executioner—but there is nothing that will come between us. I swear this on the love I hold for you."

Isabel's pretty nose twitched. "Well, at least I got your mind off . . . you know what!"

With a wry grin, Shadoe grabbed her off the settee and settled her onto his lap. "You did not. Now . . . how about that hotel room?"

Tongue River, Montana

Reading Red Sewall skirted the fringes of the river and eased the heavy-hooved gelding into a trot toward the road ranch. He'd met with no success in finding the four young heifers that had broken through the split rail fence the night before. One was due to drop her calf any day now, and he worried that wolves would get to her, and the others, before he could bring them back. Damn! He missed the boy! He wouldn't have had any trouble rounding up the heifers. He'd had a way with animals that attracted them like red ants on tender ankles.

Red had been gone since daybreak, but now returned to the road ranch, hoping that the woman he'd hired to keep up with the place would have breakfast awaiting him. Maude was something of an enigma; she claimed to have worked as a prostitute, and yet exhibited none of the qualities of such a woman. She dressed modestly and was softspoken; he liked that in women.

Presently, he dismounted and tied the gelding off. Moving onto the planked porch, he encountered Maude. A tall, bone-thin and attractive woman who wore her dark hair loose, she wore none of the gaudy pastes he'd seen covering the faces of women of the profession, and the perfume she'd dabbed behind her ears was so subtle that it hardly seemed there at all.

"Good mornin', Maude," greeted Red, removing his hat and clutching it to him.

"Did you locate the heifers?" she asked, rising from her chair.

"Not yet. Just hope the wolves haven't already taken 'em down."

"Could I help?" offered Maude.

Red's scraggy face eased into a grin. "You said so yourself, Maude, that you ain't never been on a horse."

"But I don't mind trying. Two can cover more ground than one."

Red roughly patted the arm of the woman who was a good twenty-years younger than he was. If he wasn't so set in his ways, and a confirmed bachelor to boot, he might even take the woman to wife. He'd found her on the road just east of the ranch, badly bruised and bleeding profusely from a cut at her right eye, and he'd taken her in to care for her. Maude was a sad woman, ashamed of her past, and wanting only to be accepted somewhere, by someone. It seemed that Red had become that person.

"How about if we have some breakfast, Maude? Then I'll go out lookin' fer them heifers again."

"Give me ten minutes," she said, smiling. "I'll whip up something."

Maude turned and entered the house. Reading Red Sewall, finding himself alone—a state he consciously avoided—considered relaxing a moment on the porch, but then looked up the hill. In the corral, located at the base of the hill, a spotted mare nibbled at hay while her three-day-old filly frolicked around her legs.

When Red eventually moved, there was purpose in the direction he took. At the corral, the mare trotted up to the fence for a rough pat, then followed him around the barrier until he began to ascend the hill. There, Reading Red again removed his hat, this time in quiet reverence.

The grass, awakening from hibernation after the long winter, had grown to the height of the headstones and simple wooden crosses marking the graves of those who had died. He looked from one to another, reading the names, remembering special moments he'd enjoyed with each. Then he paced off a few feet and stood before the newest grave. Scarcely before he realized he was speaking, he mumbled, "Sometimes I can't believe you're gone."

Then he became aware of the ponderosa forest surrounding him, the gentle hiss of the wind through the trees, a squirrel dropping a pine cone, the skitter of a rabbit, the rhythmic drumming of a woodpecker. The stretch marks in a single aspen tree looked like two eyes, one on top of the other and, with a smile, Reading Red remembered how John would say, "Them's the eyes of God, Red, lookin' over the souls of them that we buried here."

"You miss him, don't you?"

Red spun about to face Maude, who stood a few feet from him. Glancing back at the grave, Red replied, "I sure do. Miss him somethin' fierce."

In silent respect, Maude approached and linked her arm through Red's. She liked this kind, gentle-hearted man who often journeyed to the hill to be with those good people Maude had never known. She liked him because he had not questioned the state in which he'd found her, had never insisted that she give him the name of the man who had beaten her and dumped her on the roadway that frosty February evening.

"Got that breakfast ready?" Red asked, the emotion strong in his voice.

"I think we can fill your belly," she said quietly. "Come on, Red." Maude coaxed him down the hill.

"I sure do miss John," Red told her, stopping at the corral to pay attention to the friendly mare.

"I know you do," said Maude.

"Got this mare for him. What do you think of her?"

"She's beautiful," said Maude, touching the muzzle of the filly nibbling at her skirt through the rail. Then she turned to Red, and a strong, quiet determination reflected in her hazel eyes. "Now, you stop fretting will you, old man—" She spoke affectionately, resting her hand on his arm. "You'll be traveling over to Roscoe's at the end of the week. Perhaps you'll encounter a reason to be cheerful."

Though his heart ached, Red managed a smile. "You're a good woman, Maude. Let's go chow down on that breakfast you fixed."

By the end of the week, Shadoe and Isabel found themselves lumbering into the settlement of Casper on the North Platte River in East Central Wyoming. There they spent a long, quiet night, and resumed their journey at daybreak. Two days later, having skirted all settlements since Casper, they moved onto a trail fringing the Powder River and continued their journey northward. With the advent of Spring and warm weather, coupled with the hardier mare Isabel rode, which they'd purchased before leaving Greeley, the two travelers were easily making twenty miles a day.

On the seventh evening since leaving Greeley, Shadoe and Isabel entered the southern range of the Bighorn Mountains.

As the sun began its descent across the timberline, speckling the clearing with glimmering blood-red lights, a weary Isabel dismounted the new mare Shadoe had purchased for her and half-fell to her back upon a cool patch of grass. "I am exhausted, Shadoe McCaine," she fussed without feeling. Closing her eyes, she relished the last glimmers of the dying sun upon her face.

Shadoe moved about, performing his usual mundane chores to provide a camp for the night. Mirlo and the fettered mare were put to graze in a grass covered ravine, a pair of blankets and sturdy pieces of timber formed a tent, and within half an hour, two trout sizzled over a fire.

Isabel drew up her legs and wrapped her arms around them. The brown cotton riding skirt she wore was wrinkled, and the cuff of her ivory-colored blouse, rubbing these past six days against the pommel of her saddle, bore an ugly brown stain that would never come out. She watched the flames flicker among the rocks Shadoe had placed in a circle, and occasionally her gaze would connect to his. He reclined with his head resting on his saddle and a bit of straw tucked between his teeth.

"What are you thinking, Shadoe?"

Actually, he hadn't been thinking of anything in particular. "Of you," he responded, putting out his hand. "Come here."

She scooted on her buttocks around the fire and tucked herself into his embrace. "It's a beautiful night, isn't it?" The mountains blocked out the moonlight, only hazy patches of glittering light fringing the treeline. When he failed to respond, she asked, "When do you think we'll reach Tongue River?"

"Oh, I'd say—" His words halted as he gave it some thought. "Within two weeks."

"Two weeks. I can't believe it. I'll see my brother in two weeks." Pausing, though not for a response, she quietly spoke his name, "Shadoe?"

"Hmmm?"

"Who do you think the black man is, the one who visited me at the jail, and the one who showed you the way out of the mine?" She hesitated to add, "And the one I saw in the ravine the night we met Annie—"

"You never told me about that." His voice showed little surprise, almost as if he expected that she'd seen their mysterious visitor at times she hadn't confessed to him. Had she been wary of his reaction? It pained him that she had, because he didn't want her to be afraid of him. He'd never given her any cause that he was aware of. "Well, I really don't know who he is. Just a fella who happens to show up now and then, I'd imagine, and always at the right time."

"Quite a coincidence, wouldn't you say?"

"And just that. A coincidence."

"Poof!" Her fingers closed over Shadoe's arm and gently caressed it. "Do you want to know what I think?"

Tired after the long day of travel, he closed his eyes, his reply coming almost instinctively. "What is that?"

"I think he was a guardian angel. That night in the ravine, he warned me that you should be careful. At the jail, he said that you were in danger. And when you were trapped in the mine, he came there to rescue you."

"And why would a strange angel give a damn what happens to me?"

Isabel shrugged lightly. "Perhaps he isn't *your* guardian angel . . . perhaps he's mine. Perhaps he

401

knows how much I care for you and love you and depend on you for everything."

So sincere were her words, so sincere the speculations of the beautiful lady he held, who could paint the most mundane of situations with romanticism and love, that Shadoe was overwhelmed by the very nearness of her. He imagined that the black man had not been in the ravine at all, but was something she had merely dreamed. But he would not spoil her lovely mood by contradicting her, and he gently pulled her closer into his arms so that he might enjoy the faint softness of her thick, silken tresses against his cheek. Tenderly, he touched a kiss to the top of her head, and when she offered up her mouth, he captured the silken willingness of her kiss.

He felt the familiar ache in his loins as her hand lightly brushed his torso in its move to circle his neck. Her mouth was hot and intoxicating against his own, her tongue tantalizingly, teasingly, molding to his own searching one. How sweet was her mouth, how blissful the torment he felt as her slim, youthful hands boldly eased into the waist of his trousers to disengage the shirt tails keeping his flesh from her hungry touch.

A hot flush crept through Isabel's body as Shadoe's hands worked frantically to feel the nakedness of her flesh. When he suddenly, and without warning, rose to his knees and drew her roughly against him, she saw only the dark passion of his eyes, the matted fur of his chest exposed by her own trembling hands. Was the thrill of making love to him so powerful, so mesmerizing, that she could not remember tearing at his clothes, of him delving into her own until her breasts were bare and pressing into the hot expanse of his torso?

"Slow me down, Isabel," Shadoe rasped hoarsely. "If I don't take you now, I'll explode." In response, Isabel dragged her thigh up to press against the hard muscles of his leg straining against the tightness of denim. She had never felt such a frantic need for him, a need she sought by pure instinct, as her fingers popped the buttons of his trousers all in one motion. When her hot palms circled his hips and caressed his tight buttocks, he groaned a small protest, because the strain of his masculinity against the fabric was cruel. His body shuddered, so taut and inflamed by her erotic lack of self-control that he could hardly keep from throwing her upon her back and ripping the clothing from her body.

In the pale darkness of the Bighorn range they were soon naked, one against the other, and Shadoe eased Isabel onto her back atop the tangled mass of their clothing. His hands delved into every sensual curve and crevice of her body, and his hot, moist tongue traced paths around her passion-sensitive breasts. His groin throbbed, the evidence of his arousal straining against the flat plane of her abdomen. He tried to slow his quick, hot breath, to tame the wild, erotic kisses they shared, so that he could savor every delicious taste of her aroused body. But there was no turning back now.

Isabel gasped, thrusting her breasts against his seeking mouth, her body undulating explosively in an effort to speed their joining. And just when she thought it would happen, that he would tantalizingly invade her body, he drew himself erect, his muscles growing hard, his gaze moist with passion. She did not want any space or distance to exist between them, but for the moment, he was content to merely look down upon her. Though her thighs had parted, and his manhood probed against her . . .

there . . . he made no further move. And she thought her body would explode for want of him.

"Shadoe?" The question in her voice did not arouse an immediate response in him. "Don't you want me?"

His hands scooted beneath her, caressing her buttocks and easing her upwards. And his mouth ground out hoarsely, "Yes, yes, Isabel, I want you—" Rather than enter the moist depths of her, he folded himself across her, his mouth trailing fiery kisses over her breasts, downward . . . over her tightly constricted ribs, along the flat plane of her belly . . . and lower—

A gasp came from Isabel's full, sensual mouth. She felt her body grow rigid beneath his masterful explorations, her flesh withdrawing from the soft tickling of his thick, dark hair. Lower and lower went his caresses so that her body shuddered, so alive with molten flames that she was sure she would melt. Her self-control vanished, and when, with quaking surprise, his caresses deepened and became more intimate than she could have imagined in her wildest dreams, she closed her eyes tightly, feeling her fingers dig into the mass of clothing resting beneath her breathless body.

Isabel had never dreamed that making love could be so wild and wondrously wicked and so uninhibited. No matter how many times they were together, there were always new and powerful experiences, an omnipotence that thrust her into new universes of bliss and passion, sweet fulfillment and triumphant torture. His strokes tantalized her, undulated within her, pulsated intoxicatingly over the soft planes of her flesh . . . and when her abdomen filled with delicious, explosive release, Shadoe was immediately atop her, thrusting himself deeply into the erratically pulsating cavity of her innermost self, and his mouth was kissing hers with renewed fervor. She was mesmerized by the magnificence of his passion, inflamed by the concentrated grinding of his hips against the sweet receptacle of her womanhood, and suspended, as if in a vacuum of breathless desire, by the dark, assailing intensity of his body as it joined to her own. Their damp bodies became liquid gold, writhing together in exquisite splendor, and she lost all concept of time as she was hurled wildly into the wide Wyoming sky.

Their breathing became erratic, their concentration only on sweet fulfillment, their gazes fused and locked. Isabel felt his muscles quiver and ripple beneath her searching fingertips; she knew, by the rapid pace of their bodies as she sought to meet his rhythm and pace, that the pinnacle would soon be reached. She moaned at each exit, a hot flush writhing through her as his strokes became longer, harder and deeper. Then, with blissful torment, his body shuddered, he gasped and stiffened, and his seed exploded in hot flames between her thighs.

He collapsed atop her, his fingers entwined among the damp tresses that lay scattered beneath her, their legs entwined and their damp, sated bodies molded together. Their exhaustion was sweet, shared, their passions ever present in the aftermath of their love.

And in a quiet, husky voice, Shadoe murmured, "Damn, woman . . . you own my body and soul—"

"And your heart," she responded without hesitation, dragging in a breath as she sought to slow its rapid pace. "I want to be more important in your life than—" Looking across the clearing, she smiled, "your horse, Shadoe. I want you to love me more than you love Mirlo."

405

With a short laugh, Shadoe squeezed her to him, then, with a groan, withdrew from her. Were it not for their clothing, they would have been upon the grass when they made love, and he now pulled a blade from the edge of their crumpled clothing to tuck between his teeth. Momentarily, the same blade of grass tickled across Isabel's pert nose. "If Mirlo took off right now, I'd simply get another horse," he said. "But if you took off, my wild Louisiana lass, I'd search the world over until you were back in my arms. If you went home to your father, I would fight him for you."

She showed no modesty that she was totally naked beneath the shaded evening sky. Her fingers linked upon her gently pulsating abdomen and her pale, powder-blue eyes turned full to him, boldly sweeping over his naked masculinity and his dark, piercing gaze. "I thought eventually that you'd love me more than you loved your horse. Well . . . I do believe I've accomplished something, haven't I, Shadoe McCaine?"

He couldn't get enough of the tantalizing feminine form stretched out upon their tangled clothing: her ivory flesh softly touched by moonlight, one of her long, slim legs stretched out, while the other drew up, hiding the intimate treasure he had just taken, her full breasts still hardened after the attentions he had given them . . . and her heart, her pure, beautiful heart, thump, thump, thumping beneath her exquisite flesh. Instinctively, his hand moved to massage a path along the slim column of her neck, a finger dipping into the small pulse between her collar bones, then exploring a path between her breasts and drawing a figure eight around them. She watched the passion burning in his eyes as he aroused her flesh which was still cool ing after the love they had made, her eyes made a sweeping scrutiny of him, and there he began to gain the fullness that had aroused within her the wildest of passions.

Her gaze, glistening with humor, swept up to his. "Shadoe McCaine . . . you're not serious!"

With a wicked, half-cocked smile, he took her hand and folded her fingers gently over his erect manhood. *"You* tell me I'm not serious, my wild, beautiful Isabel."

Without prelude, and quickly smothering the feminine laugh that might have echoed across the mountain, Shadoe claimed her sweet treasure once again.

Twenty-five

Shadoe and Isabel sat atop their horses, listening to the swirling waters of the Tongue River at its junction with Pumpkin Creek. The sprawling road ranch, larger than the sod huts and tents of people calling themself a road ranch which they'd visited along their route, sat scarcely a hundred feet up from the Tongue, eerily silent this early Friday morning.

"Are you ready?" asked Shadoe, reaching across the short spanse of space to cover her trembling hand.

Isabel thought she might faint. She knew all the color had drained from her features and she was trembling so violently the mare beneath her pricked its ears. "He is there, Shadoe. My brother, my dear brother, Eduard. He is there, sleeping, possibly, behind that wall of hides and horns and antlers. Oh, Shadoe . . . if I faint, will you pick me up?"

He chuckled, even though he was as excited inside as was his beautiful Isabel. These past two weeks, a they had drawn closer and closer to their destination she had filled his head with those memories that a seven-year-old girl remembered of a four-year-old brother she had continued to adore, even believing him to be dead. Her tales had set Eduard up to th status of sainthood, and Shadoe knew that her memories were those of a loving sister who could remem ber no fault in the brother she idolized. "You're not going to faint, Isabel."

She scarcely believed that. "What am I going to say to him, Shadoe?"

"When you face him, you will know," he assured her, then coaxed Mirlo on ahead. When she did not join him, he halted, half-turned and his dark eyes gazed warmly toward her. "You're as white as a sheet, Isabel."

"I know," she responded quietly.

Drawing the stallion up beside her once again, his hand moved to the back of her neck. Tenderly, he touched a kiss to her trembling mouth. "It is all right to be nervous. I don't know your Eduard, but I'm a little nervous, too."

"Are you?" Somehow, his confession gave her the needed strength, though something deep inside continued to stall. Coming face to face with her brother was the culmination of six long months of hard travel over a two-thousand-mile spread—if you included their many detours—with many mishaps and misfortunes in between, and the sealing of a special bond, a love that would last a lifetime between her and Shadoe.

When she became aware of Shadoe's hand gently squeezing her own, she smiled shyly, then coaxed her horse ahead. Shadoe immediately joined her, and together they closed the distance between the river and the sprawling road ranch where a different kind of love awaited.

Reading Red Sewall was eating breakfast with Maude when he saw the approach of riders. "We have company, Maude," he said, rising. "I'll fetch a couple of extra plates."

Maude replied, "I'll do that. You go on out and make them welcome."

When Red moved out to the wide, planked porch, he was immediately surprised by the appearance of the man and woman now dismounting their horses. He was accustomed to grizzled old prospectors traveling through, women who were either too fat, too bony or godawful ugly, and dozens of runny-nosed kids who didn't seem to have the makings of a full brain between them. But the man was tall, slender and well-muscled, the woman, pale-haired and more beautiful than he'd ever imagined a woman could be. And there was a strange familiarity in the way she moved, in the way she smiled when, at last, she approached the porch and faced him. He had a real funny feeling about these two.

"Good morning," greeted Shadoe, propping his boot up on the first step. "I made some inquiries at a settlement down the river—"

"That'll be Roscoe's place."

"Yes," said Shadoe. "Are you Reading Red Sewall?"

"I am," replied Red. "The woman's setting a couple of extra plates. You two hungry?"

While Shadoe might have continued the polite amenities, Isabel suddenly blurted out, "We're looking for a young man named John C. Fremont Sewall. Is he here?"

A grim line assailed Red's mouth beneath the fringes of his ragged mustache. Narrowing his eyes, his gaze cut steadily between the pretty, pale-haired woman and the man who stood beside her. "What's your interest in John, little lady?" he asked.

Isabel suddenly began to tremble again. When she attempted to raise her hand to sweep back a loose lock of her hair, Shadoe, seeing its wild trembling, took it and held it firmly, giving her courage. "I have reason to believe he is my brother Eduard," said Isabel.

"What makes you think that?" Reading had not

410

meant to speak so gruffly, and immediately softened his voice. He did not attempt to hide from them the moisture now coating his eyes. "What makes you think John ain't my son?"

Shadoe had taken charge of the letter many, many miles ago. Swiftly, he withdrew it from the pocket of his shirt and handed it to the grizzled old fellow standing upon the porch. "This letter was received in New Orleans back in November. It came from here, and it came from the young man who identified himself as John C. Fremont Sewall. He wanted to know if he was Miss Emerson's brother, and she believes he is."

Silence. Red, thinking about that night when John was shot, handed the letter back. He remembered the conversation they'd had just before the boy had walked out that fateful night. He had asked about Louisiana; he had asked him how to pronounce the name he'd slowly spelled E-D-U-A-R-D. Raking back his wild, unkempt hair, Red quietly said, "John's up on that hill—" His left arm pointed to the east, "up there behind the corral. You go on—" He descended the steps. "I'll take care of your horses and bed them down. I s'pect you'll be stayin' around a few days."

As the old man moved toward a shed with their horses, Isabel tucked her hand into the crook of Shadoe's arm. "He is there, Shadoe, only a hundred yards away. I was so afraid . . . so afraid we'd get here and some horrible fate would have befallen him. But he is there, there, Shadoe! And I don't think I have the strength to move toward him."

Silence. Shadoe drew her into his arms and held her for a long, long while, his hand gently massaging her scalp beneath the thick masses of her hair. "Breathe deeply, Isabel. You will feel it returning to you, that strength you are so sure has left you. You will feel it as strongly as the love you have for your

411

brother. Now—" He stood slightly back and out-stretched his arms. "Do you wish to go alone?"

"No!" Isabel rushed back into his embrace and pressed her cheek against him. "No, I need you with me, Shadoe. I want you beside me when I am face to face with Eduard."

"Very well." They turned, Isabel tucked into the wing of Shadoe's arm, and slowly moved toward the hill where they would see the young man who had brought them on a two-thousand-mile journey.

Paul could see that his father was especially remi-niscent this evening. They had checked the drainage in the fields, gone over the work schedules with Little Jim, who was generally in charge of the operations of the plantation, and then had ridden over to Ellie's to look over the Spring foals that were just now reach-ing three months of age. One looked especially prom-ising, and Grant said that he'd like to buy the sorrel filly at a top price when it reached two years of age.

Now, they were back at Shadows-in-the-Mist, and Paul took his father's horse to the stables. "I'll take care of unsaddling and grooming them, father—" He'd always called Grant *father*, rather than the less formal *papa*, as Isabel called him, and . . . yes, Eduard, too, before he'd fallen into the Boeuf. Even at two years of age, Paul had called him father, and Grant had always wondered why not papa, like his other two children.

When he noticed Paul giving him a worried look as he contemplated the reason for his thoughtful mood, Grant smiled, wrapping his fingers around his son's shoulder. "Just thinking, Paul," he explained. "Nothing for you to worry about." Then he repeated a lighthearted order that had been his parting words to Paul frequently for the past fourteen years, "You need to relax, son. You're much too serious for a lad only sixteen."

Paul returned his father's warm smile, though it was brief, as usual. Rather than respond, he turned toward the stable, where he was met by one of the boys from the quarters. As he tucked himself into the darkness of the stable, he watched his father move toward the bend in the river.

He should have known; he was thinking about Eduard again. Paul didn't remember Eduard, since he'd been less than a year old when his brother had drowned in the Boeuf. He loved him, because he was his brother, but he didn't like him very much. When his father was thoughtful like this, it was usually Eduard's fault. If he could have any wish granted, it would be that Eduard could return home, so that his father would never be sad again.

When he entered the quarters, he stopped to talk to old Matthew. "How is Sarah?" asked Grant.

Matthew dragged his hat from his head in respect to his employer. "She be much better, Mistah Emerson. Thank ya fo' askin'."

Just then, Peculiar stepped out to the porch. "Mo'nin, Mistah Emerson."

He remembered the first time, more than twenty-three years ago, that he'd first seen the teenage Peculiar, sitting on the bare earth with frog ornaments carefully placed between her parted legs. When Ellie's housekeeper, Miss Mandy, had passed away, Grant had sent Peculiar to her, and she'd been with her and his brother Aldrich ever since. He smiled, choosing not to inform her that it was late afternoon. "How are you, Peculiar?"

"I be jes' fine, Mistah Emerson. Miz El, she done already did sent me ovah ta bring ol' Sarey some chicken soup. Mistah Dustin, he be's comin' roun' in de carriage mos' any time now ta take me home."

Old Matthew snickered, "Ya be's astin' Peculiar yere what she done wid Massah Wickley's gold dey long time ago, Mistah Emerson?"

Peculiar, her ebony features pinching in an exaggerated, and rather comical, frown, said, "Huh, what gold dat be, Ol' Matthew?"

And Grant, laughing for the first time that day, replied, "I don't reckon I will," then tipped his hat and said, "Good evening to you, Miss P. . . . Matthew."

Resuming his journey, he moved on through the quarters, speaking to the children, the women sitting on their small porches, the men coming in from the fields. His leg had been bothering him today, and his limp was more pronounced; he tried to straighten up, but his heart wasn't in it.

Very soon, he reached his destination, the small, shady clearing at the bend of the bayou, where Spanish moss hung in long, dry, gray fingers. Just a few yards down from where he leaned against the trunk of a live oak, in the shallow currents of Bayou Boeuf, a large white riverboat with peacock blue trim had once bobbed, its wheel sucked into the mud of the bayou the moment it had been rolled in by Angus Wickley's men. The Union army had burned it in 1864, but Grant could still picture it sitting there, gently rolling on the current, a pleasing sight to the people of Bayou Boeuf. There is where he and his Delilah had first made love . . . and he was sure it was where they had conceived their now absent Isabel.

Blast his rebellious, hard-headed daughter! What could have compelled her to leave the security of New Orleans, and Aunt Imogen's house, to travel with some strange man for so many miles? Why couldn't she have been a dutiful child, like Paul?

Paul: . . . how much he reminded him of Eduard: the same coloring, the same golden eyes; they'd looked enough alike at four years of age to have been twins. Eduard would have turned twenty this past March if he'd lived.

Yes . . . if he'd lived. It had been only recently that Grant had given up his dreams of Eduard being alive somewhere, not knowing his identity, and possibly happening upon his family at Shadows-in-the-Mist, drawn by the familial instincts of a small boy who had once lived here. For years he'd harbored his deepest hopes that Eduard would yet be found alive, but he knew it would never happen.

Eduard was dead; it was time to face that and go on with life. Dear God, how hard it was, though! He hadn't seen his son's body. He'd never seen the proof that Eduard was dead.

His heart tried to keep alive the hope, but his good sense reminded him in his every waking moment that after all these years that hope was slim indeed.

"Grant?"

Startled from his reminiscences, Grant spun about. There, standing not half a dozen feet from him, was his beloved Delilah, her upswept sable-colored tresses scarcely touched by passage of time, her skin smooth and flawless, like porcelain. Softening the severity his thoughts had painted upon his features, he opened his arms to her. Soon, she eased her tall, lithe figure against his hard one. "Were you worried about me?"

Delilah said, "Yes; I imagine you've been thinking about Eduard. And—I suspect you're worried about our Isabel, too."

"You know me so well," replied Grant, touching his mouth in a tender kiss to her forehead. "Isabel will return and—blast—you'll have to hold me back from taking a switch to her. Our Eduard—" He drew in a long, deep breath, then slowly expelled it, "our boy is gone, Delilah. He'll never come back."

Tears gleamed upon Delilah's lower lids as she

pressed her cheek to her husband's chest. She'd never been able to admit that Eduard was dead; she suspected that she never would. Rather than respond, and grow more sorrowful herself, she drew slightly back and smiled for her husband. "Mozelle has made your favorite for supper. I'm famished, and I don't wish to dine without you."

A tear touched her cheek, and he caught it on the tip of his index finger. Then he kissed the spot where the tear had been and turned toward the house with Delilah, to move on a slow, deliberate course toward Shadows-in-the-Mist. He loved the way Delilah rested her head against his shoulder as they walked.

They'd been married for twenty-three years; the honeymoon had yet to end. Grant liked the way Delilah made him feel. When he was with her, he could stop thinking about their lost son for a while . . . and their rebellious daughter, following an undisclosed dream.

Shadoe and Isabel had walked past a wagonload of trading goods and a healthy-looking vegetable patch before reaching a small corral containing horses and cows. Isabel's nervousness had metamorphosized into a deep contentment, and she moved gracefully around the corral, her hand now tucked into Shadoe's. All the while her topaz gaze swept over the width and depth of the hill, and into the deep fringes of the stand of ponderosa pines and aspens just beyond.

She watched for human movement, for the appearance of a tall young man with pale hair, like their father's, and golden eyes, like their mother's. Isabel could see no livestock grazing, no crops growing . . . so what would he be doing up on the hill? Then she smiled; perhaps he was a lot like the sister he would

416

soon face — a dreamer who sought solitude to nurture dreams, a worrier fretting over small, private wounds no other soul could see, feel or understand.

The presence of Shadoe gave her strength; his silence echoed the emotion he felt. In a minute, or maybe two, she would see a brother believed dead these last sixteen years. He was twenty years old now; he didn't even know that his birthday was in March.

What kind of man was Eduard? Was he kind, gentle, soft-hearted? Or was he a bully and a troublemaker? Did he make friends easily, or was he a loner? Did he have a special woman in his life? There were so many things she wanted to know of him, and all she had to rely on, to give some personal depth and character to the personality he might possess, was a single letter written by a young man who ached for love, for family, for roots. In those few lines written with childlike curiosity, she felt that she knew him almost as well as she knew herself.

Her boots moved through wildflowers . . . the dense white clusters of mountain mint, the bristly stems of blueweed, forget-me-nots and black-eyed-susans grabbing at her skirts. She watched the hill stretch out before her as her steps seemed to take her farther and farther away from the crest she was seeking. She felt the moistness of her hand within Shadoe's. Was hers perspiring, or was it his? She became aware of his steady breathing, of the way his thigh muscles tightened against the fabric of his trousers as they climbed the hill. She became aware of the silence, and its calming effect. The tremor settled within her, and she could feel the warm sun adding much-needed color to her cheeks.

Did the crest of the hill loom almost at arm's length now? Had they reached their destination? She really wasn't sure. She knew only that it seemed like

417

a very long time since they'd rounded the corral where the horses and cattle moved lazily to and fro. She knew only that it seemed like a thousand years since she and Shadoe had mounted their horses in New Orleans and began their steady journey north-westward.

A sparrow called, *tsip, tsip, teeeee-saaaaay,* in a two-part trill that was all she could hear across the distance. A meadow mouse, scurrying from them, leaped a distance of five feet out of the thicket of grass and wildflowers. But Isabel's gaze was transfixed to the crest, and when she stood there, with the earth as far as she could see now below them, she felt the nervous tremor return to her shoulders and travel a cruel, deliberate course into her neck and back.

She looked around; the wildflowers waved like flags in the gentle breeze that blew around them. Her hand was no longer enveloped by Shadoe's, and she missed the security of his grip. She felt the coolness of her skirts flapping against her ankles, her long, loose hair whipped across her cheek, which she scarcely had the strength to drag away with a raised finger.

Eduard was close by; she could feel it. Absently, she smoothed down the folds of her gown. Was the hand lifting to drag her hair to the back of her shoulders really her own? She cut a quick glance toward Shadoe, but his eyes were downcast. Perspiration dotted her forehead and began to trickle downward in streams. Oh, why hadn't she brought a handkerchief with her? She wanted to look her best when she saw Eduard, when she said, *I am, Isabel, your sister, and I have come to take you home.*

Scarcely before she realized she'd opened her mouth, she heard the words, "Where is he, Shadoe?" echo from within her like a faint whisper.

And he replied, "He's out there. Why don't you

call his name . . . and remember he is called John, not Eduard. He might answer you more readily."

She hesitated only slightly. Drawing up her hand and cupping it at the right side of her mouth, an emotional Isabel, her voice like a song, called, "Joohhhnnn . . . John Sewall . . ."

And as if the hill itself had heard her, and prepared to answer her, a breeze climbed upwards, swirling round and round, and gently flattened the tall grass still damp from the morning's dew. By doing so, it offered into view the headstones and simple crosses marking the final resting places of those whose lives had been spent at the Tongue River's junction with Pumpkin Creek.

"No . . . no . . ." She sank slowly, her skirts billowing out and settling over the cool, damp grass. "Dear Lord, no . . ." Then Shadoe was beside her, supporting himself on his knees and drawing her tenderly to him.

If he spoke, she did not hear his words. If he held her, she could not feel the warmth of him. If she had a past, she could not remember it. And a very vital part of the happiness she had expected to fill her future lay buried here, beneath a hill blanketed by forget-me-nots, mountain mint . . . and memories.

Part Four

Homebound

Twenty-six

The 28th of June, 1880

A line of live oaks created a tunnel along the roadway, deepening the shadows and closing out a mild
and everpresent threat of rain. Dustin Emerson
flicked the reins, coaxing the pair of geldings into a
trot along Bayou Boeuf very near its entrance to the
private road of Shadows-in-the-Mist.

He had visited his uncle's plantation a thousand
times, it seemed, in the past few months, so as he
entered the road, fringed the pond and drew to a halt
at the stable, he was surprised to see a rush of humans coming out to greet him. Little Jim met him
with a courteous smile.

The others who had gathered, the workers, old
and young, from the quarters, servants from the
house, and some of the family members—his father,
Aldrich Emerson, and his stepmother, Ellie, displayed curious expressions that instantly bordered
somewhat on disappointment. He had seen smiles
upon entering, but now a strange melancholy had
captured their demeanors, although they managed to
effect some semblance of toleration and cordiality.

"Did I arrive at a bad time?" asked Dustin, alighting the carriage he'd hired in Alexandria. He could
have sworn he'd told his parents to expect him back
from his business trip today, and he didn't understand why they hadn't stayed at home to await him.

Just at that moment, Grant and Delilah Emerson emerged from the house, both beaming as proudly as new parents. Their expressions, too, instantly became frozen as they saw that it was only their nephew. "I did come at a bad time!" remarked Dustin, taking his uncle's proffered hand. He couldn't help but notice its tremble, and the softly disguised chagrin in Grant Emerson's pale eyes.

"No . . . no, it isn't that," replied Grant. "Of course, you're always welcome, Nephew. It's just—" He forced his mouth into a smile as he took his wife's hand and drew it through the crook of his arm. "Our Isabel will be arriving at most anytime, and with a man she has written that she expects us to approve as a husband."

Dustin felt a frown edging onto his aquiline features. Of course, he wanted his beloved cousin to be happy . . . but with a man who was not of her father's choosing? "Oh, I see—" To change the subject from his rebellious cousin, he informed Grant and Delilah, "while I was in Baton Rouge I met a most interesting man. He claims to be a newspaperman, and he is trying to piece together the mystery of Angus Wickley's lost gold."

"It'll never happen," interjected Delilah. "Papa fully intended that the mystery would never be solved."

"If anyone can do it, this fellow can. He apparently ran across one of those gold coins in San Franciso—"

"San Francisco!" Grant and Delilah echoed the unlikely location in unison.

"Yes—San Francisco . . . and he has pieced together some other interesting information—none of which he would divulge to me—and I do believe that the fellow will show up here one day. Actually, the location of the gold is his last item of business. He is more concerned with its origin, its owner, and its intended designation. Yes, indeed, the fellow will be showing up here. I guarantee that!"

"If he can find father's gold," said Delilah, "then all the power to him. But he'd better hurry. You know that our Isabel has been as curious about the mystery of the gold as we have been since my father buried it here, and she is bound and determined to dig it up one day . . . or throttle its location out of your—" She now looked to Ellie, standing quietly by, "odd but lovable Peculiar."

Dustin snatched his hat from his head, then smiled apologetically for his mother and aunt. "Sorry . . . I don't know where my manners are."

Within a few minutes, they all sat on the gallery, sipping iced tea topped with mint sprigs and lemon, and enjoying Mozelle's apple crumb muffins. Delilah had encouraged Dustin to stay at the Shadows, rather than returning to the cottage where he would be alone, and he had agreed to do so. He wanted to see this rogue that his Isabel would try to pass off as her husband-to-be, and the more he thought about the boldness of the man, taking off with his unmarried cousin, the angrier he became.

Then, a lucky break for his mood, his thoughts were disturbed by Grant Emerson asking, "What are you thinking, Delilah?"

Delilah startled, closing her fingers over the cameo brooch at her neckline. Her lovely golden eyes met her husband's. "About our daughter," she said. "And wishing she were here."

"It'll be soon," replied her husband. Then to the now brooding Dustin, who quietly looked on, he said, "Actually, we're not sure which day she will be home. She'd said in her letter it would be this week and, as you know, it is already Thursday."

Thursday . . . two more days left for the promised arrival. Unconsciously, Delilah's gaze moved past the shoulders of the friends and family who were gathered and fell upon the roadway, upon the pond where the sun shone in glittering paths upon the still, glassy surface. There was a silence, an airlessness about the morning, almost as if the earth bearing the weight of the large, columned house was holding its breath. While she watched—praying for the emergence of a carriage bearing her beloved daughter—a wide, black shadow blotted out the sun, and only then did she notice the threat of rain spilling across the horizon. A lightning flash of pale white streaked the sky between the darkness of clouds and the deepening green of the woodline, and then, far above, rain gently began to rattle the leaves, and the encroaching dark was somehow comforting.

She is close by. I feel it . . . my dear daughter, soon to be pressed to my heart in the gentlest of hugs. . . .

The last full night of sleep Isabel had gotten had been in Topeka, Kansas. They had spent two nights there, awaiting a connecting train south, and she had thoroughly enjoyed the meals at the Harvey House Dining Hall at the end of the Santa Fe depot. The dining car of the Southern Pacific line did not offer such fine cuisine.

As she settled back into the plush seat of their private compartment in the Pullman sleeping car, she adjusted the skirts of her new camel-colored traveling dress and unpinned the matching hat with its dark brown trim and dyed ostrich feathers. Shadoe sat opposite her, his head back and his hat covering his face. He hated trains; he'd made no bones about that when he'd agreed that they would return by this mode. "I know you're anxious to get home," he had said back in Colorado. "So, Mirlo and I will make the best of it."

The best of it, indeed! For the first four days and nights of traveling, Shadoe had spent all of his time in the stock car, settling the squealing stallion that one of the railroad employees had threatened to s loose at an open doorway. They had given the chestnut mare to Reading Red Sewall, but Shadoe had refused—and properly so—to get rid of the stallion. Red had spent the better half of the first week of their visit upping his offer and hoping Shadoe would give in to the pressure.

Except for the unfortunate death of a brakeman who had been pinned between two cars, and a robbery in the second-class coach by a young Cherokee outlaw named Ned Christie, the trip had been uneventful. It had been a long, long six months since she and Shadoe had first left New Orleans, destined for Tongue River, Montana, and she was anxious to return home to Shadows-in-the-Mist.

The door into the narrow corridor between the private compartments suddenly opened. Startled from her weary thoughts, Isabel shot forward, her new hat dropping to the floor. Without hesitation, the unexpected intruder bent to one knee, retrieved the hat and politely handed it back to Isabel.

She smiled warmly . . . lovingly. "I thought you were going for dessert in the dining car?"

Since they had boarded the first train in Colorado for their journey southward, Eduard had made a point of dining at every station, and in every dining car, twice in the morning, twice in the afternoons, and at least three times between the hours of six and ten in the evening. He was as excited by his first long journey—at least, the first he could remember—as a giddy schoolboy taking his favorite girl to a barn dance. "I just came to see if you want me to bring you anything, Isabel," replied the handsome young man. "They got some real fine lookin' cakes with strawberries on 'em, an' a real purty white cream all fluffed up like a happy cloud. Want me to bring you one?"

"No, Eduard," she laughed, her slim fingers closing over his wrist. "We've been traveling, eating in dining cars, staying in hotels, and eating in dining rooms and, good heavens, you're going to be as big as a bull moose by the time I present you to mother and father."

Eduard's golden eyes twinkled mirthfully. "But they'll like me just the same, won't they, Isabel?"

"They'll love you," she continued her gentle chiding, "even if we have to roll you in wearing a barrel, because we can find no clothing to fit you."

Eduard threw back his shoulders, making a dramatic show of returning to the doorway. "Well, I'm goin' to have some of that cake with strawberries and puffed-up cream."

Instantly, Shadoe's boot rose, touching against the knee of Eduard's corduroy trousers. "You didn't ask me if I wanted any of that cake," he grinned, peering at Isabel's brother from beneath the rim of his hat.

"Do you, Shadoe? Hell—" he laughed, "my sister might be having to roll both of us into that plantation down there in Louisiana—"

"We *are* in Louisiana," Isabel reminded him. "And only a few miles out of Alexandria. You had better go and eat that cake in a hurry."

Despite his weariness, Shadoe rose lithely to his feet. Flipping his hat back on his forehead, he said to Isabel, "Do you mind if these two fellas leave you alone for a bit?"

Isabel picked up the book she'd purchased in Fort Smith and opened it to the page with the bent corner. "I think I can manage. I do declare . . . all you two think about is eating."

Shadoe bent low just then and whispered, "Food is my second hobby. Loving you is my first."

With a tenderly placed kiss to her cheek, he joined Eduard in the narrow corridor.

Isabel really wasn't in a mood to read. She watched the quickly passing, and very familiar countryside outside the train window and as she imagined the reaction of her parents when they met their beloved Eduard, she felt tears of happiness spring to her eyes. "Oh, Eduard . . . Eduard," she whispered with soft emotion. "Yes, your — our parents are going to love you. And you, too, my beloved Shadoe."

So many memories filled her at that moment: the happy times she and Shadoe had spent together, the ones that had wrenched her heart and made her believe she would never be happy again. She couldn't help but remember that morning atop the hill overlooking Reading Red Sewall's road ranch, the grass damp and crushed beneath her skirts, her broken sobs cushioned by her caring, loving Shadoe's hard chest, the way his protective arms had held her and his silence, without words, attempting to soothe her heartbreak. Would she ever forget that moment, with the wind rustling all about her, catching her skirts and whipping them up, rushing through the stands of ponderosa pines and aspens like a haunting shrill. Oh, would she ever forget that precious moment that a spry young lad had stepped from the shadow of a towering aspen and politely asked, "Something the matter, miss?"

She had drawn in a short, quick breath, scarcely able to see the blur of him through her tear-sheened eyes. Rather she had been much more aware of shadows easing across the grass and the wildflowers to grasp and cool her skin. "Shadoe . . . Shadoe," she had whispered brokenly. "Tell me please, please, tell me I'm not dreaming."

Husky, emotional laughter was his first answer to her inquiry. Then he had tightened his grip and said, with some difficulty of his own, "No, my beloved Isabel . . . you are not dreaming."

A strength with no visible source had filled her then. Her dear, long-lost brother Eduard was not an inhabitant of one of the graves exposed by the grass and the wildflowers that had been lain gently upon the earth by a sudden, precocious wind. He was there, alive, looking at the two of them with a most familiar curiosity and caring softening his youthful features. And she rose, gathering that strength and resolve, and slowly moved toward him.

She wasn't sure from where came the strength to take his hand and hold it so warmly; her knees were flaccid, and she was sure she would collapse, embarrassing herself, Shadoe, and the young man standing so timidly before her now.

"Do you know who I am?" she asked, her tear-sheened eyes unblinking, her mouth trembling.

"No, ma'am," he replied, giving her the strangest smile, and a little embarrassed by the way she held his hand while her man was looking on. "But I s'pect you're goin' to tell me real soon like."

"You wrote a letter to Imogen de'Cambre of New Orleans some months ago. I have come in response to that letter."

The young man's eyes lit up. "You come all this way from way down yonder in Louisiana jus' because I wrote a letter?" Then, politely withdrawing his hand, he asked, "Why?" though he really wasn't sure why he'd felt the need. He suspected that the woman facing him was his sister, Isabel, who had been mentioned in the *Picayune,* along with the rest of her family. When he saw tears fill the woman's eyes, John tucked his hands into his pockets and his foot shuffled out, catching upon a rock and sending it tumbling down the hillside. "Are you my sister, Miss?"

Isabel was sure that all the tears she'd ever felt in her lifetime were returning full-force, catching in her throat and making it impossible for her to speak. Then, Shadoe approached, his hand lightly dropping to her shoulder, and she felt that familiar surge of courage once again. "Yes," she eventually replied, "I believe I am your sister."

John C. Fremont Sewell was sure he would swoon

430

just like that lady he'd seen in a road play a few years ago. Quietly, not wishing to be rude, he dropped to a rock, parted his feet, then linked his hands. "Lord, Miss, I'm feelin' real odd. Don't mean to be impolite." Pulling up for a moment to remove his gold medallion, he handed it to Isabel. "This here's what I made the pencil rubbing from. Ol' Gideon said I was a wearin' it when he found me."

Almost absently Isabel took the medallion, her gaze continuing to hold the young man's features. She could see her father's image in him . . . the pale hair, the strong, square features . . . the kindness in eyes that were almost the color of his mother's . . . *yes . . . dear Lord, thank you, this is my brother.*

Reading Red and Maude, who had thoughtfully given them a few minutes to get acquainted, now ascended the hill and made an appearance. John jumped up, excitedly explaining, "This here's my sister, Red . . . this here's Isabel—"

"Kinda figgered," said Reading. "An' the fella?" His bushy gaze cut to the silent Shadoe, who immediately offered his hand.

"I am Shadoe McCaine . . . Miss Emerson and I plan to be married."

"Lord, ain't this something," exclaimed John. "So's Red an' Miss Maude. Day after tomorrow, as a matter of fact!"

"Congratulations," said Isabel.

"Yes . . . congratulations," offered Shadoe.

While Shadoe, Maude and Reading Red struck up a conversation, John C. Fremont Sewall allowed himself to be hugged. He was fairly certain he could get used to having a sister.

In the week that followed, Shadoe and Isabel grew to know John well. Isabel was especially pleased when John said one day, "You know, my real name's Eduard . . . reckon I ought to be gettin' used to it, don't you think?"

431

Maude's and Red's wedding was one of the most unusual Isabel had ever attended, and the gathering of guests was like the emergence of several isolated foreign cultures, with one thing in common; she'd never met a friendlier lot of folks.

Soon, however, the time came to begin the return trip to Louisiana, and Isabel was well aware that Eduard had a choice to make, and that the choice could not possibly be easy. After all, he'd been grievously wounded, and the man who had carried him through four feet of snow for half a day to reach the nearest thing to a doctor in the area was the man Isabel was hoping he would choose to leave. This was the same man who had raised him after Gideon Sewall had died . . . the same man who had loved him and provided for him . . . and had instilled in him the greatest sense of honor, pride and honesty that Isabel had ever witnessed . . . the same man who had journeyed twice a week to the Roscoe place, keeping up with Eduard's recovery, even when he was so down in his back that he had to be physically helped up and down from his saddle. He had soothed his aching heart while John — Eduard — was being cared for by Doc Roscoe by frequently journeying up to the small graveyard on the hill to speak to its latest occupant, his brother Gideon.

Isabel realized only then how selfish she was. How could her brother make such a choice between the man who had loved him for fifteen years and a family he remembered nothing about?

Had it not been for the newly married Reading Red Sewall, Isabel suspected that Eduard would have chosen to stay on Tongue River. That morning, as she and Shadoe had packed their few things and saddled their horses to ride to the nearest train depot anxiously waiting for Eduard to make his choice. Reading had drawn the young man — the boy he knew as John — aside in the barn. She'd not heard the words spoken between the two, but Eduard had told her much later, aboard the train leaving Fort Smith, what had transpired that morning.

"Ol' Red, he says he been takin' care of me for nigh onto fifteen years, and it's time he lives a little and stops havin' to worry about me gittin' shot over some she-male. He'll be wantin' to spend time alone with Maude, and since she's still a young woman, maybe they'll be havin' a young'un of their own . . . an' they can't be a concentratin' on it if I'm hangin' around a house where every little sound echoes like a iron-horse. So, Red, he tells me it's time I go back to folks what I belong to. So, here I am—" Then Eduard had grinned as he'd added, "But Ol' Red, I know he don't really want me to leave. He was jus' makin' it easy for me." Silence. "Isabel?" She had cut her gaze to him. "You reckon our pa and ma'll mind if I'll be wantin' to come back to Tongue River one day to visit Red and Maude?"

"I don't reckon they'll mind at all," Isabel had replied, hugging Eduard tightly. "You know, I really have to thank you."

"Whatever for?" asked Eduard, drawing back a little to favor her with that comical grin.

"If I wasn't taking you home to mother and father, they'd be angry with me for weeks . . . possibly even years . . . for running off like this with a man they had never met."

"You mean Shadoe? Hell—sorry, sis, ain't no man alive, or lady, I reckon, that wouldn't like Shadoe. I'm glad he's goin' to be family."

"So am I," said Isabel, smiling her prettiest. "So am I."

Something cool and damp suddenly touched Isabel's nose. Looking up, scraping the whipped cream from her nose, she faced a mischievously smiling

433

Eduard. "I brought you one of them cakes all covered with the strawberries and fluffy stuff, Sis," he announced, promptly forcing the bowl into her hands.

"Cost me twenty-five cents," announced Shadoe, dropping to the seat beside her. "And I had to pay that fellow up there another buck for him to turn his back so I could sneak it out of the dining car."

Isabel laughed, her hand moving out to capture each of their hands in turn. "My men. Whatever would I do without you?"

Shadoe cut a humored gaze to Eduard. "What do you think, young man, will she ever have to find out?"

Eduard pretended to think about it for a moment. Then he shook his head with exaggerated energy and proclaimed, "Nahhhh . . . don't reckon, Shadoe."

As the great iron wheels began to slow and steam filled the air outside the window, the Alexandria depot came into view.

"We're almost home," announced Isabel.

"Reckon my horse is still in the stock car?" asked Shadoe.

Edward laughed, "I'm fair certain I saw a four-legged beast being thrown over a trestle about a hundred miles back."

Isabel and Shadoe joined in the laughter, even as each . . . and Eduard . . . hid excitement, nervousness, and apprehension from each other.

Twenty-seven

The carriage clipped along at a steady pace, held back occasionally by the enthusiasm of the stallion tied at the back. Isabel almost felt guilty when they began to leave Lamourie Bayou, since she had never before passed by the cottage without stopping in to visit her uncle Aldrich and aunt Ellie. When they entered the road skirting Bayou Boeuf, Eduard began asking, "Is this our land?" every half-mile, until Isabel's laughing, though visibly nervous, response finally changed from "No," to "Yes."

"Wow." A slim, youthful finger began pointing. "Them our horses? Reckon I could ride that fine-lookin' sorrel? Them our cows? I'm real good at milkin'. Them our fields? What is that stuff? Wow, is that cotton? Look over there, Isabel! Is that Spanish moss . . . looks like an ol' lady's hair! Wow . . . this here Louisiana's really somethin'!"

Shadoe laughed, "Wait until your first trip to New Orleans, Eduard . . . and your first look at those pretty young Creole gals."

"I like gals," Eduard said, leaning across the front seat of the carriage so that his body wedged between Shadoe's and Isabel's. "That's what got me almost kil't back there on Tongue River."

"A gal's what might get me kil't soon, too," mused Shadoe.

"My pa?" Eduard drew back with the enthusiasm of

a young man ready to defend his father. "My pa ain't a goin' to shoot you, Shadoe? Heck fire—"

"Heck? What kind of word is that?" asked Shadoe, who'd never heard it before.

"Ol' Red, he says it's a lot more polite than—" His voice lowered as he said, "Hell. Said one day that people from Californie to the Atlantic, from Tongue River to this here Louisiana, they'll be sayin' 'heck' instead of—" Again he whispered, "Hell. Does sound more polite, don't it, Shadoe? Especially in front of a lady . . . an' a sister, too!"

Shadoe chuckled at the distinction Eduard had made between the two. "Sure," he responded. "Heck if it don't sound more polite."

When they were within a mile of Shadows-in-the-Mist, Isabel's thoughts began to fragment into various insecurities. Suppose her father should hate Shadoe right away and attempt to run him off; suppose he should try to file charges of kidnapping—indeed, suppose the sheriff from Alexandria was waiting on the grounds to take Shadoe into custody; suppose her father and mother did not believe the excited young man on the seat behind her was their long-lost son, Eduard. Suppose—

Oh, blast the supposes! She'd come this far, secure in her belief that everything would work out perfectly. Why did she have these doubts now that the rooftop of the Shadows—grabbing at the late evening sky across the timberline—was visible to her? She felt Shadoe shudder beside her, heard the breath drawn deeply into Eduard's lungs as he beheld, for the first time, the grand sight of the Shadows coming into view, and her own heart stopped beating for a moment.

This was it—the telltale moment when everything would work out perfectly . . . or would explode worse than any war ever to plague this land. Just as Shadoe would have reined the mare onto the private road leading to the Shadows, he drew to a halt, his smoke-gray gaze turning full to Isabel. "Suppose he won't accept me, Isabel . . . your father . . . will you still be my wife? Will you?"

"He'll accept you, and even on the remote chance that he wouldn't, you'll not be getting rid of me so easily, Shadoe McCaine!"

At that point, Eduard fell back into the plush leather of the seat he occupied and muttered, "Awe, come on, let's don't get mushy now! I've got a pa and ma an' a little brother to be meetin'."

Shadoe and Isabel, glad of the distraction from what might be a wrathful father, both laughed, Shadoe instantly clicking the horse ahead. He was counting on Grant Emerson being so happy to have his long-lost son back that Shadoe, having something to do with it, would instinctively be drawn into the circle of that happiness. Maybe Grant Emerson would forget that he'd taken off with his unmarried daughter and would simply be happy that he'd kept her safe and brought her home.

Maybe.

Little Jim ran up to the galley. "They's comin', Mistah Grant . . . Miss Delilah . . . I jes' seen 'em pull in off the road. An' Miss Isabel—she be's with two strange men!"

Grant shot up from the chair. "Two men . . . blast that girl!"

Delilah, too, arose, her hand immediately covering Grant's forearm. "Now, husband, don't assume the worst." When their sixteen-year-old son, Paul, approached, Delilah tucked her trembling arm across his shoulder for additional support.

Dustin, too, came to his feet, loudly exclaiming, "This McCaine had better be a decent man! At least one deserving of a woman like Isabel!" Then, when no one responded to his hotheaded outburst, he sank, pouting, into one of the chairs on the gallery.

437

The carriage pulled up. Grant immediately thought the man beside his daughter was a pirate: black-haired, black-clothed, and from this distance, black-eyed . . . was he also black-hearted? A rogue who had taken advantage of his daughter?

A squealing Isabel did not wait for Little Jim, now approaching, or Shadoe, sitting as still as a marble statue, to assist her down from the carriage. She hopped down and was soon drawn into her weeping mother's embrace, then her little brother's. Her father slowly approached, his eyes—under normal circumstances the same color as Isabel's—now darkening to the color of a storm-tossed ocean. "Mother . . . Paul . . . father—"

"Daughter—" Delilah hugged her tightly, "thank God you are safe. Thank God you are home."

"You should get a lickin'," chuckled Paul, again hugging her tightly.

Grant wasn't sure what held him back from the reunion with his daughter. His attention had drifted away from her, and the man who had been beside her in the carriage. Rather, his gaze had now locked to that boy whose chin had yet to sprout peach fuzz . . . a boy who looked about ready to burst wide open with happiness—

Grant's eyes misted, but he narrowed them, then tried to think of something unpleasant in his life, something that might make him angry enough not to feel the emotion now welling within him. He had held on to his hopes for years that a long-lost son might yet be found alive, but he had given up such dreams, in order that he could go on with life. If his beloved Isabel had any ideas about passing this man off as Eduard, then she'd better reevaluate her decision.

Isabel had watched his reaction; she'd seen his eyes sheen with moisture, then she'd seen anger narrow them; she'd seen the reminiscences flash across his gaze like moving pictures . . . and now, as she held her mother, her smile instantly fading, she watched him turn and walk off, soon disappearing around the pond and into the timberline parting Shadows-in-the-Mist from a gentle curve in Bayou Boeuf that had been a favorite fishing spot.

Isabel fought tears. Turning, taking her mother's hand, her other hand went out to Eduard. "Come here." She waited until he jumped down from the carriage, and when he stood beside her, she said, "This is Delilah Wickley. I want you to introduce yourself to her." Then Isabel, dragging up her skirts in two pale hands, moved toward the carriage, so that she could take Shadoe's hand and envelope it between her own. With tears burning in her eyes, she whispered, "I love you, Shadoe," then, "I didn't think this would be so hard for father."

"Do you think he recognized Eduard?"

"Yes . . . but he is afraid to believe. He's had too many disappointments in the past."

"It's going to hurt Eduard."

"No, he is prepared." Isabel touched her cheek to Shadoe's hand in a moment of affection, and to control her own shaky emotions. "He'll know what to do."

Shadoe hopped down; a narrow-eyed Little Jim took the lead of the mare and coaxed her toward the stable. Shadoe's hand now dropping across Isabel's shoulder, he watched the play of emotions, the confusion, the perplexity, easing into the features of the beautiful mother of his beloved, the woman he wanted for a wife. Delilah Wickley had said nothing, her gaze now moving gracefully — hopefully — over the features of the boy, who now crushed his hat nervously between his hands.

Without prelude, without carefully chosen words, he said, "I'm Eduard." And when it appeared that she didn't believe him, he clumsily removed the pendant from his neck, took her hand and dropped it onto her palm. "I've been wearin' this since I was a sprite of a lad."

Isabel could not bear witness to the reunion of mother and son; blinded by her tears, she now turned to Shadoe to bury her face against the folds of his black shirt. His hand, gently caressing her back, was comforting, and she found herself hoping that her mother's response would be somewhat friendlier than her father's had been.

Then she heard Delilah Wickley gently murmur, "Eduard? My Eduard?"

"Ain't nobody else's," chuckled Eduard, and was pleased to be immediately surrounded by his mother's arms.

"My Eduard—" The chain had slipped through her fingers as she hugged her long-lost son and Shadoe McCaine's strong fingers moved out quickly to catch it as it fell.

"I think I'm safe for the time being," he whispered against Isabel's hairline. When her mother called to Isabel, Shadoe immediately found himself alone, though not for long. With squeals of disbelief and enthusiasm, their small group was now surrounded by dozens of dark-skinned adults and children, weeping loudly, some uttering, "Praise Jesus!" and still others, standing back, tenderly dabbing at tears with coarse squares of muslin.

Feeling a little neglected, Shadoe found a half-barrel to rest upon. Then the negro, Little Jim, approached and asked, "You 'sponsible fo' Mistah Eduard comin' home to his mammy an' pappy?"

"I was Miss Emerson's escort," he offered, now watching as a proud, beaming Isabel turned her gaze to him.

"You in love wid de Missy?" asked Jim.

"I am," responded Shadoe without a moment's hesitation.

And Little Jim smiled widely, his gaze turning to see

the love as readable as an approaching storm in the eyes of Miss Isabel Emerson.

Soon, Delilah, Isabel, and Shadoe were moving toward the house, and Eduard, claiming he had "somethin' real important to do," moved toward the timberline where he'd seen his father disappear.

Grant Emerson stood just up from the bank of Bayou Boeuf, his hands tucked into his pockets and his pale gaze sweeping over the water. This was a favorite spot, because on that small, crumbling pier jutting into the bayou he had many times perched a precocious four-year-old son to fish for bream and *sac-a-lait*. He smiled, remembering how he'd loosened Eduard's belt and looped it at the back over a rusty old nail so that he wouldn't fall into the water.

It had taken years to accept Eduard's death, and he couldn't allow himself to hope when there was no hope, to dream when every dream was a nightmare; he couldn't allow himself to be deceived by any more pretenders—

"Father?"

Grant swung about, to face a young man very similar to himself. He could almost remember seeing a similar reflection when he'd looked at himself in the mirror a good number of years ago—more, actually, than he cared to think about. "I don't know who you are, young man," said Grant evenly, "but you're not my son."

Eduard understood the older man's hesitation. He understood the fifteen years it might have taken him to accept his son's death, and he understood that this man had been heartbroken by the loss of a young son, and by the pretenders who'd made claims. Isabel had told him on the train how each disappointment had hurt him so deeply. So, Eduard turned toward the water, approached the pier, and stooped to touch its rot-

441

ting timbers. These past few weeks of traveling and being told things by his sister had made him remember other things. He remembered this spot in the bayou . . . and he remembered a special time he had spent here with a special man.

He smiled. Without turning to face Grant Emerson, he said, "You used to loop my belt over that old rusty nail there—"

"Isabel could have told you that!"

Still Eduard did not turn, and the smile became a reminiscence easing across his youthful features. "I remember once . . . it weren't too long before I fell in the bayou, my pa had brought me an' Little Jim down here to fish, an' he sent Little Jim back for some more bait. My pa was helping me cast my line in the water an' I thought I had caught a fish an' I pulled my line real hard an' that slimy ol' worm twisted right into my hair. I was a screamin' an' yellin', an' the hook got caught in my scalp . . . an' I remember my pa promised he wouldn't tell ma that I cried . . . because I was wantin' to be a big boy—" Eduard sighed deeply, "An' I remember my pa made me promise not to tell ma either, because he didn't want her raisin' the dickens about lettin' the hook get caught in my head. So we kept a secret that day . . . me an' my pa."

Tears filled Grant Emerson's pale gaze. He had never told anyone—not even Delilah—about that incident. No one could have known . . . no one except Eduard himself. Then Eduard rose, skipped a stone across the gently washing current of the Boeuf and turned to face his father. When Grant approached, then drew him into a gentle, fatherly embrace, there was no need for words.

Grant had his son back, and that was all that needed to be said.

For two days the family celebrated. A *couchon-de-la*

was held and friends and family came from all over the state. Imogen made one of her rare treks to Central Louisiana, accompanied by Mercedes, whose personality immediately clashed with the long-time resident of Shadows-in-the-Mist, the smooth-talking Mozelle. That same afternoon that Imogen arrived, Isabel made a startling discovery.

She had been searching for a book Aimee Claire wished to borrow when she found a large wooden box sitting on a shelf in her father's study. Curiosity compelled her to open it and she began going through the items inside . . . a pair of silver spurs, a stack of yellowed letters tied in fading ribbon, a few coins and currency, then a photograph of a group of smiling cowboys. And in the middle, with large, brawny arms easily stretched across the shoulders of the men to either side of him was a very familiar face. She dragged in a small breath, then found her voice to call, "Mother . . . Shadoe—" When neither responded she rushed into the corridor with the photograph. Her mother, alarm eased across her lovely features, and Shadoe, merged into the corridor from opposite directions.

"Isabel . . . what is the matter?"

"This man . . . this is the one I met in Greeley—" Excitedly, she showed the photograph to Shadoe, pointing out the man in the middle. "Isn't this him? The one who helped you find a way out of the mine?"

Taking the photograph from her, Shadoe scraped back a lock of his dark hair. "Well, blast . . . so it is."

Delilah eased between the two. "Which man are you talking about?"

"This one—" Isabel pointed out the only black man in the photograph. "This is him. Shadoe and I both met him."

Delilah paled visibly. "You met this man? When?"

"Well . . . just a couple or three months ago."

Delilah took the photograph; she smiled, remembering the letter—his last letter—that he'd written and

443

asked the man Hotch Trumble to send on to her—a
letter in which he had sworn that he would find a way
to pay her back for the kindness her family had shown
him so many years ago. Quietly, she said, "This is
Philbus . . . Mozelle's first husband—"

"What a coincidence," said Shadoe.

"What a miracle," countered Delilah. "Since Philbus
died in a range accident this past November."

"That's impossible," said Isabel.

"Nothing is impossible," said Delilah, "where there is
love."

Then she hugged her daughter, held Shadoe's hand
fondly, as though, perhaps, a little of the miracle they
had witnessed together might rub off on her. With a
small smile, she left them alone.

Shadoe had enjoyed the love shown by the Emersons
for each other and wanted nothing more than to be
part of their family. But now, with the excitement of
Eduard being returned to the fold, he felt the time approaching that Grant Emerson's attentions would be
turned fully—and with all the wrath of a man protecting his child—toward him.

That warm Friday afternoon, Grant asked Shadoe
to ride with him. Seeing the rifle sheafed against
Grant's saddle, Shadoe wondered if Isabel's father had
already ordered a shallow grave to be dug somewhere
on the lands of the plantation he lovingly called the
Shadows, instead of its longer name. But he accepted
the invitation, and soon found himself alone with the
man who, until now, had given him little more than a
perfunctory glance.

They had ridden less than a mile from the house
when Grant Emerson drew up his horse in a shady
dell, beyond which the fertile lands of the plantation
stood knee deep in cotton. His gaze held steadily away
from Shadoe McCaine, he said, "Fine horse you have

444

there," then, before Shadoe could respond, he asked, rather matter-of-factly, "What is your interest in my daughter?"

"I love her," said Shadoe evenly, "and I want to marry her."

Silence. Grant's gaze swept over the cotton fields and the men working beneath the overhang of rain clouds. "Where do you come from, Mr. McCaine? What do you do for a living? What kind of past do you have? How do I know you're not running from the law. What is your heritage?"

"I'm not running from the law. My father was a half-breed Cheyenne renegade, and my mother was a white school teacher." Shadoe wasn't really sure why he'd divulged his parentage so early in his association with this man whose approval he very much wanted. Perhaps he could redeem himself later, when he and Grant Emerson, if it was ever to happen, became friends.

"How do I know you can take care of my daughter?"

"Well, I can, Mr. Emerson. You'll simply have to trust me."

Grant looked hard over the land, his fingers lightly resting on the pommel of his saddle. "It really doesn't matter if I trust you, Shadoe," he said after a moment. "Exhibiting trustworthiness earns a man's trust. Time ensures it. What matters is that Isabel trusts you . . . and she seems to care deeply for you. I just want to know that you're right for Isabel."

"I love your daughter, Mr. Emerson." Shadoe's attention was disrupted by a doe running gracefully along the woodline, then disappearing into the marshy darkness beyond the trees. "We are right for each other. And quite frankly, with or without your blessing, Isabel will be my wife."

"Will she, indeed?" Suddenly, Grant coaxed his horse into the clearing and started across the meadow. When he had ridden a dozen yards or so, he pulled the horse around. "Come. I have something to show you."

The two men rode in silence for half a mile through the meadow and a narrow spanse of forest, then across a stream and down the bank of the bayou. Soon, Grant pulled into a shady dell just up from the bayou, where they were given an unobstructed view of a wide green pasture. A few cattle and horses grazed there. "This is a beautiful place," remarked Shadoe. "Did you bring me here, where there are no witnesses, to shoot me, Mr. Emerson?"

Grant's mouth smiled, even while his gaze remained stern. "I just bought this tract of land at sheriff's sale, five hundred acres give or take. I had plans for it but—" Suddenly, he turned to Shadoe and asked, "Do you like my daughter?"

"Sometimes I don't," Shadoe answered truthfully. "She's blasted hardheaded at times and I'd like to shake the dickens out of her."

Grant stifled an outright laugh; he remembered feeling the same way about his Delilah a few years back, when she was young and oh, so foolish! "But you like her more often than you don't?"

"For every time that I think I don't like her, there's a thousand more times that I do. Mr. Emerson—" Pressing his forearm upon Mirlo's mane, Shadoe turned full to Grant, "I'm telling you right now that I'm—"

"I know. You have my blessing."

"—going to marry your daughter whether you like it or—" Shadoe drew himself up, his eyes narrowing "What did you say?"

Grant lifted his hat and swept back his pale hair, re placing the hat farther back on his head. "If you'd shu up long enough, young fellow, you'd have heard m say, 'you have my blessing.'" Silence. Shadoe stil wasn't trusting himself to have heard correctly. Bu when Grant said, "And this new tract, all five hundre acres of it, I want you and Isabel to have, to set u home and have a good start. Unless, that is, you're no

446

planning to settle down here."

A lump as large as Colorado rose in Shadoe's throat. He did not speak for a moment. No, it wasn't the land that made him feel emotional, though he recognized the generosity of Grant Emerson's gesture, but it was all the years that he had feared men like this one, and hated their daughters. Now, he would be part of such a family . . . and they were welcoming him, just as if he were one of them.

Momentarily, Shadoe cleared his throat. "Mr. Emerson, I will make your daughter very happy."

"You'd better," joked Grant. "Or I'll run you off the Boeuf faster than you can take a breath." Two horses appeared over the hill, half a mile away. Grant cupped his hand over his eyes, to gain a better view of the approaching riders. "There comes my boys," he said. "God . . . I never thought I'd see Eduard again. I thought—" His voice trailed off.

Closing his fingers over Grant's arm, Shadoe said simply, "I know, sir."

With a short, husky, "Welcome to the family," Grant coaxed the horse ahead. "Come on, boy. The women are at the house planning a wedding. They'll be relieved to learn that I don't plan to shoot the groom at the altar."

Soon, they joined Eduard and Paul, and together, they rode along the primeval depths of Bayou Boeuf, toward Shadows-in-the-Mist and the women who resided there.

Twenty-eight

It had been quite a morning, Mozelle and Mercedes, vying, almost violently at times, for the right to assist Isabel with her wedding attire. Finally, the argument settled and separate duties assigned, Mozelle prompted a now dressed and nervously ready Isabel to the cheval mirror. Startled by her appearance, Isabel drew a long breath, then slowly expelled it. It wasn't the wedding finery that made her feel beautiful; rather, it was knowing that Shadoe awaited her downstairs, willing and anxious to take her as his wife. A warm rush enveloped her. Her dress, a lighter shade of peach than her blushing cheeks, complemented the scattering of ivory rosettes that graced her upswept hair.

"I'll go down an' tell the preacher you is ready," offered a beaming Mercedes, who quickly left the room.

"An' good riddance to ya," mumbled Mozelle, slicing a narrowed look toward the closing door.

"Oh, do be nice, Mozelle. It is going to be a happy day."

"Sho', Missy. But dat ol' bag shoulda stayed in N'Awleans."

"Aunt Imogen couldn't have traveled alone, Mozelle. Oh, do try to be nice!" When Mozelle merely grumbled, Isabel continued, "Do I look fit to be married?" Her words ran into each other in her excited haste. "Will Shadoe be pleased?"

Mozelle, a wide grin etching deeper lines into her

ebony features, roughly plumped up the voluminous poufs of gauze that formed Isabel's veil. "Missy, if'n he ain't pleased, den I reckon he be blind."

A knock sounded at the heavy wooden door. "Isabel, your father is awaiting you."

Turning in a half-circle, Isabel called to her mother with the hesitation of a nervous bride, "I think I'm ready." The door opened and Delilah Grant stepped into the room. Isabel started to ask, *Do I look like a bride,* but the sight of her mother took her breath away. She had always taken her mother's ageless beauty for granted, but seeing her standing there in rich blue charmeuse with layers of chiffon forming the billowing skirts, her own appearance hardly seemed to matter. Her mother's bodice was ornamented with a darker blue trim, and the poufed sleeves were accented with faux pearls. "Oh, mother, how beautiful you are!" Isabel declared, finding her voice returning in bursts of pride and silent prayers that when she was Delilah's age she would look as youthful and lovely.

Delilah's perfectly sculpted features eased into a smile. "You *are* the bride, my daughter. *You* are the ones our friends have come from far and wide to see married today. *You* are the one your expectant bridegroom is wearing a path in the oriental carpet in anticipation of. Oh, my daughter . . . my daughter—" Tears sheened Delilah's exquisite eyes. "My beautiful daughter, soon to be a wife." Hugging her gently, Delilah whispered, "May your life be as full and rich and happy as mine has been with your father."

Despite her mother's hesitancy to crumple her wedding dress, Isabel hugged her tightly. "I will be happy, mother. He's a wonderful man." With a small, emotional laugh, she continued, "Finally, you will see your wild, impetuous daughter settle down and act like a lady."

Mozelle, who'd witnessed Delilah's wedding and now would witness Isabel's, looked on with pride, her fingers absently smoothing down the folds of her own gown specially sewn for this occasion, elegant in its simplicity, with lace collar and cuffs and a string of real pearls, borrowed from Delilah, lying against the dove gray taffeta. "Ya two," she said with soft emotion, "ya be cryin' all over each other, ya don't be stoppin' all dat nonsense."

Stepping back, extending her hand and waiting for Mozelle to take it, Delilah said, "Let's you and me go downstairs and witness our beautiful girl—and her father—descend the stairs." Then she leaned toward her daughter and whispered, "Don't act too shocked, but your dear old Aunt Imogen is wearing red with black trim!"

"No!" shot a dumbfounded, but wickedly humored Isabel. "She isn't!"

"I tease you not!" Squeezing Mozelle's hand, Delilah said, "Now, let's go watch this angel take a husband."

"Shoot," said Mozelle in an effort to choke back the happy emotion she felt, "I's goin' ta be watchin' de sweat ah drippin' down Mistah McCaine's collar. I's be watchin' him thinkin' 'bout turnin' tail and runnin'."

"He won't be thinking any such thing!" sweetly admonished Isabel, then looking to her mother with second thoughts, "Will he?"

"Only if he's a fool . . . or he decides to marry Imogen instead," laughed her mother in return, Mozelle's hand still enfolded within her own. "Now . . . we're going downstairs. Your father is in the corridor and will make sure *you* don't run off, either."

With a final hug for her mother and the now tearful Mozelle, Isabel raised her trembling hand as they left her alone. When the door was softly pulled to, she closed her eyes and drew in a deep breath, hoping to still the tremble of excitement she felt. *Shadoe, my beloved Shadoe . . . soon, you will be my husband!*

A nervous Isabel suddenly felt that she was in a

airless room. She thought she might faint; thus, she was relieved to hear her father's short series of raps at the door, and the calming influence of his voice. "Isabel . . ."

"I'm coming, father." She drew a long, trembling breath, then patted at the rush of color above the bodice of her gown, a dead giveaway that she was as nervous as a treed coon. Momentarily, she stood beside her father, smiling timidly, her hand moving delicately into the crook of his arm.

"You're beautiful," he said with a father's pride, touching his mouth in a gentle kiss to her hairline. "You make this old man proud."

Isabel met the loving gaze of eyes as pale of her own. "Thank you, father."

He had started to move toward the stairs, following the gentle swell of the wedding march, but now halted. "For what, daughter?"

"For accepting him." With a small laugh, she added, "for not shooting him when he alit the carriage." Her voice grew instantly serious, and she dropped her forehead against his shoulder, "For respecting my love for him, and most of all . . . for trusting me to come back home on my own."

"Don't give me too much credit for that," laughed her father, "your mother sat on me when I wanted to go after you." Patting her hand as he turned to escort her toward the stairs, he continued, "You have brought the family back together, Isabel. You brought Eduard home."

She smiled shyly, warmly, lovingly. Grasping her father's arms as if she truly needed it for support, she took her place beside him for the long, long walk to her beloved Shadoe. Her hands felt so warm and moist that she was sure she would wilt the peach-colored roses and gardenias of her bridal bouquet.

Shadoe tugged nervously at the collar of a shirt he

was sure would choke the life out of him. Eduard, standing at his side as best man, leaned close and whispered, "Having second thoughts . . . brother-in-law?"

His mouth pressed firmly into a line, Shadoe couldn't find the strength to smile. "I'm thinking maybe *she* did," he responded after a moment. "Shouldn't she have made her appearance by now?"

A disapproving glance from the minister silenced both men. Paul, standing beside his older brother, shook his head as if to reinforce the minister's reproof. As the wedding march, played at the organ by the minister's wife, rose in harmony, the maid of honor moved into place at the back of the aisle, followed shortly by the matron of honor, Isabel's cousin and co-conspirator, Aimee Claire.

When they had glided angelically down the aisle and taken their places, Shadoe turned his dark eyes expectantly toward the spiral staircase. He heard the rustling of skirts, then masculine footfalls, and when father and daughter appeared a hush fell over the friends and family who had gathered as they were stunned into silence by the vision of her.

Shadoe had always been aware of her rare and magnetic beauty, but he had never imagined that she'd make a bride to parallel the most enchanting of goddesses; there she moved with the grace of a swan, her luminescent features blushing with romance and veiled by gossamer, her peach gown of satin and embroidered tulle accented with handmade satin bows and faux pearl drops. Her slender bodice was hand-appliqued with lace trim, and her floor-length veil was edged with satin ribbons. Her thick, pale tresses had been coiffed in an upswept style, and whisper-soft curls framed her face. Then Shadoe saw her eyes, pale and smiling just for him, so filled with love and happiness that, in one swift move, the nervousness left his body

Isabel watched the expression of her handsomely attired husband-to-be, his wedding suit as dark as his hair, his jabot a bit crinkled, as if he'd been tugging at it. She thought, at first, that she'd seen his knees trembling, but as she approached on her father's arm, Shadoe . . . her dark wolf . . . the man who would soon be her husband and her life-mate, was as stalwart as a knight.

She would have continued to watch his masculine profile if the sun had not suddenly brightened at the window, sending a warm ray across the short expanse and touching her bridal veil. Her gaze slid toward the curious light, and she was sure that Shadoe's did, also. There, surrounded by the light, stood Philbus, dressed in a dark suit, smiling, lifting his hand and gently waving his fingers. With an almost imperceptible nod, he slowly turned and was consumed by the pale glow, like a candle fluttering gently, then carried away with the wind.

Much later, Isabel would not remember the words she and Shadoe had exchanged. She would recall only the minister's voice asking, "Who gives this woman in marriage?" and Grant Emerson replying, with a hesitation that had sharpened Shadoe's eyebrows, "Her mother and father do." If she had consented to be Shadoe's wife during the brief ceremony, she could not recall uttering the words. If Shadoe had consented to being her husband, the commitment was as elusive to her memories as dreams lost between the depths of sleep and a sudden and rude awakening. She remembered only a cool band of gold filigree circling the ring finger of her left hand, a masculine kiss touched lightly to her mouth, and the minister presenting, "Mr. and Mrs. Shadoe McCaine," to friends and family. She remembered the smothering attentions, pats, hugs, kisses, and congratulations of the many well-wishers who had attended her wedding. She remembered retracing her steps through the aisle of white satin and roses, and she vaguely remembered taking the bou-

453

quet from her matron of honor and flinging it into a crowd of laughing, giggling women who hoped to be the next to marry. Beyond that, the day was a haze; she felt that her feet were walking on air.

Then she sensed Shadoe's dark, loving presence and the reality that had eluded her came flooding back. "Oh, Shadoe, Shadoe, can you believe it? We are married!"

"For the past thirty minutes," he laughed, his hand circling her shoulder to press her to him.

With a slight hesitation, Isabel asked, "Did you see Philbus, Shadoe?"

Shadoe smiled sadly. "He has fulfilled his promise to your mother. Now, he has said farewell and we will never see him again . . . not in this world."

Ever so softly, she replied, "I know." And to herself, *Farewell, Philbus . . . and thank you.*

Then she drew a deep breath and willed herself into the happy mood permeating the room. The reception lasted throughout the afternoon. Food was consumed in massive quantities, guests entertained by a quartet of men from the quarters singing the Negro ballads each generation had learned from their fathers, horseshoes were pitched in fierce games of competition, children ran to and fro, and Aunt Imogen—dear, antique matriarch of New Orleans and the family—was still, at ninety-one, able to draw her fair share of male admirers.

Isabel wished that the dream and the enchantment of the day would never end. When she enjoyed a quiet moment, engaging in conversation with some of the young women of the neighboring plantations, she watched her beloved Shadoe across the crowded room, his head bent as he listened intently to his new father-in-law, his eyes occasionally cutting toward her. "Is he satisfying beneath the sheets?" suddenly asked Aimee Claire, and Isabel, jolted by the intimate inquiry, flushed as red as the roses blooming in profusion at the foot of the summerhouse.

The young women she'd grown up with on the Boeuf giggled wickedly, and at the same moment, Isabel pinched Aimee Claire beneath the edge of the table, hard enough, she hoped, to hurt.

In the weeks before their marriage, Grant had brought in a crew of men to refurbish the overseer's cottage. Shadoe and Isabel would live there until they'd built their own house on the five hundred acres at the north side of the Boeuf her father had given them as a wedding gift.

In the dark of the warm July night, lit only by the Chinese lanterns hung in profusion around the lawn, Shadoe drew Isabel up in his arms. She clasped his neck and met his gaze, the shimmering black pools of his eyes lovingly holding her own. On the lawns and the roadway separating the main house from the cottage, the stragglers among their male friends and family flooded them with raucous cheers.

Isabel dropped her head to Shadoe's shoulder and whispered, "You'd better get me inside quickly. I'll never live down the embarrassment—"

In a final display of teasing, to which he'd lovingly subjected her throughout the afternoon, this time, staged for the men who were quickly becoming his friends, Shadoe claimed his new wife's mouth in a long, passionate kiss. Then, releasing her to her stunned silence, he winked, then stepped into the semidarkness of the house he would share with his beloved Isabel.

When he finally dropped her to her feet behind the closed draperies—the first moment they'd been alone all day—he drew her close, ignoring the aroma of fresh paint and new fabrics permeating their temporary home. "I can't believe it," he mumbled against her hairline. "I am your husband . . . you are my wife."

Isabel's fingers rose to the tautness of his muscles

against the sleeve of his jacket. When she lifted her gaze to his, she realized the dream still surrounded her. She could scarcely remember saying goodnight to her parents, or feeling her mother's small kiss against her cheek and her father's loving arms folding around her. Had the customary pleasantries been spoken with her family and friends? She couldn't remember. She knew only that in all her life she'd never been happier, and she knew that today she'd been reborn. No longer was she Isabel Emerson, the tomboy, the rebellious daughter of a frustrated father and a patient mother; no longer would she don Levis in defiance of her father's wishes. That way of life had ended, and another was beginning.

"I am your wife," she uttered after a moment, almost as if she could hardly believe it herself. "Do you realize, my beloved husband, that you can never look at another woman without having your eyes scratched out? It is my right now, to keep you in line."

He chuckled agreeably, his arms instinctively tightening to draw her nearer to him. "Then you should have scratched them out today," he teased. "I just couldn't get enough of Imogen in that red and black taffeta frock—"

Isabel laughed lightly. "She was the belle of the ball today, wasn't she? I wouldn't be surprised if one of those old lechers didn't talk her out of that gown after dark."

"Well, how 'bout this lecher talkin' you out of that one," teased Shadoe, his index finger rising to softly trace the curve of her mouth. "Will I meet—" Tenderly, his lips covered her own in a long, lingering kiss before he finished with husky need, "any opposition?"

"Not from me," murmured Isabel, immediately turning her back to him. "But you have about sixty-thousand tiny buttons back here to unfasten."

"Hell . . . can't I just yank—"

"You certainly cannot!" she admonished, attempting

to still her humorous chuckle. "I want every one of those buttons in place when this frock falls to the floor. I plan for our daughter to wear it in about twenty years or so—" Her words abruptly ended. So tender was the touch of his fingers as they patiently unfastened the tiny buttons that she felt the heat of desire flow through her body. She wondered if he felt it, if he was still considering yanking down all those buttons. All of a sudden, she wished he would.

When, at last, the back of the gown gaped open, Shadoe gently turned her to face him. So searing hot was the gaze of his eyes that she thought she might faint with desire for him. When he placed his hands upon her shoulders and began to ease her sleeves downward, she lifted her own hands to his jabot to loosen it, to unfasten the rude barriers of fabric separating her from his sinewy strength.

Their warm, tender looks grew as hot as cauldrons, transfixed as they slowly, erotically, sensually undressed each other. The clothing mounted in the pile upon the floor and when they stood together, naked, Shadoe drew her against his taut chest. "You are mine," he whispered, his fingers rising to remove the pins from her upswept hair. As it fell in billowing, sun-colored tresses, he wrapped his right hand through it and brought it to his cheek. "For all time, my wild Isabel, we will be together."

"Because a piece of paper registered in a government office says we will?" she asked, accepting the small kisses he touched to her mouth.

"No; hang the marriage certificate—destiny shall keep us together. And because—" A mischievous grin raked his mouth in the half-light of the cottage, "nobody else could put up with either of us."

"Oh, I don't know about that," she teased, cuddling against him, enjoying the warmth of their bodies pressed closely together. "Right now—" As he swept her up into his arms, she murmured, "I don't care about anyone else, Shadoe. I want you . . . the night is ours."

In the silence of the late evening, his dark eyes meeting her pale, passionate ones, his mouth dipped to hers and tenderly kissed it. "My wild, rebellious Isabel . . ." Suddenly, a glint of humor eased across his gaze. "Why don't we go riding? It's a lovely night."

Drawing in a short breath, Isabel lightly struck his shoulder. "Riding! I've got other sport in mind."

With a pirate's smile, he moved toward the corridor and the marriage bed, holding her with little effort. Dropping her to the crocheted coverlet — a wedding gift from dear Mozelle — he eased between her shapely limbs and again twined his hands into the rich masses of her hair. He imprisoned her wrists, though there was no need, held down her legs with one of his powerful ones, though he knew the only movement she would will into them would be to accept him, fully and completely, when the time was right. He lowered his hands to press upon her cheeks as if to still any flinging of her lovely head, though he knew there would be no struggles this night. Her sensual, searching gaze, her parted mouth, the heat of her body molded beneath his own, grabbed him from within. Her soft breasts rose against the hard expanse of his torso and though he wanted nothing more than to be within her, taking her, driving her as wild as she was driving him, he couldn't cease his appreciative scrutiny of her.

"I've never seen a woman as beautiful as you are, Isabel. Do you have any idea how it makes me feel to know you are mine, for all time . . . for eternity?"

Her thigh rose and pressed against his narrow hip. His fingers had traveled sensually into her hairline and she could feel them gently massaging her scalp. She felt the hardness of his groin against her abdomen; within her grew her passion for him, like a vast flood that would soon consume them, body and soul. Pressing her fingers to his shoulder, then moving them

458

down his arms and onto his narrow hips, she let him know, without words, that she wanted him . . . that if their time together spanned eternity, she would never be able to get enough of him. And her husband, her lover, her kindred spirit, dipped his mouth to her own as if he'd heard the unspoken words echoing within her. Moving one hand to caress his cheek, Isabel smiled with the seductiveness of a wanton woman . . . of the woman she wanted to be in his arms this night.

Then his hands were filled with her soft breasts, caressing them, readying them for the deeper explorations of his mouth. His fingers suddenly, deliciously, scorchingly hot, traced an erotic path over the curve of her back, over the soft shapeliness of her buttocks.

"Do you know what I want, Shadoe?"

Arching a dark eyebrow, he gave her a lusty, humored look. "Well, if it's something other than what I want, I'm in a hell of a lot of trouble here."

When she suddenly reached down and touched him . . . there . . . he gave a small, surprised cry. "Oh, that . . . that, Shadoe McCaine?" she lovingly fussed at him. "You think it will fall off if it is denied?"

Finding his voice, he responded with husky need, "Well, it might—" Her fingers continued to stroke the silken evidence of his masculinity. Fighting a smile, he added, "You're torturing me, you little vixen," and in response, her caresses became longer and more seductive.

Her boldness fed a river of liquid passion into his already throbbing veins. Stiffening his body above her, he managed to whisper, "You haven't told me what you want . . . little wife."

Her fingers withdrew the torture. "I want us to have a child—"

He grinned devilishly, his dark gaze capturing her own. "I think if we keep going in this direction, we'll find we're doing everything right." Without hesitation, without further prelude, Shadoe buried himself into the moist depths of her.

With a small gasp, Isabel's body went taut, though only for a moment. She loved the sensation of him inside her; she felt wanton and free and naughty. Her passions were fired, the flames racing through her thighs and hips so fiercely that she felt that all the breath might leave her body. With teasing playfulness, her hands, circling his shoulders, drew him close, and her thighs lifted to squeeze against his narrow hips.

"I think . . . my dear . . . husband," she uttered in between the small kisses they shared, "that it is more pleasure . . . than procreation guiding you now—"

Ceasing his slow gyrations against her, his fingers drew into the fine threads of her hair. A grin raked his darkly handsome features. "I won't be arguing with you there, my love." When her sensual mouth rose to brush his smiling lips, he began to move again. "Now, hush up, and do your wifely duty."

Arching a fine, copper-colored eyebrow, her look exuded a moment of feigned sarcasm. "Wifely duties? I thought *you* were performing your husbandly ones."

The playfulness continued, his mouth teasing a path over her eyelids, capturing her uninhibited mouth again and again, dipping to the tiny, throbbing pulse in her neck, feeling the slim columns of her legs lift to surround his muscular ones as she easily matched the rhythm and pace of his manly movements against and within her.

Isabel hungered for his caresses. His arms roughly gripped her shoulders as he impaled her, again and again. Hot waves swept through her, hotter even than the humid July breeze rustling against the gossamer at the long windows and touching her skin. His thrusts grew more rapid, more frenzied, and with shameless abandon she lifted to accept him more completely.

Had mere moments passed, or an hour, or two . . . had a lifetime passed? She felt the wonderful exhaustion of their mutual throes of passion and she knew, by the tenseness of his muscles beneath her fingers, of the frantic pace with which he now joined to her, that the erotic culmination of their mutual needs was near. Then it came . . . the flood of warmth within her, the throbbing of them, together, the way it always happened, and the way he slumped, breathing heavily, atop her.

Her fingers rose to the damp strands of his hair and caressed a path along his temple. "My beloved husband, if happiness makes babies, then it has happened tonight."

Lifting his head, though he exerted great effort to accomplish it, Shadoe grinned. "How many times have we made love, Isabel? Why now, and not then?"

She shrugged tenderly beneath him and her pale eyes darkened in their attempt to see him more clearly. When he shifted from her and dropped to her side, she immediately tucked herself into his embrace. "We had other ends to accomplish before, Shadoe," she reminded him. "Now, we have only ourselves to think about, at least for a little while."

Tenderly, he said, "You will make a wonderful mother."

"Of course," she teased in reply. "Because I will have wonderful children . . . your children."

"They'll be monsters, I'd imagine."

"Oh, were you a monster as a child?"

He chuckled. "Not me. From what I've heard from your parents—"

"I was not a monster!" Despite her harshly spoken words, only love and adoration reflected in her gaze. Lifting her fingers to his taut jawline, she traced a path along it, then changed direction at his chin and traveled down his neck. When her hand rested over his heart, she pressed her cheek against it. Ever since the morning when they'd become man and wife, a nagging little curiosity had prickled her happiness. She had tried not to think about it, but now, as she lay in the

461

arms of the man she would spend her life with, the curiosity was much too great to ignore. "Shadoe?"

"Hmmmm?" His hand at her shoulder tightened.

Her gaze flickered over his strong profile, over the full, moist mouth that had just moments ago awakened her passions. "This morning when the minister said, 'Do you, Shadoe McCaine' . . . I am wondering, did you have any misgivings about getting married? Did you even for a minute think about retaining your title of bachelor, or did you marry me without hesitation?"

His dark eyes, lightly closed in relaxation, slowly eased open. "Not for a minute did I hesitate, my wild one. I've lived for the day I would become the husband of a woman like you."

Propping his head on his raised palm, Shadoe gazed over her warm, expectant features, meeting the reflection of pale, powder-blue eyes. He couldn't help wondering how long this had been bothering her. "You were worried that I would back out on you at the altar? What kind of monster do you think I am?"

She shrugged lightly, disengaging a lock of her long hair from his shoulder. "Well . . . I thought perhaps you would want a—"

"A what, for God's sake?"

"A virgin—"

Turning to his back, Shadoe chuckled. "You're the only virgin I want, Isabel Em—" He grinned wickedly. "I mean McCaine. Isabel McCaine. Now—stop this foolishness and plant that pretty head right here on your husband's chest." Then he teased, "Do you still think Shadoe McCaine is not my real name?"

She'd mentioned it only once, on the trail somewhere in Kansas, because she had thought a man on the run would want the added precaution of an assumed identity. Shrugging, she felt a passing of shame that she should question it now, when they were married. "Well, I would like to be sure."

Turning to his side, he propped his hand on his

462

palm. His eyes smiled at her. "I am a royal prince, Isabel, who was stolen away from the castle by an evil uncle who wanted my crown. I was cast out into the sea to die, and for many, many weeks I was tossed hither and yon on the raging waters, until I washed up on an empty beach. I knew I could not go back to my homeland and retake my throne, because I would surely have died at the hands of my evil uncle. So . . . I stayed here—picked the name Shadoe McCaine off a tombstone—after all, the poor fellow no longer needed it. . . . Then I settled down to wait, knowing that one day I would find my princess . . . and I would live happily ever after."

With a pretty smile, she responded, "I don't really believe this story; but I will concede one thing—"

"What is that?"

"You are my prince."

"And believe me, my darling, Shadoe McCaine really is the name my parents gave me."

"And it's a wonderful name. Thank you for letting me share it."

"You are welcome."

"Mrs. Shadoe McCaine . . . I like the ring of it, don't you?"

Tenderly, he asked her, "Nothing else would have fit you better."

Silence, Isabel tucked her head upon Shadoe's matted chest. Her hands curled together, then came to rest in the crook below her chin. "I hope you'll enjoy plantation life, working alongside father."

"It'll be the longest job I've ever held, Mrs. McCaine . . . I promise you that."

Isabel had never been happier. As she lay in the arms of her new husband, the warm July night outside the window rushed with the sounds of the bayou. She knew she could never feel safer than she did this moment.

"I love you, Shadoe."

"Not as much."

Her eyes lifted to trace the outline of his features against the pale, filtering light. "Not as much as what?"

"As I love you. We are two unique individuals, Isabel, who somehow complete each other. Now hush, go to sleep. Tomorrow is a long day. Your father is taking me over the fields."

Her eyes gently closed. Beyond the silent waters of the Boeuf, a night creature called like a sad, wailing woman, long and agonizing against the spanse of darkness enveloping them.

She had always imagined a lost love guiding that pitiful cry, a child's fears carried to full heights by an overactive imagination.

But she knew now it was merely a creature of the bayou making the night its own. She was where she belonged, safely nestled against the man she loved, and who loved her.

The passions of the night were theirs. The silent cries of the bayou folded around their gently entwined forms like protective arms. And eternity stretched before them — a ribbon of love and adoration — ready to accept their footfalls . . . together.

I love you, Shadoe. The sentiment echoed softly once again, unspoken, within her. And in the silence, her lover, her husband, her kindred spirit, hearing her sweet thoughts as surely as if she had spoken them, felt tears of happiness gather, unshed, at the corners of his eyes. He had never in his wildest dreams believed that he might find a woman as wonderful as Isabel. And he certainly didn't believe, once found, that he would deserve the love she gave to him freely, and with all of her heart and soul.

I love you, Isabel. . . . Forever . . . and always . . . far, far beyond this passionate, embracing life we shall spend together.

Part Five
Angus Wickley's Gold

Epilogue

Fraser Boothe had thought of nothing these past four years but the mystery of Angus Wickley's gold. When he had taken the assignment given him by the *Picayune,* the New Orleans newspaper for which he'd been little more than a copy boy, he had done so for only one reason . . . the position of reporter promised him by the editor-in-chief. This early Monday morning he sat in his carriage on a quiet road beside Bayou Boeuf, facing the end of four long years of chasing shadows, and leads that had taken him from San Francisco, back to New Orleans, Arizona, back to New Orleans, and even to the Hebei province in China, then back to New Orleans. He now carried beneath his right arm the burdensome portfolio with all the information he had gathered over the years. For a moment, he looked toward the elegant rooftop of the plantation, Shadows-in-the-Mist, reaching into the summer sky. As he stood there, contemplating his approach to the house, he wondered how he would begin telling the story he had been compiling in his mind for the past two hundred miles. Yes . . . how would he begin?

An intriguing gold coin, purchased from an antiquies dealer in New Orleans, had started his obsession.

Though as far as he could tell it was not an antique, he had been curious as to its origin, and the reason one might mint such a coin. He was sure that he'd fallen in love with the Chinese woman profiled on the face of the coin, and a close examination of the yew tree on its reverse through a magnifying glass had yielded the name, S. Frisco. So he had started his search there, sending a telegram to the *San Francisco Examiner*. A positive response — and a name to begin with — had immediately followed.

His editor at the *Picayune* had issued a challenge: solve the mystery of the coin, and you'll be this newspaper's first investigative reporter. *A step up, lad, wouldn't you agree, from your position as copy boy?* So, given leave, a healthy expense account, and the incentive to accomplish what might be an impossible mission, he had journeyed to San Francisco, California. There, he had met a man, so very close to death he was sure the grim reaper was reaching over Fraser's shoulder to claim him.

Beneath the covers of a massive, ebonized bed had lain the almost skeletal remains of the man whose audience he had sought that morning. The impressive Oriental flavor of the room was overshadowed by the death of its occupant, looming as imminently as the next hour.

When Fraser took the chair pointed out by the Chinese manservant, he felt a shiver as he was quickly left alone with the bedridden man. Was he in a condition to speak to him about the coin? Was he even lucid?

"You wish to speak to me about the gold coin, eh, young man?" The strong, clear voice of Argus Gaynor, one of the wealthiest men in California, did not match the dying body.

"Yes, sir. I am most curious."

"Then I suggest you not interrupt me . . . since I have very little time left." At Fraser's silent nod, the dying man continued. "In 1844 I married a Manchu maiden born of a powerful Chinese family whom I had met in the province of Hebei. As payment to her father for her hand I was to send him one hundred pounds of gold. These privately minted coins—one of which you have there in your hand—were to be proof to her father of my total devotion to Li Chu Ling. But I am afraid I was not a good husband to her, and she was unhappy. After she gave birth to twin sons, she took the smaller of the babies and fled this house, taking the gold that I was to send her father. I have never again seen the child . . . nor my wife."

"Did you search for them?" asked Fraser.

"No, of course not! I cared not about the gold; I merely replaced it with bars, shipping it on to Hebei so that her father would never know she had left me. And the woman . . . if she did not want me, I did not want her. As for the child, she left the healthy one with me; I had no need of the sick one." A withered, trembling hand crept across the expanse of covers. "Let me see the coin again." Fraser handed it to him, at which time the deep-set, half-blind eyes almost lovingly studied the profile. "She was beautiful, wasn't she?"

"Do you know where she is?"

"I've no blasted idea. I had a private detective trace her to Arizona, where I believe she deposited the sick child with a farm couple, and from there, he lost track of her. I've received reports over these past three decades that she's been seen in New York, Baltimore, London, Paris . . . even your own New Orleans. She may even have returned to San Francisco. There are many of Chinese descent here, you know."

"Yes, I know—"

"Now, go about yourself, Mr. Boothe!" Slumping into the thick folds of the bed, the old man closed his eyes. "Go away from me. I have a dying to complete—"

And he did so with haste. Before Fraser Boothe left San Francisco the following day, he learned that Argus

Gaynor had died just hours after his visit. But he had a little more to go on, and though it wasn't absolutely necessary, made arrangements to travel to the Hebei province in China, where Li Chu Ling's family lived. He thought he could visit and gather background information on this intriguing Chinese woman who had stolen the heart of a wealthy Californian. He was able to accomplish the long visit without revealing that Li Chu Ling's whereabouts had been unknown for thirty years. Then he grew lonesome for home . . . and so returned to New Orleans to spend time with his family for a few weeks. While there, he began to make inquiries, and was more than a little surprised to learn that a woman known as Li Chu Ling was employed as a housekeeper in a residence right there on Chartres Street.

He remembered sitting in the cab, looking toward the residence, then being brought from his thoughtful mood by the cabbie, wanting to be rid of him so that he could pick up another fare. Soon, he had entered a garden, walked past a battered marble figure gone as gray as any old Creole darkie, maneuvered among huge pots that might once have held summer flowers and past huge jars sinking into the soggy courtyards. Stepping up to a single step, he rapped upon an ancient, weathered door. A slim man, appearing to be about forty, answered his knock.

"Is there a Chinese woman living here?" he asked. "By the name of Li Chu Ling?"

Struck by a sudden blast of cold air, the man tucked his hands into the pockets of his smoking jacket. "We have a housekeeper named Li Chu Ling. What is your business with her?"

Explained Fraser, "I am a reporter with the *Picayune*. She may not be the woman I am looking for, but if I may have the opportunity to speak to her—"

"One moment, please." The door promptly closed in Fraser's face. Tucking his hands into the warmth of his overcoat, Fraser turned, his foot shuffling back and forth on the brick walkway. He could hear muted voices from within, a man's sharply spoken one, and a softer one, the accent strange. Then the door opened once again.

"Li will accept you. Please . . . come in. You may have the privacy of the parlor."

As the gentleman closed the door, Fraser immediately found himself facing a Chinese woman of about fifty-five years, who was slim and youthful, and who carried herself with regal dignity. The only flaw in her composure were her hands, so tightly woven together her knuckles bared white. Fraser no longer had to speculate on her identity: she bore a striking resemblance to the younger woman profiled upon the coin in his pocket.

"Who are you?" she asked in English only slightly affected by the Creole atmosphere in which she'd lived for more than three decades.

"I am Fraser—"

"I know your name," she interrupted quietly. "But *who* are you?"

"I am the man piecing together a very strange puzzle, madame . . . beginning with this coin—" His hand came up from his pocket to hand it to her. "I have already spoken with Argus Gaynor—in fact, I spoke to him just hours before his death." When she dropped into a chair, a ghastly pallor claiming her golden skin, Fraser relayed the details in the last hours of Argus Gaynor. Then he said, "Now that I have found you, I wish to find the child you supposedly left in Arizona . . . and to be told why you left him."

Tears filled her eyes. "Yes, the child . . . I have not seen him in thirty-five years. When I fled my husband, he became gravely ill. In my fear for my own life at the hands of my husband, as well as the life of the poor child, I left him with a very kind couple in the Arizona territory . . . the Pritchards, near Phoenix. I

471

had always planned to reclaim him truly, I had."

While she spoke, Argus wrote in a small notebook. "Is there a way I could identify him, if I am able to locate him?"

"What is your interest, sir?"

"Strictly selfish, madame, I assure you. If I can solve this intriguing mystery, then I have been offered a coveted position with my newspaper."

"I appreciate your honesty." At that point, Li Chu Ling took Fraser's hand and turned it, palm up. "The child will bear a birthmark right here—" A slim, golden finger traced a path from midpalm to the base of Fraser's thumb.

Discreetly, Fraser withdrew his hand. "You had one hundred pounds of gold, madame. Couldn't you have sought the best medical care for him?"

"He was beyond medical care. I suspect that he died soon after I left him." Then Li outstretched her long, slender hands. "Look around you, Mr. Boothe? Would a woman with one hundred pounds of gold live as a housekeeper all these years?"

"But . . . your husband said you took it."

"And so I did." She smiled gravely. "I lost it, near this very city, on a cold December night the same year I fled from my husband."

"Will you tell me how you lost it?"

"I was aboard a coach which broke down ten miles out of the city. The axle was repaired temporarily to allow the coach to reach the city with passengers, but all baggage had to be left on the roadside. Of course, an attempt was made to hide the trunk and the baggage in underbrush, but the following day when men from the transportation company returned, the trunk containing the gold was gone. I did not make a claim for it, because I did not want to draw attention to myself and for my husband to learn of my whereabouts. I have heard rumors over the years that the gold was found by the man who owned a plantation in the par ish of Rapides." In the moment of silence, Li Chu Ling waited for a response, which did not seem forthcoming. Then she said, "I thought I was safe until now. Will I be harmed on behalf of my late husband?"

"I certainly do not think so, madame . . . I will never divulge your whereabouts."

"But you will write a story for your newspaper, will you not?"

"I will," Fraser replied truthfully, "but I need not divulge *where* I have found you. Who would believe you had been right here beneath the *Picayune's* nose all these years?" A thought came to Fraser. "Will you tell me why you did not return to your family in Hebei?"

She smiled, sadly, reminiscently. "If I had returned to Hebei, I would have disgraced my father and he would have had me killed. So, I did the only thing I could do. I gave birth and I fled, it is as simple as that." Standing, Li Chu Ling said in dismissal, "I am sorry, Mr. Boothe, that I cannot help you further.

If he'd wanted to ask a single question more, he'd not have had the chance. She left quickly, without so much as a glance back at him.

Thereafter, it had taken more than a year to locate the missing son . . . known as Jake Pritchard and running the small ranch more than sixty miles from where his foster parents had raised a score of orphaned and abandoned children. He was a tall, slim, and noticeably weak man, and he'd not been successful at ranching, as his foster parents had. A bachelor, he had been on the verge of losing the ranch because of unpaid mortgages when Fraser found him. He had borne the birthmark, and Fraser had taken him to San Francisco, to the man who had been Argus Gaynor's solicitor for forty years, where he immediately established his claim to half his father's estate. Fraser had been with the man named Jake Pritchard when he had faced a twin brother so identical to him in appearance that they could not be told apart. Two brothers, seeing each other for the first time in their lives; Fraser was especially proud of his role in that reunion. When the three of them journeyed to New Orleans to meet their mother, it was as if they had never been apart. A very happy Li Chu Ling returned to San Francisco, to take her place as matriarch of the Gaynor empire.

Now Fraser again looked toward the house sitting serenely on a hill overlooking Bayou Boeuf. Somewhere close by, ninety-six pounds of gold had been carefully hidden away by a simpleminded slave girl in the years before the War Between the States. Flicking the reins at the hump of the harness mare, he turned her onto the private road.

He saw immediately that he'd come at a bad time. These people—the Emersons—were having a *cochon-de-lait,* and Fraser was certain the whole of the parish had shown up for it.

Alighting the carriage brought him face to face with Grant Emerson. Before he could introduce himself, Grant said, "Don't know who you are, sir, but you're welcome to stay. My wife and I are celebrating the birth of our second grandchild . . . a girl this time!"

Fraser introduced himself as a reporter for the *Picayune.* "I've come at a bad time."

"Nonsense! Stay . . . enjoy the food, and then we shall get to know each other. Perhaps you can take a story back to that newspaper of yours in New Orleans."

"Actually, sir—" Fraser smiled now, taking a place beside Grant Emerson as they moved toward the bustling activities of neighbors and friends and darkies, gathered together in celebration. "I've got quite a story to tell your family—"

Four months later

The shadows of the late afternoon crept gently across the waters of Bayou Boeuf. Shadoe and Isabel walked arm in arm, enjoying their saunter out-of-doors on this hot July day. Black children, settled peacefully on fallen logs upon the muddy banks, patiently dragged their fishing lines through the shallow waters of the Boeuf, excitedly squealing when a cork was dragged under.

"Isn't it wonderful here?" asked a thoughtful Isabel. "Surely, it must be like no other place on earth."

"I've never been happier," answered Shadoe, his cheek touching the soft tresses pinned back from her temples. "I can hardly believe we've been married four years . . . that we have two wonderful children."

Isabel laughed, "Yes, they are wonderful. Your precocious son got in the flour in Mozelle's kitchen this afternoon—"

"Marsh is a hellion, isn't he?" chuckled Shadoe with fatherly affection. "But our gentle Cosette . . . she will break many hearts in about twenty years."

"That she will."

Soon, they entered the magnificent, summer-warmed garden dominated by the gazebo, traversed the steps and settled onto the cool wooden seat. They were still like young lovers, snatching private moments, exchanging the enthusiasms of a newly formed romance, and speculating on a bright, wonderful future.

This was Isabel's favorite spot in all the world. From here she could see the glow of the sun settling across the rooftop of Shadows-in-the-Mist, the stir of activity in the quarters, and far, far across the timberline, the chimney of the new house across the bayou where she and Shadoe lived. It had taken only these four years to build a thriving place of their own, and just last month Shadoe had repaid Grant Emerson the last payment on the money he had borrowed to build the house for Isabel. Mirlo had proven his worth, siring healthy, long-legged fillies and colts that would bring a good profit at the auctions, and the land itself yielded top quality crops of corn, sugarcane and cotton.

Shadoe had found his niche in life as a planter, a father, a husband and a lover.

"I love you, Shadoe."

His mouth touched her temple in the gentlest of kisses. "Now, what brought on this sentiment?" When she shrugged against him, he whispered, "—more."

To which she replied, "More? What?"

"I love you more—"

"Oh, Shadoe . . . Shadoe . . . what would life be like without you?"

"Boring," came his immediate response.

"Boring," she laughed sweetly. "Life can never be boring on the Boeuf, what with every man, woman and child, and their uncles and uncle's uncles, all looking for papa's blasted gold."

Shadoe released a small laugh. "At least we know where it came from, don't we?"

"I guess in a way my papa stole that gold."

"I don't think he saw it that way at all."

"Do you think it will ever show up?"

"The gold?"

"No . . . the *Mary Dear*. Of course the gold, husband."

"Ellie's maid will never give up the secret. She hid that gold in a place known only to her and to God. No, ma'am, that gold might as well be on the moon for all the good it'll ever do anyone here."

Isabel sighed deeply. The secret of Angus Wickley's gold kept the mystery clinging to Shadows-in-the-Mist. In her heart, she hoped that it would never be found. It would somehow spoil things, take away the excitement . . . the enchantment . . . the lure of lost treasure. Shadows-in-the-Mist was special because of papa's gold. She prayed that it would never be found.

With fond memories of the past and her pampered girlhood, Isabel looked around the garden and fondly swept her fingers over the smooth wood of the gazebo her father had ordered built for her sixteenth birthday

Everything around her now had been new that day: the stones of the artfully laid paths, the wood freshly cut to build the gazebo, the gardens freshly dug, the flowers and the shrubs newly planted—

But no . . . everything was not new. There, in a far corner of the garden, half-buried by wildflowers and ivy, rested a large concrete pagoda, set into the ground when her grandfather, Angus Wickley, had first built Shadows-in-the-Mist. Though it was cracked and broken in places, Isabel suspected her father had built the gazebo and gardens around the pagoda in respect of the father-in-law he had never known. But somehow it seemed to fit .. a charming bit of antiquity in a garden of new ideas.

Quietly, Shadoe climbed to his feet, his hand moving out to claim Isabel's. "Come, your parents are probably pulling out their hair trying to keep up with Marsh."

"And Cosette will need to be fed soon. She is probably fussing even now."

His gaze meeting hers, Shadoe pulled his beloved wife into his arms. "All right, little wife. I will share you with our children this evening. But tonight, you are all mine."

"And willingly so," she murmured, turning with him to begin the short walk back to Shadows-in-the-Mist.

Something caught her eye—the smallest sparkle from a crack in the weathered pagoda. Could Peculiar have hidden papa's gold there—

No . . . no . . . of course, not. The only treasure I need is holding me close right now. I love you, Shadoe. As long as forever lasts. And beyond.

KATHERINE STONE —
Zebra's Leading Lady for Love

BEL AIR (2979, $4.95)
Bel Air—where even the rich and famous are awed by the wealth that surrounds them. Allison, Winter, Emily: three beautiful women who couldn't be more different. Three women searching for the courage to trust, to love. Three women fighting for their dreams in the glamorous and treacherous *Bel Air*.

ROOMMATES (3355, $4.95)
No one could have prepared Carrie for the monumental changes she would face when she met her new circle of friends at Stanford University. Once their lives intertwined and became woven into the tapestry of the times, they would never be the same.

TWINS (3492, $4.95)
Brook and Melanie Chandler were so different, it was hard to believe they were sisters. One was a dark, serious, ambitious New York attorney; the other, a golden, glamorous, sophisticated supermodel. But they were more than sisters—they were twins and more alike than even they knew . . .

THE CARLTON CLUB (3614, $4.95)
It was the place to see and be seen, the only place to be. And for those who frequented the playground of the very rich, it was a way of life. Mark, Kathleen, Leslie and Janet—they worked together, played together, and loved together, all behind exclusive gates of the *Carlton Club*.

CATCH A RISING STAR!

ROBIN ST. THOMAS

FORTUNE'S SISTERS   (2616, $3.95)

It was Pia's destiny to be a Hollywood star. She had complete self-confidence, breathtaking beauty, and the help of her domineering mother. But her younger sister Jeanne began to steal the spotlight meant for Pia, diverting attention away from the ruthlessly ambitious star. When her mother Mathilde started to return the advances of dashing director Wes Guest, Pia's jealousy surfaced. Her passion for Guest and desire to be the brightest star in Hollywood pitted Pia against her own family—sister against sister, mother against daughter. Pia was determined to be the only survivor in the arenas of love and fame. But neither Mathilde nor Jeanne would surrender without a fight. . . .

LOVER'S MASQUERADE   (2886, $4.50)

New Orleans. A city of secrets, shrouded in mystery and magic. A city where dreams become obsessions and memories once again become reality. A city where even one trip, like a stop on Claudia Gage's book promotion tour, can lead to a perilous fall. For New Orleans is also the home of Armand Dantine, who knows the secrets that Claudia would conceal and the past she cannot remember. And he will stop at nothing to make her love him, and will not let her go again . . .

SENSATION   (3228, $4.95)

They'd dreamed of stardom, and their dreams came true. Now they had fame and the power that comes with it. In Hollywood, in New York, and around the world, the names of Aurora Styles, Rachel Allenby, and Pia Decameron commanded immediate attention—and lust and envy as well. They were stars, idols on pedestals. And there was always someone waiting in the wings to bring them crashing down . . .